WITCH HUNTER

'PLEASE, SIR,' THE innkeeper said. 'But there has been another killing.'

Thulmann's expression grew grave. 'Like the others?' was all the witch hunter said.

'Mangled and ripped apart,' the innkeeper confirmed. 'Old Hans found him, out by the bog-ponds. He thinks it might be Skimmel, one of the cattle-herds.' Reikhertz looked down at the floor, fear creeping into his voice. 'He can't be certain though. There isn't enough left to be sure.'

Thulmann turned and stalked toward the door that opened upon Streng's room.

'Streng!' he shouted, pounding on the closed portal. 'Rouse yourself you filthy drunkard! The killer has struck again and we ride in five minutes!'

A WARHAMMER NOVEL

WITCH HUNTER

C. L. WERNER

For Brandon and Matt. Two friends who must be held responsible for helping to let the djinn out of its bottle.

A BLACK LIBRARY PUBLICATION

First published in Great Britain in 2004 by
BL Publishing,
Games Workshop Ltd.,
Willow Road, Nottingham,
NG7 2WS, UK

10 9 8 7 6 5 4 3 2 1

Cover illustration by Karl and Stefan Kopinski
Map by Nuala Kennedy.

A CIP record for this book is available from the British Library

ISBN 1 84416 071 8

Distributed in the US by Simon & Schuster
1230 Avenue of the Americas, New York, NY 10020, US.

Printed and bound in Great Britain by
Bookmarque, Surrey, UK.

See the Black Library on the Internet at
www.blacklibrary.com

Find out more about Games Workshop
and the world of Warhammer at
www.games-workshop.com

THIS IS A dark age, a bloody age, an age of daemons and of sorcery. It is an age of battle and death, and of the world's ending. Amidst all of the fire, flame and fury it is a time, too, of mighty heroes, of bold deeds and great courage.

AT THE HEART of the Old World sprawls the Empire, the largest and most powerful of the human realms. Known for its engineers, sorcerers, traders and soldiers, it is a land of great mountains, mighty rivers, dark forests and vast cities. And from his throne in Altdorf reigns the Emperor Karl-Franz, sacred descendent of the founder of these lands, Sigmar, and wielder of his magical warhammer.

BUT THESE ARE far from civilised times. Across the length and breadth of the Old World, from the knightly palaces of Bretonnia to ice-bound Kislev in the far north, come rumblings of war. In the towering World's Edge Mountains, the orc tribes are gathering for another assault. Bandits and renegades harry the wild southern lands of the Border Princes. There are rumours of rat-things, the skaven, emerging from the sewers and swamps across the land. And from the northern wildernesses there is the ever-present threat of Chaos, of daemons and beastmen corrupted by the foul powers of the Dark Gods. As the time of battle draws ever near, the Empire needs heroes like never before.

PROLOGUE

DARK THUNDERHEADS ROLLED across the sky, drowning out the light cast by moon and star, their brooding grey substance taking on the hue of blood where the last feeble rays of a dying sun struck them. Beneath the clouds sprawled a landscape no less sinister and menacing, no less redolent of dark powers and the malevolence of the night. Once, the sprawl of wrack and ruin had been a city, the jewel of Ostermark, a place of such wealth and power as to rival even the great cities of Altdorf and Marienburg, eclipsing even the majesty of the mighty river which flowed beneath its gates and past its streets. But such glories were now a part of its past, destined to never return.

The vibrant cityscape had been crushed and broken, naked beams blackened by fire clawed at the dark sky like lost souls reaching up from the pits of Khaine's hells.

The once teeming streets were now deserted and desolate, choked with rubble and debris and the sorry remains of the unburied dead. Marble fountains spat foul black water into weed-choked basins, stained glass windows stared at muck-ridden lanes from the sagging plaster walls in which they had been set. Everywhere the last remnants of the city's opulence fought a losing war against the decay that crawled from the hungry earth to consume what the night of doom had left behind.

A foul, clammy mist rose from the stagnant waters of the River Stir, crawling down the streets and alleys of the destroyed city, carrying with it the promise of cough, fever and plague. Like everything else around the city, even the mighty Stir had become tainted by the evil of this blighted place, its waters so choked with rubble from collapsed buildings and piers that the flow was almost completely stopped and the once clean waters were now as foul and stagnant as a toad pond.

A bloated black rat the size of a terrier crept from a crack in the only remaining wall of what had once been a resplendent merchant's residence, now was little more than a heap of blackened wood and crumbling plaster.

The whiskers on the rat's mud-spattered face twitched for a moment as the animal tried to separate the multitude of stenches that washed over it, lashing its naked tail as it sniffed out its surrounds. A carrion stench aroused its interest and the oversized rodent scrabbled across the mound of brick and timber, beady red eyes gleaming with hungry anticipation.

Not far from the collapsed debris of the high class home, another pile of wreckage groped at the night sky with talons of masonry and wood. What these ruins had been, none could now say, but they must have belonged to some tall and vast building, as the sprawl of the rubble gave silent testimony. From the height of the mound, a man might be able to see far out across the ruins, or, if some spark of wisdom guided his sight, the broken walls that demarked the limits of what had been a city, signposts to guide the lost back to the sane world beyond the desolation.

A much closer signpost had been placed upon the highest swell of the rubble. A great iron spike, some twelve feet high, perhaps once the support for the bed of a wagon or the hull of a boat, rose from the debris, pointing upwards like an accusing finger. Upon it had been lashed an old carriage wheel, the rich colours of its paint flaking away in the ill air that filled the city.

Lashed to the wheel was a bundle of sorry and ragged remains, the faded debris of a soldier's livery clinging to his pallid bones. Who he had been or what he had done to deserve such a fate, none could say, nor even if he had been alive or dead before earning his seat high above the rubble. The skeleton had long ago been picked clean by crows and ravens, and even the last scraps of meat had been stripped away by the inch-long ants that now infested great sections of the ruins. A scrap of parchment bearing the last vestiges of a wax seal was the only sign of who the unfortunate victim might have been or what he might have done. The grimy rain had faded away whatever account of his misdeeds had once been recorded there and the wind had torn away nearly all that the rain had spared, leaving the skeleton to endure its ignominious end in anonymity.

The bloated rat leapt across the uneven rubble, hopping from one mass of stone to the next, and scrabbled up the base of the iron pole, its curled claws finding an easy purchase on the corroded metal. The rodent perched on the crude wooden sign that some passerby in a moment of morbid humour had affixed to the forgotten gibbet. In dark charcoal letters that rain and fog had yet to devour, the joke-ster's hand had scrawled: 'Welcome to Mordheim'.

The vermin paid no heed to the bony remains hanging above its head; that meal had been finished long ago. The rat was more interested in the new smell its keen senses had detected, the stench of rot-ting meat and old blood.

The rat lingered for a moment upon its perch, then leapt back to the ground, scrabbling down the heap of stones then scuttling away down one of the nar-row dingy streets. There was a frantic haste to its gait, for this was Mordheim, and even rats knew better than to tempt the Dark Gods by tarrying too long in the open upon the forsaken streets.

Sounds of conflict arose from a square several score yards from where the ghastly welcome sign had been set. Once, perhaps, this had been a place where the good and great of the city might have gathered to compare fashions and gossip, to idle away the day watching ships sailing upon the river. But such frivo-lity had no place in Mordheim now. The square, like everything else in the city, had been consumed by decay. For every building that leaned sickly against its neighbour to lend it support, three had crumbled, as though some giant hand had pressed upon them from above and pushed them flat.

The square was some forty yards on a side, and within its entire expanse could be found not an inch that had not become tainted and ruined. The small garden that had been lovingly tended in the centre of the square was now choked with weeds, the trunk of the old oak tree that had shaded the flowerbeds warped and twisted. Malevolent faces seemed to stare from the mottled, sickly wood, and though the eager carrion crows gathered in the broken gable roofs that yet faced the square, the desiccated branches of the tree were absent of their croaking black shapes.

The paving stones were cracked and chipped, sickly yellow weeds stabbing upward from beneath them.

The rat crinkled its nose as it sniffed the crimson stain leading into the square, its slimy pink tongue licking at the salty fluid. The greedy vermin sniffed at the air once more, trying to decide if it was too early or too late to follow the trail to a meal. The sound of steel clashing upon steel told the vermin it was still too soon, and with an almost dejected manner, the creature crept back into the sanctity of the rubble-choked gutter.

With a groan, the warrior staggered back, his gloved hand clutching at the crimson seeping from his belly. The soldier looked in disgust at the thing that had dealt him his wound, the crimson gleaming from its dark, rust-pitted blade. His enemy did not seem to notice in the slightest that it had harmed its opponent. That the man yet lived seemed to be its only observation, indeed, if the two pasty orbs that stared emptily from the mouldering ruin of its face were capable of observing anything.

The undead thing took a shambling step towards the soldier, its decayed arm raising its rusted sword once more.

The warrior gritted his teeth against the pain surging from the cut this grave-cheating horror had inflicted upon him, struggling to lift his shield to intercept the zombie's attack. The weight of the shield seemed to have increased and he realised that slow as the zombie's thrust was, his own reactions were slower still. Once again, the rusty sword sank into the soldier's belly. A surge of pain flashed through the man's body like a bolt of fire.

With a savage cry, the soldier swung his hammer around, the heavy steel smashing against the zombie's withered skull.

The undead thing uttered no sound as its brittle bones were crushed and the maggot-infested mire of morbid fluid and greasy pulp that had been its brain was splashed across the grimy cobblestones. Rather, with a quiet acceptance, it crumpled to the ground, as if welcoming this second chance to quit the troublesome world of the living and return to the silent gardens of Morr. The warrior watched his twice-slain foe crumple, then fell himself upon the debris-ridden ground.

The soldier stared up into the darkening sky, watching as the last feeble rays of the sun turned the ominous clouds as crimson as the fluid leaking from his body.

For a moment, he fancied that it was not the sun that had so transformed the black thunderheads, but the greedy storm gods, sopping up all the blood spilt this day across the foul streets of accursed Mordheim. The warrior clenched his eyes as if to make the image disappear. So close to death, grim storm gods were not the best things to dwell on.

The duel between the soldier and his undead foe over, all sounds of conflict had ended. The ambush had been swift and sudden, felling man and undead thing alike with great speed.

There had been twenty in the soldier's warband, and the pack of rotten creatures that had attacked them had numbered at least as many. Now, the warrior could hear distinctly the moans of wounded comrades and the hideous croaking of crows.

The carrion eaters had grown bold beyond measure in the wretched environs of Mordheim, and did not bother to wait for a body to become still before setting upon it with their cruel beaks and sharp claws. Nor did they retreat any great distance when their mangled meals summoned up the strength to swat at them with maimed arms and bleeding stumps, hopping away only far enough that they might savour the wretched efforts with some assurance of impunity. The birds would then return to their loathsome repast, and no cry of wrath or pain or mercy would cause them to cease their labours.

The soldier clutched at his wound again, this time not to quench the flow of blood, but to encourage it.

With the horrible scavengers cawing and croaking all around him, death could not claim him too soon.

The sounds of the crows grew agitated suddenly, and into the soldier's dimming senses came the sound of boots rasping across the unclean cobblestones. The warrior tried to turn his head, to see who was walking towards him, but found the effort beyond him. It did not matter. Whether friend or foe, there was little more that could be done to the veteran swordsman now.

'So,' a cold voice spoke from somewhere near. 'This is how it ends.' The voice was hard and imperious, a slight lisp twisting every consonant into a sneer. It was a voice the soldier had heard before, a voice he knew well.

Though he could not see who was addressing him, the soldier knew who it was. Somehow, it did not surprise him. If anyone could have emerged from the horrible ambush alive and unscathed, that man would have been Witch Hunter Captain Helmuth Klausner.

The boots rasped upon the cobbles once more. Into the warrior's fading vision came a pale face with a square jaw and sunken eyes, nose and chin both cast in such a manner as to make the visage of a devil seem kindly.

Helmuth Klausner leaned down, his gloved hand touching the hole in the man's belly. The soldier grimaced in pain, amazed that such a sensation could still intrude upon the darkness obscuring his other senses. The witch hunter gazed indifferently at the bloody bile coating the fingers of his glove and wiped his hand upon the soldier's tunic.

'All these weeks, all these weeks of cat and mouse, lurking within these unhallowed ruins, and finally it comes to an end.' Helmuth's tone was almost regretful. 'All these long weeks, stalking and hunting, not knowing for certain who was hunter and who was prey. And now,' the witch hunter allowed himself a slight chuckle, 'now it comes to this.' He stared back down at the soldier, and this time even the mask of indifference had fallen away from the wrathful malevolence that blazed behind the witch hunter's eyes. 'Where is he, Otto?' Helmuth demanded, his words so short and rapid that even their normal lisp was clipped. 'You have seen him! He was here!'

Otto stared up into the gruesome countenance of Helmuth Klausner. Once, that face had cowed him, had broken his will with terror and fear. But no longer. He was beyond even the reach of Helmuth Klausner now. The one the witch hunter hunted would see to that. A slight laugh bubbled its way from the dying soldier's throat.

'Damn y-you...' Otto gasped. 'D-damn your... black soul... H-helmuth. May... may t-the Dark Gods... may they k-know you for... for one of their own!'

Helmuth Klausner glared at the dying man as he cursed the witch hunter. A cruel smile split the Templar's harsh features. Swift as a striking serpent he stabbed the soldier deep in his chest with the long silver dagger that he was carrying.

Otto gave voice to a gurgled rattle as life fled him. 'I'll not be seeing them for some time,' Klausner sneered down at the corpse. 'Not until my work is done. You might tell them that when you see them.'

The witch hunter rose from the carcass, his eyes surveying the carnage around him. The ambush had been a costly affair, but he had lost nothing that he could not replace. Swords were more plentiful than grain in the vicinity of Mordheim and hands to wield them cheaper still. His prey might have escaped him this day, but it would not elude him forever. Sooner or later, the light of Sigmar would find the creature he sought, no matter how deep and dark the burrow into which it crept.

Helmuth suddenly became aware of a perceptible chill, a fell odour upon the air. It was a stench of corruption rather than decay or death, the stink of evil, twisted and inhuman.

The crows rose from their loathsome meals, cawing in fright as they retreated into the shadowy garrets of the tumbledown guildhalls. Slowly, the witch hunter turned to face the source of the taint.

It stood within the shadows cast by that great malformed oak, a tall figure clothed in black. The vestment of the creature was ragged and frayed, the once elegant material torn and dirtied, hanging loosely about a figure grown too lean to properly fill it. Thin, pallid hands hung from the sleeves of its robe, the once elegant cuffs shorn away. A large gold ring dominated the finger of one of its hands, held against the shrivelled digit by a crude iron nail, a spike driven through both jewellery and the fingerbone beneath.

Helmuth smiled as he saw the ring, any question as to the identity of his adversary banished at last.

'You,' the shadowy apparition spoke, the sound less like speech and more like the creaking of wood under the attention of a midnight wind, 'and I. Things have ended much as they began, so many years ago.'

The figure strode forward, the pale, sunken face revealed in the fading twilight. The flesh was beginning to flake and peel, blotches of black necrotic skin marring the dead pallor. Great incisors, like the fangs of a rat, pushed apart the shadow's face, spreading apart the bloodless white lips. The only colour in the face was contained in the two fiery eyes that gleamed from the sunken pits that flanked its decaying nose. The eyes stared with a lifetime of hate and fury upon the figure of Helmuth Klausner, burning with a perfection of hatred that no human soul could ever hope to achieve without collapsing under the very strain of containing such malice.

Helmuth Klausner nodded his head slightly at the monster, drawing the sword sheathed at his side. 'Indeed, Sigmar could not allow such a thing as you to profane this world with your puerile mockery of life,' the witch hunter spoke, his tones cold with the extremes of his own fury. 'It is by his grace that I am the one appointed the task of restoring you to the grave you have denied so long.'

The monster stepped toward Helmuth, its pace so fluid that it seemed to glide across the cobbles. 'If there are any gods of justice and vengeance, then it is they who have guided *my* steps. I will have what is mine, I will have restored to me all that you have taken.' The creature's voice was terrible in its subtle violence, its undercurrents of ire and wrath.

'We have talked enough this night, blood-leech. The hour grows late and I have little time to waste trifling with a corpse.' Helmuth Klausner advanced toward the shadowy figure, his sword held before and across his body. The shadow drew its own blade, gliding forward to meet its foe. The dull, subdued tones of an incantation slithered into the quickening night. As they did so, the corpse of Otto began to twitch with an unnatural life...

Thus did Witch Hunter Captain Helmuth Klausner, Knight Templar of Sigmar, Protector of the Faith, drive to final and perpetual ruin the thrice-accursed vampire Sibbechai in those dark and fearsome times. Upon the streets of foul benighted Mordheim did he bring the wrath and judgment of Most Holy Sigmar down upon the foul undead abomination.

Or so say the histories written of those distant days...

CHAPTER ONE

IT WAS NOTHING much to look at really. Just a tiny little hovel like so many others that might be found beyond the walls of Wurtbad, four walls of timber tilted at an angle by the unkind attentions of time and the elements.

The thatch roof was old and ill-maintained, the roof damp and rotting where it was not missing altogether. Such was its state that the roof certainly would not survive the ice and snow of the approaching winter. Creepers and sickly yellow moss clutched at the chinking between the log walls. The awning of planks that had once shaded the front of the structure now drooped across much of the façade, one of its support poles knocked down by some long past storm. Indeed, despite everything, the dozen men who had furtively crept through the muddy, overgrown wheat field might have thought they had been led to the wrong place were it not for the thin plume of grey smoke rising from a hole in the rotten roof and the flicker of light that danced behind the sagging door of the hovel.

The foremost of the men studied the derelict structure for some time, his penetrating gaze studying its every detail. He was a tall man, lean of limb and build, his face sharp and thin. He cast a curious figure, lurking amidst the overgrown, rampant wheat stalks, dressed in his expensive shirt of scarlet and gold, his fine calfskin gloves, polished boots with massive golden buckles and long black cape edged in palest ermine.

As the man's grey eyes, like slivers of steel, watched from within the shadow cast by his wide brimmed conical hat, one of his gloved hands gripped the heavy wooden butt of a pistol. Its twin rested in a holster fixed to the man's belt beside the scabbard of a sheathed longsword. The watcher's other hand pulled at his thin moustache, a gesture that indicated a mind deep in thought. At length, the watcher scrambled back to where the other men awaited him within the cover provided by the overgrown crop.

'You were long enough,' observed one of the men crouching amidst the mud and rot. He was a short man with an unpleasantly cruel face, his features somehow suggesting both pig and hound. His hair had begun to desert him, leaving only a fringe of white, wiry hair. He wore a tunic of reinforced leather, stained black and studded with steel, and gripped a large duelling pistol in his leather-clad hands. He glared at the returned watcher, voicing the unstated challenge lurking within the piggish man's words.

'Perhaps you would prefer that we simply announce ourselves,' sneered the moustached man. 'I am certain that this murderous sorcerer would welcome us with open arms. Perhaps invite us for tea before we take him away to be tortured and burnt.' He turned from the balding man, shaking his head with disgust. 'You've made enough of a mess of things, Meisser. Just do as I tell you and we will free Wurtbad of this horror tonight.'

The leather of Meisser's glove creaked as his hand clenched about the grip of his pistol. 'See here, Thulmann,' his gruff voice snarled. 'I'm in command here! Wurtbad is my posting, its protection is my duty, not yours! I'll thank you to remember that,' the piggish man added, his voice boiling with indignation.

The other witch hunter rounded on the balding Meisser, a face livid with rage.

'I'll remember four households butchered in their beds while you stumbled about in back alleys arresting midwives and herb-sellers,' Thulmann stated, his silky tones brimming with contempt, thrusting every word like a dagger into the inflated ego of the pompous Meisser. The older witch hunter retreated back several steps before Thulmann's cold fury.

'I'll report this flaunting of my authority!' Meisser warned, eyes round with shock. Suddenly his words were brought up short as the witch hunter felt the sharp prick of steel pressed against his side. He turned his head, finding himself staring into the smiling features of Thulmann's underling. The man was stocky, with broad shoulders and a slight paunch. His leather breeches were faded and worn, his armoured jerkin filthy with sweat and dirt. The man's hair and beard were dark brown, grimy and unkempt.

The henchman grinned as he pressed the dagger a little more firmly against Meisser's side.

'You'll do exactly like he tells you,' Streng grinned into Meisser's ear.

The balding witch finder looked toward the other men lurking amidst the environs of the muddy field. They were his men, apprentice witch hunters under his command and tutelage. However, not one of them moved to extinguish the situation. Meisser might be their commander, but they recognised a fool when they saw one, and none of them were eager to follow a fool into battle.

Meisser licked his lips nervously and nodded his head in defeat.

'Nicely done, friend Streng,' Mathias Thulmann told the knife-wielding thug. 'Now if you will kindly relieve Brother Meisser of his pistol so I need not worry about a bullet in the back, we'll be on about our business here.' The witch hunter looked around him, gesturing for the apprentices to draw close in order that he might disclose his plan of attack to them.

MATHIAS THULMANN CROUCHED just outside the filthy hovel, ears listening for any sign that its occupant had detected the presence of his party, or the men he had deployed to surround the structure. He looked back at the five men he had chosen to accompany him into the witch's lair.

'I remind each of you,' his silky voice whispered. 'Guard your own lives, but see that the witch is taken alive.' Thulmann studied each man's face, making certain that his warning was understood. He met the questioning gaze of his henchman Streng.

'You certain that this is how you want to do it?' Streng asked. 'Wouldn't it be better just to put the place to the torch and have done with it? They'll be burnt anyway.'

'I want to know the reason for these atrocities,' the witch hunter told him. He thought again of the four households, slaughtered down to the last child, all of them Wurtbad's most prosperous river merchants. There was something more than simple evil and malevolence at work here. Someone was hoping to profit by these horrors. Greed was one of the simplest motives by which any crime was countenanced, but it took a truly sick mind to consider witchcraft as the solution to their ambitions. 'And I would hear who paid to have them done,' Thulmann added.

'Shouldn't you at least send him back to guard the perimeter?' Streng gestured with his head to indicate Meisser. The witch hunter captain of Wurtbad was now equipped with a sword, his confiscated duelling pistol tucked securely under Streng's belt.

'No, I want him with us,' Thulmann commented. 'I wouldn't want Brother Meisser to miss one moment of the excitement.' The witch hunter sighed, drawing his sword and pointing it at the hovel. With a shout, the men lunged forward, Streng at the fore. The burly henchman sent a savage kick smashing into the ramshackle door, tearing it from its rotted leather hinges to crash upon the earthen floor of the hovel. Streng leaped into the room, Thulmann and the other witch hunters right behind him.

The interior of the hut was small, but into that space had been crammed more paraphernalia than could comfortably occupy a room three times as large. Dried bundles of weeds and herbs drooped from the ceiling, dead and eviscerated birds hung from leather straps fastened to the roof beams.

A huge pile of bones, of every size and shape, was heaped against one wall, a collection of foul-smelling jars and pots filling a crude series of shelves beside it. The head and skin of a black cow stared at the intruders with its empty eye-sockets from the hook that fastened it to the support beam that rose from the centre of the hut. Beyond, shapeless masses dangled and drooped, drifting back into the inky recesses of the chamber.

A dozen noxious stinks fought to overwhelm the senses of the men, but no more charnel a reek assailed them than that which rose from the small fire-pit and the black iron cauldron that boiled above it. As the attention of the witch hunters was drawn to the only source of light in the gloomy shack, a dark shape rose from beside the cauldron, glaring at the intruders.

The shape resolved itself into the form of a woman, bent almost in half by the weight of her years. A shabby, ragged brown shawl was draped across her crooked spine, a collection of grey rags that might once have been a dress clothing the rest of her body. Her face was a mass of wrinkles, a spiderweb etched into the cold and colourless skin. The bones of her skull seemed to press against the wrinkled covering, showing yellow beneath the skin. Her nose was broad and sharp, like the beak of a razorbill, her eyes tiny pinpricks of malice.

Straggly white hair hung about her body, drooping as far as her knees. The hag opened her gash-like mouth, letting a trickle of spittle drool from her lips.

'So, my boy was followed after all,' the witch observed, the words leaving her toothless maw in a scratchy hiss. 'But if you think you'll be stoking a fire with these old bones, you're sadly mistaken.'

'Your unholy tricks won't protect you now, hag,' declared Thulmann, striding toward the witch, sword and pistol both pointed at her breast. 'The judgement of the god you've profaned and mocked is upon you this night!' The old crone's smile broadened, ghastly in its malevolence.

'You think so, do you?' she cackled. 'But you've forgotten Chanta Favna's darling boy!' From the black interior of the hovel, the sound of creaking wood and groaning iron issued, followed a moment later by the tottering form of the monstrous abomination the witch hunters had tracked to this, the lair of its creator and controller.

The creature was tall, forced to stoop under the low ceiling of the hovel. It was rail thin, which was fitting, since just such an object had been used to form its spine. Its body was an old burlap sack stuffed with rubbish and old dried out reeds. Its arms were long sticks, hinged at the shoulder and elbow with iron fittings. Its legs were poles, wooden feet nailed at their ends.

The monster's head was an old dried out pumpkin, upon which had been carved a leering and ghastly suggestion of a face. About its neck hung a withered, one-legged toad, a talisman that reeked of loathsome and unholy magic.

However, it was none of these features which arrested the attention of the men who had moments before challenged the construction's mistress. It was the long, sharp claws of steel that tipped each of the scarecrow's slender arms, the bladed hands that still dripped with blood from those it had slaughtered already this night.

Almost before the men could fully register its arrival, the scarecrow was upon them, lashing out with murderous swipes of its rickety limbs. One of Meisser's apprentices fell under the monster's steel claws, wriggling on the floor as he tried to push his entrails back into the gaping hole the scarecrow had ripped from his belly. The other witch hunters warded off the butchering sweeps of the automaton's flailing arms, swords crashing against claws of steel.

Thulmann fired his pistol into the ghastly pumpkin face, the shot shattering against the sorcery-strengthened shell. Streng tore Meisser's own pistol from his belt, firing at the scarecrow as its bladed hand swept toward the throat of his employer. The shot glanced off the claw, the impact redirecting the flashing talon to chew into the timber wall of the hovel.

Meisser lunged at the scarecrow as it tried to free its hand from the wall, stabbing and slashing at the unnaturally strong substance of its backbone. It seemed impossible that such a ramshackle thing could move with such deadly swiftness.

Thulmann moved to aid the witch hunter captain in his efforts, but was dealt a glancing blow that knocked him to the floor. One of Meisser's remaining apprentices shouted a warning to his mentor as the scarecrow freed its trapped arm, but the older witch hunter was too slow in recognising the danger. The scarecrow's claws slashed downward, ripping open Meisser's sword arm. With a scream of anguish, Meisser fell back, his apprentices stepping forward to protect their master. The scarecrow lashed at the swords of the two men, its powerful blows forcing them to give ground before it.

'That's it!' laughed Chanta Favna. 'Kill them all! But do it slow my pet, I want to savour every scream!' The hag's hands were held before her, swaying and jerking in time to the scarecrow's movements. Dangling from those withered claws was an articulated wooden doll, a small manikin that the witch manipulated with deft motions of her scrawny fingers. The severed leg of a toad was fastened around the mid-section of the tiny figure. As the doll moved, so too did her sorcerous construction.

From the edges of the battle, Streng noted the old hag's manipulations.

'Mathias!' the bearded henchman called out, deflecting another slash of the scarecrow's claw with a desperate sweep of his sword. Rising from the floor, half-dazed by the automaton's blow, the witch hunter looked over at his hireling. 'The witch's doll! She's controlling the scarecrow with it!'

Upon hearing Streng's words, the witch's ugly eyes focused upon the recovering Thulmann. She cackled and hissed slippery, inhuman syllables, forcing the witch hunter to meet her transfixing gaze. Chanta Favna placed all of her dark will and malignancy into her hypnotic spell, willing the witch hunter to remain where he was.

With nimble hands, she manipulated the wooden doll. In time to her manipulations, the scarecrow turned away from its hard-pressed opponents, its creaking steps turning back toward Thulmann.

Mathias Thulmann could feel the dread power of the old witch surging through his body, paralysing every nerve, urging him not to rise, commanding him to remain still. He could feel himself struggling to resist her, but it was as if his body was not his own.

The witch hunter was dimly aware of the creaking, tottering steps that were closing in upon him, yet such was the numbing power of the witch's magic that he was unable to muster any sense of haste to speed his struggles. Indeed, his entire being seemed to be in a stupor, a stupor not merely of body but of soul as well.

Only one part of his being seemed to be clear and distinct. The witch hunter's right hand yet retained its grip upon his sword, the weapon that had been given to him in the Great Temple of Sigmar in Altdorf, blessed by the Grand Theogonist Volkmar himself. Thulmann forced himself to focus upon the sword and his hand, and as he did so, the numbing deadness started to lessen. He could sense his arm now, then the feeling of warmth and control spread to his shoulder.

Chanta Favna stared in disbelief as the witch hunter began to fend off her viperous gaze. The witch's face grew dark with worry, her manipulation of the manikin hastier and more desperate. She risked a glance to see how far her automaton had come, but found it beset once again by the other witch hunters, their clumsy efforts to destroy it nevertheless managing to impede its progress.

As the witch's attention wavered, Thulmann tore himself from her lingering spell. The witch hunter surged to his feet and sprang at the old woman. 'Enough of your black magic, crone!' he cried out. The steel of Thulmann's sword flashed in the flickering light as it swept downward at Chanta Favna. The witch screamed in a howl of pain and despair as the blade bit through her wrists. The scraggly clawed hands of the hag dropped to the floor, the manikin still held in their disembodied clutch.

As the doll struck the floor, so too did the scarecrow, tottering for one moment like a puppet struggling to stand after its strings have been severed. The bundle of sticks and straw struck the ground and broke apart, the pumpkin head rolling away from its wooden shoulders.

Mathias Thulmann loomed above the moaning Chanta Favna, the witch pressing the bleeding stumps of her wrists against her body. 'Fetch brands from the fire,' the witch hunter snarled, glancing to see the surviving men from Wurtbad ministering to Meisser's hideous injury. 'See to him later!' he snapped. 'I want this hag's wounds cauterised before she bleeds out. There are questions I need to ask her.'

The witch stared up at Thulmann's menacing tone. 'I'll tell you nothing you filth! Swine!' the witch managed to forget her own agony to heap maledictions upon the witch hunter.

'Streng, go and fetch the men watching the perimeter,' Thulmann told his henchman, ignoring the curses bubbling from the witch's mouth. 'Tell them to ready some torches. I want this place razed when we leave it.' He turned his attention back on Chanta Favna. One of the men from Wurtbad held her fast while the other pressed a knife he had heated to a red glow against the bleeding stumps of her arms.

'I'll tell you nothing!' the witch managed to scream between painful shrieks.

Thulmann considered his prisoner, his face grown cold and expressionless now that the hunt had reached its end.

'They all say that,' he stated in a voice that was not without a note of remorse and regret. 'But in the end, they all talk.' Thulmann turned away from Chanta Favna, stalking toward the doorway of the witch's hut.

'They all talk,' the witch hunter mused. 'Even when they have nothing to say.'

CHAPTER TWO

THE SHRIEKS OF the old hag seemed to echo within the vast courtyard outside the massive grey-stone fortress at the heart of Wurtbad long after smoke ceased to rise from the smouldering remains of the pyre.

The assemblage of officials and lower nobility who had emerged from the fortress to observe the ghoulish spectacle began to file back through the gaping gateway. The massed crowd of commoners lingered on, watching with rapt attention every wisp and curl of grey smoke that rose from the smouldering waste. It had been they who had felt threatened by the gruesome predations of the crone's monstrosity, and it was with a mixture of relief and satisfaction that they had watched her burn.

Burning was an ugly, terrible death and Chanta Favna had been a long time in dying. Mathias

Thulmann had not departed with the rest of the officials, but had stood before the blackened scaffold to the last, lingering until the merest wisp of smoke was no more, his leather gauntlet resting loosely upon the hilt of his sword, his black cape snapping about him in the fiery breeze wafting from the conflagration.

The witch hunter had witnessed many such scenes and still they sickened him. A more wretched and loathsome end he could not easily imagine, unless it was to wallow in the depths of villainy and perversion to which such creatures willingly committed themselves.

Yes, the end of a witch was an ugly thing, but ugliness was necessary, a vital part of the grand theatre that was the very heart of such executions. There was no question of justice when it came to such things, for whatever evil witches and warlocks had perpetuated was beyond the reach of justice within the world of men, there would be a higher authority who would exact retribution upon them.

No, the execution of a witch had little enough of punishment to it, a measure of revenge, perhaps, for what that might achieve. The true purpose of such gruesome displays was for the benefit of those who observed them. The execution of a witch was a cautionary tale brought to life, a terrible parable to evoke horror and repugnance, to make the mind of the commoner shudder and cringe.

There were two ways to rule the hearts and minds of men. The noblest of souls could be held by love and devotion, but for the rest, for the vast petty masses of humanity, fear was the only thing that could bind them. And fear was the witch hunter's stock in trade.

Thulmann studied the crowd of city-dwellers, only now beginning to make their way from the court-yard. He watched them depart, fixing upon faces white with horror or glowing with satisfaction. The crowds were always the same, numbering amongst them the appalled and the self-righteous. The witch hunter grimaced as he considered the men and women, the nameless faces of the mob.

Mathias Thulmann strode away from the vast heap of ash and charred timber. The priests of Morr were standing ready, spades stabbed into the ground beside them, waiting to conduct the ashes to the unhallowed spot outside the gardens of the dead reserved for sorcerers and heretics. No marker graced the grave of a witch, no mourner wept at the passing of such a creature. A miserable end to a miserable life.

The stocky figure of Streng detached itself from the wall of a cooper's shop facing the square, a partly drained flagon of ale gripped in his grimy fingers. The bearded mercenary took another sip of his brew, then smiled at his employer.

'She took a long time, eh Mathias? I wouldn't have thought the old bird had that much squawk left in her.' Streng gave vent to a short snort of brutal amusement. 'Not after I got through with her at any rate.'

Thulmann strode past his henchman, not waiting to see if the thug would follow after him or not. 'Your skill at wresting the truth from sealed lips is quite notable, Streng, and of great value to me. But for all of that, I find it no less distasteful.' The witch hunter continued on his way, stalking through the narrow streets of Wurtbad like some grim apparition.

'Keeps you from getting your hands dirty, doesn't it, sir?' the torturer observed, his tone indignant.

'So do the labours of a dung gatherer, yet I hold him in no great deal of admiration either.' The witch hunter paused, observing that his path had brought him to the inn where he had lodged since arriving in Wurtbad. He reached into the inner pocket of his scarlet tunic, removing a small pouch. Without looking back, he tossed the object to his henchman. The pouch landed in the street to the sound of jangling silver. Streng reached into the gutter and retrieved his payment.

'Don't think your hands are any cleaner,' Streng told his employer as he counted out the coins into his hand. 'I may break them for you, but you are the one who does the catching. There is just as much blood on your name as there is on mine.' A wicked leer spread across the ruffian's face. 'I reckon we're more alike than you'd be comfortable admitting.'

Thulmann turned back from the doorway of the inn. 'There is a difference between what you do and what I do, Streng. I act in the service of Lord Sigmar. You work for crude gold and the base pleasures it can buy.'

The hireling bristled under the venomous comment. 'If you'll not be needing me further, sir, I'll be retiring to pursue some of those base pleasures, as you call them.'

'See that you are sober enough to be of some measure of use in the morning,' warned the witch hunter as his henchman retreated back along the street. Without waiting for further comment from the torturer, Mathias Thulmann stalked into the Seven Candles.

The Seven Candles was one of Wurtbad's finest inns, its cellars and pantry among the very best which the city had to offer. Its rooms were spacious, its bedding clean, its serving wenches pretty and amiable. Yet despite these qualities, the common room was all but deserted, only a pair of subdued soldiers populating the benches, both men casting sidelong glances at the sinister figure of the witch hunter as he entered.

Thulmann did not meet their furtive gaze, knowing well the mixture of guilt and fear he would find in their eyes. He had seen such looks before. Every man, if he was honest with himself, felt deep in his heart that he had failed his god in some way. Perhaps he did not attend services as often as he should, perhaps he did not pray as often as he might. Had he neglected to tithe a portion of his silver to the temple, or maybe spoken an impious thought? Sigmar was a loving god, but also a stern one. Would he readily forgive such indiscretions? A witch hunter was a living, breathing reminder that one day all failings would be judged, and perhaps sooner rather than later.

It was that guilty unease which the witch hunter's presence evoked that had depopulated the Seven Candles. As the portly owner of the inn scrambled from behind his counter to fawningly inquire as to Thulmann's needs, the witch hunter knew the question that was foremost in the innkeeper's mind, the one question which the little man would never be able to nerve himself enough to ask. *And when will you be leaving so that my custom will return?*

'Wine and some roast pheasant, if you please, innkeeper,' Thulmann addressed the proprietor as the man nervously strode towards him. 'I will sup in my rooms this evening.'

The witch hunter cast an imperious gaze across the almost vacant common room. 'The atmosphere here is rather cheerless tonight.' The innkeeper bobbed his head in acknowledgement of the witch hunter's demands and hurriedly retreated back into the kitchen to hasten his cook about preparing the Templar's meal.

Thulmann left the man to his labours and ascended the wide staircase that rose to the private bedrooms above.

Mathias Thulmann, as was his habit, had taken the finest room in the Seven Candles, relocating the previous occupant to the local magistrate's dungeon on suspicion of being a mutant. He'd have the arrogant wine merchant released upon his departure from Wurtbad, certain that the man would be a much better Sigmarite for his humbling experience.

It was part and parcel of Thulmann's philosophy that as representatives of Sigmar's continuing sovereignty over the lives and souls of the people of the Empire, witch hunters were due every courtesy and consideration. It was a reminder to every man that to be a good Sigmarite, sacrifices needed to be made, even if only such sacrifices as might be extracted from a money belt. Besides, it was well to illustrate to the common that by devoting themselves completely and fully to Sigmar they would be rewarded, not simply in the next world, but in this one as well. The respect of even the most noble could be any man's if he but had the courage, determination and devotion to prevail.

The witch hunter smiled to himself as he opened the door to his room and sank into the upholstered chair that faced out upon the chamber's view of the clustered rooftops of Wurtbad. After all, one who fought daemons and all the other misshapen abominations that lurked in the black corners of the Empire deserved a few comforts. A comfortable bed, generous provisions and a decent bottle of wine were not really so much to ask of those whose souls it was his sworn duty to protect from the things that would prey upon them.

And yet, no man was infallible. Thulmann considered again the screams of the wretched Chanta Favna as the ancient hag had been greedily consumed by the flames of her pyre.

He had nothing but contempt for creatures such as the old witch; they were beneath pity or regret. Exterminating such practitioners of foul and proscribed sorceries was a just and proper thing, a sacred obligation necessary to ensure the continued security of the Empire. But it was not only witches and necromancers that Thulmann had consigned to the flames. There had been many others, ones who did deserve some pity, ones who were not unworthy of some measure of sympathy. The evil he fought against was like a malignant plague, striking as indiscriminately as a ravenous beast. The mark of Chaos did not restrict itself to those who invited it into their souls, but could infest even the most innocent, twisting first their bodies, then their minds. Slowly and insidiously it sapped their strength until at last it corrupted their soul as completely as that of any warlock or champion of the Dark Gods.

Suddenly the source for his ill humour and harsh words to his henchman rose to the forefront of his mind. After the execution, his gaze had lingered upon a face in the crowd that had gathered to watch the destruction of the witch. It had been the face of a woman, soft and comely, filled with fascination and revulsion as she watched the flames consume the murderous crone. The spectator's face had been more to Mathias Thulmann than a remarkable countenance amidst the crowd, for it had reminded him of the face of another. It had been a window into the past, an unwelcome reminder of another pyre which the witch hunter had lit over a year past.

Mathias Thulmann could remember every moment of that incident. The report of a taint in the noble house of von Lichtberg, the swift investigation set into motion upon his arrival, the brutal attentions of Streng as he put the chief suspects to the question.

The girl had been the source of that taint, her body infested with a seed of Chaos, a mutant thing that could not be born into a sane world. She had been

innocent of any profane sorceries or heathen witchcraft, innocent of all those twisted deeds and
malevolent desires that made it so very easy to perform his duties. No, her only fault had been to heed
the advice of a crackpot physician and to love the son
of a nobleman. And for that, she had been tortured
and finally destroyed.

The witch hunter rose from his chair, the unpleasant memories coming more rapidly now. He'd
shown leniency toward the poor girl's lover, the
young Baronet Reinhardt von Lichtberg. Knowing
him to be free of any taint, he'd ordered the boy to
be released.

It was a decision that continued to haunt him. He
should have had the boy destroyed as well, for he
had seen the rage and bloodlust in those young eyes.
Indeed, Reinhardt von Lichtberg had pursued the
witch hunter across half the province of Stirland,
catching up with him in the small village of Kleins-
dorf.

Their meeting had been a violent one, but again the
witch hunter had been lenient, leaving the vengeful
youth wounded but alive following their encounter. It
was a foolish thing to have done, the witch hunter
realised, it would have been better to have the boy
destroyed for seeking to harm an officer of the Temple. But somehow Thulmann could not bring himself
to regret his unwise mercy. The knowledge that Reinhardt von Lichtberg was out there somewhere, alive,
even if thirsting for the witch hunter's blood, lessened
to some degree the lingering sense of guilt Thulmann
felt for the regrettable execution of the girl.

There was only one thing that would fully assuage that guilt. For long months now Thulmann had been on the trail of the man responsible for the girl's corruption, the old family physician of the von Lichtbergs, a villain named Freiherr Weichs. Herr Doktor Freiherr Weichs had talked the poor girl into taking a vile concoction of his own devising that he swore to her would dissipate the unborn and unwanted life growing within her belly.

But that elixir had been poison, containing the foul substance known as warpstone. Far from destroying the unborn life, it had changed it, and with it the woman herself, polluting her blood with the black filth of mutation and Chaos. Thulmann had sworn an oath to hunt down the quack physician as he watched the flames devour the girl, and had spent the better part of a year doing just that. Even as Reinhardt von Lichtberg stalked him, so did he stalk the true source of the boy's misery. That trail had led him across three provinces but at last, the witch hunter felt he was drawing near to his quarry.

Mathias Thulmann stared out of the window, gazing once more across the rooftops of Wurtbad. Somewhere amidst the bustle and confusion of the city, he would find Doktor Freiherr Weichs. And when he did, he would pile the doktor's pyre so high they would see the fire even in Altdorf.

The incident with Chanta Favna had been a necessary delay in his hunt, but now there would be no further distractions. The man who had hired the witch was in custody and would join her as soon as Meisser finished going through the motions of a trial. The man who had thought to control the river trade in Wurtbad through his scheme, and was going to discover that he'd lost not simply his wealth and position, but his life and very soul by contemplating such outrage.

It did not matter to Thulmann, in the end, that Meisser would take most of the credit for putting an end to the witch and her murderous creation, and for unmasking the villain who had made her witchcraft a part of his plotting. That the horror had been brought to an end, that the guilty would meet justice was all that mattered to him. After all, that was all that would matter to Most Holy Sigmar.

MATHIAS THULMANN LOOKED up from his meal as he heard the soft, subdued sound of knocking at his door. The interruption put the Templar in an even blacker mood and it was with an imperious tone that he commanded the supplicant to enter and state his business. The door swung inward and the portly innkeeper darted his head into the room.

'Forgive me, sir, but there is a man here to see you.'

'He can wait until I have finished this mediocre dinner you have seen fit to try and poison me with,' Thulmann snapped back. The innkeeper grew pale as Thulmann made his displeasure known, horrified that the meal had not been to the witch hunter's liking. Thulmann, considering their conversation over, returned to attacking his plate. When he looked up again, he was surprised to see the man still standing at the door.

'Begging your pardon, sir, but I don't think your visitor is the kind to be kept waiting,' the innkeeper cringed as he saw Thulmann raise a questioning eyebrow.

'You intrigue me,' the witch hunter stated in a matter of fact tone. He lifted a napkin at his face. 'I wonder what sort of man thinks himself so important that he should take a Templar knight of Sigmar away from his humble victuals.'

'He's downstairs,' the heavy-set man stammered. 'He says his name is Lord Sforza Zerndorff.' The innkeeper made the sign of the hammer as he spoke the name. 'From Altdorf. Says he's a witch hunter like yourself.'

SFORZA ZERNDORFF WAS seated upon one of the benches that rested against either side of the common room's three massive tables. Except for him, there were only two others in the room. But these were no simple off-duty watchmen, these were soldiers of a different cast, their liveries black as pitch, massive swords sheathed at their sides, huge pectorals depicting the twin-tailed comet of Sigmar hanging from massive silver chains upon their breasts.

Zerndorff himself was much smaller than his bodyguards, stocky and full in his figure where the two guards were lean and powerful. However, there was no mistaking the strength and authority of the smaller man, his piercing blue eyes considering his surroundings with a haughty air of disdain. Zerndorff idly tapped the polished top of the table with the tip of a small black-hilted dagger as Thulmann strode into the hall.

'Ah, Thulmann,' the dignitary from Altdorf said, his voice conveying irritation. 'I was beginning to think you'd perhaps gone to Altdorf to look for me. Or perhaps my messenger did not deliver my summons promptly?' Zerndorff sent a look of displeasure at the innkeeper who swiftly scuttled away into the kitchens.

'Forgive my delay, Lord Zerndorff,' Thulmann said to the dignitary. Zerndorff motioned for the other witch hunter to sit down, deciding to ignore the lack of contrition with which Thulmann voiced his apology.

'I have little time to waste, Thulmann,' Zerndorff said, 'so I will cut to the chase. I have need of someone I can trust. As you know, with the rather ugly business that has come forward in the aftermath of Lord Thaddeus Gamow's death, the entire hierarchy of our order has been restructured. There is no longer a position of Lord Protector of the Faith, instead the Grand Theogonist has appointed three witch hunter generals to share authority over the order.' Zerndorff paused, favouring Thulmann with a sly smile of superiority. 'It may be of some small interest to you to know that I have been appointed Witch Hunter General South.'

'Congratulations,' Thulmann told Zerndorff, the hostile emotion boiling within him held in check only by a supreme effort of will.

'Thank you,' Zerndorff replied, nodding his head by the slightest of motions. His smile faded away and his expression grew grave. 'I know that we have had our troubles in the past and there is no love lost between us. But I also appreciate that you are a man of conviction, that your faith in Lord Sigmar is absolute and total. That accounts for much these days, much more than any personal animosity that lies between us.'

'I understood that there was some matter you wished to discuss with me?' Thulmann interjected.

'Just so,' Zerndorff answered. 'As you can imagine, the restructuring of the order has not been accomplished without a great deal of bad feeling on the part of those whose power, or ambitions for power, has been compromised as a result of the abolition of the post of Lord Protector. The Great Temple in Altdorf is a nest of plotters and schemers these days, accusation and rumour as plentiful as sand in the desert of Araby. Everyone seeks to discredit everyone else and even the Grand Theogonist is not without his detractors. Indeed, there are some who try to connect the Grand Theogonist with Gamow's heresy, claiming that his restructuring of the order is a heretical plot to weaken the temple and reduce the efficiency of the witch hunters rather than a measure to protect against the possibility of another Gamow.

'You are an honest and loyal man, Mathias, and I trust in your devotion to the temple, even if I question your methods. There is a matter which requires a man of conviction, someone I know to be above the petty schemes and plots running rife in Altdorf. Rumours have reached my office, disturbing rumours that give me cause for concern.' The witch hunter general's demeanour became somewhat furtive and it was with a slightly lowered voice that he continued.

'You have heard no doubt of the Klausner family?' Zerndorff asked.

'The name is familiar, though I cannot say that the particulars stand out in my mind,' Thulmann replied somewhat warily.

Zerndorff leaned forward, his fingers folded on top of the table.

'The Klausners are an old and highly respected family,' Zerndorff told him. 'Very devout Sigmarites, and very zealous in their faith. Many of them have been priests and Templars over the years, and not a few of them have achieved respectable distinction. The family can trace its roots back five hundred years. They were awarded a small holding south of here in 2013, and have ruled it ever since, their district notable for its very generous tithes of money and crops to the temple. Klausberg, they named it, good farm lands, renowned for the quality of their cattle. The present patriarch of the family and lord of Klausberg, Wilhelm Klausner, is a personal friend of the Grand Theogonist himself.

'You will understand, I hope, that when I heard rumours of something strange and terrible in Klausberg why I was immediately interested.' Zerndorff's voice dripped into an almost conspiratorial whisper. 'Something is killing the people of Klausberg. Something unnatural and unholy, if the tales are to be believed.'

'What tales?' Thulmann asked, feeling himself drawn into Zerndorff's theatrics despite his determination not to suffer the man's manipulative tricks.

'Tales of men stolen from their beds in the dead of night,' Zerndorff said, 'only to be found in some field or hollow in the morning, face ripped away, innards spilled about the ground. Tales of young maidens walking home from tending their flocks and never to be seen alive again, taken by a daemon beast that stalks unhindered about the land. If we were to trust the frightened gossip that has trickled into the ears of my informants, then this daemon creature has already claimed a hundred lives, adding another corpse to its tally almost every night.'

'Surely an exaggeration,' observed Thulmann.

'Oh, doubtless the stories have grown in the telling,' Zerndorff admitted, a smug smile on his face. 'But even such tales have some truth at their root. Something is going on in Klausberg, something is killing people there. And whatever it is, it doesn't behave like an animal, an orc, a beastman or any of the other murderous things the people of our troubled land are used to coping with. There is something very unusual about the murders in Klausberg. Given the history of the ruling family, it is not impossible that some sinister enemy of the temple has chosen to wreck havoc upon their lands.'

'I have my own investigations to conduct here in Wurtbad,' Thulmann informed his superior. Zerndorff shook his head.

'You will have to set all other matters aside,' he told Thulmann. 'Instruct Meisser in what needs to be done. I want you to look into what is going on in Klausberg. I need to know what is happening, the nature of the fiend that is preying upon the lands of the Grand Theogonist's friend. I need to know if this is the opening stroke in some larger plot to discredit or destroy the Grand Theogonist's chief supporters. I have grave concerns that those behind such a plot might be secret disciples of Gamow who may yet operate within the temple. I want you to go there and learn if my fears are well founded.' Zerndorff rose to his feet, retrieving his soft, almost shapeless silk hat from its place on the table.

'I know that I can trust you to not fail the temple in this matter, and to be discreet about whom you inform of your findings,' Zerndorff spoke, his back to Thulmann. He lingered for a moment as his body-guard opened the door of the inn. When one of the soldiers signalled that all was in order, Sforza Zern-dorff strode out to the carriage awaiting him outside without a backward glance.

Mathias Thulmann watched the departing witch hunter general, his manner like a guard dog keeping a close eye on a prowling wolf. Even after Zerndorff was gone, Thulmann kept an easy hand on the hilt of his sword.

Witch Hunter General South. It was sometimes difficult to maintain faith in justice when it seemed that villainy was rewarded at every turn. Thulmann had worked with Zerndorff long ago, an association which he held no pride in.

Zerndorff was a ruthless man, callous and very ambitious. His methods were centred more upon speed and efficiency than they were upon protecting the innocent and punishing the guilty. Zerndorff practised his trade with the same wanton brutality which had characterised the Templar knights during the dark days of the Three Emperors. He gave no thought to proving guilt, even less to the possibility of executing innocent men or women. For Zerndorff, it was the number and frequency of executions that mattered. Those suspected of heresy were tried and convicted as soon as their name was made known to him, all else was simply tradition.

Breaking the suspect on the rack, wringing a confession from their bloody lips, these were nothing more than theatre, placating a secular system of law which Zerndorff felt did not apply to him. He was the sort of man who would purge a crop of weevils by putting it to the torch. Yet this was just the sort of man who had earned the attention of Altdorf, the sort of man who had been promoted to a position that gave him power over a third of the Empire. Thulmann struck his fist into the palm of his hand, cursing the inequity of Zerndorff's good fortune.

That Zerndorff had chosen Thulmann to look into the incidents in Klausberg was, the witch hunter was certain, simply Zerndorff's way of exerting his newly granted authority over his one-time associate, of reminding Thulmann of how greatly their positions had changed. That it interfered with Thulmann's own affairs made the matter all the more pleasing to Zerndorff, Thulmann was certain.

That the man he hunted might escape once again while Thulmann was on his fool's errand would not have concerned Zerndorff in the slightest. They could always find another witch to burn. Most likely, when he arrived in Klausberg, Thulmann would learn that the incident was nothing more than the work of a pack of wolves or a band of goblins, despite Zerndorff's insistence that it was something more.

The witch hunter paused as he began to consider this light dismissal of Zerndorff's assignment. True, his old rival was a petty and malicious man, but he was also a man who was obsessed with efficiency. If he had made the trip down from Altdorf, there had been more to his journey than trying to put Thulmann in his place. Zerndorff could have simply sent a messenger for something so inconsequential.

No, there must be something behind the witch hunter general's suspicions, something that Zerndorff expected to profit from by investigating. But what? The Klausners were old friends of the Grand Theogonist. Zerndorff's own familiarity with Volkmar could hardly be considered so amicable. Why then was Zerndorff so interested in the safety of a house that was so supportive of the Grand Theogonist? Did he really think to expose some conspiracy against Volkmar, or did he perhaps hope to gain control of it?

Mathias Thulmann stared once again at the door through which Sforza Zerndorff had departed. What would he find in Klausberg?

THE TINY ROOM was barely five paces wide and only a little greater in depth, its walls of bare black stone illuminated only by the flickering fingers of flame rising from the double-headed candlestick that rested below the small altar. Two doors were set against the walls to the left and right of the altar, the only interruptions in the naked stone surface, doors that connected to rooms where warmth and comfort were not considered impious and improper.

The air within the cell-like chamber was chill and carried with it the dampness of the outer walls of the old keep.

The small room's sole occupant shuddered under the cold attention of the draft, drawing the heavy wool cloak a bit tighter about his scrawny frame. He was far from young and noted the creeping chill more than any other in his household. Yet he had attended his midnight devotions here, in this small chapel set between the master bedchamber and that set aside for the lady of the keep, for more than a quarter of a century and he would not forsake his religious duties even if the grim winds of Kislev were to batter against the outside walls of the keep.

Indeed, there were few things that could quiet old Wilhelm Klausner's troubled mind in the long watches of the night sufficiently to allow him to sleep. The calming peace of casting his respectful gaze upon the heavy steel hammer resting upon the altar was one. A devout, even fanatical Sigmarite all his life, it did Wilhelm's soul good to think that the patron god of the Empire was gazing down upon him.

The hands folded in supplication before Wilhelm's bowed figure were thin and pale, blotched with dis-colourings and devoid of both strength and substance. The massive gold ring, with its rampant griffon crushing a ravening wolf under its clawed foot, hung loose about the old man's finger, as though the slightest motion might set it sliding from its perch.

The man himself was an embodiment of age and infirmity, shoulders stooped beneath the weight of years, face gaunt and lean, eyes withdrawn into their pits, dull and bleary with cataracts. His silver-grey hair hung down about his shoulders in an unkempt nest. It was not time alone that had placed its stamp upon Wilhelm Klausner, but the ultimate effect of a hard life filled with trouble and discord.

The old man lifted his head once more, his dull eyes considering the altar and its icon. Prayers slipped from Wilhelm's mouth as he repeated over and again a simple catechism he had learned long ago, a plea for protection from the denizens of the Old Night.

The old man's head snapped around from his devotions as he heard the heavy oak door connecting the chapel to his own chambers slowly open.

A man passed through the portal, broader of shoulder than the aged Klausner, with a face that was full and plump. The man's rounded head was all but devoid of hair, only a light fuzz clinging to the back and edges of his skull. His face was sharp despite its fullness, the nose stabbing downward like a dagger. There was a gleam to his soft brown eyes that somehow added to the overall air of cunning that seemed to cling about him like a mantle. He strode forward, his staff clacking against the door as he stepped past it, the large brass buckles upon his boots gleaming as they reflected the feeble light of the candles.

'Forgive the intrusion, my lord,' the steward addressed Wilhelm as the patriarch began to rise. 'I wanted to inform you that I have received word from the village.' The steward paused for a moment, setting the end of his staff against the floor and resting his weight against it. 'It would seem "the beast" has struck again. Young Bruno Fleischer, body mangled almost beyond identity.' The steward paused again, favouring his master with a look of sympathy. 'I believe that you knew him.'

Wilhelm Klausner gained his feet with a sigh. 'Yes,' he said, the characteristic lisp extending the word. 'I knew him and his father. Very old friends of the family.' The old man cast his gaze to the floor, wringing his hands in despair. 'What have I done to invite such horror upon my people?' He looked once more at his steward, his eyes pleading. 'Tell me, Ivar, am I so steeped in wickedness that Sigmar should forsake me? And if I am, why then punish my people and not myself, if the guilt for these things be mine?'

'You have broken with tradition, perhaps that is why this terror stalks the district,' the servant informed his master. 'You should have allowed your sons...'

'No!' the old patriarch snapped, strength suddenly infusing his voice. 'I'll not let my sons walk the same path as I. I love them too well to wish such a curse upon them!'

'A strange way to speak of serving the order of Sigmar's Knights of the Temple,' Ivar commented in a quiet tone. 'One might almost describe it as heretical,' he warned.

'For ten years I played the role demanded of me by tradition. For ten years I travelled this great Empire, searching out the blackest of horrors, things which haunt my mind even now.' Wilhelm Klausner turned to face the altar again. 'I did that out of love for Lord Sigmar. He knows the measure of my devotion. But I'll not condemn my sons to ruin themselves as I have been ruined!'

'For those who fend off the darkness, there is always a price to be paid,' cautioned Ivar. 'No good has ever been achieved without the sacrifices of good men.'

'Then let some other suffer that sacrifice!' Wilhelm declared, rounding on his servant. 'The Klausners have paid more than their share. I have already lost so much, I'll not lose my sons as well.' The patriarch held his hand before his face, turning the wrinkled fingers before his eyes. 'Look at me, Ivar. Anyone would think me your senior. None would believe that you served my father before me. See how the horror I have witnessed has changed me, robbed me of my time. Well, that is a sacrifice that I have made, and Sigmar is welcome to it. But I'll not send my sons to do the same!'

'That is the tradition of the Klausners,' Ivar reminded his master. 'Back to the time of Helmuth, your family has ever sent its sons to serve among Sigmar's witch finders. It is a long and noble legacy.'

Wilhelm Klausner strode toward the altar, lifting up the candlestick. 'I am not concerned with the nobility of this house, nor its legacy,' he told his servant. 'My only concern is for the safety of this family.'

The old man strode past Ivar, through the open doorway that connected the tiny chapel to his own bedchamber. The steward dutifully followed after his master.

'That also is my concern,' observed Ivar.

The chamber into which he followed his master was opulently furnished, dominated by a gargantuan four-poster bed, its surface piled with pillows and heavy blankets of wool and ermine. A glass-faced curio cabinet loomed against one wall, nestled between a massive wardrobe of stained oak and the yawning face of a hearth.

In the far corner, a writing table was set, beside it a large bookcase, its overburdened shelves sagging under the weight of the dozens of leather-bound tomes set upon them.

Ivar watched with a slight smirk as Wilhelm Klausner let his heavy cloak slip to the floor, and hauled his scrawny frame into the waiting bed. When Wilhelm was fully settled, his servant stepped forward to remove the garment from the floor, draping it loosely over his arm.

'You have served my family well,' the withered man told Ivar. 'And I have always valued your counsel.'

'Then listen to my words again, my lord,' Ivar said, punctuating his words with a stab of his gloved finger. 'There are some who will take your decision in this matter none too lightly. They will see this breaking with tradition as an ill omen, a sign that perhaps those black horrors you speak of may have warped your mind, caused a rot within your soul. Are you so certain that you are so free of enemies that you can allow such thoughts to linger within the temple district in Altdorf?'

'Let my enemies do their worst,' sneered the old man, propping himself upright amidst his bedding. 'Their yapping will avail them nothing! I still have influence of my own in Altdorf. My name is not unknown to the Grand Theogonist, nor my reputation.'

'I think that is a dangerous assumption to make,' Ivar's voice drifted back into its cautious tone. 'I served your father long before he returned to these lands, and I know how suspicious witch hunters are, seeing a heretic behind every door and an abomination of Chaos in every shadow. Trust not in the ties of old friendships and loyalties when such spectres are invoked.'

'And you would have me destroy my sons to allay the doubts of such verminous fear-mongers?' Wilhelm spat. The old man shook his head, face twisted into a distasteful scowl.

'If these murders continue, you will have to do something,' confessed the steward. 'Things cannot go on like this. When it was six or even seven, perhaps we might have been able to handle the matter more quietly. But now...' Ivar shook his head. 'No, such a thing will have been noticed. And the eyes that are drawn to the district of Klausberg will not be those of your friends, my lord. Your enemies will seize upon these incidents like starving wolves falling upon a scrap of mutton.'

Wilhelm Klausner looked away from his steward, gazing at the iron-framed window in the room's outer wall. His hazy stare considered the cold darkness that clutched at the glass, the sombre testament of night's black dominion across his lands. What things might even now be crawling under that shadowy shroud? What atrocities might they even now be plotting to inflict upon his domain?

'Ivar,' the patriarch's voice sank to a lower, tremulous tone. 'You must not let it come to this! All that I have done has been to draw my enemies away from this place, to protect my family and my people from the unholy things that would do them harm. We cannot fail in this or all has been for nothing!'

The steward strode towards the heavy outer door of the patriarch's chamber. 'Your enemies are already come to Klausberg,' Ivar told his master.

CHAPTER THREE

THE DAY WAS nearly spent when the witch hunter and his henchman reached the village of Klausberg. It was a small settlement, located almost in the very centre of the rich farmlands that composed the district whose name the village bore and as such it held a greater importance than its small size would seem to indicate.

The village served as a staging area for the food caravans that transported the harvests of the district northward to the ever hungry inhabitants of Wurtbad. At harvest time, the sleepy village would become a hub of activity, filled to bursting point with merchants and farmers, huntsmen and farriers, each man trying to outwit the other as they sought to haggle their wares or secure goods that could be transported the long distance to Wurtbad and still earn a profit. The sounds of drinking and carousing would rise from the village's single tavern long into the night as all the peasant farmers and hunters tried their best to spend the money they had spent a year earning upon long-denied revelry.

No such sounds emanated from the tavern this day, as the lowering sun cast a burnt orange glow upon the plaster and timber walls that lined the village's narrow streets. Indeed, save for the grunting of pigs and the cackle of chickens, the lanes were utterly silent, the furtive and hastily withdrawn faces that occasionally appeared at the windows of some of the homes serving as the only sign of the villagers themselves.

The two horsemen who navigated the dirty lane that wound its way through the small huddle of buildings proceeded at a wary canter, hands resting against the grip of sword or pistol. If trouble was to manifest itself upon these deserted streets, it would not find these men unprepared.

'As barren as the Count of Stirland's barracks when the gold ran out,' observed the rearmost of the two riders. Streng cast a look over his shoulder, grimacing as he saw another face slip back behind a pair of shutters.

'It would appear that Brother Zerndorff's concerns are justified,' commented his companion. Mathias Thulmann did not look over at his henchman as he spoke, but kept his eyes focused upon the road ahead. He was less unnerved than his mercenary companion by the air of hostility and fear which surrounded them as they passed each dwelling, but he had learned over the course of his career never to completely ignore attitudes of ill will. 'There is most certainly an aura of fear hanging about this place, more than might be occasioned by a pack of wolves or a band of goblins.'

'Yes,' snorted Streng, spitting a glob of phlegm into the dust. 'You'd find a more cheerful welcome in the Chaos Wastes.' The mercenary looked over as another set of shutters slammed shut behind them. 'This lot are jumping at their own shadows.' Streng paused, his leer spreading, a glint appearing in his eyes. 'There is a fair bit of money to be made here, Mathias.'

The witch hunter favoured his underling with a look of contempt. 'We're here to help these people, liberate them from whatever unholy power is at work here, not to fleece them like a couple of Marienburg peddlers!' he snapped, voice laden with disgust.

'All I'm saying is that we might help allay their fears by finding a few witches straight away. A bit of burning would do this town some good,' the henchman persisted.

'Keep that larcenous tongue quiet, Streng,' Thulmann warned. 'Or you might discover that your services are not irreplaceable.'

The bearded mercenary sucked at his teeth as he digested Thulmann's reprimand.

Klausberg's inn loomed ahead at the end of the road upon which they now travelled. The building was surrounded by a low wall of stone, and the courtyard beyond was paved, a small fountain bubbling at its centre.

Thulmann considered the mouldy stone cherub rising above the pool, spitting an endless stream of water from its bulging cheeks. The witch hunter was not unfamiliar with the quality of worldly things and as his practiced eye considered the sculpture, he found himself impressed by the level of skill and artistry that had gone into it. He turned the same appraising gaze upon the façade of the inn itself, noting the quality of its construction.

Clearly Klausberg had been quite prosperous in better times. However, a chill crept down Thulmann's spine as he took note of the sign swaying from the post above the door of the establishment. In worn, faded characters it bore the name 'The Grey Crone' and beneath the crude Reikspiel letters was the image of an old woman, her body bent and twisted by the years.

The witch hunter's thoughts drifted back to Wurtbad and the destruction of the hag Chanta Favna. He made the sign of the hammer, knocking his palm against his saddle to ward away any ill omen.

After waiting for a moment for any sign that a stable boy might scurry out from the large stables attached to one side of the inn, the witch hunter dismounted. Streng followed his master's lead, dropping from his own horse with a grunt. Thulmann handed his underling the reins of his steed.

'The service appears a bit lacking,' he observed. 'Take the horses into the stables. I'll be informing the landlord of that sorry fact.'

The witch hunter strode across the courtyard, his steely stare watching the windows of the inn for any sign of the furtive movement that had shadowed their progress through the village. He paused upon reaching the heavy oak door, banging his gloved hand against the portal. Not waiting for any response, Thulmann proceeded into The Grey Crone.

THE COMMON ROOM that dominated the first floor of the inn was spacious, a cluster of tables strewn about its vastness, a long oak-topped bar running along one wall. Several small groups of peasant farmers were scattered about the tables, nursing steins of beer and jacks of ale.

The men looked up from their hushed, subdued conversations to regard the newcomer, their eyes at once narrowing with suspicion as they failed to recognise Thulmann for one of their own. The witch hunter returned their stares with an expressionless mask, making his way toward the bar. He took especial note of the bunches of garlic and daemonroot that had been nailed to the walls and above the doors and windows, their pungent reek overcoming even the smell of alcohol within the hall.

Thulmann gripped the counter, noting for a moment the age of the wood beneath his fingers, then glanced back at the gawking inhabitants of the inn. Their hushed conversations had died away entirely now, all eyes locked on the scarlet and black clad stranger.

Presently, the landlord emerged from a little door set behind the bar. He was a short man, hair turning to grey, with large expressive eyes and a cheerful demeanour despite the gloom tugging at his features.

As he saw the stranger waiting at his counter, however, a bit of the cheer drained out of him, replaced with an air of severity. He ceased wiping out the metal stein he was holding, setting both vessel and rag upon the bar.

'I suppose you'll be wanting a drink?' the innkeeper asked, his words clipped and his tone surly.

The witch hunter favoured the little man with his most venomous smile, pleased to see some of the anger give way to fear as the innkeeper withered before his gaze. 'If you cannot show your betters deference, I suggest you at least remember to show them respect.'

He turned his stern gaze to encompass the rest of the hall. 'I am Mathias Thulmann, Knight Templar of Most Holy Sigmar, duly ordained witch finder and protector of the faith.' The hostile, sullen faces of the inhabitants of the inn remained the same.

'Aye, we know what you are,' confided the innkeeper. 'But don't expect a witch hunter to find any store of love here.' The innkeeper filled a stein, setting the beer before Thulmann. 'I'll serve you, as that is my duty, but don't expect anything more. Not here. Not in Klausberg.'

Thulmann regarded the pop-eyed man, studying the mixture of fear and hostility he found in those eyes. The innkeeper looked away, rubbing at some invisible stain.

'And why should a witch hunter find cold welcome in Klausberg?' Thulmann voiced his demand in a loud, cold voice, causing many of the gawkers to suddenly remember their own drinks. 'Is this some nest of heathens and heretics that the servants of Sigmar are treated so?'

'No,' the innkeeper replied, shaking his head, a touch of shame in his words as Thulmann cast suspicion on the man's loyalty to his god. 'But there is something, some terrible thing that is killing folks here. And them Klausners,' the man paused, looking in the direction in which the Klausner Keep would lie, 'they do nothing to protect us.'

'Wolf hunts is what they give us,' scoffed one of the farmers. 'Beating forest and field to drive out whatever starveling mongrels hiding there. As if any wolf were the cause of our troubles.'

'What makes you so certain that it isn't a wolf?' Thulmann asked.

'Ever hear tell of any natural wolf sneaking into a man's home, snatching him from his bed and all the while, there beside him his wife lies sleeping?' countered Reikhertz. 'If it's a wolf, then it's no such wolf as should be natural, but some filthy thing of the Powers!' The man rapped his knuckles on the countertop as he made mention of the Dark Gods, hoping to ward away any ill luck that might draw their attention.

'Them Klausners know it too,' commented a strawhaired farmer, his face a mask of dirt. 'They know it and they're afraid, cringing behind their stone walls when night falls, leaving the rest of us to fend for ourselves!'

'Fine lot of witch hunters they be,' sneered another of the farmers, spitting at the floor. His bravado died however as Thulmann looked in his direction, and the man wilted back into his seat.

Thulmann turned his attention back to the innkeeper, intending to question him further as to why the villagers felt their lord was doing nothing to end their ordeal, but was interrupted by the opening of the inn's door. He watched as three men entered the beer hall.

It was obvious at once that they were distinctly apart from the modest, even shabbily, dressed villagers. Each man sported a leather tunic, breeches and high leather boots that reached to their knees. Each of the men also wore a sword sheathed at his side. The foremost of the men swaggered into the inn, the others following after his lead.

The leader of these newcomers was young, his hair flowing about his head in a primped and pampered mane of pale blond. His features were harsh, his squared jaw set in a look of arrogance and disdain. As he strode into the inn, his head brushed against one of the dangling clusters of garlic cloves. The man spun about angrily, his gloved hand clutching at the bundle of herbs as if it was the throat of an enemy.

'Fools! Idiots!' the man snarled, his words stretched by a slight lisp. The farmers cringed back in their chairs as the man glared at them. 'Heathen nonsense! Yet you cling to such stupidity like frightened children! As if a bunch of foul-smelling weeds had any power against Old Night!'

He hurled the garlic across the room with a grunt of disgust, then looked away from the cowed denizens of the tavern, casting a curious glance over Thulmann as the witch hunter leaned against the counter. He did not voice his curiosity, however, but looked past the witch hunter, favouring the innkeeper with an unpleasant smile.

'And how is Miranda this day, Reikhertz?' the man asked. He glanced about the room. 'I can't see her about. I do trust that she has not taken ill?' The mocking smile twisted a bit more.

'Not at all, m'lord,' stammered Reikhertz.

'Then go and fetch her,' the young man said, his words both a warning and a command. 'The sight of her pretty face… will make that pig's water you peddle a bit more pleasing to me.'

'Your brother won't favour you causing any mischief, Anton,' protested the innkeeper.

'Ah, yes, my brother Gregor,' although his tone did not change, a subtle suggestion of menace exuded from the young man at the mention of his brother. 'Did he perhaps offer you some special service? Perhaps he offered to protect your charming daughter?' Reikhertz licked his lips nervously as Anton spoke his words. 'As if it was me you need protecting from! You should thank all the gods that a Klausner should so much as look at that little cur you sired!'

'But your brother…' persisted the innkeeper, his voice pleading. Anton Klausner slammed his fist against the counter.

'My brother is not here!' he hissed. 'Now fetch that bitch or I'll do it myself!'

'Perhaps the young woman does not favour your company,' a silky voice intruded. Anton Klausner spun around, hand clenched into a fist, glaring at the speaker. Thulmann faced the belligerent youth with a condescending smile. 'If you would learn some manners, you might find the young lady a bit more agreeable.'

'Perhaps I'll teach you a few,' Anton's voice dripped with hostility. He looked over at his two companions, watching as each of the men began to move to place themselves at the witch hunter's back, then favoured Thulmann with his snide grin. 'But first I think I'll teach you to mind your own business.'

Anton aimed a kick at the witch hunter's groin, surprised when the older man anticipated the low blow, stooping and catching his foot in his hands. Thulmann straightened up, tipping Anton Klausner to the floor as he did so. The bully's two companions had been taken by surprise as well and moved to attack the witch hunter from behind when the solid wooden seat of a stool crashed into the face of one of them. The man dropped to the floor, a senseless bleeding heap. Streng swung the battered remains of the stool at the other ruffian, causing the man to retreat back toward the wall.

'Seems to me like this is more my idea of entertainment than yours, Mathias,' laughed Streng. The witch hunter glanced over at his henchman.

'I think I was rather generous, leaving two of them for you,' the witch hunter looked down at Anton Klausner as the young man began to rise, one hand closed about the hilt of his sword. The weapon froze after it had been drawn only a few inches, its owner staring into the cavernous barrel of one of Thulmann's pistols.

'I am Mathias Thulmann, witch finder,' he informed the subdued rouge. 'I have been sent here by Altdorf to investigate the sinister affliction that has been plaguing this district.' Thulmann's silky voice dropped into a threatening tone. 'So you see, this district and what happens here are very much my business.' He motioned for Anton Klausner to stand. The subdued noble glared sullenly at the witch hunter.

'Collect your friend and get out,' Thulmann told him, gesturing with his pistol to the insensible heap lying on the floor. 'And inform your father that I will be paying him a visit shortly.'

The witch hunter watched as the browbeaten bully and his crony pulled their companion off the floor and withdrew from the tavern with their burden. When the door closed behind them, the witch hunter reholstered his pistol. The tables broke out into conversation once more, this time louder and more animated as the farmers discussed the unique and exciting scene they had witnessed. Thulmann turned around as a small glass was set upon the counter near him.

'Thank you,' Reikhertz told him. 'Sigmar's grace be upon you.' Thulmann considered the small glass of schnapps, then gestured at the bottles of wine lined against the wall behind the bar. The innkeeper hastened to meet the witch hunter's wishes. 'That Anton is a bad one, worst of a rotten lot if you ask me,' he said as he returned with Thulmann's wine.

'I shall be seeing that for myself,' the witch hunter informed him as he sipped at his wine. 'In the meantime, I need your best room for myself. You will also make provision for my man here, be it a corner of your common room or a loft in your stable. I'll be dining with the Klausners this evening, so there will be no need for your cook to prepare a good meal. I'll also desire to speak with you when I return, so keep yourself available.'

Reikhertz beamed at the witch hunter. 'Everything will be as you wish. Anything at all that I can do, you have but to ask it.' Thulmann finished his wine and handed the glass back to the grateful innkeeper. He strode away from the counter, noting the admiring looks of the farmers.

'Thank Sigmar you've come,' one of them said. 'Perhaps now there will be an end to these murders.' His declaration caused the rest of the crowd to break into a murmur of agreement and hope. Thulmann walked toward Streng. The bearded mercenary grinned back at him.

'Seems you've won quite a following,' Streng commented. Thulmann nodded in agreement as another voice rose up from the crowd praising his arrival.

'Indeed, that ugly little incident may prove beneficial,' he observed. 'How beneficial I won't know until I've spoken with that young rake's father. Still, the good will of these people is certain to be of some help.' Thulmann looked back at the farmers, toasting his health and boasting of the now swift and certain destruction of the fiend that had been preying upon them. 'Besides, these people could use a little hope in their lives.' He cast a warning look at his henchman. 'Try to control some of your excesses,' he told the professional torturer.

The witch hunter looked over at Reikhertz as the innkeeper served another round of drinks to one of the tables. 'Also, the innkeeper has a daughter. Keep your hands off her.'

The mercenary gasped with feigned injury. 'Don't worry, Mathias, these hands don't go nowhere they haven't been invited first.' Thulmann's shook his head.

'Someday,' he said, 'I hope to find some scrap of virtue in that black pit that acts as your soul.'

'If it comes in a bottle, then someday you probably will,' laughed Streng, walking toward the nearest table and snapping his fingers to gain the innkeeper's attention. Thulmann shook his head and strode out into the darkening streets.

CHAPTER FOUR

KLAUSNER KEEP WAS a massive structure looming atop a small hill some distance from the village. The keep was surrounded by unspoilt wilderness, massive trees of incalculable age surrounding it on every side, a swift flowing stream of icy water running about the perimeter of the forest from which the keep rose like an island upon the sea. As the shadows of the trees enveloped his steed, Thulmann could barely discern the twinkling lights emanating from the narrow windows of the keep. The fading gleam of the village had long since been lost.

The witch hunter pondered the isolation of the keep. In most small villages, such a fortification was commonly surrounded by the dwellings of its common folk, the better to exploit the fort's thick stone walls for protection in times of war. Here, however, the village and the keep were distinctly separated, and by more than mere distance. There was every sign that the people of Klausberg avoided the residence of their lords and protectors.

The road to the keep was obviously not heavily travelled and did not branch, but proceeded exclusively and directly to the fortress, indicating that the paths employed by the common folk of the district detoured at some great distance from the holdings of the Klausners.

And yet, perhaps it had not always been so. As Thulmann rode down the path between the trees, he sometimes glimpsed the tumbled ruin of a wall, the last outline of a building, the faint impression of a foundation crouched within the shadows of the trees. He had the impression of old stonework, pitted by time and weather, heavy with the clutching tendrils of vines.

Were these perhaps the sorry remnants of some past incarnation of Klausberg? Could it be that because the keep had failed to protect them in the past that the descendants of that long-ago village now dwelt far from the castle? Somehow, the ruins suggested an antiquity greater than that which would give credence to such a theory.

Thulmann considered what he knew of the Klausners and their history. The family first came to prominence during the era of the Three Emperors in the person of one Helmuth Klausner, a renowned witch hunter who had been a great scourge of the forces of darkness and who had been something of a hero during the wars against the vampire counts of

Sylvania. Indeed, the district of Klausberg had been awarded to Helmuth Klausner by no less a personage than Grand Theogonist Wilhelm III himself in gratitude for the heroism that marked the witch hunter's accomplishments.

Since that time, the Klausner family had been remarkable in its devotion to the Temple of Sigmar, many of its sons serving as Sigmarite priests and Templars, following the example of their ancestor. It was an exemplary history of piety, service and honour, a record which made the witch hunter question the animosity and even fear with which the people of the district held the ruling family.

Thulmann knew that a witch hunter's greatest servant was fear, but it had to be fear tempered by respect. Had the patriarchs of the Klausner family neglected to recall this important lesson when they left the service of the temple to govern their own holdings? Certainly the example displayed by the bullying Anton did not speak well for the manner in which the Klausners conducted themselves.

Thulmann had travelled beneath the shadows of the trees for some time before at last the woods opened up and he saw the keep itself standing before him.

Up close, he began to understand some of the reason the keep was avoided. It was an ugly structure, sprawled atop the small hill like some great bloated black toad. Its walls were high, perhaps forty feet, its battlements craggy and irregular, like the broken teeth of some feral hound.

The central tower rose above the main mass of the structure by another fifty feet, affording it a view that encompassed the entire district. The outer wall of the keep was without windows, its smooth black stone face broken only by the huge door which fronted it. Upon these massive portals of Drakwald timber had been carved the coat of arms that had been the Klausners' for as long as any could remember: the griffon rampant crushing a slavering wolf beneath its heel. The coat of arms was picked out in a golden trim, the only show of colour in the cheerless façade.

Thulmann rode toward the gate, addressing the armoured sentry he found posted there. The guard considered the witch hunter for a moment, holding his pike in an aggressive manner, before withdrawing through the smaller door set into the larger gate. The sentry was gone only a few minutes before the gates swung inward.

The inner courtyard of Klausner Keep was small, scarcely larger than that of The Grey Crone. The witch hunter stared up at the imposing black walls all around him. It was rather like looking up from the bottom of a well, an impression that did nothing to offset the cheerless air about the place.

Two soldiers with axe-headed pole-arms regarded the witch hunter with stern expressions while a pasty-faced boy scurried out from behind a cluster of barrels to take the reins of Thulmann's steed. The witch hunter dismounted slowly, his eyes once again staring upward at the fast-darkening sky. He corrected himself. Framed by the black walls of the keep, the view was not so much like that seen from the bottom of a well, but from the bottom of a grave.

A bald-headed, round-faced man wearing a heavy black cloak over his dun-coloured tunic and burgundy breeches watched Thulmann arrive from the raised platform that faced the courtyard. He studied the witch hunter for a moment, then detached himself from the doorway in which he had been framed and descended a flight of broad stone steps to the courtyard, accentuating each movement with a flourish of his slender steward's staff.

'Allow me to welcome you to Klausner Keep,' the steward announced as he advanced toward Thulmann. 'I am Ivar Kohl, steward to his lordship, Wilhelm Klausner.' Ivar smiled apologetically. 'His lordship regrets that he could not greet you in person, but his health has not been well of late and his lordship finds the cold night air disagreeable.' The steward smiled again, as false and uncomfortable an expression as Thulmann had ever seen.

'I can sympathise with his lordship,' Thulmann said, his eyes cold, refuting the insincere friendship proffered by the steward. 'There is much in Klausberg that can be considered disagreeable.'

The steward redoubled his efforts to put the witch hunter at ease, his smile growing even broader, his hands extending to either side of his body in a gesture of openness. Thulmann waved aside the steward's words before he could speak them.

'I've not travelled here under threat of nightfall to be turned away by a servant at the threshold,' the witch hunter stated, a commanding note in his silky voice. 'I am here to see your master, and if he cannot come to meet me, then I must go to see him.'

Thulmann pointed at Ivar's face as the man's smile slipped away completely. 'Take me to see him now, and without any further delay.'

The steward grimaced as Thulmann voiced his demand, then waved at the stable boy to remove their visitor's horse to the stables. 'If you will follow me,' he said, turning his back to the witch hunter and ascending the small flight of stone steps once more. With a last wary glance at the smothering black walls, Mathias Thulmann headed after the retreating steward.

THE INTERIOR OF Klausner Keep was no less repellent to the witch hunter than its exterior. The cold stone walls closed in upon him, even in the cavern-like main hall that opened upon the courtyard, seeming to exude some malevolent, crushing influence. The sparse furnishings which Thulmann could see within the hall, while excellent specimens of craft and skill and polished to a brilliant finish, had an air of mustiness about them, an indefinable aura of antiquity and age.

The only other items to arrest his attention were hung about the far wall, surrounding completely a monstrous hearth flanked by marble columns. These were portraits, a collection of grim and brooding countenances.

The witch hunter broke away from Ivar Kohl and strode across the vast hall to examine the portraits more closely. The steward took several steps before realising that his guest was no longer with him. Ivar cast a worried look about the hall before sighting the black-clad Thulmann gazing up at the portraits.

'The past scions of the Klausner line?' Thulmann asked as Ivar appeared at his side. The witch hunter was certain that such was the case. There was no mistaking the menacing cast of the eyes, the lantern-like jawline and thin, almost sneering lips. He had seen such a face only a few hours before when he had introduced himself to Anton Klausner.

'Indeed,' nodded Ivar, stretching a gloved hand toward the paintings. 'All the patriarchs of the Klausner family have had their countenances preserved upon canvas and placed here. From Helmuth himself,' Ivar pointed at the massive portrait that hung at the very centre of the collection, almost directly above the hearth, 'to his lordship Wilhelm Klausner,' here the steward punctuated his words by bowing deferentially to a smaller portrait on the very edge of the grouping. Mathias Thulmann studied both paintings, comparing them and the men they represented.

The portraits had all been created by masters. However much Thulmann might despise the keep itself, he had to concede that the Klausners had a deep appreciation and a keen eye for a talented artist.

Each of the paintings seemed more like a reflection of the man who was their subject. Every line, every crease and wrinkle, every expression was there, captured in paint to endure long after the bones of the real men were dust. The look of imperious command was there in every face, the severity and devotion that any witch hunter must possess to perform his always dangerous, often unpleasant calling.

Thulmann stared at the portrait of Helmuth Klausner. He was pictured as a tall man, broad of shoulder, wearing a suit of burnished plate and a wide-brimmed hat. His face bore all the characteristics of the other Klausners, but the look in the man's eyes was even more penetrating. There was stamped the fervent, feverish gaze of a fanatic, so certain and firm in the surety of his purpose as to be beyond all reasoning, unwilling to brook any question.

Even the man's image had a power about him, and Thulmann could feel its echo. Such men became great leaders, heroes of their time, or they were consumed by their own power to become monsters. Thulmann could not decide which legacy the brilliant artist had striven to capture in his intimate study of Helmuth Klausner. The background of the portrait was composed of shadows, clutching, indistinct shapes. Were they cringing away from Helmuth Klausner, or welcoming him as one of their own?

'Nelus, is it not?' Thulmann asked, stabbing a finger at the glowering portrait of Helmuth Klausner. No, the witch hunter decided, there could be no doubt. It was surely the style of the long-dead Tilean master. Truly, the Klausners possessed a true appreciation of art, and were powerful and wealthy enough to bring even a man of such fame as Nelus all the way from Luccini to immortalise them.

'Indeed,' nodded Ivar once more. He gestured back toward the portrait of Wilhelm Klausner. 'His lordship's portrait was done by van Zaentz of Marienburg, some few years before his tragic death.' Thulmann found himself eyeing the more recent painting. It was no idle boast of the steward's, certainly the portrait was crafted by no less skilled a

man than the late Marienburger. Thulmann found
himself studying the visage of Wilhelm Klausner.
There was a strength to the man, a devotion to duty
and honour stamped upon his brow, etched into the
harsh outlines of his jaw. But there was more. A slight
spiderweb of worry pulling at the corners of his
mouth, a trace of unease and doubt seeming to drain
the conviction from his stern gaze.

Thulmann turned away from the wall of patriarchs,
gesturing for Ivar Kohl to lead the way once more. 'A
fascinating collection,' the witch hunter declared. 'I
am now doubly keen to meet a man blessed enough
to have sat for van Zaentz.'

THE MAN TO whom Ivar Kohl led the witch hunter
looked more like a withered skeleton than the powerful figure in the portrait. The strong features had
grown lean and thin, the once keen eyes blurred and
withdrawn. It was only with some effort that Thulmann managed to keep from gawking in
amazement at the apparition he faced. Wilhelm
Klausner was only a few years older than Thulmann
himself, yet the man lying before him looked withered and wizened enough to be the witch hunter's
grandfather!

The thin creature who sat propped upon a mound
of pillows at the head of a gigantic bed still bore an
air of command about him, as he gestured for the
servants who had brought him a miserable supper of
soup and wine to depart. Then the patriarch of the
Klausner family cast a stern and demanding eye
upon his steward.

'This is the man who insulted my son,' the harsh words snapped from the old man's lips.

'With respect, your lordship,' Thulmann spoke before the steward could sputter a reply, 'your son is the sort of man who invites trouble upon himself. He is fortunate to be your son, otherwise he might not have fared so well raising his hand against a servant of the Temple.' Wilhelm Klausner matched Thulmann's reproving gaze.

The two men locked eyes for a long moment, as though trying to take each other's measure. Thulmann was struck by the age and tiredness in Klausner's gaze. Here was a man who knew that death was stalking his every breath, who had resigned himself to the brevity left to his days.

Wilhelm Klausner looked away, shaking his head and wringing his hands. 'I know,' he confessed in a subdued tone. 'I have done my best with the boy, done my very best to raise him as a caring father should. But perhaps it is as you say. Perhaps I have overindulged the lad.' He looked again at the witch hunter, this time with a face that was heavy with guilt. 'You see, there is a tradition among the Klausners. The eldest son inherits the title and estates, all that this family has achieved. The other sons frequently resent that, feel that it robs their own lives of any value.'

The patriarch attempted a weak smile. 'Is it any wonder that Anton should display some bitterness, or that he might need to seek ways to relieve that bitterness?'

'Maybe he should take up opera,' Thulmann commented, his voice cold and unsympathetic. A man made himself, and there was nothing that could justify to Thulmann the bullying cruelty he had seen the young Klausner display in the tavern. Cold hostility replaced guilt in the old man's eyes.

It was Ivar Kohl who put an end to the tense moment. 'My lord, may I present Mathias Thulmann of Altdorf,' the steward introduced Klausner's visitor. He pivoted his body to make an expressive bow, his hand extended toward the massive bed. 'His lordship Wilhelm Klausner,' he needlessly told the witch hunter.

'Bechafen, actually,' Thulmann corrected the steward. 'Though I do keep in touch with the Imperial city. It was such a communication that occasioned my coming to Klausberg.'

'Indeed,' said Klausner, his lisp stretching and twisting the word. 'And what do they say in Altdorf that has caused an ordained witch hunter to make the long journey to my humble domain?'

'A great deal,' the witch hunter told him. 'None of it good.'

'I believe that Herr Thulmann has come here to investigate some exaggerated rumours regarding the recent attacks in the district,' explained Kohl.

Wilhelm Klausner lifted his body from the supporting pillows.

'If such is the case, then I fear that you have come all this way for nothing,' the patriarch stated. He shook his head, a grim smile on his face. 'It is some animal, a bit more cunning and fierce than is usual, it is true, but when all is said, still only a wild beast. My hunters will catch it any day now and that will put an end to the matter.'

'They did not seem to think it was something so trivial in Altdorf,' cautioned Thulmann.

'The Klausners are an old family and still hold great influence in some circles,' Ivar Kohl explained. 'And they have not done so without earning their share of enemies, even within the temple. It is only to be expected that such enemies would exploit even the most minor of incidents to try and disgrace the Klausner name.'

'It is a wolf, or perhaps some bloodthirsty wild dog, Herr Thulmann,' reiterated Klausner. 'Nothing more.' He smiled, leaning forward. 'So you see, we have no need of your particular services.'

Thulmann smiled back. Was that what was really behind the patriarch's icy demeanour? Not the fact that Thulmann had put his antagonistic son in his place, but the fact that he did not want a witch hunter operating in his domain, stepping on Klausner's own authority?

There were many magistrates and burgomasters who clung so desperately to their own small measures of power and authority that they deeply resented someone who could take that away from them, however temporarily. But Thulmann had not expected such treatment from Wilhelm Klausner. The man had been a witch hunter himself, surely he would be above such petty and selfish politicking?

'Whether you approve or not,' the witch hunter said, 'I have been ordered by Sforza Zerndorff, Witch Hunter General South, to investigate the deaths that have been occurring in Klausberg.'

The smile faded from Klausner's face and the old man sank back into his pillows. 'If it is simply a wolf, as you say, then my business here will, I am sure, be most brief.' The witch hunter's tone slipped into one of icy challenge. 'Incidentally, just how many people has this wolf of yours killed?'

Wilhelm Klausner gave the witch hunter a sour look, clearly disturbed by the question. Ivar Kohl seemed to choke on his words as they stumbled from his mouth.

'I… they say… some twenty or so,' the steward admitted, his voice rippling with a guilty embarrassment. 'Of course not all of them might have been killed by the same animal,' he added in a weak attempt to salvage the situation.

Thulmann's expression was one of strained incredulity. 'Twenty or so?' Thulmann could not believe the enormous toll, nor the fact that even in trying to be evasive as to an exact count, Kohl would admit to around twenty victims. How high might the actual number be? 'Two phantom man-eaters that you are unable to catch?' he asked. The witch hunter shook his head. 'Perhaps you are trying to catch the wrong kind of killer. They don't seem to share your opinion down in the village. I understand that some of these people were taken from their own homes. Rather bold for an animal, wouldn't you say?'

'Perhaps the victims had a reason to be abroad at a late hour?' Kohl stated. 'Sneaking into a barn for a late night drink, or some clandestine rendezvous. Or maybe the poor fellows heard their animals becoming agitated and decided, unwisely, to see what was upsetting them. Wolves often prowl near livestock, looking for an easy kill. And they say that once a wolf has tasted man-flesh, it prefers human prey above all others.'

'Nevertheless, it might be helpful to have an outsider look into these matters,' the witch hunter told him. He turned his gaze back toward the patriarch. 'I might be able to give you a fresh insight into these killings.'

'If you are determined,' the old man sighed, shaking his head. 'I can assure you that your attention would be better directed elsewhere.' He waved his thin hand, the heavy signet ring gleaming in the flickering light cast by hearth and candle. Ivar Kohl strode toward his master. 'Prepare a room for our guest,' Klausner told him.

It was Thulmann's turn to shake his head. 'That will not be necessary, your lordship,' he told the patriarch. 'I thank you for your generous consideration, but there are questions I need to ask the common folk of Klausberg. It will be easier to conduct my investigations from the inn.' Thulmann nodded at Klausner. 'I am sure you understand,' he added in his silky voice.

'Perfectly,' Klausner replied, his tone cold. The patriarch's face split into a cunning, challenging smile. 'You will of course allow my men to assist you in your hunt. They know this district much better than a stranger such as yourself. I am certain that you will find them invaluable to your investigations.'

'Another generous offer,' Thulmann responded. 'I shall take it under consideration.' He bowed before the bed-ridden patriarch, sweeping his black hat before him. 'I thank you for your time. I will make mention of your kindness in my report to Altdorf. No need to show me out, I know the way,' he said, turning and opening the chamber door before Ivar Kohl could do so for him. The witch hunter stalked away, the heavy oak panel closing behind him. When it had shut completely, the servant spun around to address his master.

'We can't allow him to stay here!' the steward swore. 'He has certainly been sent here to spy on your affairs!' Wilhelm Klausner motioned for Kohl to compose himself.

'We will keep an eye on him,' he told the steward. 'Make certain that he intends this house no mischief.' The old man sighed heavily. 'He may be of use to us, Ivar. Our own hunters haven't been able to track down this fiend. Perhaps the witch hunter can.'

Kohl shook his head, stamping the floor with his staff. 'You can't trust a man like that!'

Wilhelm Klausner sank back down into his pillows, a sly smile reappearing on his tired features.

'Who said anything about trusting him?'

MATHIAS THULMANN STRODE down the wide, empty stairway of the keep, descending toward the vast empty hall and its collection of grim-faced portraits. His meeting with the old patriarch had been a tense affair. The old man was suspicious, and afraid of losing control.

Despite what he had said, Thulmann had read the flickering expressions on the old man's face. He was deeply disturbed by the horror stalking his district, and frustrated by his own inability to put an end to it. That an outsider had come to accentuate his own failure in this matter clearly added to his frustration and guilt over the murders. The witch hunter wondered if the old patriarch could lay aside his wounded pride and desperate clutching at his control over the district in order to put an end to the depredations of this 'beast'.

Thulmann replaced his hat and smiled. Not for a second had he even considered the old patriarch's assertions that the culprit was simply an animal. Wilhelm Klausner had lost his touch, he was no longer liar enough to put conviction in a falsehood he himself did not even slightly believe. No, there was some other agency at work here, an agency every bit as sinister as whatever dread influence had so hideously and prematurely aged the patriarch.

'Are you the witch hunter from Altdorf?' asked a voice from behind Thulmann. He turned to find himself staring at a younger version of the man he had just left. Thulmann's gloved hand dropped to the hilt of his sword, thinking that perhaps he was being called to account for the events at the inn. But, no, as he looked at the man who had spoken to him, he at once realised his mistake.

The face he beheld did not have the cruel twist to its features, the sullen anger in the eyes that had characterised Anton Klausner. This man was of a similar cast, to be sure, with the heavy brow and square jaw of all the Klausners, but there was a firmness and nobility to his countenance, qualities that had long ago faded into an echo in the withered features of Wilhelm Klausner and which had perhaps never made their mark upon the face of his younger son Anton.

'I address Gregor Klausner, do I not?' inquired Thulmann. The fair-haired young nobleman inclined his head.

'You do indeed, sir,' he said. Some of the keenness and affability drained from him and his demeanour became apologetic. 'I must apologise for my brother...'

Thulmann raised his hand, waving away the young man's words of contrition. 'Your father has already made his apologies,' he informed Gregor.

'Anton is rather temperamental,' explained Gregor. 'I have tried to curb his excesses, but sadly, I fear that he seldom listens to my counsel.'

'Your father should take matters in hand,' Thulmann advised. A guilty look came upon Gregor, suggesting to Thulmann that the eldest son of Wilhelm Klausner had voiced such opinions to the old patriarch on several occasions. Gregor quickly regained his composure and began to usher the witch hunter down the remainder of the staircase.

'It is very good that you have come,' the young man told Thulmann as they walked.

'His lordship does not seem to view things in quite such a way,' the witch hunter replied. 'I am sure he would rather settle things his own way. However long it might take,' he added.

'My father is a very independent man, very set in his ways and firm in his beliefs,' Gregor stated as they reached the bottom of the stairs and began to walk across the vast entry hall. The footsteps of the two men echoed upon the polished floor as they walked, their voices rising to the vaulted ceiling high overhead. 'But his methods are not working. We need new ideas, a new approach to putting an end to this fiend.'

'There are only so many ways to catch a wolf,' Thulmann said. Gregor clenched his fist in silent rage.

'It is not a wolf,' he swore in a low voice. 'You won't find a man, woman or child in this district who believes that, no matter how many times my father tells them it is so. Though it would be easier to believe it was some manner of beast! To contemplate that a human being could sink into such depravity sickens the soul.'

'You are certain that there is a human agency behind this then?' Thulmann asked, pausing to study Gregor in the light cast by the hall's mammoth fireplace. There was outrage, a thirst for justice about the man. Unlike his brother, it appeared that Gregor valued and cared for the people of Klausberg and their misery was something that offended him deeply.

'Several of the victims have been stolen from their beds, from behind locked doors,' Gregor said. 'What beast can open a lock? What wolf ignores swine in their pen to steal a maid from her room in her cottage?'

Thulmann nodded as he heard the conviction and emotion in Gregor's voice. There was a possibility that the young man had been sent by his father to spy upon the intruding witch hunter, but Thulmann was a good judge of character and though he had only just met the man, he felt that Gregor would be a poor choice for such duplicity.

'I am staying at The Grey Crone,' he told Gregor. 'It would help me a great deal if you would meet with me there. You have, no doubt, a great insight into your father's methods of hunting this fiend and why they have failed. Once I know what not to do, I should have a better idea of how to proceed and perhaps some inkling as to the nature of this fiend we seek.'

The young Klausner gripped Thulmann's gloved hand in a firm grasp. 'If you will give me time to fetch a cloak and have a horse saddled, I will go with you now.' The enthusiasm fell from his voice and it was with a grim expression that he continued. 'Even now, I fear that this malignant power may be working its evil.'

DARKNESS, BLACK AS pitch, cold as ice. That was what greeted the blinking eyes of Tuomas Skimmel as he sat bolt upright in his bed. The farmer cast his frantic gaze about, trying desperately to penetrate the gloom. Not even the shadows of the room's furnishings could be discerned, so complete was the blackness. The farmer gasped as he released the breath that had caught in his throat, immediately cringing as the hiss thundered in his straining senses.

What was it? What had broken his slumber? Had it been a sound? The creak of a floor-board, the rustle of a rat as it crawled through the walls of Skimmel's cottage? Perhaps it had been the icy touch of a draft whispering between the cracks in the walls, or the touch of a moth as it flittered about the room? Maybe it had been nothing more than his own mind, already overburdened with anxiety.

The fiend had struck the cottage three miles away only last week. It had been reason enough for Skimmel to send his wife and sons to stay with his mother in the village. But someone had to remain behind, to feed and look after the cattle. Skimmel's wife had considered him very brave to decide to stay alone at their home, but right now, Skimmel was more inclined to agree with her second assessment of his actions as they had made their painful goodbyes. She had said that it was foolish to stay with the fiend still abroad, and doubly foolish to do so alone.

Skimmel continued to sit frozen with fear. He could see nothing, hear nothing. He couldn't even smell anything unusual. Yet he knew. He knew that there was something in the darkness, something horrible and malevolent. Perhaps it was standing beside him, jaws stretched inches from his face.

Any moment he might feel its hot breath blasting his face, smell the stink of rotting flesh trapped between its fangs. Perhaps it was watching him even now, waiting for him to move, waiting for him to betray the fact that he was awake and aware.

An uncontrollable tremble began to worm its way through Skimmel's body. The farmer tried to fight the spasm, tried to crush it back down, keep it from over-whelming him, from betraying him.

The monster would see, it would see his legs as they shivered, it would see the goosepimples prickling his skin. It would see and it would know and it would pounce. The farmer gasped again, then gulped back another breath. Even breathing was difficult now. His body would not inhale unless he concentrated on it, and if he concentrated on breathing, then his limbs would start trembling even more fiercely.

What was that? The farmer turned his eyes without moving his head. He'd heard something, seen something in the corner of the room.

He tried to tell himself it was a mouse or a rat he had heard, tried to tell himself that the shape slowly appearing out of the darkness was nothing more than an old coat thrown across a chair. He tried to tell himself all of this as tears bled from his eyes, as the trembling of his limbs began to shake his bed.

The shape in the corner moved. Skimmel opened his mouth to scream, but no sound would escape from his paralysed throat. The trembling grew still more fierce and slowly, against his will, the farmer rose from his bed. The shape gestured to him with an outstretched hand, then it receded back into the darkness.

A CROOKED MOCKERY of a man stepped out from the humble cottage of Tuomas Skimmel. He wore a heavy cassock, grey and threadbare, trimmed in black wolf-hair about the sleeves and neck. The robed figure stared back into the gloom of the cottage and gestured once again with his thin, spidery hand. The flesh upon that hand was pale, marked by an almost leprous tinge.

At the man's gesture, Tuomas Skimmel emerged, eyes wide with terror, marching in stiff-legged-steps.

The necromancer smiled. His face was sallow, and the features were almost ferret-like in their suggestion of a malicious and scheming cunning.

Ropes of ratty brown hair dripped down into the necromancer's face as he exerted his will upon his victim. Carandini savoured the delicious terror he saw in Skimmel's eyes, enjoying it as a healthy mind might relish a glass of wine or a beautiful painting. He could just as easily have subdued the man's mind with his spell, but the necromancer preferred to watch his victim's agonies. He loathed the lowing, unthinking masses of mankind, but there was an especial hatred for the men of the Empire.

Indeed, such a man had nearly ended the necromancer's life in the Tilean city of Miragliano several years ago, an injury not easily forgotten. It was satisfying to Carandini that his knowledge of the black arts had grown tremendously since then.

The necromancer looked away from his enthralled, helpless victim, staring at the night-claimed landscape around them. He would need to be taken through the woods, led some two miles to where the ritual would take place.

Carandini pointed toward the distant trees, and watched his slave awkwardly march off into the night. How much greater would the man's terror become when he came to understand the full horror that was planned for him? He wondered idly if perhaps his heart might burst from fright when he beheld the awful aspect of Carandini's ally.

Yes, the necromancer thought as he followed after his victim, my knowledge of the black arts has grown, but it is still not enough. With the help of his ally, however, that situation would change. Carandini smiled as he considered his ambitions and their fulfilment. When he had his prize, then he would no longer fear death, whatever shape it wore. Rather, death would fear him.

Carandini hastened his steps, urging his slave to greater effort. The night was old and he was eager to complete tonight's sacrifice.

CHAPTER FIVE

THE LONG WATCHES of the night brought with them ethereal landscapes of grey worlds and fantastic visions. In the cold and chill hours, dream and nightmare clawed at the sleeping minds of men, filling their thoughts with curious sights and unquiet memories…

The sickly sweet smell of spoiled fruit and rotting cabbage surrounded the witch hunter. The darkness within the old warehouse was almost like a living thing, tangible, reaching toward him with groping claws, clinging to his clothes like some soupy vapour.

The old dry floorboards beneath his feet creaked as he made his way through the dust and filth. Plague had done its deadly work in this part of Bechafen two years before, few had been willing to return to the devastated neighbourhood with the memory of disease and death still fresh in their minds. But someone had not been so timid, and their footprints shone out from the dust as the witch hunter's light fell upon them. The hunter firmed his grip upon his sword, bracing himself. His quarry was very near now.

'So you did manage to keep my trail?' a cold, sneering voice rose from the darkness. The witch hunter froze, his eyes trying to pierce the clutching veil of blackness all around him. He directed his lantern toward the voice, casting the speaker into full visibility. He was a tall man, his black hair fading into a steel-like hue, his once aristocratic features beginning to sag and droop as age began to pick the meat from beneath his skin. He wore a bright red robe about his thin frame, the long garment hanging from him like a shroud. There were markings upon the hem of the garment, upon the sleeves and edges of its long cowl. These were picked out in gold and silver and azure hues, and they were no such symbols as any healthy mind should contemplate.

The sorcerer's empty eyes blazed into a fiery life as they considered the man who had come so far and risked so much to force this confrontation. 'I congratulate you upon your determination. Perhaps you are not quite the fool I had thought you to be.'

The witch hunter fought the uncertainty crawling through him. He had seen what this man could do, he had seen first-hand the awful, devastating power at his command. There was no question that the abominations he served were all too real, and there was no question that they had bestowed their dark gifts upon the sorcerer. The witch hunter had seen armoured knights cooked by eldritch flame in the blink of an eye. He had seen a steel gate break free from its frame of stone at a simple gesture and word from the warlock. And he had seen the unspeakable manner in which those who had died in the infernal rituals conducted by this madman to honour his foul gods had perished.

Who was he to challenge such awful power? What madness made him think he was the equal of a sorcerer?

Mathias Thulmann stared again at the visage of his foe. His face was twisted with contempt, as though it was the witch hunter and not the murderous heretic who was the deviant.

It was a face made all the more terrible for its echo of Thulmann's own. For Erasmus Kleib was the witch hunter's uncle, though madness and lust for power had long ago stripped Kleib of all that was decent and noble, leaving only a power hungry husk enslaved to the will of insane gods.

'You have no chance against me, boy,' Kleib spoke, his thin moustache curling as his face contorted into a sneer. 'You've only survived this long because I have allowed it. Some lingering trace of familial courtesy,' he gave a dismissive wave of his lean hand.

Thulmann shuddered as he considered the sorcerer's words. Could it be true? Had he indeed been able to come so far solely because of the madman's whim? He thought of his companions, his friends and comrades-in-arms. Dead, all of them, their bodies lying in graves strewn about Ostland. Even his

C. L. Werner

mentor, the renowned witch hunter captain Frederick Greiber, his throat ripped out by some black and winged horror upon the road from Wolfenburg. Doubt worked its way into Thulmann's face.

The sorcerer laughed, a short and hollow sound.

'That's right, boy,' he snickered. 'All of it, all the misery and fear, all the suffering and sorrow. All of it was needless, all of it was worthless.' The sorcerer studied the back of his hand for a moment, then looked once more at the witch hunter. 'If you ask nicely, however, I might be persuaded to allow you to leave this place.' Erasmus Kleib smiled, a look of malevolence and triumph. 'But you should be quick in your begging. I find myself becoming tired of this little game.'

The witch hunter found himself stepping back, the tip of his sword beginning to dip down toward the ground.

Despair, the rancid clutch of failure, coursed through his veins. It had all been madness, and now that madness would cost him his life. Somehow, the thought disturbed him but not for the reasons he had always imagined that it would. It was not death itself which he feared, but the thought that Erasmus Kleib would continue on after him; that once he was dead the sorcerer would continue to kill and commit atrocity after atrocity. It was the thought that Kleib would go unpunished that fuelled his fear.

One of the first lessons Thulmann had learned from Frederick Greiber suddenly came to his mind. A witch hunter did not meet the works of Chaos with wizardry of his own. He did not challenge the Dark Gods with weapons as steeped in depravity and wickedness as they. No, a witch hunter's weapons were courage and determination, to never allow fear and horror to take command of his heart, to never allow doubt and regret to weaken his resolve. He must trust completely and fully in Sigmar, armour himself in a shield of faith that would shine out into the darkness, that would challenge the terror of the night.

He must say, 'I am a servant of Sigmar, and his judgement is upon you,' and know that the strength of their god would be within him at such times. He must have faith, a faith strong enough to banish all doubt.

'No,' the witch hunter snarled, lifting his sword again. 'It is the grace of Sigmar that has brought me here. It is his determination that I shall be the one to visit his justice upon you, Erasmus Kleib, Butcher of Bechafen! And, though I perish in the doing of it, I shall see that you answer for your crimes!'

The sorcerer's face swelled with wrath. 'I see that I was mistaken,' he hissed in cold tones of subdued fury. He swept his arms wide, spreading his heavy crimson cloak about him. 'You are an idiot after all. Perhaps I shall one day answer to your puny godling's ineffectual concepts of justice, but not for some considerable time. There is much work that I have yet to complete for my own masters.' Erasmus Kleib looked at the shadows to either side of him. Thulmann could hear something moving in the shadow, the sound of claws scrabbling across rotten timber, the furtive patter of naked feet, low whispers of amusement rasping through inhuman jaws.

The witch hunter threw open his lantern to its full, illuminating the warehouse. He recoiled in disgust as he saw what the light revealed. Inhuman forms scuttled toward him from every side, shapes with crooked backs, slender limbs and long naked tails. They wore tunics of leather and loin wraps of filthy cloth, and their flesh was covered in a dingy brown fur where it was not marked by grey scars and crusty scabs.

The faces of the creatures were long and hound-like, protruding from beneath their leather helmets and cloth hoods. Beady red eyes gleamed from the faces of the Chaos-vermin, and massive incisors protruded from the tips of their muzzles.

Erasmus Kleib laughed as his inhuman allies scuttled forward to subdue the witch hunter. Thulmann could hear their chittering laughter as they gnashed their jaws and gestured with their rusty-edged weapons.

'Witch hunter! Witch hunter!' the monsters chanted in their squeaking voices. The sound of their naked feet became a dull tattoo upon the floor. 'Witch hunter! Witch hunter!' they hissed as they stalked closer still, the reek of their mangy fur heavy in the air. 'Witch hunter!' they laughed, the sharp report of their feet once again slapping against the floor.

MATHIAS THULMANN awoke with a start, hands flashing at once to the sword and pistol resting beside him on the bed. It took him only a moment to register his surroundings, to recall that he was not in

Bechafen, but in Klausberg. He wriggled his body to free it of the bed clothes that had twisted about him like a cocoon during his restless slumber, then patted at his face with the edge of one of the blankets, wiping away the cold sweat.

Dreams and nightmares. However firm his faith, however devout and complete his conviction, Thulmann seldom escaped their grasp for very long. He was only surprised that it had been the shade of Erasmus Kleib that had haunted him this night.

He'd encountered things far fouler and more horrific even than his degenerate uncle and his loathsome allies, things that made even Kleib's most heinous acts seem nothing more than the mischief of an unruly child.

Perhaps there was a reason behind the invasion of his nightmares by the dead sorcerer? There were some who said that dreams held portents of the future within them, if one but had the wit and wisdom to discern their meaning. Of course, such thought was well within the realm of astrologers, wizards and other persons of dubious morality and piety. Still, the witch hunter sometimes wondered if there might not be some truth in their beliefs for all their heresy. Were not dreams the method with which grim Morr communicated with his dour priesthood? And if Morr, the god of death, should deign to guide his servants in such a manner, who could say with certainty that mighty Sigmar, protector of man, might not use similar methods?

'Witch hunter!' came a muffled voice, accompanied by the sharp report of bare flesh striking against hard wood. Thulmann cast aside his ponderings as the sounds from his nightmare echoed through his room atop The Grey Crone. He rose swiftly from his bed, sword and pistol held in a firm grasp, and walked to the door before the person outside could knock once more.

'I've had men put to the question for a fortnight for disturbing me at such a Sigmar-forsaken hour!' Thulmann snapped as he threw the door open, frightening the colour from the already nervous Reikhertz. The innkeeper jumped back, crashing against the solid wooden wall of the hallway.

The witch hunter kept his angry glare fixed upon Reikhertz, his pistol held at the ready in his hand. 'It is courting heresy to disturb the sleep of an ordained servant of Sigmar.' Thulmann paused as Reikhertz began to mumble unintelligibly. 'Well, out with it man! What foolishness makes you court heresy before the cock has crowed!'

Reikhertz fought to compose himself, training his bulging eyes on the witch hunter. 'Fo... forgive... the... the intrusion... I... I... I m-meant n-no offence, noble... noble...'

Thulmann rolled his eyes, lowering his pistol and stepping out into the corridor. 'Despite the early hour, I begin to doubt if we will finish this conversation before the sun has again set.'

Like a mask, Thulmann discarded the anger he had assumed upon throwing open the door of his room. There was a time to intimidate commoners, to instil in them the proper deference and fear which his station demanded. But now was not one of them.

Thulmann slipped into the quiet, concerned voice of a father confessor, his eyes gleaming now not with hostility, but a keen interest in what the innkeeper had to say.

'It is clear that something of importance has happened,' he told Reikhertz, his tone now friendly and calming. 'I would hear whatever tidings you bear.'

Reikhertz swallowed hard, then nervously began to smooth the front of his woollen nightshirt. 'Please, begging your pardon, sir,' the shivering innkeeper said. 'But there has been another killing.'

Thulmann's expression grew grave. He nodded his head toward Reikhertz. 'Like the others?' was all the witch hunter said.

'Mangled and ripped apart,' the innkeeper confirmed. 'Old Hans found him, returning from frog-catching out by the bog-ponds. He thinks it might have been Skimmel, one of the district's cattle-herds.' Reikhertz looked down at the floor, fear creeping into his voice. 'He can't be certain though. There isn't enough left to be sure.'

'How is Lord Klausner attending to the incident?' Thulmann asked.

'Hans came here straight away,' Reikhertz answered. 'The Klausners haven't been told yet. Not that they would do anything about it in any event,' the innkeeper added, spitting at the floor.

'Send him to the keep just the same,' Thulmann told Reikhertz. 'If nothing else, I should like to see first-hand how Lord Klausner conducts his investigations into these killings. Then I may know better how not to conduct my own.' Thulmann paused for a moment, considering his next words. 'Tell this Hans to be certain that Gregor Klausner is informed and that I would appreciate his assistance. His knowledge of this district could prove quite useful.'

Reikhertz bowed to the witch hunter. 'Shall I have your horses saddled?' he asked.

'Yes, I'll be only a few moments,' Thulmann sighed. 'Breakfast will have to wait until I return. I expect you to see that it makes amends for my disturbed sleep.' The witch hunter dismissed the innkeeper with a gesture of his hand and Reikhertz hastened off down the hall. Thulmann turned and stalked toward the door that opened upon Streng's room.

'Streng!' he shouted, pounding on the closed portal. 'Rouse yourself you filthy drunkard! The killer has struck again and we ride in five minutes!' Thulmann lingered long enough to hear the thump of a body striking the floor and the sharp squeal of young woman, followed upon by muttered oaths and curses in Streng's sullen tones.

GREGOR KLAUSNER MET Thulmann and the still surly Streng shortly after the witch hunter had begun his ride toward the keep. Thulmann was once again struck by the competence of the younger Klausner.

Despite his naturally suspicious nature, the Templar had to admit that there was quite a bit of merit in the young Gregor. Their conversation of the previous night had revealed to Thulmann that Gregor Klausner was the polar opposite of the brash and bullying Anton.

Gregor had an eye for detail, a genuine passion for knowledge and, more importantly, a very high degree of personal morality and honour. Many times, in explaining to Thulmann the events of the past weeks, the pent-up frustration at his personal inability to relieve the suffering of the district came to the fore, breaking through his otherwise steely composure.

There had been another moment when Thulmann had observed Gregor's composure falter. When Reikhertz's daughter had brought them ale and wine, a look that had passed between the two young people. Reikhertz had quickly ushered his daughter from the room, casting a venomous look at Gregor, even more hostile than the one with which he had favoured Streng and the plump town whore he had managed to dredge up while Thulmann was away at the keep. It had been a tense moment, and Thulmann wondered at its import.

Gregor favoured Reikhertz's daughter, a situation which the innkeeper was perfectly willing to exploit in matters of protection, but also a situation which he did not condone. Suddenly Anton's behaviour of the previous night could be viewed in a new light.

Had Thulmann intruded upon a random act of bullying and arrogance, or was there something more? Anton probably knew that his brother favoured the pretty Miranda. As the younger son of old Wilhelm Klausner, the witch hunter wondered just how much Anton might resent his situation and that of his older brother.

'If it was any colder I'd be pissing ice,' snarled Streng, clapping his gloved hands against his fur-covered shoulders.

Thulmann cast a withering glance at the grousing sell-sword. 'We are about Sigmar's business. Perhaps if you considered that, your faith might keep you warm.'

'I'd prefer a set of warm sheets and the body of a hot woman,' the bearded ruffian grumbled. Thulmann ignored his complaints and turned to face Gregor Klausner. The young lord was dressed in a heavy fur coat, his head encased within the bushy mass of a bear-skin hat cut in the Kislevite fashion. Thulmann noted that both a sword and a holstered pistol hung from Gregor's belt. The witch hunter smiled. Gregor had his wits about him, even in such a lonely hour, preparing himself against not only the cold, but the unknown. There were many noblemen in Altdorf who would not have displayed such common sense and intelligence.

'This hollow that the frog-catcher described,' the witch hunter said. 'I trust that you know where it is?'

Gregor extended his hand, pointing toward a series of distant wheat fields. 'If we cut across those fields, we can come upon it from firm ground. The bog-ponds lie to the west of the woods, and south of it is an expanse of rough ground that some of the cattlemen use as pasture.'

The younger Klausner nodded at the witch hunter. 'We can make better time going across the fields than using the road. Besides, that is the route which Anton and my father's men will take.' Gregor's hard features spread in a grin. 'I rather imagine that you'd like a look at the body without my father looking over your shoulder.'

'I've made no mention of such intention,' the witch hunter told him, though there was no reproach in his tone. He motioned for Gregor to lead the way. 'The fields, then?'

The noble rode off, Thulmann and Streng following close behind him. A sharp mind, that one, thought the witch hunter. He'd possibly have made a good witch hunter himself. Indeed, given his family legacy, Thulmann wondered why he hadn't taken up such a vocation.

As they rode across the desolate fields of harvested grain, Thulmann reflected upon some of the things Gregor Klausner had told him the night before. Among the first of his revelations had been the fact that the current string of killings had not been the first to plague the district. There had been similar killings in the time of his grandfather, and his great grandfather, as any grey-hair in the town would relate in a subdued whisper if Thulmann cared to question them.

It was only by the tireless vigilance and selfless heroism of the Klausners that this horror had been driven back time and again and the lands protected from its marauding evil, or so the family tradition had it.

However, there was something more, something that disturbed even the most garrulous of the village elders. The deaths were different this time, bloodier and more savage than any of the previous ones. And it seemed that this nameless fiend was even more hungry for blood now than in the past, for all of the elders said that it had settled for far less death in their day.

Thulmann considered once more Wilhelm Klausner's insistence that the thing preying upon his district was merely an extremely clever wolf. In light of the grim tradition held by the villagers, Thulmann did not see how Klausner could honestly believe in such a theory. A wolf that had preyed upon the same district for over a hundred years? Working its mayhem in brief orgies of bloodlust and then slinking back into the wilds to wait decades before striking once again?

The old man might have been organising wolf hunts, but he could not honestly believe that what was haunting his lands was any normal animal. The old patriarch must surely be lying. Perhaps the old landholder was fearful of the scandal that might arise should knowledge of his family's grim curse become widespread. Perhaps he merely refused to believe that he might be unable to stop whatever fiend was behind his district's misfortune, and so refused to see his unknown enemy as a possibly supernatural being.

No, Wilhelm Klausner had been a witch hunter himself, he would be beyond such foolishness. He would have seen for himself the power of the Dark, seen with his own eyes some of the nameless things that haunt the night.

Thulmann wondered just who Wilhelm Klausner was trying to deceive about the nature of these

tragedies. After a long career confronting such horrors, retiring to the comfort of his ancestral home,
perhaps Klausner was no longer able to accept such
manifestations of evil.

Perhaps he needed to cling to some belief that having survived his years as a Templar of Sigmar, he had
likewise escaped from the dread clutch of Old Night.
Perhaps he could not cope with the idea that such
evil might stalk him again, rearing its foul visage
within his own lands.

Maybe he clung to the notion that his enemy was a
normal, clean animal, not some dread beast touched
by the corrupting hand of Chaos, or some daemon
emissary of the beyond. The one Wilhelm Klausner
was trying to convince might just be the old patriarch
himself.

CHAPTER SIX

THE CAWING OF crows announced that they had arrived at their destination. The three men dismounted on the very edge of the last of the fields, just where the level ground dripped away into a small wooded trench. As the witch hunter and his companions descended the dew-slicked slope, the stench of blood made itself known to them.

Thulmann could see a shape strewn about a stretch of open ground beneath the twisted, gnarled boughs of the hollow, alive with cawing, hopping scavenger birds. Several of them cocked their heads as the men advanced, favouring them with irritated looks. Streng set up a loud yell that caused the scavengers to take wing and scatter into the morning mist.

'Hopefully they haven't made too much of a mess,' Thulmann commented, striding ahead of his companions. The object that had so fascinated the crows had indeed once been a man, though the frog-catcher could easily be forgiven his inability to render the corpse a positive identity.

The arms and legs were the only parts that looked to be unmarked. The chest was a gaping wound, looking as if it had been torn open by a bear. The head was in even worse shape, little more than a mass of peeled meat resting atop the corpse's shoulders.

'Pretty sight, that one,' observed Streng, a bit of colour showing beneath his dirty beard. The witch hunter agreed. Death, horrible and unnatural, was part and parcel of the witch hunter's trade, yet seldom had Thulmann seen evidence of such unholy brutality. Gregor Klausner, unused to such sights grew pale, lifting a gloved hand to his mouth as the bile churned in his stomach.

Streng began to circle the body as Thulmann strode towards it. The mercenary stared at the ground, cursing colourfully when he found no sign of tracks. 'Ground's clean, Mathias,' he reported. 'Not a sniff of either a paw, claw or shoe.'

Thulmann bent over the corpse, casting a practiced eye upon the body. He glanced up, staring at Gregor Klausner. 'Rather savage work, even for a wolf, don't you think?'

'My father is convinced that these deaths are the work of some beast,' Gregor replied, speaking through his hand. He risked removing it and gestured at the mutilated body. 'Surely only a beast would be capable of such a frenzied act.'

'You've never seen a norse berserk,' Thulmann said. 'But this is not the work of some frenzied, maniacal bloodlust.' The witch hunter's voice grew as cold as the chill morning air. 'No, this was a very deliberate act. Deliberate and unholy. Evil has come to Klausberg, and it is fouler than any I have ever come upon.'

Gregor Klausner watched intently as Thulmann picked a long stick from the ground and began to indicate marks upon the savaged body. The noble felt his breakfast begin to churn in protest. Streng noticed the young man's discomfort and chuckled.

'Observe the lack of blood, either upon the body or the ground,' the witch hunter said. He gestured with the stick, indicating a heavily stained streak that spread away from the body. 'Except here, here alone does blood stain the ground. Note its direction. If we were to imagine it as an arrow, it should point to the south and the east. There is importance in that fact, for it is our first sign that this was a deliberate and carefully orchestrated atrocity.'

The witch hunter gestured with the stick again, this time indicating a large wound in the side of the body's neck. 'A deep, swift stab into the artery, allowing the blood to spray outward from the body. The wound is triangular, which tells us something more, for few are those who employ triple-edged blades.'

'Then you are saying a man did this?' Gregor Klausner could barely restrain the shock and outrage in his voice. Thulmann nodded grimly to the young noble.

'Oh yes, a man who wishes with all his foul, polluted soul, to become something more, no matter how abominable the price.' The witch hunter stabbed his stick again at the body. 'Observe, the mutilation of the face and skull, a feeble attempt to hide what was actually done to this man. Note the massive injuries done to the chest, the ribs peeled back to expose the inner organs.' Thulmann pointed at the messy remains of the corpse's left breast. 'Yet, what is this? Something missing, and a tidbit far too heavy to have been claimed by even the most gluttonous crow, and cut away much too cleanly to be the work of a fox or weasel.' The witch hunter discarded his stick, backing away from the body.

'There can be no doubt,' he informed Gregor. 'This is the work of a necromancer. The savage blood-letting, arranged that the precious humour might point toward the south-east, a blood offering to the profane Father of Undeath. The wound itself, delivered by a triple-edged blade, the tool of the foul elves of Naggaroth, from whom legend says the Black One learned his dark arts. Had the head not been so badly mutilated, we would no doubt find that the brain of this unfortunate had been removed, ripped from his skull by barbed hooks inserted up each nostril. The heart, too, taken, ripped from his still warm body that his vile murderer might work his loathsome sorcery.'

The young noble turned away, spilling his breakfast against the side of a tree.

Streng laughed at the sight, subduing his amusement only when he noticed the sharp look Thulmann directed at him. Gregor rose from his sickness, wiping the last of the vomit from his lips. He smiled in embarrassment, then, reasoning that his belly was already empty, stared directly at the human wreckage that had provoked him.

Gregor Klausner shook his head, trying to absorb the villainy the witch hunter had just described. It was almost impossible for him to believe that a man could lower himself to such acts of degeneracy and wickedness. Yet, there was no doubting the conviction and certainty in the witch hunter's words.

'Why?' was all Gregor could say. 'Why would any man commit such an outrage? What could he hope to accomplish by working such an atrocity?'

Thulmann's expression became troubled. 'If I knew that, I should be a great deal…'

'Riders,' interrupted Streng, drawing his sword. The witch hunter turned, his hand loosely resting upon the wooden stock of his pistol.

Horsemen thundered down the hollow, brush and fallen branches cracking beneath the hooves of their steeds. There were a dozen of them, hard men wearing heavy coats over their suits of sturdy leather armour. They favoured Thulmann's party with looks that bespoke obvious annoyance, seemingly more interested in the witch hunter's party than they were in the mangled thing that lay sprawled upon the ground near them.

Thulmann was somewhat surprised, however, when one of the horsemen forced his way to the fore of the group. He was wrapped up in the mass of an immense bear-skin cloak, the fur of its collar rising so high as to cover his cheeks. A rounded hat of ermine was crunched down about his ears. Even so, what little flesh of his face was left exposed was pale and tinged with blue and there was a trembling shiver to his lean frame.

'You should have waited for me and my men,' the lisping voice of Wilhelm Klausner hissed from his shivering lips. 'As lord of this district, propriety would dictate that you allow me to conduct you about my lands.' Wilhelm Klausner cast a disapproving eye on his son Gregor, who averted his eyes in a shame-faced fashion. 'But then, there are quite a few people, I find, who are not bound by the laws of propriety.'

'With all respect, your lordship,' Thulmann bowed slightly to the old patriarch. 'I felt that it was important I see the body at once, before it was disturbed.'

Wilhelm chose to ignore the suggestion in the witch hunter's tone. 'I can hardly imagine that such a sorry spectacle might have anything important to tell,' the old man stated. 'If you have seen the work of a wolf once, that is enough.'

'But it isn't a wolf,' protested Gregor, fire in his voice. 'There is something else at work here, something evil.' Gregor noted his father's unchanging expression. The young Klausner stepped forward, gesturing at the maimed corpse of Skimmel. 'This was not the work of a wolf, or any other beast!' Gregor declared. 'Just listen to this man, father, he will tell you! He will show you how wrong you are!'

Wilhelm Klausner looked away from his son, casting a sceptical glance to where Mathias Thulmann stood, his gloved hand still resting upon the grip of one of the pistols holstered on his belt. 'I am certain that the witch hunter has been quite convincing in his observations.' The old man smiled thinly, the faint whisper of a laugh hissing from his throat.

'But you forget that I too was once a witch finder. I know only too well how that grim calling preys upon the mind and soul, twisting them until one sees evil everywhere and a monster lurking within every shadow. Were I to give free rein to such morbid fancy, I myself could gaze upon those savaged bones and spin speculations just as wild and horrifying as those this good fellow has no doubt been relating.'

Wilhelm Klausner clenched a bony fist, shaking it at his son. 'But such sick imaginings would not be true. You should be wary in what you listen to, and what you choose to believe.'

The witch hunter studied the old patriarch. There was something new about him, something lurking just beneath the surface, something that might drive a man to any act of desperation or folly.

There was fear in Wilhelm this morning, carefully hidden, yet no less prodigious than that which might fill a witch's eye as she lay upon the rack. It was something more than the fear and suspicion his own presence might account, nor had it been evoked by the bloody corpse strewn about the ground.

No, there was something else that occasioned the old man's terror, something that had not manifested itself until he had laid eyes upon his son Gregor. A quick glance told Thulmann that whatever fear was bubbling up within Wilhelm Klauser was absent from the countenances of his companions, even the glowering Anton and the obviously discomfited Ivar Kohl.

Mathias Thulmann stepped toward the mounted men, noting at once that several of the old patriarch's troop let their hands slide toward the hilts of their swords. The Templar chose to ignore the menacing motions, instead focusing his attention firmly upon Wilhelm Klausner. 'With all respect, your lordship, it seems you have forgotten the lessons you should have learned in your prior calling. The world is far less pleasant than we might have it. There are times when evil is everywhere, there are times when monsters do lurk in the shadows.'

'Not here,' swore the old man. 'Not in Klausberg. You are allowed to operate within my lands only by my indulgence. Do not give me cause to revoke it.'

'I will linger in this district until this unholy butcher is brought to ground,' Thulmann's silky voice intoned. 'Your sovereignty extends to secular matters, but I am an agent of the Temple and beyond your will to command. It is by my indulgence that I have so far chosen to respect your authority and try to operate within your auspices. In future, I shall reconsider such courtesies.'

Wilhelm Klausner's lips twisted into a snarl, swiftly punctuated by a snort of disdain. 'Chase your phantoms from here to hell for all I care!' The patriarch glared again at his eldest son. 'Come along, Gregor, leave this man to his shadow-hunting.' The old man extended his hand toward his son, indicating that he should join the company of riders. The angry expression melted from Wilhelm's face, replaced by a look of shock when Gregor remained unmoving.

'I cannot, father,' the young noble said, his voice a mixture of defiance and regret. 'I think that Herr Thulmann is correct in this matter. Look for yourself, father! These horrible acts are not the work of a simple wolf. There is something evil, unclean about these deaths! Why can't you understand that? Perhaps it really is the curse the villagers speak of.'

Wilhelm Klausner doubled over in his saddle, overtaken by a fit of violent coughing. Two riders moved in to support the old man and prevent him from falling from his steed. After a moment, Wilhelm straightened his body, waving aside the supporting arms of his steward Ivar Kohl and his younger son Anton. The patriarch locked eyes with Gregor. 'I would not have believed you to give credit to such contemptible legends,' Wilhelm sneered. Another fit of coughing wracked the old man's body. He looked over at his steward.

'The keep, Ivar,' the old man said weakly. 'Leave these fools to their foolishness.' As the steward helped Wilhelm turn his horse, the old man gripped the arm of his younger son.

'I leave the hunt in your hands, Anton,' he said in a rasping whisper. 'Do not fail me.'

'I shall not,' declared Anton, his words sharp and strong. He watched as Ivar led his father's horse away, then turned his gaze back upon Mathias Thulmann and Gregor. There was an air of triumph and superiority about the younger Klausner now, his cruel face scarred by a victorious leer.

'You heard my father,' Anton said. 'I am now master of this hunt. If you will remain, then you shall do as I say. Otherwise you shall pursue your foolishness elsewhere and leave this matter to men of true quality.'

Mathias Thulmann tipped his hat to the gloating huntmaster. 'I think there will not be much to discover once you and your mob have finished trampling every inch of ground in the hollow, and to follow your lead would be more foolishness than I care to contemplate at present.' The witch hunter turned, motioning for Streng and Gregor to return to their horses. Anton Klausner watched the trio depart, his face darkening with rage at the Templar's disparaging remarks.

'Witch hunter, I've not dismissed you!' Anton Klausner spat. Thulmann froze in his ascent up the slope.

'There are very few men who speak to me in such a tone,' the witch hunter told him, not deigning to turn around. 'You are not one of them.' Thulmann continued his climb. 'I suggest that you remember that,' he added darkly.

Anton Klausner fumed as he watched the three men ride off, the colour growing ever more vibrant in his face. 'Come along, you scum!' the lordling snapped as he jerked his horse's head around. 'I want that animal's head on a spear before nightfall. Then we'll see which of Wilhelm Klausner's sons is the fool!'

CHAPTER SEVEN

MATHIAS THULMANN AND his companions sat astride their horses, staring back down at the hollow from the vantage of the overlooking fields. The Templar shook his head and sighed in disgust.

'Superstition, ignorance and fear are the greatest armour the Dark Gods ever crafted for themselves,' he commented. 'Against the folly of the human soul, even the might and glory of Sigmar is hard pressed to persevere.'

'I am certain that my father can be shown that he is wrong,' Gregor Klausner told Thulmann, a defensive quality in his voice. Clearly the implication that the three failings he had spoken were to be found in abundance in the Klausner patriarch had offended Gregor. Even from a man like the witch hunter, he was not about to hear ill spoken about his father.

'There are none so blind as those who refuse to open their eyes,' observed Thulmann. He lifted his hand to forestall the angry protest that rose to Gregor's lips. 'It would aid me immeasurably if your father could be brought to accept the true nature of the horror that has visited itself upon this community, but I fear that no amount of evidence will sway him. He refuses to accept this thing not because he disbelieves, but because he knows it to be true.'

'That cannot be!' snapped Gregor. 'My father is a virtuous and courageous man! He served the temple for ten years as a witch finder! He is no coward!'

'I did not say that he was,' Thulmann's voice drifted into the low and silky tones that so often caused condemned heretics to confide in their seemingly sympathetic accuser. 'Not in the sense you mean. But courage and virtue have their limits, and I think that Wilhelm Klausner long ago met and surpassed his own. When he put aside the mantle of a witch hunter, I think he also imagined that he had put aside the duties demanded of one who takes up that calling. Now, perhaps, he cannot bring himself to call upon the man he once was, cannot bring himself to do what needs to be done.'

Gregor grew quiet as the witch hunter spoke, considering the Templar's words, much of his anger dripping out of him as doubt flooded in to take its place.

Thulmann noted the exchange of emotions, considering how close his suppositions about the elder Klausner might have come to hitting the mark.

'Shall we scout around the edges of the hollow, Mathias?' Streng inquired, jabbing a meaty thumb back toward the trees. 'Maybe pick up the heretic's trail?'

'No, I don't think that will serve any good,' the witch hunter replied. 'We seek a man, not the animal of Wilhelm Klausner's fancy. And even a madman knows the value of a decent path. No, if there was a trail to be found, the hooves of Anton Klausner and his thugs will have destroyed it.'

'Then how do we proceed?' Gregor Klausner asked.

Mathias Thulmann was quiet for some time, considering what little he had learned since coming to Klausberg. A decision reached, he stared once more at Gregor. 'I think we might uncover much if we were to perhaps delve a bit deeper into this curse the villagers speak of. There might be something to learn, something that might put a name to this fiend we hunt.'

Gregor Klausner nodded his head. 'There are extensive records of my family's history kept in the keep. If there is any truth to the curse, then it will be in those records, if it is to be found anywhere.' The nobleman grew silent, a distant look entering his eyes, and he turned a suddenly grim face back upon the witch hunter. 'But first, I think there is something you should see,' he said.

THE FOREBODING WOODS that bordered upon Klausner Keep had been frightful, shadowy apparitions when Thulmann had first seen them upon his twilight ride to the fortress. In broad daylight, they were no less unsavoury and disquieting. The trees were twisted, gnarled things, as though the trunks were writhing in silent torment. The bark was discoloured in leprous splotches, the leaves more often coloured a sickly yellow than a healthy green.

Streng reached out his hand to inspect one of the branches that overhung their path, only to have the wood crumble away into a reeking dust as he touched it.

'They call it "the blight", and have done so for as long as any can remember,' explained Gregor as Streng tried to wipe the filth from his hand, only to have the piece of bark he was employing for the task crumble away in a similar fashion.

'Are many trees so afflicted?' Thulmann asked.

'No, only those near the keep. My father believes that it is some deficiency in the soil,' Gregor stated.

'Strange that there should be such a patch of unwholesome ground at the very centre of all these productive fields and orchards,' observed Thulmann. He suddenly brought his horse to a halt, nearly causing the trailing Streng to crash his own steed into Thulmann's animal.

The witch hunter dismounted and strode into the bushes beside the path, the bracken crumbling softly beneath his booted feet. He extended his hand, brushing a twisted clutch of brambles away from an object partly buried in the diseased loam. It was a section of slender stonework, possibly once part of a column or pillar. The witch hunter studied it intently for some time, his hand slowly running along the fine curves and sharp angles.

'Elves lived here once,' Thulmann stated.

'There are quite a few such ruins still scattered about these woods,' Gregor told him. 'Though many of them have long since been broken up and used by the villagers and farmers to construct their homes.'

The witch hunter rose from the broken column, striding back toward the path, a new sense of unease about his bearing. The elves were a strange and fey race, mysterious in their ways and deeds. They were a magical people as well, tapping the unnatural winds of magic with a skill unknown to mere men, a proficiency which men of Thulmann's calling often took as certain evidence of the corruption inherent in the elder race. They were a people not to be trusted, as the ancient dwarfs had learned at great cost, and their ruins were haunted places, echoing with the lingering traces of the enchantments worked by their long dead builders.

Thulmann wondered if there might not be some manner of connection between the existence of these ruins and the affliction that Gregor had named 'the blight'. Indeed, the witch hunter could only conjecture whether 'the blight' might not itself be a symptom of the greater affliction now plaguing the district.

'So old Helmuth Klausner built his fortress upon the bones of the elves,' Thulmann said, his gaze straying in the direction of the keep, which loomed unseen somewhere beyond the overhanging trees. 'I wonder if he truly appreciated what he was doing.'

* * *

'DRINK THIS,' THE woman spoke in a stern voice, lifting the bowl of steaming broth to the old man's mouth. Wilhelm Klausner screwed his jaw tight and turned his head in protest.

'I'll have none of that,' the woman scolded him. She was younger than the old man who lay muffled within the mass of blankets and furs piled atop his bed, her long red hair just showing the first hint of silver. She was pretty, a woman who might once have claimed beauty before the hand of time had begun to caress her plump, robust frame. Her cheerful visage and ruddy, healthy glow of her skin were the utter antithesis of the withered, gaunt apparition who grumbled at her from his cavern of bedding.

An observer would never have guessed that Ilsa was two years her husband's senior.

'This soup will warm the chill that you let sink into those stubborn old bones of yours,' Ilsa said, her round cheeks lifting in a smile. Her husband turned his head to face her.

'Am I master in this house or not?' he growled, his lisp stretching the words into a hiss. 'Damnation woman, if I don't want to drink your concoction, then let me be!'

Ilsa cocked her head at Wilhelm's vituperative outburst. 'Indeed, and I suppose it was I who told you to go racing out into the morning frost like a starving halfling.' She lifted the bowl to the old man's face once more. 'Now you drink this, unless you like having ice-water in your veins.'

'Her ladyship is right,' conceded Ivar Kohl. The steward was leaning against the side of the hearth, nursing the fire with an iron poker. He had shed the heavy furs from his morning ride, replacing them with his black livery and robe.

'You see,' beamed Ilsa Klausner triumphantly, 'even nasty old Ivar thinks you should do what's good for you.' With a sour look at his servant, Wilhelm opened his mouth and allowed his wife to feed him. Ilsa persisted until the bowl had been drained down to its final dregs.

'Satisfied?' Wilhelm grunted as his wife withdrew the empty bowl. He did not have time to await a reaction, however, but at once doubled over as a fit of coughing seized him. Ilsa reached forward, a concerned look on her face.

'Whatever possessed you to go rushing out into the cold like that?' she asked, trying to soothe away the coughing with her tender caress. She glanced back at the steward. 'You are smarter than this Ivar!' she snapped. 'He's not a young man any more!'

'His lordship can still present a very fearsome figure when his anger is upon him,' protested Ivar. 'And your husband was most determined about his course of action this morning. I doubt even you would have stopped him.' Ilsa turned her attention back toward her husband as the fit subsided.

'You are too good to me, Ilsa,' the old man said, his gnarled hand touching her cheek. 'All the gods smiled upon me when they put you in my life.' Wilhelm drew his wife's hand to his lips, then sank back into his mound of pillows. 'I can imagine no greater treasure in this world than the love of a woman like you. You, and Gregor and Anton,' the patriarch smiled as he spoke the names. 'The house of Klausner can never have been more fully blessed.'

Ilsa rose from her husband's sick bed, discreetly wiping a tear from her eye. 'Listen to you prattle on like some hen-pecked cuckold. Now you sit still and rest.' She turned a stern gaze upon Ivar Kohl. 'He needs his sleep,' she told him.

'Ivar, stay a moment,' Wilhelm called out, his voice a tired rasp. 'There are a few things I wish to go over with you.'

Ilsa favoured both men with a reproving look.

'As you will have it, but only a moment,' she declared. 'Then you get some rest,' she ordered her husband, wagging a scolding finger at him. Ivar Kohl watched her withdraw, closing the door after her.

'Has she gone?' inquired the patriarch. His steward listened at the door for a moment, then nodded his head. The old man waved at Ivar, beckoning him to the side of the bed.

'This witch hunter is a menace,' Wilhelm told his servant.

Ivar Kohl shrugged. 'Perhaps, but it is just possible that he might discover who did kill that unfortunate wretch we found in the hollow,' the steward told Wilhelm.

The old man reached out, grabbing Ivar's arm.

'I don't care about that!' he hissed. 'You've seen Gregor! He is fascinated by that man and what he is, tagging after him like an eager puppy.'

'It is only natural,' explained Ivar. 'He is a Klausner after all. The trade is in his blood. Now, if you would only allow him to go to Altdorf...'

Wilhelm's clutch on his steward's arm tightened, bringing a gasp of pain from the man. 'I've told you, I'll not see my sons robbed of their life and happiness as I was! While I still draw breath, they'll not!'

Kohl gasped in relief as Wilhelm's strength failed and the old man sagged back into his pillows, releasing his grip. The steward tried to smooth the rumpled sleeve of his shirt.

'You've done all in your power to steer him away from that path,' admitted Ivar. 'But you cannot defy fate. Perhaps Gregor is meant to…'

'I'll defy the gods themselves,' Wilhelm stated, his voice barely a whisper, 'if it will keep my family from harm.' He laughed weakly, holding his withered hands before him. 'Once I thought I could save the entire Empire from the clutch of Old Night with these hands. Now I only want to protect my own.'

'You shall,' the steward assured him. Wilhelm swung his head around to look at Ivar once more.

'I will!' the old man exclaimed. 'This witch hunter, he must be kept away from Gregor.'

Ivar Kohl nodded in sympathy, but spread his hands in a gesture of helplessness. 'There is only so much we can do,' the steward told him. 'He is an officer of the temple. Even you have no authority over him.'

'I want him kept away from my son,' the old patriarch repeated, his gnarled hand closing into a fist at his side.

MATHIAS THULMANN STOOD before the object Gregor had led him to. It was some distance from the path, almost completely covered by the grasping, sickly weeds. It had taken little time to clear them away however, the fragile things crumbling at the touch, a cold breeze sweeping away the filmy dust.

The witch finder discovered that the chest-high diamond-shaped plinth was no elven relic, but something of much more recent construction, and cut by human hands. Indeed, with his knowledge and eye for quality in works of art, Thulmann could readily appreciate the skill and craftsmanship that had gone into it. The black marble plinth was topped by a small stylised griffon clutching a heavy warhammer in its upraised claw, one of the many symbols of the cult of Sigmar, one that had been quite popular two centuries past. Beneath the statue was a bronze plaque. Thulmann read the inscription.

'The sacrifices of forgotten martyrs are remembered always,' the witch hunter read aloud.

'Hmmph,' sneered Streng, spitting into the brambles. 'Looks like this thing was pretty well forgotten for all its fancy words. Otherwise you can bet your boot some enterprising wretch would have turned that fancy plaque into bread and ale.'

'The people of this district are a very superstitious sort,' explained Gregor. 'They would not desecrate such a shrine even if they did know of it. I only discovered it when hunting hares several years ago. It was apparently constructed by my great-grandfather, to commemorate the deaths in the village that had preceded the demise of his own father. I wanted you to see this, to show you that in the past, my family has not always regarded the curse with scorn.'

Thulmann looked away from the plinth, his eyes wandering across the landscape around them. 'These trees are old,' he stated. 'Even two hundred years ago they would have been large.'

'What's that have to do with anything?' Streng asked, not following his employer's train of thought. Thulmann stared at the brutal mercenary.

'Why place a monument, especially one that has obviously been constructed at such great expense, where no one could see it?' the witch hunter elaborated. He turned his gaze toward Gregor. 'Unless of course it was not meant to be seen. Perhaps your ancestor felt guilt for the deaths he associated with the family curse, felt an obligation to honour what he considered their sacrifice, but at the same time was ashamed to display that obligation openly.' The Templar turned away from the plinth and his thoughts.

'I need to examine these records you have mentioned,' he told Gregor.

CHAPTER EIGHT

THE BROODING MASS of Klausner Keep seemed to swallow Thulmann and his companions as they rode through the black gates. Once again, the witch hunter had the impression of some vast and noxious toad squatting atop the hill, surrounded on all sides by a wretched and diseased forest and the crumbling relics of an elder age. Even in daylight, the unpleasantness of the small courtyard and the black stone walls was not lessened.

Gregor Klausner conducted the witch hunter and his henchman into the vast entry hall, leaving the horses to be tended by servants. The young noble turned to speak with Thulmann as he led the way.

'The library is located on the northern face of the keep. The records we want to examine will be found there,' he explained. The young noble turned as he saw the black-clad shape of Ivar Kohl descending the broad staircase. 'Excuse me please,' he told the witch hunter.

Ivar Kohl regarded Thulmann with an oily look, a false smile forcing itself to his features. He continued to descend the stairway as Gregor hurried toward him. 'Master Gregor,' the steward addressed the noble. 'I trust that your morning has been... productive.'

'My father, Ivar, how is he?'

The steward adopted a posture not unlike that of a lecturer delivering a dissertation. 'Well,' Ivar began, 'your father is not a young man. I am afraid that the excitement and tragedy of the scene in the hollow has upset him greatly. And the chill of this morning has disordered his humours. He is not so resistant to the caprices of temperature as he once was,' Ivar stated regretfully.

'I should go to him,' Gregor declared. The grin on Ivar's face spread, becoming a touch more genuine. He reached out and gripped the noble's shoulder.

'Yes, you should,' agreed the steward. 'Your father is resting at the moment, but I am certain that seeing you would do him more good than any amount of sleep.'

Gregor nodded. He looked back toward Thulmann and Streng. 'I shall only be a moment, I wish to check upon my father.' He looked back toward the steward. 'Ivar, please conduct Herr Thulmann and his associate to the library. I shall join them shortly.'

'Ivar, conduct those men out of my home,' a harsh, commanding voice spoke from the top of the stairs.

All eyes turned upon the gaunt, sickly figure that stood there, lean frame swaddled in a heavy cloak. Wilhelm Klausner glared down at the witch hunter for a moment, then swung his gaze upon his son. 'In fact, you can see them out of my district. I don't want them here, scaring the peasants and filling their heads with all sorts of morbid nonsense.'

Ivar Kohl took a reluctant step toward the witch hunter, but a sharp glance from Thulmann froze the servant. Thulmann advanced to the base of the stairway, looking past Gregor at the skeletal figure of his father.

'There is still evil abroad in these lands, your lordship,' Thulmann said, his silky voice rippling with menace. 'While it is, there is work for me to do here.'

'Then you refuse to accept my wishes?' the old patriarch snarled. 'That is unwise.'

'Father,' interrupted Gregor, climbing the stairs to stand beside his sire. 'Herr Thulmann has come here to help.'

'He's come here to undermine my authority!' corrected Wilhelm, his lisping voice rising with his anger. 'Come here to twist this entire district against me with his bogey stories and shadow-chasing. But I'll not have it!' The old man shook his thin hand at Thulmann. 'You forget just who I am, witch finder. I am no petty burghomeister to be bullied and frightened by your tricks. I am not without my own influence, and I shall bring it to bear upon you if you continue to defy me. The elector count himself has dined within these walls, and I have sat to supper with two emperors. Need I remind you that the

Grand Theogonist is one of my oldest and dearest friends?' Wilhelm laughed, a low dry rattle that slithered from his throat. 'Defy me and you will wind up burned at the stake yourself as an apostate!'

Thulmann stood his ground, meeting the patriarch's challenging gaze. 'There is a monster at work in your district, Klausner. I will leave when it is ash and blackened bone and not before. No threat from you will change that.'

Wilhelm Klausner's face twisted into an animalistic snarl, but before the patriarch could give voice to the invective boiling up within him, another fit of coughing wracked his body. Wilhelm crumpled into the arms of his son, allowing Gregor to conduct him back to his room. Thulmann watched the two Klausners withdraw, then faced Ivar Kohl once more.

'His lordship is not quite himself,' the steward apologised. 'These killings and his unwise venture this morning have disturbed his thoughts.'

'I will conduct my inquiries in the village today,' Thulmann told the servant. 'Perhaps when I return I will find his lordship in a more conciliatory mood.'

'That would be for the best,' Ivar Kohl nodded his head enthusiastically. 'I am sure that when this sickness passes you will find his lordship much more agreeable.' Thulmann lifted a warning finger.

'Cooperative or not,' he said, 'I will be back. You might relay that information to your master.' Turning on his heel, the witch hunter stalked from the hall. Streng paused to snort derisively as he passed the steward, then followed his employer into the courtyard.

Ivar Kohl watched the door close behind the two men, the false pleasantry slipping from his face, his usual mask of cunning rising to take its place. Sick or not, Wilhelm Klausner was correct, the witch hunter was a menace. Possibly one that might have to be attended to in a more direct manner. Still, while the perpetrator of last night's atrocity was still abroad, the witch hunter might have his uses. There was no reason to act in a hasty and irreversible fashion.

Not yet, at least.

UPON HIS RETURN to the inn, Mathias Thulmann found the common room of The Grey Crone crammed with people. As the witch hunter strode through the door, the excited murmur of the crowd died away and every face in the building turned in his direction.

The witch hunter scrutinised the crowd, seeing old men stooped with age and young, burly lads just beginning to grow their beards. They were garbed in simple homespun or furs, or else in modest fabrics such as might be found clinging to the frame of merchants and traders in any town in the Empire. It was a cross-section of Klausberg that faced Thulmann, men from the lowest classes and men from what passed for the wealthy elite of the village. They were men who under normal circumstances would not have deigned to walk the same side of the street as one another. But these were not normal times, and a grim and dreadful common purpose had united them and brought them here.

Streng muscled his way past the witch hunter, the thug's hand dropping to the hilt of his sword. The mercenary did a quick count of the sullen, expectant faces looking at them. 'Aren't you the popular one?' he muttered to his employer from the corner of his mouth.

Streng discreetly removed his hand from his weapon. In a louder voice he said: 'I don't know about you, Mathias, but I could do with some ale to wash away the chill from our ride this morning.' Streng left his master's side and strolled toward the counter where Reikhertz stood wiping his hands upon his apron.

'It seems your custom has improved, friend Reikhertz,' Thulmann said in his silky voice. The familiar tone nearly caused the innkeeper to drop the flagon he was handing to Streng.

Reikhertz cast a nervous glance at the mob.

'Can I help with something perhaps?' the witch hunter asked the foremost of the men, a rotund fellow with brightly striped breeches of white and red and a bronze-buttoned leather vest. Thulmann's tone was imperious and the surly merchant retreated from his gaze. The witch hunter turned his attention to the man standing beside the merchant. He was tall and black-bearded, his bare arms rippling with muscle. Thulmann guessed that the man was a blacksmith.

'Aye,' the man said, 'you can start by telling us what you and those damn Klausners intend to do to stop these murders!' With every word, the mob surged uneasily, their courage bolstered as their spokesman gave voice to the source of their fear and outrage.

Thulmann did not speak at once, but stepped toward the bar, leaning his back against the hard wooden surface, adopting a practiced pose of unconcern and inoffensiveness.

'A glass of wine, if you would, Reikhertz,' the witch hunter told the innkeeper. 'Red, and in a glass, if that is achievable.' Thulmann turned around, taking his time to answer the smith's question, allowing the crowd's mood to simmer.

He needed these people angry. Anger was a poor cousin to courage, but it would suit his purposes. These people were afraid of the thing that was preying upon them, and that fear might keep their lips closed when Thulmann needed them at their most active.

'For my part,' the witch hunter said, nodding to Reikhertz as the nervous man set his wine down on the counter and scuttled away, 'I intend to bring a halt to these atrocities.'

'And what about his lordship?' an angry voice snarled from the back of the crowd. Thulmann took his time to answer, sipping at his wine. Beside him, an increasingly uneasy Streng watched the discontent grow within the crowd.

'As for his lordship,' Thulmann commented, setting his glass down once more, 'he is convinced that a wolf is preying upon his district.' The statement brought an incredulous murmur from the gathering. 'In fact, one of his sons is leading a hunting party to look for the animal even as we speak.' The murmur grew into an angry roar.

'Sure you know what you're doing?' Streng asked in a low whisper.

'Rest easy and continue drowning your wits,' Thulmann told his underling.

'Klausner plays games!' growled the smith, his deep voice roaring above the crowd. 'He plays games while our people die!'

'Yes!' shouted a second voice. 'He's safe behind his walls with his family, while our brothers and sons, wives and daughters are dying!' Thulmann listened to the fury swell within the mob, waiting for his opportunity.

'Our people die!' snarled a third man. 'Our blood to feed the damn Klausners and their curse!'

'The Klausner curse,' Thulmann's voice rose above the crowd, projected to the very back of the room, a trick often employed by actors upon the stage and taught to every Templar and priest of Sigmar. The crowd grew silent again, staring once more at the man whom they had come here to confront. 'I have heard much of this curse, but know little,' the witch hunter continued when he saw that he had the attention of the room. 'I have seen for myself the remains of one of this fiend's victims, a cattleman named Skimmel who was found in the early hours of this morning.' The news brought a shocked gasp from some in the crowd who had not given full credence to the rumours that had already been circulating about the village. 'His lordship thinks these crimes are the work of a wolf. I know better. I must know more.'

Thulmann strode away from the bar, stepping to the fore of the crowd, his keen gaze sweeping across the faces filling the room. 'You, the good folk of

Klausberg are the ones to whom I must turn if we are
to put an end to these atrocities and bring this insidious fiend to justice. You must tell me all that you
have seen, all that you have heard.' Thulmann let his
lean features spread into a grim smile. 'Together, if
we keep our faith in Sigmar, we will overcome this
evil.'

The witch hunter's quick, impassioned words had
their effect, and a new murmur, this one of excitement and cautious hope, rippled through the room.
Thulmann smiled as he watched his handiwork take
root. Now he needed to cultivate it and force what he
had planted to bear fruit.

A small, mousy man broke away from the crowd,
nervously approaching the witch hunter.

'I can help you, master witch finder,' the little man
said, wringing his hat between his hands. 'You see, I
have seen the daemon for myself,' the little man confessed when he was aware that he had Thulmann's
attention.

At the bar, Streng overheard the little man's story.
He grumbled into his ale and drained the last dregs
from his flagon. 'There are times when I truly regret
deserting the army,' he mused. 'I have a bad feeling
that this is going to be one of them.'

'I'm sorry, sir, but I be closing early. You'll have to
come back tomorrow,' the butcher informed the man
who had just slipped into his tiny shop. The rebuked
customer stood in the doorway of the shop, a perplexed look contorting his pale features. He brushed
a ratty string of oily hair from his face as the butcher

rounded the counter, tossing his stained apron on the floor.

He glanced about the shoddy interior, staring with keen interest at the bisected pig carcasses hanging from hooks fixed to the ceiling, at the barrel of dismembered chicken refuse that would be later ground into meal for hogs, dogs and the least discriminatory of the town's human denizens. The smell of blood and the buzzing of flies occupied the visitor's other senses.

'It will only take a moment,' he told the butcher. 'Some sausage and a bit of pig's blood to boil it in.' The butcher shook his head, hastening toward the door and hurrying the robed man before him as though he were a wayward duckling.

'No time, my friend,' the butcher told him. The big man paused, his eyes narrowing as he looked more closely at his guest. 'I don't think I've seen you here before,' he commented with an accusing voice.

'Humble means,' the pasty faced man returned, shrugging his shoulders in apology and resignation. 'I fear I cannot often afford decent meat but must make do with what I can provide for myself.' He froze for a moment, staring at a haunch of meat resting on a wooden platter, trying to decide what exactly it had come from. The crawling blanket of flies that clothed a fair portion of it did little to aid his study.

The butcher snorted with distaste. 'Poacher, eh? Lord Klausner will catch you soon enough, rabbit-catcher, and then you'll be for it.' The man laughed grimly. 'He might even try and lay the terror on your head if you're not careful. He'd be just as happy to put the blame on a two-legged wolf as a four-legged one.'

The customer chuckled nervously. 'That would certainly be an unpleasant turn of events,' he muttered. His speech trailed away as he stared at a cow head lying atop a wooden box, its lifeless eyes staring back at him, its thick tongue protruding from its dead mouth. 'All the more reason for me to procure some of your provender,' the man said hastily as he saw the butcher advancing toward him. The big man was not moved, pushing his ill-featured patron back out the door.

'Sorry friend,' the butcher mumbled, turning to lock the door to his shop. 'Afraid you'll have to live on rabbit a bit longer. Big doings at the inn, and I'll not miss a moment of it.'

'Is that so,' the pale man asked, glancing in the direction of The Grey Crone. There was indeed a steady stream of traffic flowing into the building. He tried to recollect his sketchy knowledge of Imperial holidays. 'The Festival of St. Ulfgar?' he asked as the butcher completed his task.

'No indeed!' the butcher scoffed. 'The witch hunter is there, taking statements from any who will give them.' The butcher turned, walking quickly in the direction of the inn. 'Finally, somebody's going to put an end to these killings,' he called back as he raced away.

Carandini scowled as he heard the villager's words, quickly sheathing the triple-edged dagger he had been holding beneath the voluminous sleeve of his tattered grey cassock.

He had feared something like this. Things had been stalemated for several weeks now, but the arrival of this witch hunter would give a new strength to the enemy. The necromancer scuttled off down the nearest alley, trying to remain inconspicuous. Strangers were common enough in Klausberg, even under the current pall, but he wanted to take no chances. This close to achieving everything he had ever hoped for, he was even more paranoid than usual about putting his own neck in jeopardy.

The necromancer hastened to where he had tethered his sickly mule and rode off to bring the ill news to his confederate.

NIGHT HAD FALLEN by the time Carandini returned to his lair, a small and abandoned shack five miles outside the village. Even so, the necromancer was obliged to wait for nearly an hour before his ally put in his appearance. Carandini turned away from his small fire as he heard the swish of clothing behind him. The necromancer could barely make out the white face that rose above his confederate's black clothing, even with his supernaturally keen night sight. Carandini rose to his feet, wiping the dirt and soot from the front of his cassock.

'Forgive my tardiness,' the shadow said. Carandini could just make out the movement of the speaker's mouth within the smoky darkness that surrounded him. 'I was unavoidably delayed.'

'You have not been discovered?' demanded Carandini, his hand closing about the small vial he had sewn within the lining of his cloak.

'I am not so reckless as to jeopardise all that we have worked for,' the shadow hissed, his powerful tones redolent with resentment. 'There is nothing in this world or the next more important than the prize we will claim.'

'A permanent and lasting end to both of us is something that I should hold of greater importance!' Carandini snapped. 'It might be of interest to you to know that a witch hunter has come to Klausberg. You must be more cautious than ever! If it is even suspected…'

'I have known about the witch hunter's arrival for two days now,' the other told him. 'I watched him ride from the keep the first night he was here.' Carandini rounded on his companion, fury swelling within him, forgetting for a moment even the habitual loathing and fear which his ally caused in his heart.

'You knew about him and said nothing!' the necromancer shouted incredulously.

'Would you have informed me were our positions reversed?' the shadow asked calmly, his deeply accented voice twisted with a cruel mirth.

Carandini scowled and retreated back toward the fire. There was truth in his ally's words, Carandini would indeed have kept the information to himself, in hopes that he might find some way to use the witch hunter against his associate when the time came.

It did not disturb Carandini that his companion did not trust him, neither of them were such fools as to trust one another any more than a miser would trust a dwarf with his money-belt. They were useful to one another right now, but once that usefulness had run its course, their fragile alliance would come to an end, and the one who struck first would most likely also be the one to triumph. No, their mutual capacity for treachery was something of an unspoken understanding between them; what disturbed Carandini was the felicity with which his associate had predicted what shape his plots might assume when that time came.

'Do not brood so,' the shadow hissed. 'There are ways that we might turn this man's arrival to our advantage.' Carandini looked up sharply, his face twisted with suspicion. 'Our mutual advantage,' the shape added.

'Being burned at the stake is not something I should find advantageous,' spat Carandini. 'And I dare say that it would not do yourself any great amount of good.'

'We can arrange something to dispose of this man, certainly,' the shadow hissed, slowly circling the fire. 'If he hunts a beast, then perhaps we should let him find a beast. But consider this,' the voice dropped into a slithering whisper. 'We might do better than simply kill him. We might direct his attention to where it will serve us best. The enemy of our enemy,' the figure grew quiet as he considered his idea.

'His presence here interferes with our plans,' stated the necromancer. 'I had to abandon my choice for the next ritual because of his presence in the town.'

'The rituals will proceed,' the shadow assured Carandini. 'Nothing can be allowed to prevent them. You will simply have to find another viable sacrifice. However, it is wise to plan for every contingency.'

EMIL GUNDOLF SLOWLY picked his way through the trees, lips pursed as he whistled a low, mournful tune. He had walked this way countless times, yet never had his spirits been so low, his fears so great. Evil was abroad in Klausberg, striking everywhere, striking anyone. It was dangerous to be abroad at night.

He cast a nervous look over his shoulder, staring at the now distant light twinkling from his home. He could be at home now, safe and warm beside his wife and children.

The thought of his wife and daughters caused the forester to grip his axe a bit more securely. He fastened the top button of his coat and strode onward. Whatever fiend was abroad, it could be no more deadly than an empty belly, of that Gundolf was certain. And if the blight really had spread from the Klausner estate into Franz Beicher's timber, then Gundolf could expect a very summary dismissal from Beicher when the merchant discovered that his logging grounds had become corrupted.

Warmed by such grim pragmatism, Emil Gundolf continued to whistle and walk through the maze of rail-thin trunks.

He did not see his attackers, for they set upon him in darkness and silence from behind.

A heavy hood was slipped over his head before Gundolf could even open his mouth to scream, and powerful hands tore his axe from him.

The forester struggled as he was pushed and pulled, striving to overcome the tremendous strength of his captors. He soon realised that he was no match for those that held him, but Gundolf had no delusions regarding what his fate would be if he allowed them to drag him away.

Every step he tried to stamp the feet of his attackers, tried to smash an elbow or a shoulder into the face or stomach of one of his unseen adversaries. Sometimes he was rewarded by a grunt of pain or a muttered curse, sometimes the grip upon him would lessen slightly. But never enough, never would his captors weaken enough to allow him to slip their clutches.

Emil Gundolf thought of his wife, his tiny twin daughters, waiting nervously beside the hearth, waiting for him to return. Within the cloying darkness of the suffocating hood the forester shouted, screamed in impotent anguish, but the mask smothered the sounds. Tears welled up in his eyes, dampening the cold leather.

After some time, his captors brought him to a halt. Gundolf was gasping for breath beneath the hood, fighting to pull every scrap of air through the heavy leather. Sightless, with his arms now bound at his sides, he was unable to brace himself when his captors threw him to the ground. Gundolf groaned as his foes kicked and rolled his body into position upon the cold damp earth.

'That will do,' a cold voice spoke from somewhere above him. The last thing Emil Gundolf heard was the sound of his wool shirt being cut open and the wet flop of his guts as they spilled from his torn belly.

CHAPTER NINE

MATHIAS THULMANN SAT before the small table that rested within his room at The Grey Crone, staring intently at the old map of the district he had acquired from the village scribe. It was a crude thing, and now bore the irregular splotches and blemishes the witch hunter had daubed onto it.

Each splotch was accompanied by a number, and each number accompanied an entry in the cloth-bound chapbook in which Thulmann had written all the information he had gained from the villagers. He rubbed his eyes, cursing once again the ethereal weapons of the Dark Gods: ignorance, superstition and fear. They had certainly been working overtime upon the people of Klausberg. The peasant farmers, tradesmen and rugged foresters were jumping at every shadow, cringing at every sound in the night, certain that the perpetrator of these vile crimes (which they had named the Klausner daemon) was near. Thulmann had hoped to learn something of value. Perhaps he had, but separating it from all the chaff of panic and superstition was going to be a monumental task.

He read one of the entries in his chapbook, sipping at a glass of wine from the bottle Reikhertz had provided him with. It was a perfect example of the confused nonsense that he was coming up against in his inquiries. A swineherd had gone out at night to investigate the agitated sounds of his hogs. Turning from the swine pens, he had nearly expired from fright when he had seen the evil eyes of a daemon glaring at him from the dark loft of his barn.

A few quick questions about the daemonic eyes and their size in relation to the dimensions of the loft, had convinced Thulmann that they were not nearly so large nor so extraordinary as the man had imagined them.

The witch hunter drew a line through the record. The swineherd's account was almost certainly a case of mistaken identity, in this instance a harmless owl transformed by shadow and fear into some emissary of the Ruinous Powers, one of many accounts Thulmann was finding himself drawing marks through.

It was a strange paradox. On the one hand he had Wilhelm Klausner, who, for reasons of his own, refused to admit the possibility of the unnatural no matter the evidence that might be presented. On the other hand he had the people of Klausberg, who were seeing a ghoul behind every tree and a blood-hungry fiend under every haycart.

Thulmann looked again at his map. There were several marks that were made not in the blue paint with which he had denoted the peasants' accounts, but in bright red. These denoted incidents that could not be disputed, incidents that were without a doubt the work of the witch hunter's quarry. For at each of those sites, some forsaken soul had met a gruesome and hideous death.

The witch hunter counted them again, shaking his head at the enormity of the horror that had struck this community. Twenty-seven. Twenty-seven red marks. Twenty-seven lives ended by this unholy marauder.

Thulmann studied the locations of the victims, trying to decide if there was any pattern to the fiend's carnage. But there was nothing. North of the village, east of the village, south, west. In woods and in fields, pasture and bog, it seemed to make no difference.

Thulmann sighed in frustration at the turn his thoughts had taken. Klausner's mythical wolf would have chosen some sort of hunting ground, its methods and actions betraying its simple brute intellect. If the enemy were a simple beast, it should have displayed such character from the beginning, stalking a particular sort of prey and only under particular conditions. But this fiend must be something else. Thulmann wondered if the killer's disordered mind still clung to any sort of purpose, or had the killings themselves become all the purpose they needed?

Those who dabbled in the black arts did so at the peril of not only their immortal soul, but their very ability to reason.

Once again, Thulmann found himself considering the foul Erasmus Kleib. He had all too readily dismissed the sorcerer as a madman, falling into the same trap that had caused his mentor to underestimate their foe, at the cost of his life.

Kleib had been a twisted and evil man, but he had not been truly insane. He had been all too aware of the horror and perversion of what he did; he had appreciated in the full that his actions were lawless and murderous. That great intellect, that powerful mind had been twisted, tainted, but it had not been broken. It was not the base cunning of a madman that had allowed Erasmus Kleib to remain at large, committing his atrocities, for so many years, but the wicked application of that tremendous intellect. It had been all too easy to call him a madman, as if that would excuse his seduction to the ways of evil.

Thulmann considered if he might not be doing the same with the Klausberg fiend. He removed a thin volume, bound in leather, from an oilskin pouch that rested upon the covers of his bed. Speaking a quick prayer for guidance to his patron god Sigmar, he opened the slender tome.

It was a simple thing, employed by many witch hunters. Upon the pages of the slender book were drawn many of the symbols and signs employed by those who practised the darker aspects of wizardry. The more potent sigils and scripts employed to create the full designs were absent, but enough were present to allow the witch hunter to recognise such symbols should he encounter them. It was a book Thulmann consulted only with reluctance, for even such reduced emblems of sorcery disquieted him, but there were times when its usefulness could not be denied.

He flicked slowly through the worn pages, trying to match one of the patterns he saw there to the arrangement of crimson splotches upon his map.

A sharp knock upon the door roused him from his tedious labour. The witch hunter rubbed at his eyes again, slipping the thin volume back into its sheath.

After hours of study, Thulmann decided that his sudden inspiration was an unlikely one. Whatever foul ritual his nameless foe was perpetrating, the sites of the killings did not seem to be a part of it. None of the symbols he had tried to impress upon the map had fit, no matter how complex. There were always other murders, other deaths that did not conform to whatever pattern Thulmann tried to establish.

A sudden chill crawled along the witch hunter's spine. Unless the fiend were crafty enough to slay simply to break such a pattern. If that were the case, it would truly take the hand of Sigmar to outguess the monster.

Thulmann sipped at his glass of wine, grown warm from his neglect, as he walked across the room and opened the door. He half expected to see Reikhertz the innkeeper, following his established custom of inquiring as to the witch hunter's needs before seeking his own bed. Instead, Thulmann was surprised to find Streng standing there. An uneasy alarm crept into him. It would have taken no mean matter to make the mercenary leave his drinking and gambling after their collection of statements had been completed.

'Seems you need to update that doodle of yours,' Streng said, a wicked grin on his face. 'Reikhertz just let a very distressed fellow in. Insists he needs to speak to the witch hunter.'

Thulmann set his glass down with a groan. 'My ears are fairly bleeding already with the imaginings of these people. If I have one more hell-hound described to me by some oaf who wouldn't know a troll from a fox with the mange, I swear that the lout will be introduced to a tall tree and a short drop.'

Streng scratched his scraggly beard. 'Not that sort of thing he wants to see you about,' the mercenary informed him. 'Seems this fellow had a brother. A brother who went out tonight and never came back.'

Thulmann stared intently at his henchman, his irritation forgotten. 'Go on,' he told him.

'Well, this fellow gets worried when his brother doesn't come back. So he leaves his brother's wife and children safely locked up in the house and goes out looking for him.' The mercenary looked over at the map sprawled across the table. 'You better stock up on red paint,' Streng nodded toward the table. Thulmann reached behind him, snatching up his weapons belt from where it lay draped over the bed frame. Pausing to grab up his hat and cloak, he joined Streng in the hallway.

'Have the Klausners been informed?' he asked in a low voice.

'Not by our man,' Streng told him. 'But in a village this size, you can bet that they have more than a few eyes and ears.'

Thulmann strode toward the stairs. 'Then we'd better be quick. I'd like a little time to examine the surroundings before Wilhelm's men arrive to run us off,' the witch hunter said as he descended the stairs.

THE MOONS OF Mannsleib and Morrsleib were low in the darkened sky as the witch hunter and his party made their way through the maze of thin, pole-like trees. He had taken a reluctant Reikhertz along with them, as well as the brother of the slain man to act as their guide.

The brother, one Fritz Gundolf, had been no less reluctant than the squeamish Reikhertz to accompany Thulmann on his gruesome expedition. It had taken an exertion of his authority and a few thinly veiled threats to impel Fritz to lead them to his brother's remains. Having seen the mutilated body once, Fritz was visibly horrified at the prospect of revisiting the horrid scene, taking long pulls from the squat clay bottle of ale Reikhertz had provided him with, trying to bolster his courage and numb his fear.

A chill wind whipped Thulmann's cloak about as he followed the light cast by the lanterns borne by Reikhertz and Streng, desiccated leaves swirling about his every step.

He glanced about him, remarking once more upon the remoteness of the area. They were so close to the heart of the district, and yet to the witch hunter, it felt every bit as lonely here as on the slopes of the Grey

Mountains or the haunted domains near the dreaded Drakwald Forest.

There was an ugly reason for this, one which Fritz Gundolf had repeated to him. The Klausners might be the lords and masters of the district, but they were not well-loved and their black-stoned keep and its surrounding forest were openly shunned by the common folk. It had been the rather diminished value of the land adjoining that of the Klausners that had prompted the Gundolfs' employer, a Klausberg lumber merchant, to purchase the property.

Only the lure of money could give any of the people of Klausberg reason enough to linger so near the ill-favoured family's holdings.

What had the Klausners done to earn such enmity, the witch hunter wondered? True, the younger son, Anton, was a vicious and foul-tempered brute, but Wilhelm Klausner himself seemed a fairly considerate lord, his inability to put a stop to the murders notwithstanding, and Gregor Klausner was a bright and honourable man, one who had a deep commitment and affection for the people of the district.

The villagers and farmers could certainly have done much worse by way of rulers. Why then the resentment and fear? Was it some legacy from the Klausners' careers as witch hunters?

Thulmann knew only too well the fear and nervous suspicion a witch hunter evoked in all he encountered. But was that enough to explain the stigma that clung to the Klausners, or was it something more? Time and again over the course of the night, Thulmann had heard hushed voices speak of the dread curse that hovered about the patriarchs of the Klausner line, the horrible thing that would ravage the land until it bore the elder Klausner's soul back with it to the blackest pits of the Dark Gods.

Ahead of him, the lanterns came to a halt. Thulmann advanced, joining his companions. Streng and Reikhertz were looking at Fritz. The forester was turned around, his back facing the direction in which they had been travelling.

The trembling man took another pull from his bottle, spilling the fiery liquor about his shirt. With his other hand, he stabbed a finger at the trees behind him.

'That way,' the man choked as the alcohol stung his throat. 'Emil is in there! And ain't nothing you can do to make me go no further!' he swore, staring at the witch hunter with a mixture of terror and defiance. Thulmann nodded, drawing one of his pistols from its holster.

'Very well, friend Gundolf,' his silky voice spoke. 'But you will remain fixed to this spot.' He wagged the barrel of his gun at the subdued peasant. 'I warn you, even in poor light I am an excellent shot.'

Thulmann stalked ahead and gestured for Streng and Reikhertz to accompany him. A part of him disliked threatening the forester, he had after all done his duty and had already displayed a commendable degree of fortitude by returning to this place despite the possibility that whatever had killed his brother might still be abroad. Yet another part of him understood that only by keeping Fritz more afraid of him than whatever had killed his brother would Thulmann keep the man from fleeing back to his hovel as soon as the witch hunter was out of sight. It was an unfair and brutal sort of efficiency, but that did not lessen its effectiveness.

The smell of blood and excrement announced the body long before the light from the lanterns revealed it. Thulmann deftly relieved Reikhertz of his lantern as the innkeeper withdrew to vomit beside one of the spindly trees.

The form sprawled across the grass had spilled its guts in an entirely different fashion.

Thulmann stepped closer, holding his lantern high to reveal as much of the sorry form and its surroundings as he could. Once again, blood stained very little of the ground, most of it splashed across the ground in the familiar south-easterly direction. The body itself was hideously mangled, but the witch hunter had some idea what he was looking at, and what he was looking for.

A cursory glance showed Thulmann that the forester's belly had been slashed open, his intestines and stomach removed and placed on the ground beside the corpse's left boot. Further mutilation had occurred in the chest, the ribcage again cut open and spread.

This time it was not the heart that had been removed, but the lungs. The witch hunter's mind swept back to an incident three years before, in a small town just outside Talabheim where a fledgling daemonologist and necromancer named Anatol Drexel had practised his foul arts. One of his rituals had been to expunge the 'breath of life' from a corpse by puncturing its lungs.

According to blasphemous texts written by no less terrible a personage than the infamous Doom Lord of Middenheim, doing so would make the corpse ideal for a sort of grisly pseudo-resurrection as one of the undead. But if that was what had been done here, why had the perpetrator of this atrocity left the body behind, where it was certain to be discovered?

'This wolf is getting pretty damn artsy, eh Mathias?' Streng chuckled with morbid humour. He looked away from his employer, delivering a gruesome description of the corpse for Reikhertz's benefit. Thulmann ignored the renewed sound of retching and leaned down, inspecting the corpse a little more closely.

Once again, the blood had been drained from the body, but this time the bloodletting had not been achieved by a stab into the jugular vein, but by the more crude method of slitting the victim's throat. The witch hunter looked again at the spread of the blood on the ground. This was not the precise spray-effect that had marked the site of Skimmel's death, but the more sloppy effect of liquid discharged from a bowl.

The witch hunter stood back, studying the scene in its entirety. There had been less care made with this murder, the ritual fashion was there, but it was less efficient, less precise. There had been no attempt at further mutilation to obscure the intentions of the culprit, and the bloodletting had been crude compared to the single deep stab that had ended Skimmel's life.

There was an overall suggestion of haste and carelessness about this killing. Thulmann considered what this might mean. Was the killer losing patience with whatever sorcery he was trying to work, or perhaps there was an element of timing to his magic, and the time left to him was growing short?

Perhaps the fiend he sought was becoming frightened, worried that he might be caught now that an outsider was investigating the killings. But such a conclusion would mean that the fiend did not fear the Klausners, who had been hunting him now for over a month. Thulmann wondered if he dare follow that notion where it might lead him.

'Our wolf has a friend,' Streng interrupted. Thulmann looked over at his henchman. Streng was pointing his foot at an impression on the ground. 'Boots, and rather fine ones,' the mercenary commented. 'Much better than that poor dead bastard is wearing,' he added with a nod of his head toward the feet of the corpse. Thulmann did not need to shift his gaze to recall that Gundolf had been wearing a set of badly patched fur boots.

The mercenary moved about, setting his foot beside another impression in the ground. Unlike the first, this mark was somewhat smaller than Streng's foot, though it was likewise the mark of a heeled boot, not unlike a cavalryman's. 'Might even be a third one,' the henchman told Thulmann. He gestured toward a deep mark beside one of the trees. 'Of course, it is only a partial and the man might have slipped when he made it, which would have stretched it a bit.'

Thulmann nodded in approval. 'The Count of Ostland lost a good scout when you deserted,' he observed. 'Though I imagine that the longevity of his sergeants has improved in your absence.'

The witch hunter began to stalk the area, inspecting the ground for footprints. 'A good deal of tracks coming from that way,' he pointed the barrel of his pistol in the direction that they themselves had come.

'Aye,' agreed Streng. 'That's how they brought the sorry bugger here. He must have tried to dig his feet in every step of the way to judge by the marks.'

Thulmann circled the area again, inspecting the ground for further clues. After several minutes, he straightened, shaking his head in disgust. 'They may have been sloppy in everything else,' he hissed, 'but they made certain to leave no sign of where they went after committing their little atrocity.'

'We might find something when the sun comes up,' suggested Streng.

The witch hunter shook his head.

'We are on borrowed time already,' he told his underling. 'I think it is asking too much of even Sigmar to be free of Klausner's meddling that long.' A sudden idea caused the witch hunter to break into a sly smile. 'Of course, we might avail ourselves of his hospitality while he concerns himself with this occurrence.'

Thulmann considered his idea a bit more, letting a slight laugh slip from his mouth. 'We might even find him rather accommodating if he thinks he is keeping us from discovering this spectacle.' Thulmann cast one last look at Gundolf's body, then motioned for Streng to withdraw.

'Let's fetch Reikhertz and send him on his way, and tell that man Fritz to keep a close tongue.' Thulmann smiled again. 'It wouldn't do for his lordship to know we've been here. Not until I'm ready, at least.'

CHAPTER TEN

THE WITCH HUNTER found Klausner Keep in a great deal of agitation as he and Streng rode their steeds toward the imposing structure. Every window seemed to have been lit up, blazing with light and making it look as if the black toad of the keep had suddenly opened a chaotic multitude of eyes. The mouth formed by the gates of the keep yawned wide, and Thulmann could see riders galloping from the fortress, half their number holding aloft flickering torches that betrayed their advance. The horsemen thundered down the path, the hooves of their steeds flinging mud and pulped leaves in every direction.

Thulmann watched them advance with an elaborate calmness. Beside him, Streng caressed the stock of his crossbow.

The foremost rider pulled his horse savagely to a stop only a dozen feet or so from where Thulmann and Streng's horses stood beside the road. The sudden halt brought the rest of the company to a disordered stop, men and mounts grunting in protest. Anton Klausner curled his lip as he considered the witch hunter.

'Such unpleasant things one finds upon the roads after dark,' the young lord said, his smouldering eyes locking with Thulmann's. 'I should have expected to find you occupied elsewhere.' Anton's expression turned into a look of suspicion as much as contempt. 'Or were you unaware of the latest killing?'

'I am well aware that the fiend has struck again,' Thulmann returned, choosing to ignore the rogue's baiting tone. 'And you might have found me investigating the matter had my guide not deserted me.'

'And you thought to conscript a new one from the keep?' Anton Klausner's smile was every bit as unfriendly as an orc's. 'Somehow, I don't think you will find my father eager to bend on his knee to please you. We are well capable of catching a simple wolf.'

'You've done a fine job of it so far,' observed Streng, shifting his position so that the bolt of his weapon was aimed at the brash noble. Anton Klausner gave the henchman a murderous look.

'Your pet vermin is speaking out of turn, witch finder,' he hissed. 'Keep him in line lest I be forced to teach him some respect.'

'You are welcome to try,' Thulmann told him, his silky voice remaining level. 'Of course, he isn't so restrained as I am when it comes to putting swaggering hotheads in their place.' Anton Klausner's hand shot to the hilt of his sword. Thulmann could hear the nervous muttering of some of the other horsemen, uncertain whether they should aid their master, uneasy about raising arms against an agent of the temple.

'Stop it at once! This bickering is pointless!' Ivar Kohl manoeuvred his steed between the two men. He glared for a moment at Anton, who reluctantly let his hand slip from his weapon.

'You must forgive Master Anton's rudeness, Herr Thulmann,' the steward said, his face displaying the false pleasantry it habitually slipped into. 'The news of this latest tragedy has shocked and disturbed his lordship, indeed all of us, greatly.'

'I am certain that it has,' Thulmann stated, keeping his eyes on the scowling Anton. 'In fact, it was on this point that I journeyed to the keep. I wish to discuss with his lordship how we might bury our differences of opinion in this matter and combine our resources.'

'You will find that my father is indisposed,' Anton said, fairly spitting the words. Kohl cast another hostile look at the young noble. When he turned his attention back to Thulmann, he was once again displaying his oily smile.

'It is true that his lordship is still very weak, but I think that he would receive a man such as yourself,' Kohl told the witch hunter. 'It is a pity that you were unable to verify this tragic account. I am certain that the patriarch would be most anxious to hear any news about this matter.'

'As I have said,' Thulmann informed the steward, 'my guide let his fear get the better of him. No matter, I doubt if we would be able to find anything in the dark in any event.'

Ivar Kohl nodded his head, chortling with enthusiastic agreement. 'Oh doubtless, doubtless. Nothing more foolish than crashing into trees in the pitch of night. Still,' Kohl shrugged his shoulders, a gesture that somehow reminded Thulmann of an over-eager vulture, 'the simple folk of this district would not be so understanding. They would take any delay on the part of his lordship in this matter as a sign that he was disinterested and unconcerned. So, for us, I fear, this foolish venture is unavoidable.'

Kohl turned his gaze back on Anton Klausner, gesturing with a sidewise motion of his head that the young noble should get his men moving again.

'I do hope that you and his lordship can come to an agreement,' Kohl told the witch hunter as Anton's men began to gallop off down the path.

The steward turned his own horse around. 'Rest assured, Herr Thulmann, we will send word back to the keep in the unlikely event that we discover anything.' With a slight wave of his hand, Kohl joined Anton and the pair set off in pursuit of the departed soldiers.

'There goes a man who is quite pleased with himself,' commented Thulmann as he and Streng continued their own journey. 'A man who is trying to be deceitful is always the easiest to deceive.'

The witch hunter reflected upon the exchange as they continued to ride. Clearly the steward Kohl had been the one in command, a certain sign that Wilhelm Klausner did not trust his son Anton with the task of beating Thulmann to the location of Gundolf's body, even to mollify his son's inflated ego.

He could appreciate the elder Klausner's position: he could ill afford to let an outsider solve these crimes, and was desperate to maintain his edge over Thulmann. At best, to allow such a situation to occur would certainly cause his perception of power and authority in the district to diminish greatly. At worst, perhaps the patriarch feared the unearthing of some old legacy of the Klausner clan, some evidence that the curse was more than a simple fable. No doubt Kohl had orders to rearrange the murder scene when he came upon it, to mislead or confuse the Templar's own investigations. Perhaps it might even resemble the work of a wolf by the time Kohl was finished with things.

Thulmann also pondered the absence of Gregor in the hastily assembled hunting party. By all accounts, Gregor was the more intelligent and capable of Wilhelm's two sons, and certainly Thulmann's own impression of the young noble did not contradict such an evaluation.

Why then had Wilhelm sent Anton rather than Gregor? Was there some motive behind the patriarch's decision, or had Gregor refused to be a party to Wilhelm's deceptions and intrigues? The young man did have a very deep-seated sense of honour, one that might be very easily offended by Wilhelm's plotting.

Certainly, Gregor had displayed a much more helpful attitude than his father and seemed just as eager to end this menace to the people of Klausberg as the witch hunter himself. Such feelings would not lend themselves well to old Wilhelm's desperate and selfish attempts to maintain his authority.

Thulmann decided that when he reached the keep, he would speak with the young Gregor openly about what he had learned from his study of Gundolf's corpse. Sharing such intelligence with the young noble might further ingratiate Thulmann into Gregor's confidence, and the witch hunter was in desperate need of at least one ally at the keep.

WILHELM KLAUSNER WAS indeed indisposed when Thulmann arrived at the keep. The servant had conducted the witch hunter and his henchman to a small parlour in which he had found the patriarch's wife seated in a high-backed chair knitting a shawl with a pair of long iron needles. The woman smiled when she saw the witch hunter, apologising profusely for her husband's inability to receive visitors. He had not been in the best of health lately and recent events had not improved the situation at all.

'I am afraid that you are to blame for some of the worry he feels,' Ilsa Klausner told him. 'These terrible killings have been distressing him horribly, sapping his strength. But I think it was your arrival that really weakened him,' she confessed. 'He has lost his old self-confidence. I think he takes your arrival here to mean that others have lost confidence in him as well.'

'I am not here to usurp his lordship,' Thulmann said, seating his lean form in the chair opposite the lady. 'My only concern is to learn what is behind these outrages and put an end to them.'

Ilsa Klausner bent forward, severing a strand of wool with her teeth. 'I understand that, Herr Thulmann. But you must understand, protecting this district is my husband's duty, and one he takes very seriously. I am afraid that he takes your being here as something between an insult and a challenge.' The woman smiled, setting aside her handiwork. 'I know that a person should not speak so openly with a man in your profession, you are so unaccustomed to people speaking their mind. But that is how I see things between yourself and my husband.'

The sound of boots clicking upon the tiles of the floor caused Ilsa to look away from the witch hunter. Thulmann followed the woman's gaze, not entirely surprised to find Gregor stepping into the room.

'Ernst said that we had guests,' Gregor said as he walked toward his mother's chair. He leaned forward, allowing the older woman to kiss his cheek. Straightening, he bowed his head toward Thulmann. 'I am sorry that you have again been cheated of a decent night's sleep, Herr Thulmann.'

'It is another quality of the insidious practices of the forces of darkness that they must wait for the most uncharitable hours in which to work their devilry,' the witch hunter said. 'One becomes accustomed to irregular hours.' Thulmann's eyes narrowed. 'Of course I was rather surprised not to find you with your brother. We passed him and his men on the road coming here.'

Gregor and his mother shared an awkward look for a moment. Ilsa was the first to look away and speak. 'My son did want to go. He insisted, but my husband forbade him,' she stated. 'My husband is a very cautious man and he felt it would be far too reckless to jeopardise both of his sons upon such a potentially dangerous excursion.'

'It is just as well that you did remain at the keep,' Thulmann told the young noble. Gregor Klausner's expression became one of cautious interest. 'You see, there were some things which I wanted to discuss with you. I have learned quite a bit since we parted ways, but I feel that I need a man of your insight to evaluate the facts I have collected.'

Ilsa started to rise from her chair. 'That means, I suppose, that you have men's business to discuss,' she said. Gregor motioned for her to sit down.

'No need to leave, mother,' he said. 'When Herr Thulmann was here last, he expressed a wish to see the family records. I think that we can have our discussion there just as easily as here.' Gregor turned his head back towards the witch hunter. 'Herr Thulmann, shall we withdraw to the library then?' He extended his hand to indicate the open doorway through which he had made his own entrance.

The witch hunter nodded and rose from his chair. He bowed again to Ilsa Klausner.

'Give my regards to your husband,' the witch hunter said. The woman smiled up at him as she returned to her knitting.

'Assuredly,' she told Thulmann. 'But not until you have finished your business with my son,' she added with a conspiratorial wink. Thulmann marvelled at her for a moment, then followed Gregor from the room.

THE LIBRARY WAS a large room, dominating one corner of the keep. It might once have been a barracks of some sort. Thulmann could still see the remains of wooden beams sunken into the perimeter walls of the room, the last remnants of walkways and ladders that had once provided archers with access points to the narrow windows set some fifteen feet above the floor.

Now the vast hall had been fully converted, mammoth wooden bookcases filling the centre of the room. Each was at least ten feet in height, and at least three feet in depth. Doubled upon one another, sometimes in ranks four and five long, the cases made a maze of the old chamber. Each was filled almost to bursting with thin folios and monstrously bloated tomes, mounds of cylindrical scroll-cases and stacks of unbound parchment and paper.

The musty odour of rotting wood and mould was thick and heavy about the hall. Thulmann smiled to himself as he was conducted into the room. How many times had he stood in rooms exactly like this stalking some obscure shred of knowledge? For every second of terror spent confronting some loathsome visitation of the Ruinous Powers how many hours had he spent rummaging about in some dusty old library?

'Your mother is quite a remarkable woman,' Thulmann told the young noble. Gregor looked away from lighting a number of candles fixed into the claws of a candelabra shaped like a wrought-iron sea monster standing at the centre of a small desk.

'That she is,' Gregor admitted. 'She has a sharp mind and a proud spirit, and isn't afraid to let anyone know it. When my father went away to serve the temple, Ivar Kohl tried to run the estate his own way, as he had when my grandfather left, but my mother wouldn't let him. She had her own ideas, and was not about to let Kohl push her around.'

Gregor chuckled as he slipped into his recollections. 'I have to say, even old Ivar would have to confess that she ran things very well until my father returned.'

Thulmann only partly heard what Gregor was saying, his attention instead fixed upon the large map of the district hanging upon one of the walls. The witch hunter could see more detail was present in this work than the one back in his rooms at The Grey Crone.

He stared at it for some moments, studying its every line, imagining red splotches upon its surface. There had to be a key, something that would make these killings take up some semblance of reason. It was like one of the cryptograms such groups like the Pallisades played with. Once the code was discovered, the message would stand revealed. But what was the code? And what was the hideous message it concealed?

The witch hunter looked away from the map, staring intently at Gregor. 'I need your help,' he told the noble. 'You are aware that another life was taken this night. I have seen the body, and it was not the work of any brute beast. My associate,' Thulmann indicated Streng, who had slouched down into a heavy chair and was studiously inspecting a portfolio of exotic Bretonnian woodcuts, 'found tracks this time. Footprints of at least two men.'

Gregor considered Thulmann's statement, striding back and forth behind the desk as he turned them over in his mind. 'Then it is not one fiend we are seeking, but some dark conspiracy!' he exclaimed.

'The secret, I feel, is somehow tied into your family history,' the witch hunter told him. He waved his arm to encompass the towering bookcases behind him. 'Somewhere in these records may be the clue we need to learn the nature of this fiend.' The witch hunter clenched his fist. 'And once I have put a name to this pestilence, then I may be able to guess its intentions, and predict where it will strike next.'

'And destroy him,' Gregor stated.

'And destroy him,' the witch hunter concurred.

CRUEL EYES STUDIED the two-storey, half-timber structure. The night was nearly spent, the moons already retreating toward the horizon. There was not much time left in which to act, but Carandini was nothing if not a careful man. He wanted to give the poison every chance to work its course.

A few of the brutish farmers had been quite large, and it might take the poison a little longer to run its course through bodies so laden down with meat and muscle.

The necromancer looked at the rotting thing beside him. He had long ago lost any sense of horror at the many appearances assumed by death. In fact, to him there was nothing quite so wondrous as watching that almost mystical transformation as a living body became a corpse, to see the corruption work its way through the flesh, as tissue withered and bones broke through the weakened flesh.

The necromancer smiled at the stiff, still figure. His pale hand patted some of the mould from the front of its tunic, stopping when the rotted cloth began to fall apart. Dismayed, Carandini instead concentrated on stuffing the creature's dangling eye back into its socket. He found the organ reluctant to return to its place however, popping free whenever he removed his hand.

Annoyed, Carandini produced his dagger and pounded the greasy, staring object into the zombie's skull with the hilt of the weapon.

Turning from his gruesome maintenance, the necromancer stared keenly at the house once more. He had come upon it shortly after dark, creeping across the farmyard to the brick-lined well that stood before the house. The poison had gone in, and he had slunk back to the shadows. It had been hard not to laugh when the wife of one of the farmers had emerged to retrieve a bucket of water from the well.

The woman could not imagine how astounding they would find this evening's gruel. Indeed, they would never eat anything else ever again.

Carandini motioned for the creature beside him and the five others like it to advance. The necromancer followed after his loathsome creations. He would allow his zombies to enter the structure ahead of him, let them discover if anyone still lived. After all, a knife in the ribs or a hatchet in the head would not do them any great deal of harm. Nothing that couldn't be made right by a few incantations and a little baby's fat.

The walking corpses stalked towards the door, their movements stiff and silent and began to batter on the heavy door with their decaying fists.

The necromancer watched the windows of the house. If anyone was still inside, they could not fail to hear the commotion. However, no light appeared in any of the windows, and the only sound to rise from the structure was the howling of a dog. Carandini smiled. If he ever tired of trying to unlock the secrets of death, he might make a successful career as a professional poisoner back in his native Tilea.

After a few minutes, the relentless pounding of the zombies caused the door to collapse inward with a resounding crash. Carandini heard the frightened yip and the angry snarl of a dog as his undead slaves marched inside. The necromancer waited a few moments more to follow after them, then with swift, scuttling steps, made his way into the residence.

The main room of the farmhouse was a shambles, furniture tipped over, part of a rug pushed into the embers in the fire-pit where the covering was now slowly smouldering.

Carandini strode towards the hearth and pulled the rug from the fire, stamping out the fledgling flames with his boots. It would hardly do for the place to burn down. The necromancer looked up from his task, his weasel-like face grinning as he spied the large iron pot that had fallen to the floor. As he had known, there was some still-warm gruel at the bottom of the pot.

Another thing that the Tileans despised about the people of the Empire – their predictability. They were so disgustingly easy to predict, their thoughts regimented and unimaginative. It was no wonder that all the great thinkers and artisans were Tilean born and bred. The necromancer smiled again – as his scheming ally would learn soon enough for himself.

Carandini made his way from the living room, throwing aside the heavy fur curtain that separated a niche at the rear of the room. He peered into the gloomy space beyond, staring at the simple straw mattress, at the filthy fur blankets, at the two bodies lying sprawled upon the floor.

Carandini pursed his lips and tutted as he saw the corpses. 'Must have been something they ate,' he muttered, wiping a stringy lock of hair from his face.

The necromancer went back into the living room, this time following the small hallway, finding another tiny room at its terminus. The hanging here had already been torn down, and the necromancer could see two gaunt figures standing above the straw bed. He shuffled into the chamber, oblivious to the reeking corpse-things, and smiled down at the two bodies curled upon the bed.

There was no need to feel for any sign of warmth or pulse, the purpling tinge of the corpses told the necromancer that his poison had done its work. He looked at each of the stationary corpse things. They did not glance at him, but remained motionless, their colourless eyes focused on the wall.

'Take these into the other room,' Carandini told his slaves. There was no real need to speak to them, it was the exertion of the necromancer's will that caused the zombies to obey his commands, but there were times when Carandini slipped into his old habits.

The corpse-creatures bent forward, almost in perfect synchronisation, and pulled the two bodies from the bed. Carandini did not linger to see his slaves complete their task, but slipped back into the hall, climbing the stairs that led to the upper floor of the dwelling.

At the top of the stairs he found another of his zombie slaves, this one standing idle over the body of a very fat and very old woman. A small dog dangled from the monster's arm, worrying the rotted flesh viciously. The zombie was oblivious to the damage being inflicted upon it, its vacant stare contemplating the floor.

As Carandini came forward, he extended his will. The zombie lifted its free arm and brought its skeletal fist smashing down into the skull of the dog. The animal gave a muffled yelp, then fell to the floor, its weight snapping the arm it had been worrying like a twig. Carandini stared down at the dead animal, then looked up at his rotting creation. A look of annoyance crawled across his features. The necromancer pulled his dagger and grabbed something dangling from the zombie's face. With one deft stroke, he cut the veins connecting the recalcitrant eye to the creature's skull and tossed the disagreeable organ down the stairs.

'Take that,' the necromancer ordered, pointing at the old woman's body with his knife, 'below.' Once more he did not wait for his creation to obey, but continued down the narrow hall. A sudden sound made the necromancer pause. It did not sound like one of his creations blundering about, he thought. Carandini paused then hurried into a room at the far end of the hallway.

He found another of his creatures here, its skull-like face looking blankly at the wall. The bed was actually equipped with an iron frame, though the bedding itself was the usual pile of straw covered by furs and blankets. Two bodies were sprawled here, but they did not interest Carandini as much as the others had. No, it was the tiny shape nestled between them, the tiny little shape that sobbed with a fear its small mind could not fully appreciate.

The child's eyes were locked on the grisly shape of the zombie, not even looking away when the necromancer glided towards the bed.

'Oh,' Carandini said, his voice soft. 'You poor little thing,' he reached forward, picking the child from between his dead parents. The boy began to cry as the necromancer held him. 'You have been a bad little thing, haven't you?' the necromancer said. He exerted his will, causing the zombie to pull the child's father from the bed. He could hear the other two zombies pulling bodies from one of the other bedrooms. The child hid his face in the fur of Carandini's cassock, and the necromancer gently patted his back.

'You really should have eaten your gruel like a good little boy,' Carandini told him, striding from the room ahead of the over-laden zombie. He paused in the hallway, shifting his grip on the boy and removing a small object from a pouch on his belt. His associate's contingency was a small thing, and something of an enigma to Carandini. He was not entirely sure how it would benefit them to have the witch hunter discover it here, but such had been his confederate's directions when he had given it to Carandini.

The necromancer let the small object fall to the floor with a metallic ping.

Carandini walked ahead of his zombies, willing them to bring the bodies into the living room. It would be much easier to perform the ritual over all the bodies at once. The little boy began to cry again in the necromancer's arms.

Carandini set him down, smiling at the dirty-faced blond child. The child's face was dripping with tears and a thin stream of snot dangled from his nose.

'Now then,' the necromancer said, 'don't cry so.' His eyes lit up, and he let a false enthusiasm spring into his tone. 'You know, I might have something for you if you're good and quiet.' He took a few dried berries and a tiny glass vial from a pouch on his belt.

So utterly predictable, these men of the Empire, Carandini thought as the boy stuffed the berries into his mouth. That was why his confederate's ploy was unnecessary. Because the witch hunter would not be escaping the trap Carandini had set for him.

CHAPTER ELEVEN

THE WITCH HUNTER shut the heavy wood-bound volume closed with a crash, pushing it across the table from him in disgust. He reached to his face, pulling away the tiny pair of pince-nez reading glasses he had adopted upon beginning his labour and rubbed his eyes, then snatched up the cup of now-cold tea a servant had brought to the library some hours ago.

The witch hunter made a sour face as the drink chilled his lips, cursing once more whatever thrice-damned sadist had constructed Klausner Keep. He could imagine a Kislevite kossar catching a cold within the gloomy damp of the fortress, with its infinite drafts and omnipresent chill. It had been a steady struggle to keep warm, and several times he had pondered casting some particularly uninformative volume into the hearth to augment the sparse heat being generated there. It had been a tedious vigil, delving into the massive collection of portfolios, books and uncollected manuscripts through the small hours of the morning and on until now, somewhere beyond the dreary walls, the sun was at its full height.

The sound caused the head resting on the other side of the table to shoot up, Gregor Klausner sputtering in surprise. The young noble cast an ashamed look over at the witch hunter.

'I am sorry, Herr Thulmann,' he said, trying to stifle a yawn. 'I must have dozed off for a moment.'

'Yes,' sighed Thulmann, pulling another massive old history toward him and flinging the cover open. 'You did,' he said, eyes locked upon the coarse yellow paper, 'about four hours ago.'

Gregor looked at the witch hunter, his face incredulous. 'Four hours?' He reached toward one of the cups, recoiling when he discovered that the tea had gone cold. 'Did I miss anything?'

The witch hunter kept his eyes on the pages before him. 'Streng ran out of questionable wood cuts about the time you took your nap and left, most likely to avail himself of the wine cellar or a chamber maid, whichever he happened upon first. Then about an hour ago Ivar Kohl returned, quite pleased with himself, though that quickly passed when I told him I wouldn't be needing to see the scene of the latest murder since I had already been there.'

'I should have thought he'd have told my father and had you removed from the keep,' commented Gregor.

'Perhaps he was too tired,' Thulmann answered, an uncertain quality to his voice. 'Of course, with somebody as duplicitous as your father's steward, I doubt his motives are quite so simple. Still, he's let me alone.'

Gregor rose from his chair, walking around the table to glance down at the book Thulmann was perusing. The young noble's brow knitted as he tried to decipher the scrawl.

'The career of Gustav Klausner, head of your line about three hundred years ago,' the witch hunter informed him. 'Volume eight of sixteen,' he added in a weary grumble.

'Have you found anything that might be of help?'

Thulmann looked up from the book, closing the ponderous volume. An ironic smile tugged at his face. He lifted a thick pile of parchment sheets from the tabletop. 'My notes,' he informed Gregor. 'Your family has quite a colourful history, as you might imagine.' He let the papers drop back to the table, rubbing his eyes again. Gregor leaned forward and read what the witch hunter had written.

'Renzo Helder, Hierophant of Nuln; Detlef-Erich von Engelstoss, the Ghoul-lord; Faustine Kurtz, the Black Witch...'

'It reads like a roll-call of the chamber of horrors in Marienburg,' the witch hunter told him. He pointed his finger at the volumes strewn about the table and the nearby floor. 'One could hardly accuse your ancestors of being idle.'

Thulmann took his notes from Gregor, leafing through them. 'I've tried to eliminate a lot of the chaff. We know that the foul art of necromancy is involved, so I have concentrated my efforts on that arena, eliminating such villains as...' Thulmann glanced over the top sheet, picking one of the names he had written down and then crossed out, 'Grey Seer Kripsnik. One of your father's investigations. Then there are the ones whom we know to be dead,' he rummaged through the notes again, choosing another name he had drawn a line through. 'For instance, Giselbrandt Vogheim, one of the disciples of the late and unlamented Great Enchanter. They still have his skull on public display at the temple of Morr in Carroburg.' The witch hunter shook his head and sighed. 'Even so, there are fifty-seven names on my little list.'

'Surely we could eliminate the older names,' observed Gregor. He gave voice to a soft laugh as he picked up the heavy tome Thulmann had been perusing. 'I mean, is it really necessary to go back three hundred years to put a name to our fiend?'

'It might be,' Thulmann informed him, his voice carrying a sense of deadly seriousness. 'The filthy art of necromancy has at its heart a twisted search for immortality, and it is a testament to the power and twisted genius of some who practise that art that they can extend their lives well beyond the span granted to them by the gods. Some can even bind their spirits to their bodies after death and motivate their own corpses into a gruesome parody of life.' Thulmann smiled thinly at the young noble. 'Who can say how long such a creature might harbour a grudge, and your ancestors have certainly crossed the path of more than a few of them.' He lifted the notes again.

'For instance, your grandfather was responsible for bringing down the profane Nehekharan vulture god cult established by the deranged wizard Tefnakht in Averheim. While he did succeed in bringing Sigmar's justice to the sorcerer, he himself was not satisfied that all of Tefnakht's followers had been captured. Your great grandfather made battle with a creature calling itself Khanzhik Vasalov somewhere near the Kislev border. His account relates that he took all the necessary precautions in disposing of the creature, but one can never be entirely certain with vampires.'

The witch hunter ruffled through his notes again. 'We might even go so far back as the progenitor of your line, Helmuth Klausner, who relates that he destroyed a vampire calling itself Sibbechai in the cursed city of Mordheim over five hundred years ago.' Thulmann set the pages down.

'Even your father has his share of skeletons in his history,' he told Gregor. 'He tracked down the vile Enoch Silber in Helmsgart, although that loathsome individual escaped before he could be burned at the stake for his crimes.'

Thulmann paused, recalling his own encounter with the insane 'Corpse Collector' in the catacombs beneath Talabheim. The witch hunter still shuddered at the recollection of the madman's collection of 'bits and pieces', each crawling or screaming with an unnatural vitality. Silber was not Thulmann's best choice, being far too demented for the care and craft he had seen exhibited by the mind behind the

Klausberg crimes, yet he was not a possibility the witch hunter wanted to dismiss out of hand. 'Then we have his encounter with the necromancer Dragan Radic, who was discovered looting old barrow mounds in Sylvania. There is an interesting fact that escaped your father, although he hung Radic, there have been recent reports of the necromancer being seen in the Ostermark.'

Thulmann shook his head again. 'Any one of these disgusting creatures might be behind your district's affliction. Or none of them, I have only just scratched the surface of your family's history. As you well know, it was common practice for all the Klausner men to offer their service to the temple.'

Gregor turned away. 'Yes,' he sighed, 'a tradition which my father has broken with. He has forbidden either of us to follow that tradition. He fears that by serving the temple we will somehow invite great tragedy upon ourselves.'

When Gregor turned back around he found the witch hunter staring at him intently. 'For myself, I would like to serve, to become a champion of Sigmar and purge this land of the forces of the Old Night. It would somehow give me a sense of worth, make me feel that I truly deserve to inherit the family fortune and the right to wear the name of Klausner.'

'And your brother?' Thulmann said, his voice low.

'I think he resents my father's edict even more than I,' Gregor told him. 'Anton has always lived his life under a shadow. Mine, I am afraid. He's lived his life knowing that everything he saw, everything he touched, would one day be inherited by me. I imagine that makes him feel somehow less important than me, as if he didn't matter as much. Becoming a witch hunter would have given him purpose, made him feel that he had worth and value.'

'And yet, if anything, your brother is more eager to please your father than you are,' Thulmann pointed out. Gregor conceded the issue.

'Yes, and he has always done so,' he said. 'Anton has always tried to impress my father, in whatever way he can. He might not like my father's edict, but he would never question him about it.'

The door of the library suddenly swung inward, causing both men to turn around in alarm, Thulmann's hand sliding toward the pistol resting beside his papers on the table. Standing in the doorway was a grimy, flush-faced man wearing a tunic of studded leather over his stained breeches and shirt. Streng grinned through his unkempt beard.

'Sorry to disturb you, Mathias,' he said, hooking his thumbs in his belt. 'Thought you might be interested to know that our friend struck again last night.' Streng's smile grew broader as he elaborated. 'It seems our foe is getting bolder. They wiped out an entire household this time.'

'What?' exclaimed Gregor, shock and fury filling his voice. Thulmann motioned for the young noble to be silent.

'Where did this happen?' the witch hunter asked. 'And how did you come to hear of it?'

'Not far from here,' the mercenary answered. 'Only a short ride. Heard about it from one of his,' Streng pointed a finger at the young Klausner, 'brother's bully boys.'

'Well, that answers our questions about why Kohl was content to leave me here,' Thulmann said in disgust. 'They must have discovered this atrocity last night.'

'Could be,' agreed Streng. 'But shouldn't we go and have a look anyway?' There was a note of enthusiasm in the thug's voice.

'Kohl might have overlooked something of value,' Thulmann said after a moment of thought. 'In any event, we shall be no worse off than we are now.' He looked over at Gregor Klausner. 'I imagine that you want to come as well?'

'Try and stop me,' Gregor told him, the lisp stretching his words. Thulmann studied the determination, the smouldering outrage in the young noble.

'Then let us be on our way,' Thulmann said.

BENEATH THE SHELTER of the few rotting beams that were the last remains of the old cottage's roof, Carandini sat, his gleaming eyes focused upon the grisly object he had set upon the ground. It was a noxious thing, a large preserved hand.

The withered claw was wrapped round with dirty grey-green cloth, upon which the faintest outlines of script could still be seen. It was old almost beyond belief; the man to whom it had belonged in life had been born well before even Sigmar had walked the lands of men. There was the blackest of sorcery about the claw, both in the fell magics that had preserved it down through the ages and the lingering power of the spirit of the man to whom it had originally belonged. Mighty had the vanquished tomb king Nehb-ka-menthu been in life, and some of that power remained in his severed hand.

Carandini stirred from his half-sleep as the claw began to twitch. The necromancer leaned forward, staring intently as the limb began to move.

The spirit of Nehb-ka-menthu was still tethered to his hand, trapped between the worlds of death and life, even that of unlife. It could see far beyond the mortal world, even into the ancient past or the unwritten future at times. And what that spirit saw, the hand could relate.

Carandini had dipped the fingers of the claw in ink before setting the ethereal spirit of the old tomb king to watch over the farm house he had visited the previous night. It would watch and wait, reporting all those who came and went.

The necromancer stared as the claw began to scratch its picture-script upon the sheets of human skin that Carandini had set beside it on the ground. The necromancer was attentive to remove each sheet as they filled up with the claw's observations, so that the ghoulish oracle might have a fresh page upon which to write.

Carandini smiled as he read the hieroglyphs. The prey was almost in the trap.

CHAPTER TWELVE

THE HOUSE WAS fairly nondescript on the outside, like so many other half-timbered structures that dotted the countryside throughout the Empire. A small number of log outbuildings and a barn with a thatched roof completed the small compound. The log fence that surrounded the buildings had clearly been neglected, tied together by bundles of rope and twine in places where the ground had given way, sagging forward in awkward angles in others.

As Thulmann's party rode toward the small farm, the witch hunter spied a half-dozen horses tethered to a hitching rail between the buildings. A number of men exited the structure as the witch hunter approached. At their head was Anton Klausner.

'You have the nose of a vulture,' Anton said as the witch hunter rode through the gate. 'We only just found this place ourselves.'

'Then you must have spent a fair time riding circles around this place,' Thulmann stated, having seen the poached earth left behind by the hooves of Anton's men's horses. Whatever tracks there might have been to follow, Anton and his men had obliterated them, trying to impair the witch hunter's own hunt. Clearly, the tracking skills of Anton's group had not yielded any great success, leading the frustrated nobleman back to the farmstead.

'How bad is it?' Gregor asked, his face drawn with concern. Anton sneered up at his brother.

'Not a man, woman or child left alive,' he declared. 'He even killed the Brustholz's little dog. This is certain to stir up the village this time. They might even turn on our friend the witch hunter,' Anton hissed. 'People are so very fond of... dogs.' The brute chuckled, gesturing for his followers to mount.

'I grow tired of what passes for your wit,' Thulmann warned the brash ruffian as he climbed into his saddle. 'And I'll not tolerate any further interference from yourself and Kohl.'

'It is you who is interfering,' Anton snapped coldly. 'This is my father's land and it is his job to defend it!'

'These lands are still a part of Sigmar's Empire,' Thulmann retorted in a voice every bit as devoid of warmth. 'You and your father might remember that.'

'When the messenger my father dispatched to Altdorf speaks with your superiors, it is you who will be reminded of your place,' Anton warned. He whipped his horse's head about with a savage tug of the reins and spurred his steed into a gallop. His comrades quickly followed his example, thundering out of the gates in his wake. Thulmann watched the horsemen disappear down the muddy path.

'You know,' Streng commented, looking askance at Gregor, 'I am really starting to not like your brother.'

Mathias Thulmann dismounted, tying his horse's reins to a fence. The witch hunter cast his gaze across the compound. There was no sign of life, not even a single chicken or goose. He would have expected the animals to remain, bound by habit to the place despite the death of their owners. However, if these deaths were indeed the work of the fiend he sought, then perhaps the animals had sensed the unnatural nature of the events and been frightened into flight.

He knew that it was not uncommon for dogs to sense the workings of sorcery, and not unheard of for lower animals to also be disturbed by lingering traces of magic.

Thulmann withdrew one of his pistols from its holster as Gregor and Streng dismounted. He looked over at the two men, his eyes lost in shadow beneath the brim of his hat. 'Be on your guard,' he cautioned them. 'There is something not right here.'

Gregor nodded his own understanding, checking that his sword was loose in its scabbard. Streng simply grinned, pulling his crossbow from its sheath on his saddle.

'Expecting trouble?' the warrior asked, an eager note to his speech.

'Just keep an eye open,' Thulmann told him, striding toward the house.

* * *

THE FRONT DOOR had been battered from its hinges, lying upon the earthen floor just inside the threshold. It was a fitting precursor to the scene of destruction and horror that occupied the room beyond. Furnishings, meagre and fragile to begin with, had been toppled and destroyed, wooden tables and chairs crushed and shattered in a mindless rage, clay pots and jars broken to shards that crunched underfoot as the witch hunter strode into the room. But it was the sight at the centre of the room that arrested their attention.

The bodies had been piled like cordwood, stacked in a precise and cold manner that was utterly at odds with the reckless destruction that surrounded them. All wore their nightshirts, their exposed skin pale and tinged with a sickening purple hue. Vacant eyes stared out from rigid faces that were locked in the last grimace of some agony, their hands contorted into frozen claws.

There were ten in all. Anton Klausner had been right, the fiend had spared neither woman nor child.

'The bastard,' Gregor swore as he laid eyes upon the evidence of mass murder. 'There is no end fitting enough for such scum!' He smashed his fist against the wall in impotent fury.

'Rest assured, we shall find this monster, and bring it down,' Thulmann told him. He slowly circled the mound, staring intently at the bodies.

'Well, it seems Anton and his lads didn't do too fine a job of searching this hovel,' Streng stated with a macabre humour. The mercenary lifted a clay bottle from the floor, holding it to his ear so he could hear its contents slosh about. 'Any wagers on whether it is ale, mead or beer?' he asked.

'You should include poison on your list of liquors,' Thulmann said. Streng arrested the bottle's advance a hand's breadth from his lips. With a nervous look, the mercenary lowered the bottle, dropping it to the floor with a crash.

'Is that how this was done?' asked Gregor, struggling to maintain his calm. These might not have been mighty nobles or great scholars, but they had been people, good hard-working Klausbergers. To see them slaughtered in such a cold and ruthless fashion offended every sensibility in the young man's body and filled his heart with a fiery need for revenge.

'There are no marks of violence that I can see,' the witch hunter informed him. 'Apart from some scratches that are hardly of enough import to have caused death. Indeed, I rather suspect that they were caused after death, when, for whatever reason, the fiend decided to construct this morbid testament to his evil.' Thulmann turned away in disgust from the piled dead. 'No, our killer employed some foul venom to work this evil, or else some sending of the blackest magic.'

Gregor shuddered at the possibility. To kill without a sword or weapon of any sort, to simply mutter an incantation, make a few gestures and then invoke death. It was a horrible thing to contemplate.

Thulmann began to inspect the room, looking for any clues as to the motivation and purpose for this last atrocity. There had been something more to this act; it had broken entirely with the pattern set by the other murders. No lone woodsman, no solitary farmer lured from his home in the dead of night, rather an entire household slaughtered under their own roof!

Did it bespeak some final sacrifice, an end to the fiend's blasphemous rituals? Or perhaps these people had not been so innocent as they seemed. The villain he sought had associates, and perhaps it was they the witch hunter now gazed upon, given a treacherous reward by their unholy master. Whatever the truth, Thulmann held out a vain hope that some clue might yet linger within the charnel house, something left behind by the perpetrator of this act and not discovered by Anton Klausner and his men.

'Search the floor above,' Thulmann told Gregor and Streng as he peered into the little sleeping nook set to one side of the room. 'Look for anything out of the ordinary.'

Streng nodded in understanding, patting Gregor's shoulder and motioning for the noble to follow him.

The two men climbed the stairs, the rickety steps swaying beneath Streng's heavy tread. The mercenary paused at the top of the stairs. He stared down at a tiny crumpled shape, turning it over with his foot, then bending down to extract the rotting object clenched in its jaws. It was a human forearm, the flesh so decayed and rotten that in places the bone peered through. A large section had been stripped completely bare by the dog's fangs.

'Rather unusual toy for anybody's dog, don't you think?' Streng said, letting the loathsome object fall. The mercenary continued on, ducking into one of the side rooms.

Gregor stared down at the rotted limb. His mind cringed as he considered how it might have come to be in such a place. For the first time, something of the true nature of the man they hunted impressed itself upon him and Gregor appreciated in full the horrible power arrayed against them.

As the noble began to turn away from his fascinated study of the rotted arm, his eyes caught a slight glitter upon the floor. He took a few steps and bent forward to retrieve the small metal object.

When he saw what he had picked up, he stared at it as though he held a lethal serpent in his grasp. Gregor's limbs began to shake, shivering with a palsy of terror. He could feel his stomach churning, his bile fighting to purge itself from his body. The noble's vision began to blur, refusing to accept the thing his eyes beheld.

It was a ring, a simple band of gold. Its face bore a shield-like device, upon which had been etched two figures. One was a griffon rampant, and beneath its clawed foot it crushed the shape of a slavering wolf. Gregor closed his fist around the object, refusing to accept the importance of what he had discovered. How often had he gazed upon this ring? How often had he seen it, clinging to his father's frail fingers?

'Come along now,' Streng's voice intruded upon Gregor's terrified thoughts. The noble snapped out of his fear, stamping it down as he forced control back into his frame. The mercenary looked at Gregor with a glint of suspicion in his eye. 'Find anything?' he asked.

'No,' stated Gregor, discreetly slipping the ring into his pocket. 'Shall we try the other room?' he asked.

'If it's as small as this one, I think I can manage on my own,' Streng told him. 'You go down and see if Mathias needs any help.'

GREGOR STEPPED DOWN into the central room of the cottage, gripping the creaking banister with a hand that had not entirely ceased trembling. He looked over to find the witch hunter emerging from the back room, a bit of mouldy cloth impaled upon a long iron needle gripped in his hand.

'I found this back there,' Thulmann told him. 'Rather shabby even for a peasant, wouldn't you say? Stinks worse of death than those over there do.' The witch hunter shook the offensive scrap from the end of the needle. 'It's my guess that our friend did not work alone when he did this, and his assistants were of a most unusual sort.'

'We found an arm bone upstairs,' Gregor told the witch hunter, 'clutched in the jaws of a little dog. It looked like it had been a month in the grave.' The noble's expression suddenly changed, his eyes going wide with alarm, his mouth dropping open with shock. A gasp emptied his lungs and it was with a trembling hand that he pointed at the witch hunter.

Thulmann spun around to see what had drained the colour from Gregor's face. He sprang back as he saw the pile of corpses begin to twitch, as the topmost of them began to lift itself with awkward movements. The rigid expression locked upon the dead woman's face did not change, nor did any sound issue from her frozen mouth, but a ghastly intent emanated from her dull eyes.

'Zombie,' the witch hunter hissed in a mixture of alarm and loathing. He lifted his pistol, bringing it to bear upon the animated corpse. It crawled from the pile, falling to the floor with a heavy thud, then awkwardly began to gain its feet once more, ignorant of the ankles that had snapped beneath its ungainly descent.

'Streng!' Thulmann called out as the rest of the slain family began to stir.

The witch hunter pushed Gregor toward the door. 'It's a trap! Get the horses!' he ordered the young noble. The harsh commands snapped Gregor from his horrified paralysis and he raced out into the yard, only to be brought up short a few feet from the collapsed doorway.

Six stumbling, shambling shapes had emerged from the barn, bits of hay still clinging to their rotted, dripping frames. They must have lain hidden beneath the hay when Anton had made his search, only to emerge now to close the trap. Gregor met the empty, vacant stare of the skull-faced horrors, then withdrew back into the house.

'No good!' he told Thulmann. The witch hunter had backed up nearly to the stairway, the shuffling zombies slowly closing in upon him. 'There are more outside!'

The witch hunter snarled under his breath, firing his pistol into the nearest of the corpse-creatures, exploding its skull. The thing took another stumbling step forward, then collapsed, tripping up two of its fellow abominations. 'Damn it Streng!' Thulmann called out.

The mercenary appeared at the head of the stairway, his crossbow gripped in his hands. He took in the situation with a calm, chilling detachment, then aimed his weapon. The bolt smashed through the arm of one of the decaying horrors that was now stalking through the front door, pinning the rotting limb to the wall.

'I shouldn't stay down there if I were you, Mathias,' the mercenary said. Gregor and the witch hunter followed his example, slowly ascending the rickety stair. The silent, stumbling figures shuffled after them.

'An excellent suggestion,' Thulmann commented, drawing his second pistol and firing over Gregor's shoulder into the rigid face of the foremost of the monsters. The bullet tore through its skull, exploding from the back of its head in a spray of greasy brain matter. The zombie sagged to its side, flopping on the floor like a fish out of water.

Thulmann slammed the smoking pistol back into its holster, swiftly retreating up the stairs. Gregor followed in his wake, slashing with his sword to keep the undead horrors at bay. His sword ripped and tore at the clutching arms that reached out toward him, tearing the lifeless flesh, spilling rank and gluey blood.

'Mathias,' Streng called down as he reloaded his crossbow. 'Probably a bad time to point this out, but there's no way down from here.' The mercenary aimed and fired, the bolt punching harmlessly through the chest of one of the undead monstrosities.

'What about the windows?' Thulmann snapped, reaching forward and pulling Gregor back as the clawing hand of a zombie nearly fixed upon the young noble's arm. Thulmann lashed out with a sidewise slash of his longsword, bisecting the putrid creature's face. The zombie stumbled back, arresting the advance of its fellows, then began to lumber forward once more, teeth dripping from its injury.

'No good. They're too narrow for a fox to slip through,' Streng snarled in disgust. 'Made to keep thieves out.'

'They also serve to keep us in. I fear I underestimated terribly the cunning of our enemy. It seems he isn't adverse to playing the hunter himself.' Thulmann suddenly noticed a shudder pass through the oncoming horde.

For a brief moment, they were still, but it quickly passed. The witch hunter did not have long to wonder about the cause. The controlling influence of the zombie master had isolated one of the monsters from its fellows, guiding it toward the piled mass of straw and bedding that was heaped in one corner of the room below.

Thulmann watched in fascinated horror as the monster fumbled at its pocket, removing a small tinderbox. With dull, idiot movements, the rotten fingers began to work the mechanism.

'Streng, shoot the one in the corner over there!' Thulmann cried out. The mercenary aimed and fired, the bolt punching through the corpse-creature's neck and burying itself in the monster's shoulder. The zombie did not so much as flinch. Thulmann swore.

Below him, Gregor sliced the clutching hand from one of the creatures, a bubble of black blood oozing from the stump.

'We could use an idea right now,' the noble said. 'Maybe push through them after their friend gets its fire started and they start to retreat?'

Thulmann shook his head, his sword crunching into the collarbone of the zombie that had slipped into the space vacated by the one Gregor had maimed. The zombie pitched sideways, breaking through the banister and crashing to the floor below. No sooner had it hit the ground then the corpse began to pick itself up, broken rails protruding from its chest.

'They won't retreat,' the witch hunter stated. 'These things are simply a mockery of life, enslaved completely to the will of the one who called them from their graves. They will keep pursuing even as the entire building comes down around us!'

Streng fired another bolt into the zombie down below. The thing crumpled as its knee exploded, pitching forward into the flickering flames that were beginning to rise from the heap. The mercenary gave voice to a colourful curse as the burning creature rose, its skin and clothing afire. Its task completed, the burning automaton limped across the room to join its fellows.

'Wait a moment!' exclaimed Gregor as he watched the flames rise. 'If we can't go down, perhaps we can go up!' Thulmann glanced overhead, observing that the roof was simply thatch thrown over wooden beams.

'Streng!' he cried. 'Find something to stand on and knock a hole in this roof! We'll keep these creatures at bay.'

The mercenary hurried off, slipping into one of the rooms. Thulmann and Gregor could hear the mercenary tip some heavy object over, then the sound of him savaging the ceiling with his sword. The two men continued to back up the stairs, the undead horrors shambling after them in eerie silence. Below, one entire side of the room had become engulfed in fire, the flames quickly spreading through the dry wood and even dryer thatching of the roof.

'He'd better hurry,' Gregor grunted as he slashed at the zombie reaching toward him. The creature stumbled back, its arm dangling uselessly from its cloven shoulder.

A shout from the side room caused both men to turn their heads. 'You go first,' Thulmann ordered Gregor. The noble opened his lips to protest, but the expression in Thulmann's eyes brooked no question.

The noble slashed once more at the zombies climbing the stairway, then turned and raced toward the room. He found that Streng had tipped over a heavy wooden wardrobe, the most lavish furnishing they had yet seen in the hovel. Overhead, sunlight shone through a large hole that had been cut through the thatching.

Gregor sheathed his blade, then climbed atop the wardrobe. Stretching his arms, he jumped toward the opening, catching the beams that edged the hole and pulling himself up onto the roof.

Gregor paused for a moment, looking around him for any sign of Streng, but he could not see the mercenary. Smoke was rising from a section of the roof only twenty feet away, and he could see tiny fingers of fire peeping between the thatching. He looked back down into the hole.

'Herr Thulmann!' he shouted. 'There is not much time!' He waited, watching the room beneath the hole, with many a nervous glance at the creeping smoke and flame. Suddenly, a shadow moved across the floor. The eager, hopeful look on Gregor's face faded however, when a purple-skinned figure shuffled into view, surveying the room with sidewise swings of its torso.

The zombie paused for a moment, then lifted its head, staring straight up at Gregor with its dull, vacant eyes. The noble cringed back as the monster reached up toward him. Cursing, Gregor slid down towards the low end of the roof, lowering himself from its edge with his hands and dropping to the ground.

'Nice to see that you made it,' Streng called out to him. Gregor turned about to see the mercenary seated on the back of his horse, the reins for Gregor's and Thulmann's own steeds clutched in his meaty hands.

'Nice of you to wait,' Gregor snapped. The bearded mercenary chuckled.

'I risk my neck only when it might serve a purpose,' Streng told him. 'I didn't see any way that dropping back down would help the situation.'

'But your master! He's still in there!' As Gregor spoke the words, a look of regret came upon Streng.

'We have to go back for him!' exclaimed the young noble.

'Back into that?' Streng said, his voice sombre. Gregor turned to regard the cottage. The lower floor was almost entirely engulfed in fire now, the plaster peeling away as the flames devoured the beams beneath them. Thick black smoke billowed upwards into the sky, turning the afternoon into twilight. The noble stared down at the ground, shaking his head.

'I vow that I will not rest until this fiend is made to pay for his crimes,' Gregor swore.

'A commendable oath,' a silky voice told him. Both Gregor and Streng turned their heads to see the witch hunter emerging from the billowing smoke. His hat was gone, his thin face stained by soot and the long cloak upon his back was torn, but otherwise he looked none the worse for his ordeal.

'I thought they had you,' stated Gregor. Thulmann nodded to the young noble.

'I will admit that there was a moment when I thought the same,' he confessed. 'Some reckless desperation seemed to come upon them and they pressed me harder than before. One of them even slipped past me. I was forced to turn my back to them and trust to the grace of Sigmar to preserve me as I raced toward the opening friend Streng provided us with.' The witch hunter shook his head as he recollected his near escape. 'I dropped down on the other side of the building, somewhat alarmed not to find you two awaiting me.'

Thulmann turned and regarded the blazing structure. A figure could be briefly seen shambling towards the doorway, its body wreathed in flame. But even as it staggered forward, its knees buckled and it fell to be consumed by the fire. 'It seems our enemy desires to swap the roles of hunter and prey,' Thulmann told his companions. 'This might mean he's worried that I might be close to guessing his purpose and thwarting whatever diabolical plan he has in his mind.'

The witch hunter climbed into the saddle of his horse. 'We proceed with care now,' he cautioned. 'For our enemy has become doubly dangerous.'

CARANDINI GLARED AT the scrabbling mummy's claw, hissing with rage as he read the inscription upon the page. The necromancer rose to his feet, pounding his fist into his hand.

'Did you truly think it would be so easy?' the low voice of his confederate spoke to him from the deep shadows at the back of the ruin. The necromancer turned around with a start, visibly flinching from his surprise. He tried to recover his composure, determined to show no weakness before his nebulous ally.

'I had not expected you,' he said. 'Not so... soon. Are you certain that it is safe to be out?'

'My being here is not without some slight danger,' the shadow conceded. 'But no more than I am willing to risk.' The voice grew stern. 'Certainly less dangerous than your failure to kill the witch hunter.'

'My plan was flawless,' spat Carandini, glaring into the shadows. 'There was no way he could have escaped!'

'And yet, to judge by your reaction, he has,' observed the necromancer's associate. Carandini scowled, pulling his ratty hair from his face.

'I suppose that you could do better?' he challenged. He cringed back as the dry, rasping laughter of his ally echoed through the ruin.

'I can and I shall, little man,' the shadow told him. Carandini could feel the air grow cold, the chill touch of the tomb caress his face as his ally began to call the foulest of powers into his body. The necromancer fancied he could see a ghostly green glow burning from the eyes of his confederate. The necromancer watched in rapt fascination, promising himself that one day such power would be his.

'It is done,' the shadow spoke as the glow began to fade and the temperature began to creep back.

'What is done?' Carandini asked, a keen quality to his voice.

'What needed doing,' the shadow declared. 'I have called upon my own resources to salvage this situation from your bungling. The witch hunter will never reach the keep alive. My hounds shall see to it.'

CHAPTER THIRTEEN

FROM AN OVERLOOKING rise, the witch hunter watched as the flames devoured the last of the cottage, his keen gaze alert for any sign of unnatural movement among the rubble. He'd always read that creatures such as those that had attacked him in the house were amongst the lowest and simplest of the undead, and that destruction by fire would be sufficient to end their unholy existence. But Thulmann was a cautious man and waited until the smoke began to lessen. Satisfied, he holstered the pistol he had been reloading and turned toward his companions.

'Shall we withdraw and inform his lordship that his district is now lessened by one farm?' he asked Gregor. The young noble's face was grim, his eyes filled with a distant melancholy. Thulmann could imagine the man's thoughts: one's first encounter with the restless dead was always a profoundly disturbing experience. He guessed that Gregor was at that point where he was questioning the power and wisdom of Sigmar to allow such profane things to walk the earth. Thulmann himself had faced a similar dilemma when he had first seen the power of the necromancer's arts in a crypt beneath Wolfenburg over a decade ago.

'Lead the way, Streng,' Thulmann told his henchman. 'I want to be back at the keep in time for his lordship to invite us to dinner.'

Streng grinned at the comment, urging his steed to turn around and gallop off in the direction of Klausner Keep. Gregor extracted himself somewhat from his brooding thoughts and followed Streng's lead.

Thulmann studied the man for a moment. In the face of such unholy visitations, it was all very well to question the power of the gods, the witch hunter thought, so long as one drew the correct conclusion. Anything else was the first step on the path of heresy. Thulmann hoped that Gregor would reach the right conclusion.

THEY WERE RIDING along a path that wound through a tangle of woods that bordered on the area where Thulmann had found the ruined remains of Emil Gundolf the forester. That fact, and the growing darkness, made the witch hunter's skin crawl with a sense of unease. There was no doubt it was a cheerless, friendless region.

The moon overhead bathed everything in a disconcerting grey illumination, fighting a hopeless struggle against the ascendant shadows. Even the crickets had fallen quiet and the only sound that accompanied the clop of horse hooves was the rustle of wind-blown leaves blowing between the trees. Thulmann patted the neck of his white steed as the horse gave a nicker of fright.

Ahead of him, he saw Streng's steed come to an abrupt stop. The mercenary swatted the animal with the end of the reins, but the horse remained resolute, whickering in protest as Streng tried to urge it forward. 'Something's gotten into him,' Streng said, looking back to his master.

Thulmann did not reply, instead looking past the mercenary at the gaunt shape that had ghosted out of the trees and was now standing in the centre of the road, as if in challenge. It was large, the size of a yearling calf, its shoulders broad, its frame squat.

Despite the encroaching gloom, Thulmann could make out its lupine outline, could catch the gleam of bared fangs. However, more hideous than the wolf-like creature was the stink that emanated from it, a foul and carrion reek.

The eyes of the creature regarding them glowed with an unholy light, like glittering pools of green pus.

'What in the name of Holy Sigmar?' marvelled Gregor. Thulmann paid him no mind, his head snapping around as he heard a twig snap among the trees. Three more pairs of glowing eyes stared back at him from the darkness. A swift glance to the other side of the road showed four more creatures creeping between the trunks.

'Ride for your life!' the witch hunter shouted, digging his spurs into his mount's flanks. His charger thundered down the path, smashing into the snarling creature that stood in its way. Thulmann heard the snap of breaking bones as his steed rode down the wolf, but did not hear the creature give voice to any sound of pain.

He glanced back to observe Streng and Gregor riding hard after him, the broken remains of the first wolf snapping at them as they passed, pulling itself after them with its front legs, leaving its broken midsection to drag along the ground behind it. More successful were the half score of sleek shadows that erupted from the trees, loping after them with swift, tireless bounds.

Thulmann ripped one of his pistols from its holster and fired back into the pursuing pack. The bullet caught one of the wolves dead on, throwing its body upwards. It was a killing shot, but the witch hunter did not expect the eerie blue flame that erupted from the wound, nor the long drawn-out howl that emanated not from the wolf, but from the wisp of grey smoke that spilled from its injury.

The other members of the pack paid no attention to their companion's demise, loping after the three men without breaking their stride.

'By all the hells!' shouted Gregor. 'What are they?'

'More creatures of the necromancer!' Thulmann called back. 'We must outrun them,' he added. 'I only have two silver bullets, and I've used one already.'

The riders continued to barrel down the path, their hellish pursuers close behind them. The heavy breath of the terrified horses resounded in Thulmann's ears, but from the sleek shadows loping after them there came not the slightest sound. He turned his head to check their position, horrified to find that the pack was only about a horse length from catching up to them. And they were gaining. He looked ahead, spying a fork in the road.

'The left path!' shouted Gregor. 'If we can just keep ahead of them, a little longer we can reach the keep!'

Almost in unison, the men turned their animals toward the left. The sudden manoeuvre spoiled the leap of one of the wolves as it pounced for Thulmann's steed. The black-furred brute struck the ground, rolling hard. Yet the creature was hardly phased by its ineffective leap, gaining its feet almost at once and loping after the rest of the pack.

They were now travelling through the relatively healthy trees that bordered on the region afflicted by what Gregor had called 'the blight'. The trees here were older, their trunks gnarled, their branches thick. They cast their shadows upon the road, covering it with darkness.

The fleeing riders had to trust to the instinct of their steeds, and the straightness of the path. Thulmann prayed that no branches had fallen since the road was last cleared, so nothing might lie upon the path to trip their steeds. If any of the horses should stumble at such breakneck speed, their rider could be killed by the fall.

The horses were gasping now, their strength and vitality waning from the long chase and the terror the wolves evoked in their hearts. They could not sustain the pace much longer. Behind them, the tireless wolves maintained their unnatural, unwavering stride. Thulmann drew his second pistol, firing another bullet into the pack. There was a flash of blue fire, another long, unearthly howl. At least there would be one less when the pack caught them.

A new sound suddenly intruded upon the nightmarish chase, the soft babble of flowing water. Thulmann recalled the road that led to Klausner Keep. A small stream wound through the diseased woods; the sound had to be coming from that. If so, they could only be five or ten minutes' ride from the safety of the fortress. Could the horses maintain such a cruel pace for that long?

'By the light and glory of Holy Sigmar, bane of the unlight, I abjure you!' Thulmann shouted back at the pack.

It was an incantation from the rites of exorcism as practised by some of the Templars of his order. Of course, there were all manner of preparations and paraphernalia that were needed to complement the ritual, things the current situation did not really lend itself to. Still, perhaps it might cause the unholy things to flinch back, recoil in fear for a moment. Every last second might save them now.

The wolves did arrest their pursuit, the sleek shadows coming to a stop in the middle of the path. For the space of a heartbeat, it seemed that the simple prayer had broken the strength and will of the unholy pack. But the illusion swiftly faded, for as the next second came to pass feral snarls and wheezing growls hissed from the gaunt frames. With a redoubled savagery, the undead wolves bounded towards their prey once more.

'Nice going,' Streng commented, rolling his eyes. 'Now they are mad.'

'They were already going to kill us,' Thulmann retorted, trying to urge his tiring horse to greater effort. The small wooden bridge that spanned the stream was ahead of them, the witch hunter could see its black mass separating the gleam of the slow-moving water. 'We are close now!' he shouted.

The three men thundered across the span, the hooves of their animals flying across the wooden surface. They had no intention of stopping on the other side, but a startling occurrence caused them to pull their steeds to a halt.

An icy chill seemed to surround them, and a peculiar odour, like singed hair. There was a bright flash of light and a sound not unlike the crack of lightning. An agonised howl punctuated these events, and when Thulmann looked back towards the bridge, he could see a shape lying upon it, grey smoke rising from its still form. The rest of the wolf pack was glaring at him with their glowing green eyes as they paced back and forth along the far bank.

Thulmann dismounted, pulling his sword from its scabbard.

'You sure that's wise?' Streng called to him as Thulmann strode toward the bridge. The witch hunter did not hear him, too perplexed by what he had just felt and witnessed.

It was lighter here, a break in the trees allowing the light of Mannslieb to illuminate the scene. Now the witch hunter could see the full horror of the things that had stalked them through the woods. They were monstrously oversized wolves, almost as large as the extinct great Sylvanian wolf, and certainly more vile. Their flesh clung to their bones like wet paper, their pelts were mangy, the black fur missing in clumps and patches. The patches of naked flesh were clearly necrotic, the pale bodies of maggots crawling about in the meat.

The faces of the animals were likewise decayed, their muzzles bare and skeletal. Their gleaming eyes were utterly ethereal; Thulmann could detect no sign of any physical eye behind their fire. The monstrous hounds glared back at their observer, snarling and growling in frustrated bloodlust.

The witch hunter turned his attention to the wolf lying on the bridge. It was rapidly decaying, even as he watched it, the skin peeling away and the fur withering. It was as if all the years the ghoulish creature had cheated its grave had been thrust upon it. Soon, there was only a pile of bone, and even these began to crumble in upon themselves.

'Truly you are blessed by Sigmar,' Gregor said, his voice subdued by the awe of their miraculous escape. The witch hunter shook his head.

'No, this is not the work of Sigmar,' he said, a haunted quality to his words. 'I have heard old folk fables that claim the restless dead cannot cross moving water. But never have I read or encountered anything that would give such legends credence.'

'Well, there is your proof,' said Gregor, pointing at the dwindling remains on the bridge.

Thulmann again shook his head.

'No, there is something fouler than legend at work here,' he declared. 'Can you not feel it all around you? A crawling in your skin, a greasiness in your breath, the chill of the crypt slithering across your bones? It is the stink of decay and corruption.' Thulmann could see by Gregor's reaction to his words that the young noble had indeed felt the same sickening sensations.

'What does it mean?' he asked in a sombre tone.

Thulmann looked back across the stream at the pacing pack. 'The same force that gave those obscenities their mockeries of life,' he said. 'I have seen abominations destroyed in just such a manner, in the madhouse of Enoch Silber's unholy experiments. A necromancer takes pains to preserve himself from that which he calls from the tomb.'

Gregor Klausner recoiled from the witch hunter's statement. 'But that can't be,' he protested.

'It can and it is,' stated Thulmann flatly, his eyes cold and stern as they looked into Gregor's. Both men turned as Streng rode towards them.

'Seems like that lot want another chance at us,' the mercenary swore. He hefted his crossbow, grinning at the witch hunter. 'Think this would do any good?' he asked.

'Not any appreciable damage,' Thulmann told him. 'Holes punched through dead flesh have little effect. But I have something here that they won't shrug off so easily.' Thulmann removed his powder flask from his belt and a silver ball from his cartridge case. The pack stopped their pacing, fixing him with their luminous gaze. The creatures gave voice to a final snarl of anger then fell back, slinking into the night.

'Our friend has quite a mixed bag of tricks,' commented Streng as he watched the wolves disappear into the darkness. Thulmann turned his own gaze back upon the stream.

'Yes,' he said in a low whisper. 'A mixed bag indeed.'

MATHIAS THULMANN THREW open the front door of the main hall of the keep. His cloak was torn, his clothes stained by soot and sweat, his boots covered in mud and the greasy pseudo-blood of the zombies he had battled at the Brustholz farm. However, it was the look of cold, cruel menace upon his face that caused the servant who had met his party at the door to race away in search of Ivar Kohl.

Thulmann ignored the departed servant's admonishment to await the steward, and began to climb the stairway at the side of the hall. Gregor Klausner followed after the witch hunter. Streng strode toward the blazing fire set beneath the hanging portraits of the Klausner patriarchs, turning when he reached the hearth, trying to warm the numbness from his backside.

'What the devil do you think you are doing?' cried out Ivar Kohl's heavy voice. The steward stood below, in the main hall, glaring up at the witch hunter as he ascended the steps.

'I am going to have words with your master,' Thulmann snapped, not bothering to look at the irate steward. Kohl muttered a colourful curse and hurried up the steps in pursuit.

'His lordship is sleeping,' the steward told the witch hunter.

'In that case, I will wake him,' Thulmann informed the man, not looking back. Ivar Kohl's face reddened and he flung himself up the stairs ahead of the two men.

'I said that his lordship is not to be disturbed,' he repeated, extending his arm to block Thulmann's progress.

The witch hunter glared at Kohl. 'Remove your arm or I will have my man break it,' he snapped. Stunned by the violence in Thulmann's voice, Kohl retreated, his continued protests sputtering as they tried to form on his lips.

'Perhaps I should speak with him,' Gregor said when they stood outside the door of his father's room.

'No,' Thulmann told the young noble. 'It is time your father heard the situation laid out before him in no uncertain terms. He will face reality this time, and Sigmar take his precious ego!' The witch hunter knocked once upon the heavy wooden portal, then flung it open.

Wilhelm Klausner was resting in his bed, his frail body nestled amidst its mound of pillows and furs. His wife sat beside him on the edge of the mattress, feeding her husband a bowl of medicinal broth. Both of them gave a start when the witch hunter strode into the chamber.

'What is the meaning of this!' rasped Wilhelm, raising his body from the bed. 'How dare you!'

'He forced his way past me,' explained Kohl, squeezing his way into the room behind Gregor. 'I'll have him removed at once.'

'Think about leaving this room, and I'll snap you in chains,' snapped Thulmann. 'I've had enough of your plotting and scheming. Any more of it and I will put you somewhere where you can't interfere.'

'You arrogant dog!' hissed Wilhelm, his wrinkled face contorting into a mask of fury. 'I'll have you know I've made them aware of your heavy-handed posturing in Altdorf.' He wagged his emaciated finger at the witch hunter. 'I am the authority here, and when my messenger returns from seeing the Grand Theogonist, you will receive a most forceful reminder of that fact!'

'Father, please,' protested Gregor, stepping towards the bed.

Wilhelm cast a pained look of disappointment and contempt at the young man.

'I'd not have expected my own son to side against me,' he stated. His wife set a restraining hand on her husband's shoulder, but he shook it off. 'I expect disappointment from Anton, but this treachery hurts me as keenly as the knife stabbed into my heart.'

'At least Gregor is doing something to put a stop to the horror that is at large in your district,' Thulmann informed the sickly lord. He tossed a filthy, rotting object upon the bed. It was the bloated, purple-hued hand of one of the Brustholz zombies. Wilhelm recoiled, staring in horror at the loathsome object.

'I have been attacked twice this night by things that by all rights should have been quiet in their graves,' stated the witch hunter. 'The massacre at the Brustholz farm was a trap, a cunning trap laid for me by the insidious fiend who has conceived these atrocities. No sooner had your son and myself arrived than the slaughtered family took to their feet in a ghastly parody of life, motivated by the murderous will of their killer. We were attacked again on the road here, hunted by wolves, your lordship. Wolves that feel no pain and have bale-fires instead of eyes.'

Wilhelm Klausner began to tremble, a confused look coming upon his face. 'Can this be?' he gasped.

'Yes, it is, father,' Gregor told him. 'I was there, I saw these horrors for myself.'

'We were saved from the devil dogs by a most unusual phenomenon,' Thulmann said, his silky voice carrying a hint of challenge. 'The wolves were unable to pursue us across the stream that borders your estate. Indeed, the one that did so dropped dead instantly, crumbling into dust as we watched it. Most unusual, wouldn't you say?'

Ivar Kohl blanched at the implication in the witch hunter's voice. It was with a visible effort that he regained some measure of calm. 'Any peasant can tell you that the unquiet dead are unable to cross running water,' he stated. As the steward spoke Gregor stared at his father and shuddered, his hand seeking out the ring he had secreted in his pocket.

Thulmann swung his unremitting gaze on the steward. 'Something destroyed the monster,' he stated. 'Something more tangible than peasant superstitions.'

'There are a great many elf ruins on my lands,' Wilhelm said. The witch hunter turned back toward him, impressed by the even, level quality to the man's words. 'Perhaps it was some lingering enchantment of the elder race that preserved you and destroyed the wolf?'

'Perhaps,' Thulmann conceded, though the dubious quality in his voice said that he was far from convinced. 'Or perhaps there is another reason.' The witch hunter stalked toward the door. 'I will finish my consultation of your family records, then you will provide me with an escort back to the village. I don't have the time to continue placating your pride, Lord Klausner. Cooperate with my needs and we will rid your lands of this menace.'

The witch hunter looked over at Ivar Kohl and smiled thinly. 'Wherever it might hide itself,' he added.

GREGOR KLAUSNER REMAINED behind in his father's room after the witch hunter had withdrawn. Ivar Kohl was not long in making his own excuses, hurrying away like some mammoth spider slinking back into a dark corner. Gregor walked over to his mother, asking her to leave him alone with the patriarch.

The woman nodded her head, kissing her son and withdrawing to her own room, telling Wilhelm to call out if he needed anything.

Gregor smiled at his mother's statement. Even with an entire household at her beck and call, she preferred to see to her husband herself.

'Gregor,' Wilhelm said, clutching his son's arm. 'Dear Gregor, can you really appreciate the horror of what you involve yourself in?'

'I have seen it for myself, father,' Gregor said, his tone defensive. 'And I have fought it with courage.'

'Courage?' Wilhelm chuckled scornfully. 'Do you think you know the meaning of that word? I pray you never have cause to discover what real terror is!' He stabbed a warning finger at his son's chest. 'But if you continue on the path you walk now, you will! I tell you again, Gregor, have nothing more to do with that man!'

Gregor did not hear his father's words, however, for he had been frozen to the spot when the old man's claw had reached toward him. There, upon his thin, spindly finger, was a gold ring, the device of a rampant griffon and a slavering wolf impressed upon its device. Gregor clenched the hand in his pocket, feeling the object there dig at his palm. It was impossible, the young noble thought. The ring in his pocket was the same as the ring on his father's hand.

'You can't begin to understand what is going on here,' Wilhelm continued. 'I pray that you never need to.' He pulled his son downward so that he could stare up into Gregor's eyes. The old man's face was moist when he spoke. 'Leave the witch hunter to his business, Gregor. Stay out of it.'

'I can't,' Gregor told him, pulling away. 'These atrocities must end. Our people cannot go on suffering, not knowing which night death will come to them.'

Wilhelm sagged back into his bed, defeated.

'If that is your decision,' he said, his voice empty and hollow. He looked over at his son, and this time there was no mistaking the trickle of tears. 'Whatever happens, know that I love you. Know that everything I have ever done has been to protect this family.'

'I know that,' Gregor assured him. He walked away from his father's bed, back out into the corridor. He needed time to think, to consider the enigma that preyed upon his mind. He was not sure whether to feel relieved or alarmed by the discovery that his father's ring was still upon his hand. And that conflict of emotion worried him even more.

Wilhelm watched his son depart and shook his head.

'Forgive me,' he whispered.

THE BLACK-ROBED figure smiled down at the bound form stretched out beneath his feet. The captive tried to scream, but the heavy linen gag stuffed into his mouth muffled the sound.

'I'm afraid that it is too late for that to do any good,' the robed man said, a regretful tone in his voice. He gazed upward, studying the sky. The great bloated mass of Mannsleib filled the night, but it was not with the greater moon that the stargazer was concerned. He was awaiting the emergence of Mannslieb's smaller brother, the dim, darkling moon Morrslieb, sometimes called the 'moon of sorcery'. There was a truth to such fables, for the influence of Morrsleib was beneficial to enchantments and wizardry.

A cold wind caused the clawing tree branches above them to sway, the crawl of dead leaves upon the ground melding with the creak of the wooden limbs. The stargazer looked back down at the bound man.

'Not so very long now,' he told him, removing the gleaming blade from its sheath on his belt.

THE LONELY HOWL of a dog echoed through the blackness, like the mournful wail of a lost soul. The analogy was not at all improper, the man with the blade thought. This was the hour of lost souls, when the restless dead were at their most powerful. The blasphemous writings of Kadon, the high priest of thrice-accursed Morgheim, claimed that it was at this hour, when the watches of the night were at their longest, that the Supreme Necromancer had raised the first corpse from its grave.

There was a great, unholy power at such times, a power made all the more potent still by the emergence of Morrsleib from behind its brother.

The sorcerer looked again at his chosen sacrifice, savouring for a moment the fear he saw crawling through the man's eyes. Oh yes, he could feel the power, feel its dread influence clawing at his spine. He knows what is going to happen, the part he is to play. A magical ritual was not so very unlike a theatrical production, the sorcerer considered. The success of the performance depended on much the same things: the quality of the props, the location of the theatre. And of course the selection of the actors. Was the wizard truly skilled enough to do justice to the performance demanded of him? Was the fair-skinned sacrifice really so fair, his blood really so rich and vibrant as it seemed?

We shall soon find out, the sorcerer thought, as he watched Morrsleib appear overhead.

THE KNIFE STABBED quickly, sinking deep into the sacrifice's neck. A spasm of thrashing and trembling gripped the man's body as life spilled from his frame. The robed figure above him wiped the crimson from his blade, sliding it back into its sheath. It had played its part. Now it was time to close the circle, complete the ritual.

'BY THE THREE thousand torments of Nagashizzar do I defile,' the crisp, clipped tones of the sorcerer sounded. The gruesome object clutched in his hand began to crawl with maggots. The man's lip curled in pleasure as he saw the loathsome worms, then dropped the organ to the ground where they could continue their cannibalistic work.

'By the four names of power do I desecrate,' the man hissed again, this time holding the bisected eyes of his victim. The organs began to decay, dripping into a watery filth that sizzled upon the ground and yellowed the grass.

'By the might of He Who Was, He Who Is, He Who Shall Be Again, do I destroy!' The sorcerer cast the stringy material he had removed from the sacrifice's skull into the brass brazier resting before him. The smoke that arose from his offering seemed to swell with the ghastly impression of a death's head.

THE MAN IN black robes hurled the organs from him, wiping his hands in disgust on a heavy strip of leather. The wet, gleaming things collapsed upon the ground beside the body's foot. He bent down toward the corpse again and cut a lung from the man's chest. With the organ clenched in his fist, he called out into the night.

'To Phakth do I give the breath of life,' the man cried out. 'That he might speed upon the wings of justice and undo the works of wickedness.' He bent down, extracting the other lung.

'To Ptra do I give the breath of life! That his glory might shine out into the darkness and banish the dominion of night.'

The black-robed figure returned his attention to the corpse, cutting the body once more. He rose with another piece of the corpse.

'To the watcher at the gate, Djaf the jackal…'

CARANDINI CONSIDERED THE wretched ruin of his victim. He flicked his wet, sticky hair from his face. Invoking the dread powers always excited him. He never felt more alive than when he was working the fell sorcery of death. The necromancer turned toward his associate, who had remained silent throughout the ritual.

'It is done?' he asked.

'It is done,' the necromancer assured him, a proud quality to his voice.

'It had better work this time!' the shadowy figure warned. Carandini fingered the vial secreted in his cassock.

'I have told you before,' he said. 'We must wear them out. They can't keep up with us forever.'

Carandini favoured his confederate with a superior smile. 'I should think you'd have learned patience after all this time.'

THE BLACK-ROBED man stared down at the ruin of his sacrifice. There was nothing more to be done, the ancient ritual was complete. However, there was another part to it, something that had been added much later. The robed figure fell to his knees, hands closing about each other. He bowed his head, shutting his eyes so that he might not see the blood staining the ground.

'May Lord Sigmar forgive the doubts and fears of the flesh and honour the sacrifice of this noble martyr, who has died that evil may not prevail,' the man said. Slowly he rose to his feet, motioning for his associates to rejoin him. His thoughts turned away from the gruesome act he had committed, the ancient pagan rite he had performed. Instead, he considered the troublesome witch hunter. Things were swiftly coming to a head, their enemy must strike soon. The witch hunter was an unnecessary complication.

One that would have to be removed.

His face set into an expression of grim determination, Ivar Kohl removed his robes and made his way back to the keep.

CHAPTER FOURTEEN

MATHIAS THULMANN SCARCELY looked up as Reikhertz crept into his room, a plate of steaming sausage and boiled cabbage held before him. The odour was enough for the witch hunter, his brow lifting in surprise.

'I had thought you to be a more devout Sigmarite than that,' he commented, still regarding the map laid out upon the table. His words caused the innkeeper to freeze.

'Your pardon, sir?' he muttered, his voice a nervous squeak.

'You expect a servant of Holy Sigmar to fortify himself on that?' Thulmann asked. 'Take it away,' he added in disgust. The innkeeper flinched away at first, then began to bristle as he considered the witch hunter's high-handed tone. Before he fully knew what he was doing, the innkeeper's mouth was open once more.

'Look here, just what sort of food do you think I can afford to keep feeding you?' he snapped. 'I've yet to see any sort of coin from you, not that I've asked for any,' he hastily added when he saw Thulmann look up. 'I am just saying that this isn't the Nine Crowns in Nuln. I can't afford to keep feeding you better than I do myself.'

Thulmann regarded Reikhertz with an angry gaze, his finger stroking the thin moustache on his upper lip. Eventually, he reached into the pocket of his scarlet vest and withdrew a pair of gold crowns, which he tossed to Reikhertz. The innkeeper caught the coins with his free hand, his face dropping into an expression of stunned marvel.

'I ask no man to sacrifice more than he can afford,' Thulmann told him, a note of apology in his voice. 'There are times, however, when I forget that not every man is as privileged as I. You've been most helpful, friend Reikhertz, a true servant of Sigmar.' The witch hunter pointed to the coins gripped in the man's hand. 'Take that, go and get us a lamb, the best spices you can round up in this village and see that it is enough to feed both an innkeeper and a Templar.'

Thulmann smiled. 'Whatever is left, I am sure you can find a use for.' He looked back to the map, focusing on the marks he had made upon it.

Reikhertz stood in the doorway a moment, considering the sudden change that had come upon the witch hunter. He strode forward. 'Please don't misunderstand,' he told Thulmann. 'We really do appreciate how you are helping us. I know, everybody in the village knows, that you are doing your best to…'

'But my best isn't good enough,' sighed Thulmann, leaning back in his chair. 'Oh, I am making progress, but so is this fiend I am hunting. He grows more bold, more desperate every hour. And it is your people who pay the price for every day I fail to…'

'You sound as if you're giving up,' Reikhertz interrupted. 'If that's the case, then I'll be giving these coins back to you and ask you to kindly leave my house.' The emotion in the man's voice brought a smile to the witch hunter's tired face.

'No, friend Reikhertz,' Thulmann said. 'I'll not rest until this animal is made to pay for his crimes. But it is a frustrating hunt,' he pounded his fist against the map. 'I know that the key lies in the murders themselves, each one is a part of some ghastly whole. If I could only find the pattern, I would know what this monster is up to and where he may strike next.'

Reikhertz withdrew toward the door. 'You sound like a man who's lost and can't see the forest through the trees,' he observed. 'Maybe what you need to do is stand back and try to see things a different way.' The innkeeper stepped aside hurriedly as Streng pushed his way past him, a beer stein gripped in his grimy paw. There was a twisted grin on his face.

'Drinking again, and at so early an hour?' commented Thulmann, disapproval dripping from his voice.

'Still drinking, Mathias,' the mercenary shot back. 'I have to stop for it to be "again".'

'Well, this might sober your sodden brain,' Thulmann said, rising to his feet. 'From now on, we pay for what friend Reikhertz is gracious enough to provide us with.' The witch hunter smiled as his henchman's expression grew grave. 'That includes anything from his cellars.'

'As you say, Mathias,' the thug said in a surly tone. He cast an angry look over at Reikhertz, then turned back to his employer.

'Might interest you to know that our friend has been busy again,' the mercenary reported. 'A fellow has just come in – says he's found another body. Wanted me to report it to the witch hunter.'

'What?' gasped Reikhertz. 'Another murder? Who?'

'Farmer named Weiss, apparently,' Streng told him. 'Same as that second fellow we found, Mathias. Didn't take the time to try and hide who it was, just did his business and went his way. Mind you, the fellow downstairs didn't stay around to note too many of the particulars.'

Thulmann snatched up the map from the table. Reikhertz was leaning against the wall, a pained expression on his face. 'Old Weiss,' he muttered in solemn reflection. 'Used to drown cats by the old mill when he was in his cups, but a good man just the same.'

'Where did this take place?' Thulmann demanded, thrusting the map under Streng's nose. The mercenary stared at the map for a moment, brow knitted in concentration as he struggled to read the names marked on it.

'A dry stream bed near someplace called Dagger's Reach,' he said. Reikhertz walked over, taking the map from Thulmann and pointing out the relevant feature, a jagged fang of rock situated amidst a tangle of fields and wood. The witch hunter spun about, removing a heavy brush from a pot of pigment resting on his table. He daubed a bright crimson mark where Reikhertz had indicated.

The witch hunter sat down again, studying the map intently, trying to perceive how this new atrocity might fit into any of the patterns he had been trying to impose upon the murders. After a few moments he pounded the table in frustration.

'There is a pattern,' he swore. 'I know there is! I am just too much a fool to see it.' For the umpteenth time, he began to draw lines between the murder sites with a stick of chalk, snarling every time they did not merge into anything resembling even the most esoteric shape.

Reikhertz and Streng watched Thulmann work with bewildered interest.

'My credit good for one more stein?' Streng asked the innkeeper from the corner of his mouth.

'I'll join you,' the innkeeper told him. Both men turned, only to find that the hallway was blocked. Gregor Klausner, wearing a bicorn hat and a heavy grey cloak trimmed in rabbit fur, stared back at them. Reikhertz only spared a brief glance at the young noblemen, then locked eyes with the plump young woman with her arm about Gregor's waist.

'Back to your work!' he snapped at his daughter. Miranda withdrew her arm, setting it on her hip.

'Gregor wanted to see the witch hunter on a most urgent matter,' she snapped back. Father and daughter glared at one another for a moment. It was the daughter who looked away first.

'You see that they ain't helping themselves to my ale down there,' Reikhertz told her in a stern voice. Without another word, Miranda retreated back down the hall.

'It really was my fault,' apologised Gregor. 'Don't be too hard on Miranda.'

Reikhertz transferred his glare to the lord. 'You're the son of Lord Klausner, and that puts certain obligations upon me, certain privileges custom dictates I extend to you.' Anger flared up in his voice and he jabbed a finger toward Gregor. 'But those privileges don't extend to the person of my daughter.' Reikhertz started to stalk out into the hallway. Gregor caught him by the arm.

'I've been nothing but proper and honourable with your daughter,' he told the innkeeper. Reikhertz brushed the young noble's hand away as though it were a noxious insect.

'I appreciate what you've done for us,' the innkeeper told him. 'But you're a Klausner all the same. Being the best of a bad breed doesn't make you any more decent.' Reikhertz took a deep breath. 'You know my father was killed by your family. Not an easy thing to forgive or forget.'

'That is a fact that might have been worthy of knowing,' interrupted Thulmann. Unobserved by the other men, he had risen from his table to listen to the tense conversation.

'You'd heard enough stories like it the other night,' Reikhertz told him. 'It is not something I like to talk about,' he added.

Thulmann looked at him expectantly and the innkeeper continued in a subdued voice. 'It was near on twenty winters ago, I was only a boy, but I can recall every detail. His,' he pointed toward Gregor, 'grandfather was dying, health fading quite fast. Then the daemon came. My father was one of its last victims.'

Thulmann nodded his head in grim appreciation of the tragedy Reikhertz had alluded to. A sudden flare of inspiration filled his eyes. 'Do you know where your father was found?' he asked, gesturing for Reikhertz to come over to the table. Soon all four men were staring down at Thulmann's heavily marked map of the district.

'It was over near the old crossroads that lead to…' the innkeeper's voice caught in his throat. His finger had been following the road, but when he reached the site he wished to indicate, he found a bright crimson splotch. 'But you've already marked the spot,' he muttered. 'How did you know?'

Thulmann shook his head. 'I didn't. That mark shows where a herb grower named Jannes was killed. This is very important, Reikhertz. You say your father was the last of the daemon's victims?'

Reikhertz shook his head. 'No, there was a midwife, Lucina Oberst. She died a few nights after my father. She was the last. But I don't remember exactly where they found her. Someplace near…' he looked away as he saw still another crimson splotch where he had been about to point. 'What does this mean?'

Gregor looked away from the map, grasping the importance of what they had chanced upon. 'There were six victims back then,' he told Thulmann.

'Yes, and I would wager that each of them died at a spot already marked on my map,' the witch hunter declared. 'Thirty years and the killer strikes in the exact same places.'

'But it has never been this bloodthirsty before,' protested Gregor. 'They haven't killed six this time, they've killed twenty-nine times, if we discount the massacre at the Brustholz farm.'

Thulmann nodded. 'Yes, that atrocity was a trap designed to dispose of me, not a part of whatever foul ritual these other murders are a part of.' He began drawing lines between the first six murders, snarling in disgust when they did not match up. Then he noticed a curious fact. Both of the marks that Reikhertz had indicated, also murders from three decades ago, were not among the first six killings.

'Reikhertz, the other murders thirty years ago, do you recall where the bodies were found?' The innkeeper leaned down again.

'I remember. It's the sort of thing a person doesn't forget.' He pointed out the scenes, each, not surprisingly, already marked in red. Thulmann saw that only three of them were included in the earliest killings. Realisation began to dawn on him. He drew a connection not between the current killings, but those long ago, finding himself staring at a hexagonal shape. Then he looked back to the other murder sites he had bypassed in drawing his shape.

A sudden understanding filled him as he began to draw the connecting lines between these. A pentagon was soon described upon the map.

The witch hunter leaned back in something approaching triumph. 'There is a connection, a pattern,' he declared. 'I did not see it because there is not one here, but two. The hexagon, the squared circle employed by mystics to protect them from daemons and other malign supernatural forces.'

'The dire wolf at the bridge!' exclaimed Gregor. Thulmann nodded.

'Then we have this other figure,' the witch hunter indicated the pentagon. The murder sites used to form it were spaced much more widely, completely enclosing the first shape. 'The pentagon is employed by daemonologists and necromancers to invoke the forces of death and ruin, to summon and bind the blackest currents of sorcery.' Thulmann's voice grew contemplative. 'Not one ritual, but two. One designed to protect, the other...' He stared at the multitude of other marks upon his map, those that had not yet been fitted into a pattern. Gregor noted the witch hunter's area of study.

'You can add another mark to your map,' he told Thulmann in a sombre voice.

'There's a man trying to reach the bottom of a cask of ale downstairs who already told us,' Streng interjected.

'Then you already know that Otto the frog catcher was killed last night?' Gregor asked. The other three men in the room stared at him.

'No,' sputtered Reikhertz. 'They said it was Weiss,' the innkeeper seated himself on the edge of Thulmann's bed, shaking his head in disbelief. The witch hunter grabbed Gregor.

'Where was the man found?' he demanded, his words clipped by his excitement. The young noble tapped the surface of the old parchment, indicating a spot some distance from the place where Weiss had been found.

'This horror compounds itself,' Thulmann commented as he marked the spot. 'Two murders in one night. This man Otto, what condition was his body in?'

'A terrible sight. One of Anton's men found him and said that he only knew it was Otto because his frog bag was lying nearby.' Thulmann leapt to his feet when Gregor had related his information.

'Go to the shrine of Morr and bring back the priest,' Thulmann ordered Streng. The mercenary grinned, handing his stein to Reikhertz and departing at a brisk jog.

'The priest?' asked Gregor.

'I need to know exactly how each of these,' the witch hunter gestured at the marks on his map, 'died. You see, there is not one fiend plaguing Klausberg this time. There are two.'

AFTER THE DOUR mortuary priest had left, Thulmann smiled in triumph at the white chalk lines that swarmed across his map, describing a number of hexagons and pentagons. He looked over at the expectant faces of Gregor and Streng. Reikhertz, disturbed enough by the grim business, had withdrawn to meet his afternoon custom in the tavern down below.

'Two,' Thulmann repeated. 'Two necromancers at work.' He gestured at the complex network of pentagons and the solid ring of hexagons. 'One conducts the rituals that form this hexagon. He is less cautious about his craft, taking no pains to hide the nature of his ceremonies. The other plies his trade farther afield, mutilating the bodies when he is finished with them. His handiwork composes this pentagon.'

The witch hunter gave a sigh. 'But the question remains, what is the purpose of these atrocities, and why have they become so much greater than those in the past? Unless...' Thulmann glanced over at Gregor. 'Perhaps these unholy degenerates are not working in concert with one another, but rather seek to undo each other's rituals.' He stabbed a finger at the map again. 'The killings that form the pentagon, from the beginning they were not the same as what was done thirty years ago. Something new, something outside the established pattern. Perhaps something meant to break that pattern?'

'Then finding the one won't yield up the other,' groaned Gregor.

'Removing one of these predators may expose the other, if we can take the fiend alive,' Thulmann told him. 'If these sorcerers are at odds, then they must know something of one another. More than we know about them, in any event.' He looked back at the map, staring at the only partially formed figures he had drawn. 'The pentagon needs two more points to close the current pattern,' he said. 'But the hexagon is nearly complete. Only one more red mark to seal it. If the pattern holds, the fifth and sixth sacrifices that compose the six-sided circle will occur on coincident nights.'

'That would mean the killer will strike again tonight!' exclaimed Gregor. Thulmann smiled grimly.

'Yes, but this time we know where his ritual will take place,' the witch hunter told him. 'And we will be ready for him.'

'I'll alert my father, gather some soldiers from the keep,' Gregor stated, turning to leave the room.

'That would be unwise,' Thulmann's sharp tone brought the young noble to a halt.

Gregor turned slowly, a questioning look on his face. The witch hunter gestured for him to look at the map again. 'The hexagon, the protective circle, do you see what lies at its heart?' Gregor's eyes widened with shock as he saw Klausner Keep lying perfectly within the hexagonal pattern. It could be no coincidence that the keep lay at the very centre of the figure, there was some dark purpose at work.

Gregor pondered once more the sickeningly familiar ring he had discovered amidst the carnage of the Brustholz farm. If the keep was at the centre of this web of horror, then most assuredly Wilhelm Klausner was the centre, the cornerstone, of the keep. But what possible reason could there be that might drag his father into such gruesome and horrific occurrences?

'I fear that the man we hunt is not unknown within the halls of your household.' Thulmann rose to his feet, gathering up the hat Reikhertz had procured to replace the one he had lost to the burning farmhouse and the heavy leather belt from which dripped his pistols and sword.

'No, we will keep what we have learned to ourselves,' Thulmann declared. 'Then we may be sure that our quarry will not be expecting us.'

'Just the three of us then?' asked Gregor. Thulmann nodded.

'Right and justice are with us, Gregor,' the witch hunter stated. 'They are all the reinforcements we shall require.' Streng gave his employer a sarcastic grin. Thulmann turned on him, his voice sharp. 'You doubt the might of Sigmar?' he snapped. Streng shook his head.

'Not at all,' the thug said. 'I just respect it more when it is wearing plate mail and the colours of the Reiksguard.'

A HALF-DOZEN MEN were scattered about The Grey Crone's common room when Thulmann and his companions descended the stairs. The witch hunter paid them little heed, striding toward the bar where Reikhertz was busy serving a large man with a bald head and a massive moustache.

'We'll be needing our horses, friend Reikhertz,' the witch hunter said. The innkeeper paused and nodded to the Templar. The heavy-set man he was serving turned around, looking over Thulmann with a sour look on his rugged features.

'The man was serving me, witch finder,' he snarled. Thulmann gave a thin smile in return and turned to walk away. 'I was talking to you, witch finder,' the ruffian called after him, stalking away from the counter.

'But I was not talking to you,' Thulmann retorted with a dismissive voice. The bald man dipped his head in a slight mockery of a bow.

'Of course not, you only talk to wretched old ladies,' he sneered. 'Talk 'em into saying all sorts of silly things so you can burn 'em and hang 'em and whatever else tickles your fancies.'

Thulmann's eyes narrowed, his face slipping into a mask of sullen anger and indignation. He shook his hand toward his assailant.

'As a duly appointed servant of Holy Sigmar,' Thulmann warned him, 'I can tell you that your words flirt with heresy. Since you are obviously drunk, I am prepared to be lenient and ignore your impious remarks.'

'Oh, is that so?' snorted the ruffian. His hand slid to his belt, pulling it around so that the sword sheathed at his side was in ready reach. 'I'm not some poor defenceless woman that you can beat and abuse. You'll find me a much colder vintage than that.'

'I suggest you go home and sleep away these bottled spirits that so affect you,' Thulmann told him. There was a sharpness to the witch hunter's words now, and a crueller glint in his eyes than there had been moments before. 'Before I begin to take offence to your belligerence.'

The swordsman laughed, looking about the room, his face lifted in amusement. From the base of the stairs, Streng and Gregor watched the situation unfold. Streng gripped the young noble's arm to prevent him from interceding in the coming confrontation.

'I can't tell you how much it frightens me that I might cause you offence,' the swordsman snickered.

He leaned forward, his face a hand's breath from Thulmann's own. 'Tell me, would it offend you if I were to say your precious Sigmar isn't fit to lick the piss from Ulric's boots?'

The witch hunter leapt back, meeting the swordsman's dancing blade with his own sword. His attacker seemed shocked by the older man's speed, but quickly regained his composure, pressing his attack. The other patrons in the room scattered, chairs clattering to the floor, leather jacks and clay steins spilling ale and beer as the men gripping them rose hurriedly, giving the two combatants ample room to fight.

'Blasphemy and heresy,' the witch hunter snarled above their crossed steel. 'You had best hope that my sword finishes you, friend.' The swordsman's eyes displayed a flicker of fright at the cruelty stamped upon Thulmann's words. He withdrew a pace, the witch hunter at once capitalising upon the opening and pressing his own counter attack.

The clash of steel rang through the common room as the blades of the two combatants flashed, struck and parried.

The bald swordsman's earlier bravado began to fade, and his movements degenerated into ever more frantic and desperate swings. By contrast, Thulmann worked his blade with a cold, judgmental manner, parrying his opponent's every move with a delicate turn of wrist and waist.

The swordsman cried out in alarm as Thulmann's blade penetrated his defences and slashed his shoulder. 'I hope the sight of your own blood does not offend you,' the witch hunter said, his voice rippling with a sadistic mockery. 'You'll see a fair deal more of it before I finish with you.'

The swordsman cast a desperate look behind Thulmann, then redoubled his frantic efforts at defence. As the man fell back before Thulmann's advancing blade, a scream of agony sounded from the back of the room.

Streng wiped the blood from his knife on the grimy surface of his breeches even as his victim clutched at the wound in his neck. The heavy pistol fell from the rat-faced man's hand, and a moment later, the back-shooter joined his weapon on the floor, body shuddering in its death agonies.

Seeing his comrade down, Thulmann's opponent directed a wild swing at the witch hunter's head, trying to slip past the witch hunter as he reacted to the erratic attack. Thulmann deftly ducked the wild swing and slashed his sword along the man's ribs. The swordsman staggered away, slamming into the base of the counter as he slipped to the floor.

The witch hunter strode toward him with slow, deliberate steps. His enemy lifted his blade in a last attempt at defence, but his fading strength was unequal to the task and the heavy length of steel clattered to the floor.

Thulmann sneered down into the man's pained features, then stooped down over his body, rummaging in the man's pockets.

'They meant to kill you,' exclaimed Gregor, rushing to the witch hunter's side.

'Yes,' Thulmann said, rising from the wounded swordsman, holding the small leather bag he had withdrawn from the man's tunic. 'They were paid to,' he kicked the leg of the bald man. 'This scum was supposed to keep me occupied while his associate put a bullet in my back. Isn't that so, swine?' By way of answer, the swordsman gave voice to a dull groan of pain.

Thulmann looked back toward Gregor. 'I think you will find that the Klausner treasury is missing a few gold crowns.' Thulmann's eyes hardened into chips of ice. The witch hunter reflected upon the pattern he had discovered, upon the situation of Klausner Keep at the very centre of the web, and upon Gregor Klausner's timely arrival. Had he come to relay information, or to find out how much the witch hunter already knew? Thulmann gave voice to the suspicion his instincts forced to the fore of his thoughts. 'Are you certain you came here alone?'

Gregor pulled back in shock. 'You don't mean to think that I...'

'Let's ask this vermin,' the witch hunter replied. But when he turned to speak to the wounded man, he found that it was too late. His blow had punctured one of the man's lungs. The only thing that would be coming from his mouth now was a thin trickle of blood. 'Heathen wretch,' Thulmann hissed. 'He might have held on a few moments more.'

'The other one's dead too,' Streng informed him.

'My thanks, friend Streng,' the witch hunter replied. 'To show my gratitude, you may keep the money you removed from his person.' The mercenary nodded, clearly not entirely pleased that his employer had guessed about the second bag of gold.

'I swear to you, Herr Thulmann,' protested Gregor. 'I never laid eyes upon these men before. On my faith in Sigmar, I swear it.'

'He may be right about that,' observed Reikhertz, peering over the counter at the dead man slumped against his bar. The innkeeper's face wrinkled in annoyance as he saw the blood spreading across the floor boards. 'These two were caravan guards. Came in with the last wagon train from Wurtbad.'

The name of the city gave Thulmann pause. Could it be that these men had nothing to do with the Klausners and Klausberg? Had they perhaps been hired by the same man who had employed the witch Chanta Favna to slaughter his business rivals? It was not entirely impossible that the merchant might not have some means of working his revenge even from a dungeon cell. Still, his instinct told him that the man who had paid these assassins was much nearer at hand.

'Perhaps things are as you say, Master Klausner,' Thulmann said, his voice uncertain. 'In any event, you know too much for me not to trust you a little longer.' The witch hunter's face slipped into a thin smile. 'We will find out tonight if that trust is misplaced.'

Fuming from the witch hunter's words, Gregor could only nod his head in understanding. Thulmann indicated the door, motioning for the young noble to precede him. Streng paused to remove a brass buckle from the dead man lying against the counter, then produced a knife to cut away the bronze buttons from his tunic. A sharp growl from Thulmann caused the mercenary to rise from his ghoulish labour, stuffing the few trinkets he had looted into a pocket. Slamming his knife back into its sheath, the mercenary hurried after Thulmann.

When they had gone, Reikhertz came around the counter to study the dead man a little more closely. His face again wrinkled in annoyance.

'Nasty...,' he muttered. He turned and shouted to his remaining patrons. 'Right, that's nasty. Help me clean it away now!'

IVAR KOHL STALKED the corridors of Klausner Keep, his face dark and brooding. His spies in the village had reported that the two sell-swords had failed in their task to kill the witch hunter. The steward hissed in anger as he considered how disastrous things could have become had either of them lived long enough to say who had paid them to murder the Templar. Perhaps Sigmar truly was lending his aid to Kohl's purposes.

Of course, the survival of the witch hunter might also be taken as a token of divine intervention. Bruno Fleischer had been quite an accomplished blade in his own rights, and Kohl had been quite confident in the swordsman's ability to despatch the Templar, especially with a second man to stack the odds in Fleischer's favour. The steward cursed again. It was bad enough that things had become so complicated and drawn-out. The meddling of a witch hunter was the last thing he needed, especially since it seemed he might be coming close to guessing the truth.

The steward strode into the kitchens, ignoring the servants who scurried out of his way, knowing better than to cross the grim Kohl in his current mood. Ivar Kohl soon faded past them, his black livery melding with the shadows that hung heavy about the short hallway that led to the wine cellar.

There was no question about it: the witch hunter was a threat, and a pronounced one. He would have to be dealt with. Kohl would arrange a more certain course of action, perhaps send for a professional assassin rather than trust again to the capabilities of ex-soldiers.

Kohl found himself within the dingy confines of the cellar. Ranks of wine racks filed away off into the gloom while mammoth casks and barrels of beer loomed against the walls. The steward strode toward one of the beer barrels, its surface covered in cobwebs.

He slid his fingers into the tiny groove just under the steel rim of the barrel, depressing the tiny stud he found there. The top of the barrel slid back, exposing a small compartment within. Kohl reached down and withdrew the heavy black robe and gleaming gold-hilted knife he found there.

Threat or no, the steward considered, the witch hunter would have to wait. Tonight's ritual would complete the pattern and close the circle. It was too important to put off, and any delay would undo all that had already been done. Ivar Kohl shuddered as he considered the horror of such a disaster. No, nothing could be allowed to stop the ceremony.

He spoke a short prayer to Sigmar that no more rituals would be needed after this one, that it would be the last.

CHAPTER FIFTEEN

DARKNESS HUNG HEAVY across the land. Clouds, thick and dark, had been blown down from the north, casting a pall across the gleaming face of Mannsleib. The moon could only be dimly seen behind the cloud cover, a dull glow behind the dark, nebulous shapes, flaring brilliantly during the infrequent breaks between the clouds. The same chill wind crawled about the ground, causing leaves to skitter and trees to sway.

It was a night made for horrors, when even the most sceptical city dweller might ponder the darker mysteries of the world and pause before every shadow, jump at every unseen sound.

Through the darkness, two shapes crept from shadow to shadow, pushing a third before them. Wet, wailing sounds could dimly be heard shuddering from the leading figure, her white dress standing out brilliantly against the landscape when she chanced to linger between shadows. Her body was young and shapely, a thing of delicate curves and slender smooth-skinned limbs. She was shivering beneath the thin covering of white homespun, damp with the sweat of fear.

The woman's steps were awkward and ungainly despite the gracefulness of her form, and it was with groans of pain that she stumbled and fell, her choking sobs muffled by the filthy linen sack that had been thrown over her head.

Her name was Deithild, one of five daughters of Reimar Stoss, one of Klausberg's numerous shepherds. In her twenty years of life, she had never experienced much that had been remarkable or exciting, and her ambitions did not extend beyond the prospect of a dreary marriage to seal some business dealing of her father's. The terror that had been stalking the district had been the first discordant note in her life, breaking up the harmony and pattern of her days.

Now, instead of taking turns to tend the flocks, her father took the entire household with him, determined that the horror stalking the land would not glut itself upon his valuable animals. This night, however, Deithild had begged away from helping her sisters, claiming illness with such conviction that even her suspicious father had not pressed the issue.

However, instead of long hours of restful slumber, the young woman had found herself awakened in the middle of the night. The terror that had been prowling Klausberg had reached out to claim her, snatching her not from the chill of her father's pastures, but from the supposed safety of her own bed.

'Pick up the pace, bitch,' snarled one of the brutish men following her, his leathery hand jerking sharply on the rope that bound Deithild's hands behind her back. The woman wailed into her cruel hood as she was forced back to her feet by the painful pressure working on her arms.

The two men wore rough leather breeches, tunics of wool and crude boots of hide and fur. Swords hung from their hips and one of the men fingered the stock of a pistol holstered across his belly. Their faces reflected the simplicity of the minds behind them.

They were men who took a sadistic delight in the labours which they were sometimes called upon to perform, the sort of unscrupulous men that might be found in the service of any noble family, much like an ill-tempered guard dog, creatures tolerated purely for their usefulness.

These men had made themselves very useful over the past few weeks. Certainly, their nocturnal labours had been greatly different from their usual duties – the beating of peasants who refused to pay their tax, torching the wagons of merchants that thought to escape paying Lord Klausner for the privilege of passing through his lands. Still, the escalation of their brutality did not disturb the two unduly. Certainly these nocturnal sojourns for Ivar Kohl paid much better than any tasks they had before been charged with before. For men without conscience, that was enough.

Deithild was leaning against a tree, trying to gather breath between her terrified sobs. The brute holding the rope jerked her around, spilling the girl to the ground. His companion gave a short bark of amusement.

'Now you've gone and got her all dirty,' he laughed.

'Pick the wench up. Kohl will skin us if we're late,' the other snarled. His companion stepped forward, his hairy hands grabbing a hold of Deithild's arms. He paused in lifting her, moving one hand to slide down the length of her leg. The captive tried to wriggle out of his clutch, but her strength was not equal to the task.

'Shame to waste a fine cut of meat like this on Kohl,' the brute holding the girl commented. He laid his neck on the woman's shoulder, blowing his hot breath through the sacking. 'What say you? If you're be nice to us, maybe we'll let you go.'

'Enough of that!' snapped the man holding onto the rope. 'We don't have time to bounce the wench. Kohl's expecting us.' The other kidnapper licked the bare shoulder of their captive before withdrawing.

'It just seems like a waste, that's all,' the thug said. He looked back at the bound woman, raising his voice so that she could hear every word. 'I mean taking her out there, to him. To be cut up like something at a butcher's shop.' Deithild fell to her knees again, shuddering and sobbing, wailing with horror. The man holding the rope gave it a savage tug, pulling her back up.

'She faints and you're carrying her,' growled the brute holding the rope. His companion laughed again.

* * *

IVAR KOHL STOOD beneath the shadows cast by the broken stone wall. It was a curious thing, the steward thought. The blocks did not seem to have been mortared but rather fit into one another with such precision that nothing more was needed to hold them in place. Most likely some old elf trick, the steward shrugged. There were many mysteries surrounding the elder race. He doubted if men would ever uncover them all.

The steward cast a nervous eye overhead, licking his lips nervously as he saw the darkening clouds. This was a problem he did not need. The emergence of Morrsleib had to be timed correctly for the ritual to have its full effect. Kohl did not want to trust to any diminishment of the power of the ancient rite. For a moment, he almost wished he knew some sorcerous tricks that would banish storms.

The steward smiled at the thought, chiding himself for such weakness. *That way lies heresy*, he told himself.

Kohl cast a sour glance at the man standing beside him, then looked away when he heard the faint sounds of someone making their way through the woods. He retreated a bit deeper into the shadow, but as he listened further, he could hear the now familiar muffled sobs and wails of a sacrifice as the doomed soul was led to the place of ritual by his thugs.

A fanatic gleam flared up in the steward's eyes. He looked again at the figure standing beside him, nodding his head. The man helped Kohl into his black robe, then handed the steward a golden dagger.

'Pray to Sigmar that this is the last,' Kohl said, striding out into the clearing to greet the approaching figures. He could see his men leading their charge forward. A sickly smile crept onto Kohl's features. Sigmar forgive him, but a part of him hoped it wouldn't be.

'STAY WITH THE horses,' Thulmann said, his voice sharp and cold. Gregor Klausner glared back at the witch hunter.

'I tell you again that I had nothing to do with those men at the inn,' he said for what felt like the hundredth time that night. As before, his declaration did not impress the Templar.

'We will soon find out, won't we?' There was no mistaking the tone of menace in Thulmann's words. They stood within the trees bordering the Klausner estate, gazing down upon the clearing where the witch hunter had predicted that the next ritual would take place. The witch hunter had brought them here directly after the events at The Grey Crone, secreting them among the trees. All three men had shared watch duty, waiting until their insidious quarry showed himself. Gregor had begged the witch hunter to spring as soon as they had seen the two men lurking at the edges of the clearing, but Thulmann had called for them to maintain their vigil, awaiting the arrival of the other conspirators and their victim.

'Streng,' the witch hunter hissed. The bearded mercenary looked up at him from where he crouched close to the ground. 'Master Klausner is remaining here. Kindly relieve him of his armaments.' The witch hunter smiled thinly at the young noble. 'Purely so you might not be tempted into any injudicious actions,' he explained. Gregor scowled as he lifted his arms and allowed Streng to remove his sword belt and pistol.

'Nothing personal, you understand,' Streng told him. The mercenary cast an appraising eye over the sword he held. 'Of course,' he considered, a greedy glint in his eyes, 'if you are a heretic I'll get to keep these.' He grinned back at Gregor. 'Nothing personal of course.'

'An end to your chatter, man,' snapped Thulmann, drawing both his pistols. 'We've work to do.'

Gregor Klausner watched the two men slip into the darkness, slinking toward the clearing where they could now see three figures approaching. Gregor knew they had to be the other heretics and their captive. A cold determination swelled up within him. He stepped away from the horses, removing the tiny pocket pistol Streng had not known about. It was an old thing, a relic captured by some long dead Klausner during a crusade in Araby. Since that time, it had served the Klausners well. It would do so again this night.

Of that, Gregor was determined.

SWEAT BEADED KOHL's brow as he stepped toward the approaching men. This would be the one, he could feel it. This would be the one that would put an end to the horror. It had to be. It had to work this time. Kohl fingered the hilt of the dagger nervously as he advanced.

A sharp crack and boom intruded upon the silence. Kohl crumpled to the ground as his knee exploded, bursting apart as though an ogre had smashed it with a hammer. The ceremonial dagger flew out of his grasp, skittering off into the dark. Kohl winced in agony, rolling onto his back, fighting to keep from blacking out from the pain surging through him.

He could see a man emerging from the trees, black cloak billowing about him, his face hidden in the shadow cast by the brim of his hat. Smoke rose from the pistol gripped in his left hand. He pointed with the other into the gloom. Ivar Kohl felt disgust and rage swell over his pain. The witch hunter! He should have known.

'Draw your steel, you sons of blaspheming slatterns!' Thulmann roared, his voice burning with outrage and challenge. The pistol in his hand roared in turn, spitting flame and smoke. The ruffian holding the rope that bound the captive woman gave a cry of agony. He released his grip, falling to the ground and rolling in agony as he clutched the weeping crimson mask that had moments before been his face. The woman dropped to her knees, screaming in terror into the sack that covered her head. The other brute turned to run.

'Going somewhere, friend?' hissed Streng, emerging from the trees opposite Thulmann and plunging Gregor's sword into the fleeing villain's stomach. The man gasped, hands flying to his injury, trying to staunch the stream of blood and bile.

Streng smashed him aside with the engraved hilt of the sword, knocking him to the ground. The mercenary lifted the pistol gripped in his other hand, sighting across the clearing at the dark-garbed man who emerged from the trees. The pistol cracked and roared, the impact of the bullet spinning the man as he ran toward Thulmann, a cavalry sabre clenched in his fist. Kohl's assistant cried out as he fell.

Thulmann strode toward Ivar Kohl's prone body, holstering his pistols and drawing his sword. A look of indignation, wrath and disgust pulled at the witch hunter's features.

He glared down at Kohl. If he was surprised to see the steward's face underneath the black robes, Thulmann did not let it show. He pricked the injured man's throat with the point of his blade. Kohl's eyes grew wide with horror. Thulmann smiled down at him coldly.

'Oh no,' his silky voice had a quality of malevolent mirth about it. 'You don't die so easily, or so quickly.'

Across the clearing, Streng removed the linen sack from the sobbing Deithild's head. He paused to admire the cast of her pretty features, then busied himself undoing the knots that bound her hands.

He fumbled with the knot for some time, one dirty paw clutching at the woman's chest, ostensibly to support her. The mercenary looked up at her, a lewd smile on his crude features. 'Sorry about that,' he told her, doing nothing to remove the groping fingers. 'Everything's going to be all right. Isn't nobody going to hurt you while I have anything to say about it.'

As he freed her hands, Streng braced himself for a slap to his jaw. Instead, such was the woman's relief at her rescue that she wrapped around Streng's neck, crushing him in a fierce hug, her face buried in his grimy tunic as she sobbed with relief.

Streng smiled above her embrace. 'Very nice to see you feel this way about me,' he grinned.

Mathias Thulmann set his heel on Kohl's chest, pinning the injured steward to the ground, then inspected the man's wound. His leg was pumping a steady stream of blood; already a small puddle of it was congealing around the man. Thulmann swore under his breath, sheathing his sword and pulling a laced handkerchief from his vest.

'It won't do to have you bleed out on me, Master Kohl. Not until you've answered a few questions.'

'I'll tell you nothing!' Kohl snarled through his pain. The witch hunter tore the piece of fabric, then wound it around the steward's bleeding stump. He smiled in cruel mockery at the heretic as he pulled the makeshift tourniquet tight.

'Yes,' he chuckled grimly, 'I do believe I have heard that one before.'

'Thulmann!' Gregor's voice shouted from the night. Thulmann turned his head to see the young noble emerging from the trees, a small pistol clutched in his hand. Before the witch hunter could react, the gun gave a sharp bark and yellow fire, grey smoke and lead death erupting from its barrel. The echo of the discharge was almost immediately drowned out by a burbling wail of anguish.

The witch hunter turned his head in the direction of the sound. The man Streng had earlier shot was lying in a spreading pool of gore, a dark depression in the middle of his forehead. The man's dead hand was closed around a dagger.

'Friend Streng,' Thulmann called out. The mercenary was looking over at his employer, having extracted himself from the thankful embrace of the young woman as soon as he had heard the pistol shot. 'Your slovenly marksmanship will cost you five gold crowns,' the witch hunter declared. The mercenary shrugged his shoulders, turning his attention back to Deithild's gratitude.

Thulmann looked over at Gregor. 'Thankfully your own was much better,' he said, smiling. The young noble nodded his head in acknowledgement of both the spoken compliment and the unspoken apology.

Gregor Klausner stared in horror and loathing at the prostrate form of his father's steward. Anger, the righteous indignation of a man who had sworn to put an end to the horrible crimes committed against the good folk of Klausberg, boiled within him. But the emotion was subdued by the sick horror that drained the colour from Gregor's skin, that gnawed at the pit of his stomach and his soul.

Ivar Kohl, a man he had known all his life, a man who had in many ways acted as his father's surrogate when Wilhelm Klausner had gone away to serve the temple of Sigmar. A stern and unpleasant individual, one who Gregor had feared more than respected as a boy, who he had tolerated more than liked as a man. But to see Kohl unmasked before him as the perpetrator of such heinous acts of heresy and wickedness was a thing beyond belief. Yet the evidence, the unquestionable evidence of his own eyes, was laid out before him.

The young noble thought once more of the ring hidden in his pocket, that talisman of the Klausner line. The sickness swelled as he desperately tried to tell himself that his fears were impossible. How could his own father be a party to such crimes? Yet why else would his oldest and most trusted servant be lying upon the ground, the witch hunter's bullet in his leg? How else could a Klausner ring have come to be lying upon the floor of the Brustholz farm?

'What are you going to do with him?' Gregor pointed down at the figure of Ivar Kohl. The subdued steward glared back at him. Thulmann pulled the wounded man to his feet, ignoring the cries of pain the steward uttered as his weight pressed against the wound.

'As a duly appointed representative of Sigmar's Holy Order of Witch Hunters, it is within my authority to question my prisoners in any provincial or municipal structure I deem suits my needs,' the witch hunter told him. 'I am sure that Herr Kohl will not object greatly if we escort him home.' The witch hunter looked away, shouting over to Streng. 'What about those two?'

'They're done for,' Streng replied, casting a sideways look at each of the wounded men squirming upon the ground. 'The one you shot won't last another five minutes. The one I stuck is spilling his belly, might take him a few hours to finish bleeding out.' The mercenary spat at the writhing man. 'A load better than the vermin rates,' he snarled, much to the approval of the woman who still held him in a fierce embrace.

'Well, see that they are both finished and hurry it up,' the witch hunter snarled. 'We're going to take Master Kohl here back to the keep. There will be work for you to do when we get there.'

Streng's face split in a bloodthirsty grin.

CHAPTER SIXTEEN

THE WITCH HUNTER's boots clicked across the floor of the keep's entry hall. He cast an imperious gaze across the dimly lit room, then focused his attention back on the frightened servant who had admitted him and his party. The man kept looking over at the sagging, bleeding figure of Ivar Kohl with an expression that was a mixture of shock, wonder and even a fair degree of satisfaction. The steward was not well loved by his staff.

'Gregor,' the witch hunter spoke. 'Escort Streng and my prisoner down to the cellar you spoke of.' During their ride back to the keep, Gregor Klausner had related that his great grandfather, a morbid and intensely zealous man who had expired in the act of scourging himself with a steel whip in his later years, had maintained a gruesome reminder of his years as a witch hunter. Beneath the wine cellars, in a sub level, he had built a torture chamber, equipping it with all the vicious implements of his trade. It was an ugly little room, and though it had never been used, it still seemed to echo with the sounds of screams. Thulmann had smiled grimly, commenting, 'Sigmar provides.'

The two men carried their injured captive away. Streng sneered into the semi-conscious heretic's ear. 'Many's the time you went past that room, I'll wager,' the mercenary laughed. 'Didn't ever think you'd be visiting it yourself though?' Pushing their near insensible prisoner, the two men disappeared down one of the corridors opening onto the great hall. The shocked servant watched the men leave.

'You,' Thulmann's silky voice snapped, causing the servant to spin around. 'Take this girl to the kitchens. Get her some food, some decent clothes and a bit of good wine to burn the chill from her bones.' The witch hunter gestured and the servant took the hand of the pale, trembling girl who lingered upon the threshold. Deithild pulled away in fright.

'It's alright, child,' Thulmann's soothing tones told her. 'This man will take you somewhere warm and get you something to eat.' He fixed the man with a warning look. 'No harm will come to you.' Deithild reluctantly allowed herself to be led away, pausing before Thulmann to return his cloak, which the Templar had thrown about her when they had left the site of Kohl's abortive ceremony.

The witch hunter smiled in return, watching the rescued woman be taken away. As soon as she was out of sight, the smile dropped into something unfriendly and filled with anger. Thulmann lifted his gaze toward the stairs.

It was time for a reckoning.

MATHIAS THULMANN GLARED across the bed chamber, his wrath fixed upon the withered man nestled within the mammoth bed. The witch hunter's face twitched in barely restrained fury. He pointed a gloved finger at the chambermaid who was fluffing pillows in a corner of the room.

'Leave us,' he snarled. The tone in his voice caused the girl to set down her work and hurry from the room with only a single, worried glance to her bed-ridden master. 'Now,' the witch hunter added in a hiss when she did not move fast enough.

Thulmann's anger was matched by that of the aged Wilhelm Klausner. 'How dare you?' the old man growled. 'I'll not put up with this nonsense any longer!' He reached his hand for the bell rope beside him, tugging it furiously. Distantly, the jangle of the bell could be heard sounding somewhere within the keep below.

'You'll find your steward is otherwise occupied,' Thulmann informed the patriarch. 'He is with my man, down in your torture chamber, your lordship.' The scorn in his voice was like the edge of a knife. Wilhelm Klausner flinched away, his already pallid skin losing yet more of its colour.

'Oh yes, your lordship,' Thulmann pressed, noting the old man's anxiety. 'The fiend that has been prey-ing upon your district has been unmasked at last.'

The witch hunter's hand closed about the hilt of his sword, the knuckles whitening beneath his glove. 'By Sigmar, you are more of a monster than any of the vermin you sent to the stake!' he spat. The violence in his words caused Wilhelm to regain much of his composure, the old man rising up to the Templar's challenge.

'Who do you think you are to speak to me in such a fashion, in my own home?'

Thulmann began to pace, his hand opening and closing about the hilt of his sword. He stalked past the small writing table situated near the corner of the room, its surface pitted by age beneath its sheen, a well-worn Book of Sigmar dominating its surface.

Above the table, fixed to the wall was a wooden plaque upon which had been fixed the seal of Sigmar, the sigil of the twin-tailed comet that was given to every witch hunter. Thulmann scowled as he considered that it had once been worn by the patriarch. It was a struggle for the witch hunter not to rip it from its fixture. 'I have not dragged the story in its full from Kohl,' he snarled, turning away from the offending plaque. 'But be certain that I shall. My man is a hedonist, a thug and a drunkard, but when it comes to the art of torture, he is a prodigy. What little I did glean from his semi-coherent ramblings already turns my stomach. Preying upon your own people! Offering them up in pagan sacrifice in return for some sorcerous protection!'

'You dare!' shouted Wilhelm, his entire body trembling from the emotion swelling up within him. 'I deny these filthy allegations! How dare you accuse me, I, who have served the temple and the Empire with devout loyalty my entire life!' The old man's withered claw rose, swiping at the air. 'Get out of my house!' he roared.

'You have no authority here, your lordship!' spat Thulmann, stalking forward like some great beast. 'This farce is at an end!' he added with a snarl. 'All you deny is the glory and might of Holy Sigmar!' The door began to open behind him, a liveried servant moving to enter in answer to Wilhelm's summons. The witch hunter grabbed the handle, slamming the portal shut in the man's face.

'You, a servant of Sigmar,' the witch hunter sneered, voice dripping with venomous contempt. 'Be thankful that I was in time to stop your steward from completing the obscenity he contemplated this night. It will be one less crime to answer for when you stand before Sigmar and are judged for your blasphemies.'

The Templar stalked past the foot of the bed once more, passing before the old man's massive wardrobe and a glass-faced cupboard that held musty relics from Wilhelm's time of service to the temple.

Wilhelm Klausner seemed to wilt as he heard Thulmann's words. He lifted a trembling hand to his mouth. 'You… you stopped…' A look of absolute terror came upon him and he gave voice to a rattling sob that seemed to surge from the very pits of his soul. 'Now we are doomed,' the old man groaned.

'You were doomed and damned when you chose to forsake the might of Sigmar and put your faith in profane sorceries to preserve you from evil,' the witch hunter rebuked him. The door behind him opened once again. This time it was no servant, but a livid Anton Klausner who stood outside. The younger Klausner stepped into the room, his face contorted with his own indignant fury.

'What the devil are you…' The young noble's words were cut off as he spoke. Thulmann's gloved hand shot from the hilt of his blade, striking Anton across the face with the back of his hand with such force that the young man was thrown to the floor, falling beside the hearth. Thulmann glared down into Anton's face as the boy reached for his own weapon.

'Draw that blade but an inch,' the witch hunter growled, 'and I shall paint that wall with your life's blood, be you guilty of your father's heresies or no.' The cold, chill manner in which Thulmann spoke his threat caused Anton to back down, the young Klausner daubing at the thin trickle of blood dripping from the corner of his mouth.

The boy turned his gaze from the glowering witch hunter to the withered old man on his sick bed.

Anton stared in bewilderment at the expression on his father's face. Written upon that aged visage was misery and defeat and shame, emotions Anton had never before seen exhibited by his always stern and stalwart father. More, there was the agonised appeal in old Wilhelm's eyes, the desperate cry for pity and understanding and forgiveness.

Anton felt contempt boil within his heart. After all these years, long years of trying to prove his value to the old man, and now it was his father who showed himself to be of no value. Wilhelm Klausner had given everything to his eldest son. To Anton, he had given only his name, and Anton had taken great pride in that name and in the long history of honour and tradition that graced it. The name of Klausner was what made him important, made him better than the swineherds and farmers. He could clearly see the guilt in his father's face, more evident even than the old man's shame and fear.

Wilhelm Klausner had given Anton his name, and now he was taking even that away from him, staining it with such crimes that he had drawn the attention of an outlander witch hunter.

The youth bared his teeth in a feral snarl, picking himself from the floor and storming from the room, slamming the door behind him. Thulmann again fixed Wilhelm with his harsh gaze.

'I know not how deep this heresy runs,' he spat, 'but I will find out! I will learn the root of this madness that has infected you and your household and I will burn it from the face of the Empire!'

ANTON KLAUSNER SMASHED his fist against the hard stone wall, giving voice to an inarticulate howl of animal rage. How dare that old man! How dare he! Anton would not have believed anything the witch hunter said, anything that anyone said. But he had seen the truth in his father's eyes, the dismal guilt and self-loathing, the resignation to a long-deferred doom.

The youth howled again. He would not cry, he would not shed a tear for the old bastard.

Anton looked below to see Gregor racing up the steps, taking them two at a time. The other Klausner son had finished conducting Streng and his prisoner to the old dungeon and was now desperate to reach his father, to hear for himself Wilhelm's reaction to the witch hunter's accusations.

Despite the firm conviction that gripped Thulmann, and Gregor's own disturbing discovery of the family ring at the Brustholz farm, the young noble could not bring himself to believe his father guilty of participating in such an unholy conspiracy.

'What has happened?' Gregor called out to Anton as he approached his brother, seeing the violent distress on Anton's face, the blood trickling from his bruised mouth and savaged hand.

Anton's gaze was as cold as the winds of Kislev. 'Ruin,' Anton answered. 'Ruin has come upon us. Your witch hunter friend has destroyed us.' Anton's face twisted about into a grim sneer. 'Oh, maybe you,' he laughed without mirth. 'You'll still get the title and the lands and the power! But all I had was the name, the name of Klausner and the legacy of honour and valour that accompanied it!' He clenched his bruised fist. 'It's being stripped away! The witch hunter won't leave that! When he is finished, there will be no honour left!'

'He is with father?' Gregor asked. The murderous hatred in Anton's eyes caused him to recoil.

'That sick old heretic bastard up there is no father of mine,' he spat, storming past Gregor, shouting for his ruffian cronies. Gregor watched his brother, shaking his head, then continued on to his father's room.

GREGOR FOUND THE witch hunter pacing across his father's room, his body trembling with every step, his hand clenching and unclenching about the hilt of his sword. The old man on the bed seemed even more shrunken and withered than before, looking like a pile of old, tired bones. Something had been taken from his father, some vital spark, and its absence had diminished the old man hideously.

Thulmann turned on Gregor as the young noble entered. The Templar's face retained its mask of grim judgement and for a moment, Gregor actually thought that he was going to draw his sword.

'This does not concern you, Gregor,' the witch hunter told him. 'If there is one man in this entire district who is innocent of this heresy, it is you.' Thulmann closed his eyes, a tiny fraction of his rage escaping him in a sigh. 'Your marksmanship earlier this evening proved that.' When he opened his eyes, the intensity flared up again. 'Leave this room.'

The young noble stood his ground. 'He is my father,' Gregor said. The words caused Wilhelm's face to twist in pain and an agonised groan to hiss from his wasted body.

'He is a heretic and a murderer,' Thulmann snarled. 'He knew about his steward's blasphemous practices. At best, he turned a blind eye to them. At worst, he condoned these profane rites.'

Or orchestrated them, Gregor thought, his eyes turning toward the Klausner coat of arms fixed above the hearth and considering the ring that bore that heraldry still secreted in his pocket. He looked again at his father. The old man lowered his eyes, as though too ashamed to face his son. Gregor shook his head. 'Whatever he has done,' he repeated. 'He is my father.'

'Whatever he has done,' echoed Thulmann. He sneered at the patriarch. 'And what have you done? To what depths of obscenity have you sunk? How many people have you seduced into this loathsome sorcery?' He shook his fist at the old man. 'I will have my answers,' he warned. 'By the temple, I'll have my answers, if I have to rip them from you with whip and knife!'

Gregor clutched at the witch hunter's arm. 'You would not dare!' he gasped in horror.

Thulmann's expression grew grave. He could sympathise with the young noble's emotions, the affection and love he had always known for his father were not so easy to banish. Still, for the sake of all those who had been so ruthlessly slaughtered, he would not be dissuaded from that which needed to be done.

'I'll have my answers,' he repeated coldly. 'Leave now.' The witch hunter stabbed his finger at the door. 'Now!' he snarled. Gregor strode instead to the small side door that led to his father's private chapel.

'You are wrong,' he said, his voice heavy with doubt even as he said the words. 'My father couldn't...'

'He has,' Thulmann spat, glaring once more at the wretched creature on the bed. 'Look at the guilt gnawing at him, the shame of his unmasking. Wilhelm Klausner, witch hunter,' Thulmann snorted in contempt. 'Wilhelm Klausner, necromancer and sorcerer is nearer the truth.' He looked at Gregor, studying the younger man's face. 'You know that I'm right.'

Gregor swallowed the lump that swelled in his throat. 'I will pray for you. Pray that Sigmar will rid you of these hideous delusions that beset you.'

'Pray instead for your father's black soul, that Sigmar might show it some of the mercy this animal never showed his victims,' the witch hunter retorted.

'Do not harm him,' Gregor warned. 'I will be able to hear all that occurs in this room.' Wilhelm clenched his teeth in agony as he heard his son's words. The witch hunter merely nodded.

'I will not do him injury,' Thulmann said in a chill hiss. 'Not until he ceases to answer my questions. When that time comes, you can help me destroy this legacy of evil, or you can become a victim of it. That choice I leave to you.'

Gregor said nothing more, but left the room, slamming the chapel door behind him.

'Don't harm him,' Wilhelm implored in a dry rasp.

Thulmann stared down his nose at the wasted old man. 'My sons are innocent of the evil I have been guilty of. I would not let it touch them.'

The witch hunter smiled back, an expression as cruel and malevolent as any that had ever been cast in stone upon the Great Temple's gargoyles.

'Convince me,' Thulmann commanded.

CHAPTER SEVENTEEN

ANTON KLAUSNER AND his three closest cronies galloped down the winding path through the blighted
woods that surrounded Klausner Keep.

The young noble's mind brooded upon the drama
he had left unfolding in the fortress behind him. He
refused to accept the events, lashing his steed to
greater effort as anger welled up within him.

The horror that had been preying upon the countryside was no doing of his father, it simply could not be.
What end would it serve? These killings did nothing
but weaken the power and authority of the Klausners
within their own district. No, this outlander witch
hunter had some other motive behind his accusations,
some conjuration of the family's enemies. He had
twisted the old man's feeble mind into believing these
falsehoods, into accepting them as the truth.

Such were the lies Anton told himself. He did not care overmuch if his father really was guilty of that which he had been accused, nor did he really find himself disturbed by the thought of the old man ending his life screaming upon a rack or tied to a stake.

All his life, Anton had tried to measure up to the old man's ideals, and yet, when he had become old enough, when he was at last man enough to go forth and earn his own legacy of honour and accomplishment, the spiteful old tyrant had denied him the opportunity. Gregor, dear Gregor, the elder son, would inherit the title and the lands and the power.

What would Anton have if he did not go out and win it for himself? Nothing, only the name of Klausner and the aged heritage of tradition and honour that was a part of that name. Now even that was going to be taken from him. Anton was not going to allow such a thing to happen.

Anton glanced aside at his men. They would show this witch hunter. They would go out and find a more expedient culprit for the murders, find him and bring his mangled body back to the keep, show this outlander swine how wild and baseless his mad accusations were. He would pull his father out of the pit of dishonour and scandal he had dug for himself and which the miserable, thoughtless fool was seemingly resigned to.

Anton sneered as he imagined the old man's gratitude. Perhaps then he would see his younger son's worth and value. All the young noble need do now was settle on which miserable wretch from the village he would say was responsible for the murders.

The horses thundered across the tiny bridge that spanned the stream where Thulmann and Gregor had had their remarkable escape from the undead wolves. There was still a darkened stain, like a burned outline, upon the wooden surface where the wolf had been destroyed. Anton paid the crossing no notice, intent upon his own dark thoughts. However, when the horse of one of his comrades gave a sharp whinny of terror, the young man gazed around him in alarm.

They had ridden into the narrow pathway that snaked its course among the sickened trees and crumbling elf ruins, where not so long ago Anton's own brother had been beset by the restless dead.

Dead things stirred once more upon the edge of the blighted wood, prowling the borderlands of the Klausner domain. Anton could see them shambling out from behind the trees in a rotting, mouldering horde. Limbs picked clean of flesh groped toward the riders as grinning skulls opened their jaws in sound-less howls of battle. Rusted swords and crumbling axes lashed out.

Anton could see that one of his friends was down already, his horse gutted by a corroded axe. Three of the skeletal horrors loomed over the thrown rider, their weapons rising and falling like the hammers of clockwork bell-ringers. The screams of the man weakened, then stopped.

'Holy Sigmar!' Anton shouted in terror. The youth tore his sword from its scabbard. One of his friends tried to ride through the horde as they began to converge upon the path ahead. The man's steed slammed into the rotting figures, bowling the first few ranks aside as though they were tenpins. But as it plunged deeper into the host, the charge lost its impetus, the horse was slowed by the clutching hands and by the rusted blades that tore at its legs and flanks. A ghastly wail like the sound of a soul tossed into the Pit exploded from the rider's lungs as the skeletons pulled down his weakened steed, and he disappeared beneath the bodies of his foes.

Anton Klausner lashed out desperately as the skeletons continued to pour from the trees, his sword smashing into bleached skulls and decayed shoulders.

Sometimes, his blows would splinter the bone, crashing into the fleshless horrors with such force that their animated bodies would come apart, falling into a jumble of shattered bone and rotten armour. Other times, he would only succeed in causing a crack in the sorcerously reanimated bone, and the unfeeling monster would continue to press forward, requiring repeated blows to finally arrest its advance.

Anton struck to the left and right, his blows finding targets wherever he turned. In the span of only a few seconds, he brought down five of the undead abominations, and still they came at him, neither noticing nor caring about the fate of their comrades. There seemed no end to the monsters. To every side, Anton could see only the grinning, fleshless heads of things newly called from their graves.

Beside him, his last companion finally faltered, flinging his sword into the face of one of his skeletal attackers and jerking the head of his horse so sharply that he nearly overturned the animal. The skeletons rushed upon him, even as he spurred his mount to flee.

The horse galloped away, seven of the undead monsters clinging to it, either by means of their claw-like hands or the rusty blades they had buried in the animal's flesh. The terrified animal raced across the bridge, carrying its horrible cargo along with it. The skeletons held firm, however, and soon dragged the faltering brute down by means of their continued attacks. Not so very far from the scorched timber that marked the dire wolf's destruction, the undead warriors hacked Anton's friend to bits.

Anton did not see his comrade die, however. Beset on all sides, at last several of the monsters penetrated his own desperate defence. His horse gave vent to a sound that was almost eerily human as it was dragged down.

Anton tried to fend off the blows that followed as his horse struck the ground, and he along with it, but grasping claws ripped his sword from his hand. The young noble looked up, his vision filled with the grinning, eyeless countenances of his unnatural enemies. Rusty swords and crumbling spears were raised above him, poised to strike.

'No,' Carandini's voice slithered from the night. The necromancer pushed his way through the mouldering ranks of his soldiers, his children of the grave. 'This one does not die so easily.' He stared down at

Anton, a greasy smile working itself upon his face. 'I think that my friend will want to see this one.' Carandini snapped his fingers and the skeletal warriors seized Anton Klausner, dragging the screaming man from beneath his horse.

Carandini followed behind the skeletons as they carried their prisoner into the darkness.

'Oh yes,' the necromancer hissed. 'I am most certain that he will be pleased to see you.'

GREGOR CLOSED THE door behind him, lingering for a moment just beyond the threshold. He could hear the angry voice of the witch hunter shouting in the room he had just left, haranguing his father once more. Much softer, almost inaudible, were the old patriarch's subdued responses. Gregor fought to keep the emotion from his face. He needed to be strong now, not give way to the hopeless despair that gnawed at him. There was a way out of this horror, there had to be.

The young noble's face dropped as he fingered the ring in his pocket. He considered the possibility, nay, the probability that his father truly was guilty of all the witch hunter accused him of. The thought had preyed upon Gregor for days now, and it was one that even his love for the old man could not fend off.

The ring old Wilhelm had worn afterwards could have been a copy. Tradition held it that the patriarch's ring was the same one worn by Helmuth Klausner five hundred years ago, handed down from father to son along with the title and lands. But who was to say that it was the same ring? There could have been any number of copies made over the years, perhaps with the originals buried in the vaults with the men who had worn them in life. If such was the case, Wilhelm would have known this and had one of these rings taken from the old graves when he discovered that his own had been lost.

Gregor knew what he must do. He must help the witch hunter. He must do his duty to the Empire, to Sigmar and help discover the source of this horror that had overwhelmed his father's mind. But Gregor also knew what helping the witch hunter would mean; he knew what fate Thulmann would put his father to.

On the road back to the keep, Streng had taken a sadistic pleasure in describing the atrocities he would visit upon Kohl, gleefully illustrating for the wounded steward how flesh might be scraped from bone without the victim losing consciousness.

Gregor knew that Thulmann would not spare his father from similar torments simply because of his position or his former role as a witch hunter himself. He had seen the outrage, the fury in Thulmann's eyes. He took the descent of a former witch hunter into such vileness as a personal affront, a slight upon the temple itself.

Thulmann would not rest until every life taken by Wilhelm and Kohl had been avenged through torment. Gregor felt sorrow and regret for the lives that had been lost. For Kohl, he could summon not even the shadow of pity, but his father, how could he leave the old man to such a miserable end?

Gregor turned, walking toward the altar. He needed to pray, needed to beg at the shrine of his god that the madness that had risen up to devour his world could be pushed back, that all could go back to what it had been. He stopped when he saw a figure crouched before the altar, its form covered in a long black cloak. The shape moved its head, the hood falling away from a head of greying hair.

Ilsa Klausner smiled at her son, a pained expression that spoke more than Gregor wanted to hear.

'How long have you been here?' Gregor managed to ask after a few moments.

'Long enough,' his mother responded, her voice old and dry. 'Long enough to know that it has all come to an end.' She looked toward the door through which Gregor had only moments before passed. Her face was moist with the shimmer of tears. 'You knew?' Gregor gasped. 'You knew about this all the time?' A new horror squirmed through Gregor's soul. The woman shook her head.

'No,' she told him. 'I did not know. I did not know because I did not want to know. I loved your father. I still do and always shall, whatever that may cost me.' She looked deep into her son's eyes. 'And know this, Gregor, above all else, he loved us. We were his light, his life, his soul. Whatever he did in his life, he did it because he wanted to protect us, to keep his family safe. That was all that mattered to him. Whatever he has done, it was not toward some selfish end. It was to keep us safe.'

Gregor extended his hand, leaning against the wall to support a body that had suddenly grown weak.

He had just begun to resign himself to the fact that his father was a monster, a bloodthirsty beast who preyed upon the countryside with his unholy hunger. Now his mother had bolstered his doubts and rekindled his fears.

'I think, whatever he has done, whatever secret he and Ivar shared, it is a very old secret.' Her eyes hardened even as her voice grew quiet. 'Remember, Ivar was your grandfather's steward before he served your father. And Ivar's grandfather was steward before him...'

Gregor's eyes grew wide with shock as he considered the path to which her mother's frightful statement might lead. He thought again of the old monument buried, hidden, within the blighted woods. He thought of the old legends, stretching back into the mists of time. The Klausner daemon. How aptly had it been named, for it was not a daemon that sought to prey upon the Klausners, but the Klausners themselves who were the daemon.

'You should go to him,' Gregor said in a soft voice. 'Before... Before the witch hunter...' Ilsa Klausner shook her head.

'He would not endure the shame of it,' she told him. 'And, may Sigmar forgive me, I could not see that sort of pain in his eyes.'

Gregor thought of the crushed, degraded and humiliated creature that had gazed upon him from his sick bed and knew that his mother was right.

'Then all we can do is pray,' the young noble said, dropping to his knees beside his mother. 'All we can do is pray that Sigmar will take my father's misguided soul before the witch hunter begins his work.'

'A FAMILY SECRET then?' Thulmann's sharp words lashed out like the barbed end of a whip. 'Some unspeakable pact between your ancestors and the Dark Gods?' The witch hunter slammed his hand against the polished headboard with a violent thump. 'Speak damn you! I will know how far back this profane taint extends itself! I've seen the hidden monument on your property! I've heard the legends they whisper in the village! Tell me when this night-mare began! Confess, man, and lessen the taint that has swallowed your soul!'

Wilhelm turned his eyes toward the ceiling. They were dull, almost lifeless, filled with a terrible weari-ness. His lips trembled as if stricken with palsy. When he spoke, it was in a rasping croak. 'The ritual was never meant to go so far,' he said, almost imploring his accuser to believe him. 'Ever before, it had only taken six to complete the circle.' He could see the fiery gleam burning in Thulmann's gaze and has-tened to explain further. 'The circle was meant to protect, to safeguard the keep and the lands around it. Nothing more!'

'You sent six innocent souls to their graves and you call that nothing!' snapped the witch hunter.

Wilhelm drew himself back, a fragment of his old strength surging into him.

'Six peasants, six dullard farmers and swineherds who could not even write their own names. Six sorry specimens of humanity to preserve the line of

Klausner, to produce sons who would carry on the fight to the enemy, who would serve the temple as its sword and hammer.'

Wilhelm's voice trembled with the violence in his words. It was an echo of the argument he had heard Ivar Kohl use upon him many times, an echo of the last words he had heard uttered by his own father upon his deathbed. It was an argument that even now, Wilhelm fought desperately to believe.

'I notice that you have forbidden your own sons to carry on that tradition,' Thulmann sneered. 'Reconsidering the hypocrisy of your heritage? Deciding to embrace your pagan beliefs in full perhaps? Does that explain why so many have died, to proclaim your loyalty to your new masters?'

Anguished horror filled Wilhelm's face, the horror of a guilty man desperate to explain the motives behind his crime or desperate to have them believed.

'No! I have never allowed my sons to know of this hideous legacy! I would not let them be destroyed and damned as I have been! That is why I forbade them to serve the temple, and why I took measures to ensure that the ritual need never be performed again! I could never allow them to become what I have become.' The patriarch's words drifted off into a miserable sob.

'But something went wrong,' Thulmann snapped, not giving the old man a second to compose himself. 'Something went wrong and it was not six who had to die. Nor seven. Nor eight,' with each statement, the old man covered his ears and moaned in horror. 'What were you hoping to accomplish! What went wrong with your profane rites this time!'

Wilhelm's eyes had become black pits of despair. 'The enemy had some new trick, some powers it had never had before. Only the blood from half the deaths stains my hands, the others were the work of... it. It performed its own rites, its own dark sorcery, and those rites undid the power of Kohl's rituals. With every new murder, the circle of protection began to weaken. Ivar had to kill again and again just to maintain the circle's power.' The old man looked at Thulmann again, and the fear the witch hunter saw there was of such intensity that even he had never seen its like. 'You stopped him tonight,' the old man's finger shook as he pointed at Thulmann. 'The circle is broken now, and it will come and kill us all.'

'What will come?' Thulmann demanded, the hair on the back of his neck prickling with foreboding.

'The enemy that has haunted my line since the very beginning,' the old man replied. His voice dropped into a horrified hiss as he spoke the name, the strength seeming to drain out of him once more as the syllables left his lips.

'Sibbechai.'

ANTON KLAUSNER WAS thrown to the ground, his arm tearing itself open upon the jagged rubble. The youth ignored the pain, however, scrambling behind a crumbling block of stone. He stared in fear at the silent, skeletal shapes that had carried him through the woods to this place, their fleshless claws clutching his arms and legs with grips as strong and chill as the glacial ice of Norsca. The cold wind pulled at the lingering scraps of rotting leather and links of chain armour that clung to their limbs and ribs.

The animated corpses did not return his gaze, did not appear to still notice the captive they had brought here.

Anton's hand closed about a mass of fallen masonry. If he could strike quickly, before the weird, unnatural spark that motivated the dead warriors asserted itself once more, perhaps he could destroy his captors or at least give some account of himself before they hacked him to ribbons as they had his friends.

There were only four of them, the others had stayed behind, patrolling the section of road where Anton had been ambushed. Even so, it was bad odds, one weaponless man against four undying things from beyond the grave. They were odds that gave Anton pause, made him delay before leaping into a reckless and desperate fight. The decision to act or not was soon taken from him.

The already cold atmosphere of the ruined cottage suddenly became even colder. Anton shuddered, shocked to see his breath forming into icy mist before him.

A foul, revolting stench swelled about the ruin, the stink of something long dead, something necrotic and decayed, something rife with a corruption even more loathsome than his silent captors. Fear gnawed at the very depths of Anton's soul, a fear so profound, so complete and all-consuming that his stomach purged itself without warning and a warm foulness dampened his legs.

Tears coursed down Anton's face and the block of masonry fell from his shaking hands. His breath stopped, even his heart seemed to slow.

It was there, the young noble knew, in the darkness behind him, lurking within the shadows cast by the few remnants of the building's roof. It was something horrible and foul, something of such unholy terror that the mere sight of it would destroy him.

Anton began to weep freely now, the sounds harkening back to the crib, back to the multitude of childhood phantoms and fiends that had prowled the nursery until his cries had brought his nanny running with a lantern to chase them away again. He would not look at it, he would not see it. He would close his eyes and hide his head and wait for nanny to chase it away. Whatever happened, he would not turn. He would not look at it.

Anton Klausner shifted his position, turning his body to face the darkness. Despite his terrified conviction, an urge had come upon him, a command that seemed to burn into his brain, a compulsion that did not originate from his own mind but from another's. His eyes grew wider and wider until they seemed that they might pop and the only sound that now came from him was an inarticulate whimper.

A part of the darkness glided forward, moving more like a wisp of smoke than any mortal's step. The shape was tall and thin and decayed. It wore a long black robe about its reed-like shape, a robe with a leather collar that looked as though it had been stitched together from the wings of bats. Chains and leather cords dripped from the garment, each string ending in some morbid talisman. Here, a cord of severed human and inhuman ears, there the tiny pickled hand of an unborn infant. Upon the hem of the garment the picture-writing of long-dead Khemri had been stitched in golden thread.

The arms of the figure were long and cadaverous, the hands protruding from the sleeves of the robe. They were thin and desiccated, the skin grey, corrupt and rotten. Long nails, like the talons of a vulture, tipped each of the fingers, the enamel hardened into a shiny brown surface that resembled the back of a corpse beetle.

The apparition's head was shrunken and withered, little more than a skull with a thin covering of grey, leathery skin wrapped about it, its bald pate covered by a rounded cap of black velvet from which grinned the skeletal face of a dead bat. Long, pointed ears flanked either side of the misshapen head, looking as though they had been cut from the head of a wolf and stitched onto the monster's skull. The face of the creature was that of a death's head, the nose fallen away long ago, the eyes withdrawn into their pits, lips pulled back from the oversized jaw. The teeth alone carried with them a hint of vitality, shining like polished ivory, the eye-teeth grown into ghastly, rat-like incisors.

The vampire's smouldering eyes suddenly gleamed with a terrible and unclean vigour. The creature stretched forth its hand and Anton could do nothing except obey the unspoken summons.

The youth took a slow, shambling step toward the ancient monster. The vampire closed its eyes, hiding their unnatural light, and its shrunken chest drew a deep breath.

'A Klausner,' the thing's voice hissed like leaves crawling across a grave. 'I will never forget the smell of that blood, no matter how many lifetimes have fallen into dust.' The vampire's eyes blinked back into unholy life. Its corpse-face stared at Anton, the leathery flesh pulling back into a malevolent grin. 'The hour has indeed grown dark,' it observed.

The vampire shifted its gaze to consider the man who had approached from behind the unmoving skeletons.

'A most rare gift,' Carandini said, bowing his head slightly in deference to his ally. 'Something to display my commitment to our common purpose.' The necromancer smiled ingenuously, not caring that the undead monster might read his expression. 'Something to display my loyalty,' he added in what was only marginally a servile tone.

'One that is appreciated,' the vampire said, its withered face puckering into a sneer. 'What other things have you observed this day?' it asked, the hollow voice brimming with suspicion.

'The witch hunter has stopped the Klausner's ritual,' Carandini told the vampire. 'Without any new blood to bolster it, the protective circle will collapse. We shall be able to proceed very soon.'

The necromancer smiled as he added the lie to the truth. The witch hunter had indeed stopped the ritual, but that event's debilitating effect upon the wards had been much quicker and more profound than he wished his confederate to know. Carandini had seen with his own eyes his skeleton warriors carried across the stream that marked the boundary, the line over which the restless dead could not normally cross. He had seen, too, those same skeletons unharmed by that passage.

The vampire smiled back at Carandini. It knew that it could not trust the mortal, any more than any of the living could be trusted. It knew what Carandini had seen, ripping the images from Anton Klausner's mind. The circle was already down. The necromancer's usefulness was at an end.

The monster fought down the urge to destroy the sneering, scheming wizard. Did he dare to think that his feeble deceptions would trick Sibbechai, that his transparent manipulations would trap the vampire? Did he think that the vampire would fall upon the Klausner pup like some blood-hungry von Carstein, slaking its thirst for vengeance upon this sorry mortal while the necromancer stole past the defeated wards and made off with the real treasure?

'How shall we proceed?' the vampire asked. The necromancer smiled back at him.

'In a day or so, the wards will lose their power. Then we can strike,' he replied.

'Perhaps they are already weakened,' the vampire said, voicing the thing they both knew to be the true. 'I am not so easily dissuaded as one of your battlefield relics,' the monster observed, enjoying the flare of anger that worked itself onto Carandini's face as he heard Sibbechai diminish the necromancer's powers.

'I would remind you that your curs could not cross the wards either,' the necromancer retorted. 'I would also remind you that you did not know the secret rites that would weaken those same wards.' The necromancer smiled coldly at the vampire. 'For all your knowledge,' he added with another sneer. 'Besides, even if you could cross, there is the problem of gaining entry to the keep. Something one of your kind should find difficult.'

The vampire grinned back, an expression as much of menace as of triumph. The scheming idiot had solved that problem on his own, though he did not see it. Sibbechai shifted its gaze to the trembling, transfixed Anton. Carandini followed the gesture and what little colour there was in his pasty skin faded. Sibbechai let the necromancer's understanding of what he had done sink in.

'A very fine gift,' the vampire hissed. It closed its eyes, picking into the tangle of thoughts and emotions crawling within Anton's soul. Sibbechai opened its eyes again, releasing a fraction of its control over the youth. There was an irony, a deep irony to what the vampire had in mind now, though it had long ago ceased to be human enough to appreciate it. The vampire tilted its arm, exposing its wrist. With the talons on its other hand, it slashed through the rotten skin. Thin black filth oozed up from the injury.

'I offer you what your father has denied you,' Sibbechai told the youth. 'I offer you purpose. I shall raise you above the peasant cattle. You shall become an aristocrat of the night, and mighty shall be your name. Men will tremble in fear of you and your power shall know no end.'

The vampire's face twisted in macabre mirth as it read the crude, simple desires and the smouldering resentments of the young noble. 'I shall help you to avenge the dishonour your father has brought upon you and he will know the power and strength of your will before he dies.' The vampire released the rest of its control over Anton Klausner. The youth shook, trembling still with the unnatural terror which the vampire's presence evoked. But he stood his ground, for all his shivering, for all the fear in his eyes.

'Drink,' Sibbechai said, lifting its bleeding wrist. 'Drink and all that I have promised will be yours.' *In so much as you shall be my slave until I tire of you.*

The vampire sneered as he saw the youth struggle with his decision. It already knew how Anton would decide, knowing the young noble's mind better than he knew it himself. Anton lowered his head, his warm lips touching the cold, clammy skin of the vampire. He sucked at the dark liquid drooling from the monster's wound. Sibbechai let only the smallest portion pass Anton's lips before wrenching its arm away.

'We share the same blood,' the vampire hissed, watching as Anton staggered and fell, overcome by the power now racing through his body. The vampire looked over at Carandini, studying the necromancer's anxious face. 'Be not dismayed, necromancer. I shall go myself. You may remain behind, where it is safe.'

'I would happily accompany you,' Carandini protested, hands toying with the cuffs of his cassock.

'Your newly found valour,' Sibbechai shook its head, its voice rumbling with a dangerous mirth. 'Why does it fill me with such…' the vampire paused as though struggling to find the right word. 'Uneasiness?' it said at last.

'No, you shall stay here,' Sibbechai proclaimed. 'I shall go.' Its voice slipped into a malevolent whisper. 'I shall reclaim that which is mine!'

CHAPTER EIGHTEEN

'SIBBECHAI.' THULMANN REPEATED the name. He cast his thoughts back to his study of the Klausner family records. It was the name of the vampire that Helmuth Klausner had hunted to the cursed city Mordheim and destroyed five hundred years ago. The witch hunter knew that a vampire's destruction was sometimes a nebulous thing and that at certain times, and by certain rites of such horror that they defied the most morbid imagination, such creatures could be called back from the realm of the dead. He also knew that a vampire was like a dragon: age did not diminish its potency but rather increased its power and malevolence.

What might this creature Sibbechai have become after five hundred years?

Wilhelm dipped his head in a solemn nod. 'Yes,' the patriarch said. 'The great shadow that has haunted my family from the very beginning. A vampire sorcerer, a monster of loathsome and awful power. One of that most obscene of the profane breeds of vampire – a necrarch.' The old man spoke the last word only as a frightened whisper. Thulmann made the sign of the Hammer as he heard the evil name spoken.

A necrarch. Vampires were an unclean, loathsome kind of being, lurking among the people of the Empire like wolves prowling among sheep. Except during certain times of decadent permissiveness on the part of past aristocrats and nobility, it had been the witch hunters' duty to root out these monsters and destroy them.

Many were their breeds and diverse were their powers, but above them all, there was one kind that was feared even by the servants of Sigmar: the vampire sorcerers known as the necrarchs, a foul kindred of undead wizards who looked upon the living not simply as prey, but as subjects for their unholy experiments.

There was a foul and abhorrent tome, kept under lock and key in the lowest vaults of Altdorf's Great Cathedral, a book of such vile evil that only the most pure and devout of Sigmar's servants were allowed even to see it. The *Liber Mortis* of the mad necromancer Vanhel.

Thulmann had been permitted access to the *Liber Mortis*, allowed to study fifteen pages of its ghastly text for the space of two hours, a brutish, illiterate temple guard standing at his shoulder, watching him for any sign of corruption. Even now there were times when Vanhel's spidery script would boil up within the witch hunter's mind, disturbing his slumber, robbing his food of its taste and perfume of its scent.

It was a poison of the soul, a tainted knowledge that corrupted all who contemplated it. A glimpse had been enough, perhaps even too much. But in that glimpse, Thulmann had read of the necrarchs, of their foul nature and their abominable ambitions. Vanhel himself had been frightened of them, calling them the 'Disciples of the Accursed'. He related the foul prophecy of the progenitor of their bloodline, W'soran, a prophecy that the necrarchs hoped to fulfil. For, like the Great Necromancer himself, the necrarchs dreamed of a world that was still and quiet and cold.

Other vampires sought power over the living, in one way or another. The necrarchs sought a way to destroy all life, to scour the world of every living thing and leave it as a shadow peopled only by the restless dead.

If this Sibbechai was one of the filthy breed of the necrarchs, then the Klausners had good reason to know fear.

'It was long ago, in the Time of the Three Emperors,' Wilhelm continued. 'The land was rife with war and ruin. Plague was everywhere. In those days, the name of Klausner was not so well known, they were just another family of merchants. Then plague came to the town of Gruebelhof.' Wilhelm looked at the witch hunter, and it was a look of pain, the mark of a man who was about to confess some great shame.

'The plague struck down most of the Klausner line, laying low the old and the young, wiping away in an instant almost three generations. The priests and healers could do nothing, even when one among the priesthood bore the same name.

'Helmuth watched in horror as the plague devoured his family. At last, only his brother Hessrich and Hessrich's wife and daughter remained. Hessrich was determined to save his family, and did not intend to leave their survival in the hands of the gods. He had learned a few heathen practices from an old witch who dwelled outside the village, petty magic that might make his family resist the plague. Hessrich saw the potency of the hag's spell and he left Gruebelhof in search of a sorcery mightier still, a sorcery that would make his family immune to the disease.

'In his absence, the heathen rites practised by Hessrich's wife were discovered by their neighbours. She was denounced as a witch, put in irons and cast into jail. Helmuth pleaded desperately to save them, but he was powerless before the will of the townspeople and his brother's wife and their young daughter were burnt at the stake.'

Wilhelm paused, licking his lips nervously as he considered the next part of the tale. 'The smoke was still rising from their pyre when Hessrich returned. He had found the knowledge he had sought. He had travelled to a shunned and haunted tower and been captured by the thing that dwelt there. Despite his terror, Hessrich had pled with his captor to release him so he might find the magic he needed to save his family. In its twisted humour, the vampire had offered not only to release him, but to give him the knowledge he needed as well. All Hessrich had to do was drink the vile liquid that coursed through the monster's veins and be inducted into its unclean brotherhood. Hessrich died in that nameless tower, transformed into one of the undead. The newborn monster took a name of power, discarding forever the name of Klausner. Its new name was Sibbechai and it was a man no longer.

'Sibbechai's rage was great and terrible when it learned what had been done, for the salvation of Hessrich's family had been the only lingering shred of humanity left in the creature. It massacred over half of the already plague-wracked town before the priests were able to drive it away. Amid the carnage wrought by the thing that had been his brother, Helmuth swore a grim oath to atone for the horrors of Sibbechai and not to rest until the vampire had been destroyed.

'Across the Empire he hunted the beast, stalking it through lands haunted by war and disease, until at last, the monster came to the cursed ruin that had been the great city of Mordheim. It was there that Helmuth confronted the monster and terrible was their battle. After hours of combat, Helmuth fell and the vampire leapt after him in a frenzied madness of bloodlust and hate. In its violent pounce, the monster did not see the broken spear gripped in Helmuth's hands. It impaled itself upon the weapon and with a final shriek of malevolence and profanity, it died.'

'But the monster did not stay dead,' observed Thulmann, listening intently to every nuance in Wilhelm's tale. Wilhelm shook his head.

'Helmuth was too fatigued from his battle to destroy the remains properly and he was compelled to leave the shunned ruins. It took him three days to gather together a strong enough force of fellow witch hunters and mercenary hirelings to return. When he did, they found no trace of the vampire's body.

'Helmuth prayed that some foul beast, some nameless creature of Chaos from the Cursed Pit had devoured Sibbechai's remains. But it was not so. Within a year, as he scoured the Empire, purging it of sorcerers and mutants, Helmuth learned that the vampire had survived. It eluded his efforts to track it down, lingering just beyond his reach, a vengeful spectre waiting to strike at him whenever he let down his guard.

'So it has ever been for the Klausners,' Wilhelm continued. 'The men of the Klausner line have always tried to hunt down this loathsome beast, but never have they succeeded in destroying it. Over the centuries, many of the descendants of Helmuth have fallen victim to the vampire Sibbechai and the threat of the fiend's undying lust for vengeance has never diminished.'

Thulmann was quiet for a moment as he reflected upon the old man's story, pacing the room as he contemplated the tale. At length, he spun about, his voice snapping like a whip. 'But this does not explain the foul necromancy your family is guilty of. You have told me the reason for it, but not its cause! To save yourselves from the vampire, yes, but how did this abominable practice come to be? How did corruption burrow its way into the pious legacy of the Klausners?'

'It has been with us from the beginning,' Wilhelm relented. 'It was Helmuth who first performed the ritual of protection, so the family he made for himself after the era of the Three Emperors might not be claimed by his undead enemy. And the ritual has been handed down ever since, tied into the title and legacy. At the end of his life, each father inducts his eldest son into the secret.'

'And have you told Gregor yet?' the witch hunter demanded. The old man wilted back into his covers, a long sigh shuddering from his chest.

'No,' he protested. 'I have told you I would not let this evil touch my sons. That is why I forbade them to become witch hunters, forbade them to continue the hunt for Sibbechai. I felt that if the vampire was let alone, if the monster was not hounded and if… other measures… were taken, it would have no reason to menace this house any longer.' Wilhelm's eyes shone with a desperate eagerness. 'Don't you see? This was to be the last time there would be any reason to perform the ritual! I was going to bring the shameful tradition to an end!'

'By making peace with an undead monster who lusts after the death of the world?' Thulmann sneered. His eyes narrowed as he fixed upon the subject Wilhelm was trying to avoid. 'How did Helmuth learn this loathsome ritual? What was the source of his knowledge?' The old patriarch looked away, refusing to speak.

'I will find out,' the witch hunter's voice was like steel. 'Either now, or after my man has torn your old body into an open wound!'

THE BURNING EMBERS of Sibbechai's eyes flared within the darkness, tiny pinpricks of malice floating amid the shadows of the night. The vampire strode between the rotting trees, its unnatural vision allowing it to navigate flawlessly through the pitch black that had fallen across the land as the moons once again were consumed by the brooding clouds overhead.

The vampire stared at the sombre sky, its face twitching with the faint echoes of memory. It had been on just such a night, so very long ago, that it had nearly been destroyed, that it had been cheated of its vengeance. Sibbechai had long ago ceased to believe in such things as fate and destiny, but there was something terribly fitting that the hour of its long-denied victory should mirror that of its ignoble defeat.

The vampire rotated its skull-like head, watching the wretched thrall it had created from Anton Klausner. There was still much of the man within the thrall, it had not been dead long enough yet for the thoughts and cares of life to fade. Sibbechai struggled to remember what it had been like to have such vibrant emotions surging within it, struggled to try and capture the faintest trace of the man it had once been. It could remember the events, remember the places it had walked when alive, the people it had known, the things it had done. But the vampire could no longer feel the emotions that had been attached to those places and persons. It knew that it had loved a woman and a tiny baby girl, but it recalled that fact with distance and coldness, as though it had been another who had felt such things.

Sibbechai could remember leaving the village, and finding the haunted tower where it was said a sorcerer lived. It could still see the corpse-visage of the thing that had killed the man Hessrich Klausner and put in his place the vampire Sibbechai. The vampire could remember too the horror and loathing it had felt for its condition in those days and weeks after it had been transformed, only its lingering love for its family keeping it from going mad.

That link was severed when Sibbechai had returned to its village, severed by flame and fire. Severed by Helmuth Klausner, the man who had been its brother.

The vampire looked again at Anton Klausner, and the skull-like face peeled back in a gruesome smile. So very like Helmuth this one was, bristling with ambition and petty jealousy, filled with cruelty and brutality. Helmuth Klausner, the man who had lusted after his brother's wife, who had bristled with resentment and envy every time he saw Hessrich's family pass him upon the street. Helmuth Klausner who, to indulge his bitterness and innate cruelty had become a witch hunter and begun a vicious purge of the township, all in the name of cleansing it of the wickedness that had drawn the plague there.

When it had returned to the town, Sibbechai had been stunned that Helmuth's cruelty had dared to claim even his own family, imprisoning and torturing his own niece and stepsister and then condemning them both as witches to be burned at the stake. The vampire was not so naïve now. All life was treacherous and cruel, self-serving and unpredictable.

Helmuth and his followers had managed to overcome the vampire, for in those days, Sibbechai did not fully understand the power of what it had become, nor was it so detached from the emotions that had flowed through it in life as to be inured to the grief that wracked its dead heart.

Rather than destroying the vampire outright, Helmuth had decided to imprison and study it. It was a foolish decision, for he underestimated how powerful the undead monster was and when the sun again set, Sibbechai had escaped the jail with ease. But the witch hunter had captured more than just the vampire, he had also taken from it the thing it had stolen from the tower of the elder necrarch, the thing it had hoped would save its family from the plague.

Sibbechai clenched its bony fist, the old withered flesh creaking as the knuckles cracked. It would reclaim that tome, that grimoire of ancient secrets and profane lore. It had read and understood enough of the book to know the power that was contained within its pages. That power would belong to Sibbechai again.

The vampire stared once more through the darkness, peering past the twisted trees. It exerted its malignant will and the Anton-thing turned its eyes upon the necrarch.

'As you command,' the thrall hissed.

The vampire strode out from amongst the shadowy boughs, stalking across the path, ignoring the dismembered corpses that only hours ago had been its friends and comrades. The vampire walked toward the small bridge and the stream it spanned.

Anton hesitated for a moment as it reached the bridge, new senses warning the fledgling vampire of the faint echoes of power that yet coursed about the barrier. Then he stepped out onto the wooden planks, striding with purposeful steps across the span. From the blackness of the wood, Sibbechai smiled.

The protective circle was no more. The power that had guarded the Klausners for centuries had been banished. Now nothing would stop Sibbechai from reclaiming its own.

Not the dead.

Not the living.

CARANDINI SAT UPON the cold, wasted ground within the ruins of the farmhouse, his eyes narrowed as the intellect behind them slithered through the twisted corridors of his mind.

Events were proceeding swiftly, threatening to slip beyond the necromancer's ability to control. Now, so close to all that he hoped for, so close to the knowledge that he desired, things were at their most dangerous.

The vampire was becoming reckless, something that Carandini had not anticipated. He had expected the monster to be shrewd, certainly, and he understood that Sibbechai was not so foolish as to trust the necromancer any more than he trusted it. But he had not imagined that a creature who had waited centuries might become impatient when the goal was so very near at hand.

Sibbechai had set off on its own, to confront the Klausners and the outlander witch hunter in person. Carandini was at a loss to understand such a foolish action. He would have stayed safe within the darkest depths of the forest and sent wave after wave of reanimated warriors to assault the keep, not setting foot inside until he was certain that no living thing remained within its walls. That was the way to be sure. The vampire's way courted calamity.

Perhaps it was true what was whispered about the bloodline of the necrarchs, that all of that unholy brotherhood were insane, or perhaps there was indeed a cleverness in Sibbechai's insanity. Perhaps the monster was not so contemptuous of Carandini's powers as it tried to appear. Perhaps it feared the inevitable confrontation between them when victory was at last theirs.

The necromancer smiled as he considered this pleasant thought, that his knowledge of the black arts was enough to impress one of the undying necrarchs. Maybe the vampire felt it had good reason to put itself at risk, intending to seize the prize and escape with it before Carandini could react to the monster's treachery, perhaps even leaving the necromancer behind to contend with the witch hunter, should the vampire leave the man alive.

Quite clever, in its way, if such had been the vampire's purpose. There was only one problem with Sibbechai's plan. Sibbechai was a vampire, and as such needed a place of sanctuary when the sun bathed the land in its golden rays.

Oh, the creature had taken such pains to keep its lair hidden and secret from Carandini, but the necromancer had discovered the cave with Sibbechai's casket all the same. Carandini had continued to 'search' for the vampire's refuge ever since to deceive the monster into thinking its secret was still safe. For who continues to look for something they have already found?

Oh yes, Sibbechai would attempt some treachery, of that Carandini was most certain. But the vampire would have a rather interesting surprise when it slunk back into its cavern to hide from the sun and rejuvenate its unclean vitality within its casket.

The necromancer was quite pleased with his plotting. It was rather like a game of regicide, only as a mortal man, Carandini had a slight edge over his supernatural opponent. For a man was not bound by the same rules as a vampire. Carandini stared out into the night, chuckling as he imagined Sibbechai's reaction when it saw what had been left in its coffin.

A sudden movement in the shadows caused the necromancer to stand. Only eyes as unnaturally attuned to the night as Carandini's could detect the low, slinking shapes that crept about the fringe of the ruined farmhouse walls.

The necromancer hissed under his breath, fumbling about within the secret pockets of his gown. It seemed that the vampire had not been derelict in making its own treacherous plans. Carandini cursed his overconfidence. He should have prepared for something of this sort, should have brought the entire host of his animated soldiers back with him instead of the feeble quartet that had taken hold of Anton Klausner.

The low, grisly snarls of Sibbechai's rotting wolves sounded from the darkness. Even as Carandini willed his skeleton warriors into action, mangy lupine shapes lunged at them from the night. The wolves smashed the slow-moving skeletons to the ground, ignoring the fleshless talons that tore at their maggot-ridden flesh as their jaws worried and savaged the brittle bleached bone of their foes.

Carandini cursed again, spinning about just as another wolf lunged out of the night, the black-furred beast streaking toward him. The necromancer flung a foul grey powder into the zombie animal's face, causing the wolf's muzzle to disintegrate into a steaming white ash. The wolf crashed to the ground, its body shuddering as the powder continued to eat its way down the length of the creature.

The necromancer cast more of the powder into the second wolf that lunged for him. The creature's leg crumbled, spilling it to the ground in a writhing pile of fur and swollen entrails. The other dire wolves rose from the mangled remains of Carandini's warriors. There would be no help from that quarter for the necromancer. His hand sifted the bottom of the small elf-skin pouch that held the consuming dust.

Carandini's face twisted into a look of horror as he considered how much powder remained as opposed to the number of Sibbechai's wolves that now began to circle him with hackles raised. He did not find the calculation to be a favourable one.

The monstrous wolves prowled about the embattled necromancer, their rotting muzzles scrunched into feral, hungry visages. The lights that shone in their wasted eye sockets gleamed from the black shadows of their skulking forms. Warily they paced, awaiting the ideal moment to pounce. The necromancer stared back at them with cold resignation.

The hollow, deathly howl of the pack leader sounded in the darkness and like a midnight wave crashing upon the bow of a ship, the wolves leapt upon their prey.

CHAPTER NINETEEN

'THE VAMPIRE'S GRIMOIRE,' Thulmann proclaimed as the idea came to him. He saw shock flare up in Wilhelm's eyes and knew that he had struck upon the truth. The witch hunter considered how much sense his guess made. Helmuth Klausner had captured his vampire brother, a vampire that was of the sorcerous necrarch breed. It made sense that he would have seized whatever book of spells the monster carried, spells, perhaps, that it had hoped to use to protect its family from the plague. It also explained something else that had been nagging at the witch hunter.

Wilhelm had tried to describe the vampire's motive as being a centuries-long quest for revenge. With another of the polluted breeds of the vampire, Thulmann might have believed the old man. It was known that while vampires did not feel emotion the same way as living men, they were still capable of many of the baser emotions like hate, lust, envy and spite. But a necrarch was something different. In them, even the most base of emotion seemed diminished, if not absent altogether.

No, they were motivated by something colder and less human even than hate. The necrarchs only cared about their sorcery, their store of profane knowledge. The quest for supreme mastery of the black arts was the one thing that drove their inhuman hearts, even as it consumed their minds and souls.

Revenge would not have kept a necrarch haunting the Klausners. But the repossession of some tome of blasphemous knowledge might.

'Helmuth kept the vampire's spell book,' Thulmann declared again. Fury swelled up within him as he recalled his own sickening glimpse into the *Liber Mortis*. 'Sigmar's Blood! How far into the pit of heresy and evil does this family's madness run!'

Wilhelm shook his head with what strength remained to him, an imploring look on his wrinkled features. 'He never sought to become some nightmare of sorcerous power,' the old man gasped. 'No, he sought to use the works of the enemy against itself! To fight fire with fire! To use the foul magic that had destroyed his brother in the service of Sigmar, to scour the Empire of the filth that festered within it!'

'Your ancestor was a heretic and a warlock!' spat the witch hunter, violence in his eyes. 'Recall the scriptures: "Suffer not the necromancer, shun his works. By smoke and by fire shall they be consumed and blessed shall be the land whose sorcerers are ash." So said Sigmar in his wisdom. Your ancestor would have done well to heed the voice of his god.'

'He served Sigmar,' Wilhelm growled. 'As have all the Klausners!'

'Even Hessrich?' Thulmann directed his comment like a sword. 'Whatever lies Helmuth told himself to justify his purposes, he was heretic and worse. Better men than him have paved the road of their damnation with the noblest of intentions. But it was damnation awaiting them just the same.' The witch hunter's voice trailed off, the image of Lord Thaddeus Gamow suddenly springing into his mind and the horror that exalted figure had caused. He broke from his recollection, glaring down into the old patriarch's eyes.

'I want what the vampire has tried to take from this fortress for five hundred years,' he told the old man. 'I want the book!' Wilhelm sank back into his pillows, a sad smile on his face.

'I cannot give it to you,' Wilhelm said.

Thulmann pounded his fist against one of the posts that supported the bed's canopy.

'Unrepentant wretch,' the witch hunter hissed. 'Is it not enough that this book has been allowed to taint and corrupt this family for hundreds of years? Is it not enough that it has drawn unspeakable evil to these lands like moths to a flame? End this horror! Give me the book so I can destroy it and put an end to this nightmare!'

The smile remained on the old man's face as he shook his head. 'Some things are not destroyed so easily,' he said. 'Even if I could, I cannot help you.'

Thulmann sprang forward, his gloved hand pointing accusingly into the patriarch's face. 'Cannot? Or will not?'

'Whichever you like,' Wilhelm sighed. 'It is the same.'

Thulmann turned away from the old man, pacing the room once again like a caged lion. 'I will find out,' he said. 'I *will* find out.' He turned to face the old man again. 'I will not hesitate to put you to torment if you refuse to confess all to me and renounce this filth that has tainted your legacy!'

A part of Thulmann desperately hoped it would not come to that. The old man would have to die for his crimes, there was no getting around that, but the thought of putting this man, who had once been a hero of the temple, a champion against the dark, the thought of putting such a man to torture sickened Thulmann.

Then there was Gregor to consider. Despite all he had learned, Thulmann was still certain of the young man's nobility and character. He would spare Gregor as much misery as he could. The execution would be hard enough, the youth did not need this as well.

The witch hunter shook his head in disbelief as the old man still refused to speak. 'I give you until I return to reconsider your position,' he said. 'Fortunately, I have another prisoner at my disposal.' Thulmann's voice slipped into a threatening growl. 'If you still pray to Sigmar, pray he tells me what I want to hear.'

* * *

THULMANN STALKED ACROSS the room, knocking upon the door that connected to the small chapel. He swung the door inward, only slightly surprised to find two figures kneeling before the altar instead of one.

'Lady Klausner,' the witch hunter said, dipping his head, yet keeping one wary eye on the room behind him and the old figure lying upon the bed. 'I did not mean to interrupt your prayers.'

'Sigmar knows what I would ask of him,' Ilsa Klausner returned. 'I am sure he would welcome a respite from hearing an old woman pleading over and again for the same thing.' The woman rose to her feet, looking squarely into the witch hunter's eyes. 'Tell me, will it be quick?'

A look of regret came on the witch hunter and there was a touch of genuine pain in his eyes. 'That I cannot say.' He turned his head to look back at the bed ridden patriarch. 'It depends on him. There is much that must be done this night.'

Ilsa nodded her head in understanding. 'Then I should prepare some tea,' she said. 'Would you like some tea, Herr Thulmann? I promise not to poison it, should that thought have occurred to you.'

The witch hunter smiled thinly and shook his head. 'I am afraid that I can only allow myself to trust one Klausner right now,' he apologised. 'I am sure that you can understand my position, given the circumstances.'

'Well,' sighed Ilsa Klausner. 'I think I will find some tea for myself then.' A suggestion of fear and anxiety crept past her air of resignation as she started to leave. 'That is, if I am still free to do so?'

Thulmann motioned for her to proceed. 'I need to speak with your son,' he told her. 'There is something I need him to help me with,' he added as he saw the fear swell up in Ilsa's eyes. The woman cast a lingering look at her son, then retreated through the small door that connected the chapel with her own room.

'There really is no hope, is there?' Gregor said when she had left.

'For your father,' the witch hunter replied. 'No. He is guilty of such crimes that his life must be forfeit.'

'And for the rest of us?' Gregor asked, a tremor in his voice. He had heard the dark tales that were sometimes whispered, tales about overzealous witch hunters who, having found one member of a family guilty of sorcery had then scoured the length and breadth of the Empire to destroy the entire line.

'He claims that only he and his servant knew what was going on,' Thulmann said. 'I believe him, in that much at least.' He placed a reassuring hand on Gregor's shoulder. 'A man is not damned by the sins of his father, he must damn himself. Two of the most famous members of the Order of Witch Hunters were Johann van Hal and Helmut van Hal, both of them direct descendants of the infamous necromancer Frederick van Hal.'

Thulmann paused for a moment, recalling the skeleton swinging from his own family tree, the black sorcerer Erasmus Kleib. Like the van Hals, the existence of such a foul taint upon his lineage helped to strengthen his spirit and resolve, fill him with a consuming need to atone for the misdeeds of his wicked relation.

Gregor's face was contemplative for a moment as he too considered the witch hunter's words, appearing to find some reassurance for himself in them. He had hoped for some reassurance for his father's fate. 'Must he... must he be put to the torment?' Gregor asked in a subdued, fearful whisper.

'Unless I can pry the secrets he refuses to relate from Kohl,' the witch hunter sighed. 'I have to go below and see if Streng has broken Kohl's determination yet. I need someone to remain here and watch the patriarch.'

'You would trust me with such a task?' marvelled Gregor.

'You are intelligent enough to know that you would not be doing the old man any service by helping him escape. He would be hunted across the land like an animal, and his soul would assuredly be damned to the darkness.' Thulmann smiled grimly. 'Besides, I have seen the strength in you, the honour and courage that makes me think the taint that has attached itself to your line does not run deep. You would never be able to help a murderer escape justice, to let innocent blood go unavenged.'

Gregor watched as the witch hunter stalked away. A part of him was proud that Thulmann trusted him enough to bestow such an important duty upon him, that childish part that still believed in honour and duty, that still looked with wonder and awe upon the great deeds of the Templars. The other part of him seethed with silent rage as it watched the witch hunter leave, so certain that he could trust his evaluation of Gregor's character. The part that saw past the codes of honour and devotion and obligation. The part that saw one brutal, simple fact.

His father was going to die. Slowly or quickly, his father would die.

THE DOORMAN MAINTAINED his position within the massive entry hall, watching from the shadows as the witch hunter descended the stairs and made his way down the corridor that led to the cellars. The Templar was going to join his henchman, no doubt. The doorman did not envy Ivar Kohl when the witch hunter arrived.

It had been a strange and fear-fraught night. The dramatic entrance of Gregor Klausner and the witch hunter's entourage, a bleeding Ivar Kohl in tow. The horrific story told by the shepherdess the men had rescued from Kohl. Then there had come the raised voices emanating from Lord Klausner's room, the ghastly accusations of the witch hunter echoing down from the heights of the keep. The doorman wondered where it would all lead.

He was certain that things would grow worse before they became better.

The sound of the heavy iron door ring pounding against the massive wooden portal brought the servant out of his gloomy reflections. He strode across the hall, swinging the heavy wooden panel inward. He was somewhat surprised to see Anton Klausner on the other side. As the doorman held the portal open, Anton stepped inside, without any of the swearing or slapping that had characterised his exit earlier. The younger son of his lordship had left the keep only a few hours before, brimming with anger and outrage. The night air seemed to have done the young Klausner a great deal of good, for it had certainly cooled his temper, though his skin was very pale. The young man must be frozen to the bone, thought the servant.

'Welcome back, Master Anton,' the doorman said. Before he could elaborate, the pale young man turned, staring back into the blackness of the courtyard with an intense gaze.

'Enter this house freely and of your own accord,' Anton said into the night. The doorman glanced outside, trying to determine who the noble was addressing. Darkness and shadow seemed to become solid, just beyond the threshold. The doorman flinched away from the sudden chill, from the charnel stench, but it was already too late. A thin, almost skeletal hand shot out from the darkness and with one deft motion broke the man's neck like a twig.

The shadow glided over the twitching corpse of the servant. Anton bowed before its advance, following in the apparition's wake. Sibbechai paid the vampiric slave no further mind. The thrall had achieved its chief purpose. There were strange limitations to the power of the undead, one of these being that they could not cross the threshold of a dwelling unless first invited by one of its occupants. The corpse-face of the vampire smiled as it again considered how the necromancer's scheme had turned against him. Sibbechai wondered how long it had taken the wolves to finish its erstwhile ally.

'There,' Anton hissed, pointing a pale hand to the stairs. 'The Klausner is up there.'

Sibbechai's smile grew wider, the grotesque fangs gleaming in the flickering light cast by the hearth. Soon, all that had been taken from it would be restored.

CHAPTER TWENTY

THE WITCH HUNTER's cloak billowed after him as he swept down the narrow stairway that burrowed into the basement levels of the keep. Thulmann's mood was as black as the garment he wore.

The revelation that the Klausners had never been the pure and pious champions of the temple that legend and history proclaimed rested ill upon the witch hunter's heart. If such a noble lineage as the Klausners could be so grotesquely tainted, then there truly was no saying how far corruption had sunk its fangs into the fabric of Imperial society.

Despite Thulmann's reassuring words to Gregor, the taint of his family was more ghastly and hideous than anything Thulmann had ever heard of. This was no case of a lone madman profaning the name of his family by his misdeeds. This was a tradition of horror and heresy that stretched back hundreds of years, back to the very foundation of the line. Van Hal had been but a single man, Klausner was a dynasty, the entire honour of its name nothing but carefully maintained illusion. Whatever lies they told themselves, however they might justify their sorcerous heresy, the Klausners were every bit the filth they hunted in the name of Sigmar.

Perhaps Gregor could redeem the name, reinvent the line? Certainly it would fall to him, because Thulmann did not see Anton rising to such a thankless task. It would take many lifetimes to atone for the crimes of their ancestors, many generations to wash away the evils of the past.

First though, this foul tome of sorcery that had tempted Helmuth Klausner to his fall had to be destroyed. Thulmann could not allow such a profane work to exist.

He thought again of the spidery script of van Hal crawled across the pages of the *Liber Mortis*, the taint of madness dripping from every word. He would sleep better knowing such a work had been purged from the face of the world. It might not be within his power to decide the fate of the *Liber Mortis*, but it was within his power to destroy the grimoire of Sibbechai. There could be no redemption for the House of Klausner while the source of their corruption remained intact.

The witch hunter's steps carried him to the heavy iron door that closed off the old torture chamber from the rest of the cellars. It was something of a testament to the erratic eccentricity and morbidity that had infected the Klausner patriarchs that such a room, devoted to such a purpose, should be situated here, where servants would constantly be passing by it as they hurried about their duties, rather than hidden away in some dark corner.

Torture was a vital tool of the witch hunters, fear of torment was something that had broken many a witch and set many a sorcerer into flight, thereby revealing himself. But it was still a despicable tool, for all its necessity, and one that the Templars did not display for all to see. The location of this room was exactly that, the open flaunting of what the long dead patriarch had been and what he had done.

A groan sounded from beyond the door, followed by a harsh snarl in Streng's brutal tones. Thulmann lifted his gloved hand, banging on the cold iron surface of the door. 'Sigmar protects,' the witch hunter said. It was an arranged code between himself and his henchman to indicate that all was well and that he should open the door.

Thulmann knew that he was taking a risk by conducting his investigation here, but he also knew that it was the quickest way to unmask the conspiracy at work, to flush out the rats who had been associated with the heresy.

The witch hunter did not care overmuch for his own safety. His life and death were almost inconsequential things to him. He had left a sealed report of his discoveries with Reikhertz back in the village, instructing the innkeeper to ride to Wurtbad and deliver the report to the temple of Sigmar there should Thulmann fail to return by dawn. He was certain that the simple tradesman would follow his instructions, and the report would soon come to the attention of Sforza Zerndorff.

His own death would not help the Klausners, Thulmann concluded grimly. Just the opposite, they would be trading the surgeon's knife for the headsman's axe, for Zerndorff would not be so careful about trifling matters of innocence and guilt. If the Witch Hunter General South read that report, he would come with a small army and blast Klausner Keep into rubble.

Streng pulled the door inward, a glowing iron rod clenched in his upraised hand, ready to dash the brains from any unwanted visitor who might be accompanying the witch hunter.

The mercenary stepped back when he saw that Thulmann was alone. The witch hunter slipped past him, his icy gaze considering the dank, miserable room he had entered.

It was like stepping into the study of a Solkanite inquisitor. Iron manacles hung from steel staples fixed to two of the walls. A massive fire pit had been hacked into the stone floor, a large bellows looming beside it to ensure that the flames would be as hot as the breath of a daemon. Gibbets and small iron cages that seemed too small to hold a human body no matter how contorted hung from the beams overhead.

A dusty wooden rack held a grisly assortment of pincers, tongs, bone saws and even a few implements that Thulmann did not recognise and whose use the witch hunter was not too eager to contemplate. A gigantic iron sarcophagus dominated one corner, its surface morbidly cast into the image of a praying abbess.

Thulmann had employed such 'iron sisters' before; sometimes the mere sight of such an instrument of slow and agonising death was enough to break the will of a heretic. Beside the iron sister sat the cruel framework of a Tilean boot, a ghastly device that made a slow and exacting art of breaking every bone in the foot of its victim.

Ivar Kohl was bound to a long wooden table that dominated the very centre of the chamber. The steward's hands were locked into an iron bar, his feet bound likewise at the other end of the table. Thick ropes connected the iron bars to the pulleys that were fixed to either end of the table.

The rack, a fiendish invention concocted by some long forgotten sadist; a loathsome device, but one that was as necessary to Thulmann's trade as the sword and the pistol.

The man bound to the table did not react as the witch hunter stared down at him. Kohl's face was pale, beads of sweat dripping from his brow, jaws clenched against the steady and persistent pain. Thulmann glanced down at the man's injured leg, noting with some alarm a faint trace of crimson splattered upon the surface of the table.

The steward was already weak from his wound, and might not be able to withstand being put to the question for long.

'Has he said anything?' Thulmann snapped as Streng shut the iron cell door with a metal crash.

'I've only had him an hour,' protested the merce-nary. 'Haven't even pricked his skin or scraped his bones yet.' Streng grinned down with sadistic antici-pation at his prisoner. 'Don't worry, he'll be talking soon enough.' The grin grew wider. 'But not too soon I hope,' he added.

'I care not about your bloodthirsty amusement,' Thulmann snapped at his underling. 'Get this wretch talking!'

'I was about to introduce Herr Kohl to my little friend here,' Streng gloated, brandishing the red hot iron and ignoring his employer's reprimand. 'He'll be singing like one of the divas of Altdorf's theatre dis-trict in a few moments,' he added boastfully. The shape stretched upon the rack whimpered pitifully as Streng drew closer.

Thulmann lifted his hand, motioning for the tor-turer to hold back.

'My associate is very eager to be about his work,' the witch hunter said, his silky voice frigid with men-ace. 'Give me a reason to keep him off you and I shall. All you need do is tell me exactly what I want to hear.' Kohl groaned as he heard Thulmann speak his threat. The steward's eyes were open now, staring with wretchedness and defeat at his captors. Thul-mann fully appreciated the resignation in that broken gaze.

'I know that you were taught these profane rituals by your master,' the witch hunter stated. 'He has con-fessed as much to me.' Thulmann smiled as he heard the captive groan again as whatever hope he had that Wilhelm Klausner might be able to save him was dashed. 'Though it took me some time to get that much from him,' the witch hunter said. He smiled as he continued. 'He was most adamant that he knew nothing of what you were up to. Perfectly willing, eager even, to place all the blame for these heretical acts upon your head.'

Kohl growled, then sobbed in agony as he heard Thulmann describe the patriarch's betrayal of his servant. It was of no importance to Thulmann that he had told a lie. The greatest obstacle facing him would be Kohl's loyalty to his master. Once that was destroyed, the steward would be only too willing to tell Thulmann whatever he knew.

'Lord Klausner would not…' Kohl sputtered through his broken, swollen lips. The witch hunter pounced upon the steward's desperate protest.

'Your master is concerned with saving his own neck now,' Thulmann told the steward. 'He is perfectly willing to paint every person in this household as a heretic if he thinks it might keep his own neck from the noose. Or him from sharing your position on the rack,' the witch hunter added with a slight maliciousness.

'I have served him faithfully,' Kohl cried. 'All that I did was as my masters ordered.'

Thulmann chuckled grimly, his gloved hands running along the length of a set of grotesquely oversized tongs. 'I seem to recall an epitaph of that sort,' he mused. After a pause, he gasped in mock recollection. 'Oh yes, Macherat, the captain of Vlad von Carstein's Sylvanian guard. I think they inscribed that on the ten-foot stake they impaled him on. Took the swine a week to die, so they say.' Thulmann stared coldly at the prone man. 'But I imagine that you will be more forthcoming than Macherat was.'

Kohl screwed his eyes shut, unable to maintain the witch hunter's intense stare. 'Lord Klausner gave me a parchment upon which he had transcribed the rites he wanted me to perform. He said that they were meant to protect his family, to hold back the forces of Old Night.'

Thulmann nodded his head as he digested his captive's words. 'So old Wilhelm never showed you any book, any record of spellcraft? He only gave you this parchment, written in his own hand?' Thulmann began to pace across the chamber. 'Tell me, is this how Wilhelm's father instructed you in performing this ritual as well?'

The witch hunter watched as the remaining colour in Kohl's face drained away. Clearly the steward was not very comfortable with Thulmann knowing of his involvement with the earlier crimes. The time for soft words and false kindness was over. The witch hunter stormed across the torture chamber, slamming both hands down upon the surface of the rack.

'I know full well the extent of your evil, Ivar Kohl!' Thulmann spat. 'And you will answer for every atrocity that has blackened your loathsome soul! But first you will tell me how you learned these obscene practices and then you will tell me where it is!'

'Where what is?' the steward's broken voice squeaked. The witch hunter leaned down, his face only inches from that of his prisoner.

'The grimoire,' Thulmann hissed. 'The source of all this evil. Helmuth Klausner's tome of sorcery.'

GREGOR STOOD BESIDE the door of his father's chamber, staring in silence at the old, withered figure of the patriarch. The old man stared back, his gaze filled with such shame that Gregor knew the witch hunter would not have to kill his father now. With the ugly secret revealed, everything Wilhelm had been was gone.

No one would remember the hero who had hunted the darkest corners of the Empire in his pursuit of the enemies of man. No one would remember the gracious ruler who kept his lands safe and prosperous. Perhaps no one would even remember his all-consuming love for hearth and home, his limitless devotion to his family.

'I am so terribly sorry,' the old man croaked at last. 'I never appreciated how this could affect you and Anton. I never thought that my crimes might shame you. The risk to myself I never gave a thought, but I would not have allowed you to be hurt by my deeds.' There was an imploring quality in Wilhelm's voice. 'Please understand that. I would never have allowed any harm to come to either of you. Everything I have done has been to keep you safe.'

Gregor detached himself from the wall. 'I do understand, father,' he said as he walked toward the bed. 'But you must understand something. You must understand that it was not your place to take all those lives, no matter what you hoped to achieve, no matter who you hoped to protect. No good can come from such a thing. Can't you see that?' A moan of despair rattled from the aged frame of the patriarch.

'Now,' he said. 'Now I understand. I could not before, or perhaps I simply would not. Kohl explained to me the dark secret of our family, and your grandfather, upon his deathbed, told me what must be done to keep our line from harm. I recoiled in horror as they revealed these things to me. I did know it was evil, but I persuaded myself that it was a necessary evil.'

Wilhelm grasped his son's hand, the old man's withered claw closing about Gregor's fingers with a strength that surprised his son.

'You must get away from here!' the old man told him. 'When the sun rises you must gather your mother and Anton and leave this place.'

Wilhelm's face flared with anger as he saw the questioning look on Gregor's face. 'Don't question me in this! If you ever honoured and loved me, obey me this last time! It is not safe here any longer. I thought it would not come, that it would leave us alone if we left it alone.' A haunted, miserable light crept into the old man's watery eyes.

'You cannot placate evil,' he told his son. 'You must hunt it down and destroy it, never tolerate it to thrive, never suffer it to live. That has been the great crime of our family. We feared to face our enemy, and hid ourselves behind spells and walls crafted from innocent blood. But the walls are gone now,' Wilhelm cautioned. 'There is nothing to keep it away now. That is why you must leave.'

'What is coming, father?' Gregor asked, his curiosity kindled. Wilhelm lifted his withered frame from the bed, his wrinkled face peering into that of his son.

'Death,' the old man hissed in a voice that was more shudder than speech. The heads of both men spun around as a loud crack roared through the room. The heavy oak door exploded inward, slamming against the floor as its twisted hinges rattled across the chamber.

A chill froze the room and with the cold came a stink of graves and blackening blood. The flickering candles dimmed as a shadowy shape billowed across the threshold, two pits of corpse-fire glowing from its darkness veiled face.

Gregor could feel the terror stab into the very core of his being like a dagger of ice. He could feel the breath in his lungs freeze, feel the blood in his veins congeal, the strength in his knees crumple.

The young noble found his gaze riveted to the embers that smouldered from the face of the dark shadow, transfixed like a small bird beholding the approach of a serpent. On the bed behind him, Wilhelm gave name to the unholy visitation.

'Sibbechai,' his voice shivered. The burning eyes of the shadow turned towards him and the dark shape drifted forward, the feeble light in the room illuminating its rotten flesh, mouldering raiment and skeletal figure. The skull-face of the vampire curled into a malevolent sneer, the withered face pulling back from the gleaming rodent-like fangs.

As the vampire surged forward, the motion caused such a wave of horror in Gregor that he found his terrified paralysis overcome. The youth tore his sabre from its sheath, the sound of steel rasping against leather somehow invigorating him with its simple normalcy.

The vampire didn't even glance in his direction; its burning eyes instead transfixed Wilhelm Klausner. The undead creature reached a withered claw towards the bed.

'You won't have him!' Gregor shouted, lunging toward the monster, his steel held before his body like the lance of a knight. In his terror, the young noble had reverted to base instinct, all his martial skill forgotten.

The crude attack did not fall upon its intended target. As Gregor lunged, a powerful grip closed about his neck, lifting him from the ground. Anton's cold hand ripped Gregor's sword from his grasp as if he were plucking a toy away from a child.

Anton stared into his brother's face, his ghoulish eyes filled with contempt and triumph. With a sweep of his arm, Anton hurled his brother across the room, Gregor's body slamming into the wall with such force that the plaster cracked and rained about him as he fell.

Anton Klausner grinned at his fallen sibling, the thrall's cold flesh pulling away from the monster's gleaming fangs. The beast took a step towards the stunned man, but the horrified gasp that sounded from the patriarch's bed caused him to pause, turning to face his mortal father with a look of bitter victory.

'Anton!' the patriarch sobbed. 'Not Anton...' The corpse-lights burning in the face of Sibbechai flickered with amusement as the old man's agonised wail crawled through the room.

'Yes,' the Anton-thing hissed. 'It is I, your second son. Your reserve in case anything should happen to your darling heir.' The malevolence in the vampire's voice struck the old man like physical blows. 'The son you denied purpose. The son who received nothing from you except his name, until you stripped even that from him.' Anton turned his gaze, gesturing toward the malignant shadow beside him. 'But I have found a new father. One who has promised me purpose. One who has promised me power.' The thrall's hand closed about the bed post, his unnatural strength causing the wood to splinter. 'Let me show you that power, old man!'

An inarticulate snarl from the Sibbechai brought Anton up short. The vampire thrall turned towards its master, cringing before the elder necrarch's displeasure liked a whipped cur. Sibbechai waved its claw, gesturing for its slave to withdraw. Then its smouldering gaze returned to the wizened patriarch.

'You have something that belongs to me,' Sibbechai's words bubbled from its putrid mouth. 'I will have it returned.'

'Rot in the grave you have so long cheated!' Wilhelm shouted, his voice cracking with fury. What the vampire had done to Anton had caused such wrath to well up within him that even the necrarch's aura of fear was not enough to subdue it. The vampire watched with amused interest as the old man rose from his bed. 'You'll get nothing from me!'

With a speed that belied belief, the undead monster surged forward, its cold hand grasping the bottom of Wilhelm's chin, forcing the old man's head back at such a violent angle that it seemed his back would snap. The vampire's lifeless, decaying breath washed over Wilhelm's face as it glared down at him.

'I tire of these games,' Sibbechai said. 'You will tell me what I want to know or I will kill every living thing in this district and drown you in their blood. Then I will force life back into your swollen corpse and repeat the process.' The vampire's fingers twisted, the claw-like nails tearing Wilhelm's skin.

Sibbechai's eyes glowed more intensely as it saw the old man's blood weeping down the front of his nightshirt. 'Tell me where it is, Helmuth's *Das Buch die Unholden*. Your end can be quick, or it can be longer than you are possible of imagining.'

'Sigmar rot you, carrion worm,' Wilhelm managed to snarl. The vampire forced the old man's head back still further and Wilhelm could feel the strength and anger flowing through its clutch, threatening to overcome the control of the vampire's malicious intellect.

'You will tell me where it is, you weak-willed fool,' Sibbechai promised. The vampire's gaze shifted as a figure struck at it from behind. Once again, its slave Anton intercepted Gregor's attack, catching the naked steel in its bare hand. Instead of cleaving through the vampire's cold flesh, however, Gregor felt the blow resonate back up his arms. It was as if he had just struck a granite wall. Anton twisted his hand, snapping the blade he held, then lunged at the man who had been his brother. Sibbechai's foul visage spread into a smile as it saw the patriarch's eyes go wide with a miserable despair.

The vampire released its hold on the old man, spinning about and ripping Anton from Gregor's chest. The thrall slunk away, staring at its master with resentment and terror. Sibbechai locked its arm about Gregor's neck, lifting the young noble back to his feet. The vampire spun him around so that Wilhelm could see his older son's face. Sibbechai's lips drew back in a savage grin.

'Perhaps you do not value your own life,' it hissed. 'But what of your son's?' Sibbechai laughed as it saw the anguish that wracked the old man. The vampire pulled at Gregor's hair, forcing his head to tilt and expose his neck. A thin line of black fluid, like stagnant water, dripped from the vampire's fangs. 'Nothing to say?' its malicious voice rasped.

'Tell this monster nothing!' pleaded Gregor. Sibbechai forced the youth's head back even further, stopping his words with a pulse of pain.

'Be quiet boy,' the undead thing snarled into Gregor's ear. 'This does not concern you. This is an arrangement between...' the vampire's voice dropped, its tones slithering with a mocking scorn, 'gentlemen.'

Sibbechai raised its voice once more, directing its attention back toward the old man. 'But will you do it, Lord Klausner? Will you save your boy from death? Or will you watch him die?' The vampire uttered another snort of tittering laughter. 'Or perhaps worse than death,' it threatened. Wilhelm could see the vampire slice its palm with one of its long nails, could see the black blood of the monster begin to weep from the injury. Sibbechai began to move its hand toward Gregor's lips...

'Anything!' the old man cried. He began to lunge for the vampire, but was held fast by the interceding figure of Anton. Wilhelm struggled feebly in the grasp of his undead son, watching as the fiendish figure of Sibbechai threatened Gregor with the same fate. 'I'll do anything, just release my son!'

Sibbechai gazed at the old man for a moment, its corpse-face studying that of Wilhelm Klausner. 'Where is the book?' it hissed.

'I will take you to it,' Wilhelm offered. 'Just release Gregor.' The vampire seemed to consider the old man's offer, then inclined its head ever so slightly.

'Your father is a wise man,' its rotting voice purred into Gregor's ear. Its hand closed about Gregor's face, flinging him across the room. The youth crashed against his father's heavy oak wardrobe. For the second time, Gregor fell to the floor but this time did not rise.

Sibbechai smiled at Wilhelm, displaying its rat-like fangs. 'If you play false with me,' it warned, 'we shall return here and you will watch me do all that I have promised. Perhaps I shall even leave the slaughter of your household in the capable hands of your sons.' Sibbechai surged forward, one diseased talon pressing against Wilhelm's cheek. 'Where is the book?'

'In the cemetery,' the old man choked. His eyes were fixed upon the unmoving figure of Gregor. A grim determination filled him.

'I will take you to where it is kept,' he said.

'THE DARK GODS will feast on your soul, you filthy maggot!' Mathias Thulmann growled into Ivar Kohl's bloodied face. 'Damn you, confess your iniquities! Repent your evil ways!' Kohl's head sagged weakly against the surface of the rack, a trickle of blood dripping from his mouth. The witch hunter's gloved hand lashed out, striking the man's face once more. 'Do one decent thing with your wicked life! Help me to destroy this evil, to wipe its taint from this family forever!'

Thulmann had been interrogating the unrepentant steward for the better part of an hour, his questioning growing more intense and enraged with every passing moment. Every ploy he had tried to break Kohl's resolve, every trick and deception had failed. Just when the steward's will seemed to break, the man would dredge up some new strength from some black corner of his being.

The loyalty of Kohl would have been commendable in a healthy mind, but the witch hunter found the presence of such a virtue in the murdering sack of filth laid out before him whipping up his fury like lamp-oil thrown upon a fire. It might take days to break the man, and there was a dread gnawing at the witch hunter, a foreboding of doom that told him he did not have days, perhaps not even hours, to wrest the hiding place of Helmuth Klausner's book of spells from the steward.

Words began to sputter from Kohl's broken lips. Thulmann leaned down, hoping to hear the heretic's whispers. Instead, the steward spat a mouthful of blood into the witch hunter's face. A satisfied smile flickered on the captive's battered visage.

Thulmann pulled away, wiping at the filth with a silk handkerchief. He glared down at the man, then looked over at Streng. The mercenary was grinning at his employer, openly enjoying Thulmann's discomfort and growing frustration.

'Got you, did he?' Streng chuckled. The witch hunter paid the jibe no attention but gestured toward the brazier of hot coals and the three irons that were nuzzled within them.

'This vermin will talk,' Thulmann swore. Streng dutifully retrieved one of the irons, its tip smoking and glowing from the heat.

'I'm not so sure that is a good idea,' the torturer commented. 'You might be better leaving him be for a time.' Thulmann snatched the cruel implement from his henchman.

'When I want your advice, I'll ask for it,' he snapped. The witch hunter moved the heated iron toward Ivar Kohl. Yet as he did so, the already tormented man's body shuddered, seeming to collapse upon itself. Thulmann dropped the iron to the floor, grabbing the front of Kohl's robe.

'The book!' the witch hunter snarled into the heretic's face. 'Helmuth Klausner's grimoire! Tell me where it is!'

Streng strode past Thulmann, staring intently at their prisoner. At length, he reached out and turned the man's head, finding no resistance. Streng wiped his hand on the remains of Kohl's robe then stepped back.

'You'll have to speak louder if you expect him to hear you now,' the mercenary observed with a shrug. 'Or maybe send for the priest of Morr again.' The witch hunter swallowed an enraged curse. Streng grinned over at him. 'I told you to hold back a little.'

Thulmann turned away from the dead man, crushing his fist into his palm. He knew that Streng was right, it had been the overwhelming need for haste that brewed within him that had caused this. He had pressed Kohl beyond what the man's already weakened frame could endure. Now there was only one place he could go to learn what he needed to know.

'We'll start on the old man then, eh?' asked Streng, not able to hide the brutal anticipation in his voice. Thulmann sighed with resignation and bowed his head.

'Yes,' he said. 'Wilhelm Klausner is the only one now who can tell me what I need to know.'

The witch hunter turned, stalking across the chamber and opening the iron door. As the door opened, a terrible scream echoed down from above. Thulmann glanced over at his henchman, then raced back up the stairway, his sword in one hand, a pistol clenched in the other.

The nagging foreboding that had been haunting him was surging through his mind now as the screams were repeated, echoing down the cellar stairs. The sounds spurred Thulmann on, and soon the Templar was leaping up the steps three at a time.

Even so, he knew that he would not be in time to thwart whatever dark doings were afoot.

The witch hunter sprinted down the empty corridors of the keep, running towards the sound of frantic voices and frightened sobs. Then something else made itself known to him, a chill that plucked at his skin, a foul carrion stench that assailed his nostrils. The nagging foreboding that had haunted Thulmann exploded into tragic reality. He soon found himself standing in the main hall, his pistol sweeping about the chamber as he entered it.

A mob of terrified servants was huddled near the roaring fireplace, as though seeking protection from the stern-faced Klausner patriarchs captured in pain hanging from the wall behind them. Even a cursory glance told the witch hunter that every man and woman among them was trembling with fear.

Upon the polished floor of the hall, he could see three bodies lying in crumpled heaps, servants who had tried to stop whatever foulness had visited the keep this night. Pools of blood glimmered in the flickering light cast by the hall's torches.

'They took him!' a woman's voice shrieked. Thulmann turned toward the speaker, surprised to find that the terrified words came from the normally calm, precise and collected Ilsa Klausner. The noblewoman pointed her shivering hand toward the main door. Thulmann's gaze regarded the portal, finding that the heavy oak door had nearly been wrenched from its fittings.

'Who did they take?' the witch hunter asked, his sharp tone lashing at the frightened mob like a stream of ice water. He already knew what the answer would be.

'His lordship,' a blond-haired groom muttered, his voice a feeble croak.

'They were monsters!' a young chambermaid gasped. 'They weren't human!'

The girl's words brought a gaggle of hysterical confirmations to her claim, as each witness struggled to be heard over the others. Above the babble, the witch hunter heard something that at once arrested his attention.

'Anton? Who said that one of these intruders was young Klausner?' the witch hunter demanded. A pair of burly manservants stepped away from the crowd.

'We saw him when Rudi and Karl tried to stop him,' one of the men said. 'It was the young master. But he was wild and his strength was that of a daemon!'

'It was not my son,' Ilsa Klausner swore as she came forward. 'Whatever it was, it was no longer my son behind its eyes.' She fixed Thulmann with her wretched gaze. 'I know enough of my husband's former profession to recognise one of the undead when I see it. It was a vampire, like the thing it was with.'

Thulmann spun around as a shape rushed at him from behind. It was only by chance that he did not fire his pistol and explode the skull of the man who ran towards him down the corridor. Streng drew his bulk to a sudden stop, exhaling sharply as he considered how near he had come to getting killed by his master.

'Tardy as ever,' the witch hunter sneered, replacing the pistol in its holster.

'Miss all the fun, did I?' Streng asked, still visibly shaken.

'The vampire was here,' Thulmann told him. 'It came and took the old man. Anton was with it, which is how it gained entry to this place. The boy is a monster now as well.' A sudden thought occurred to the witch hunter. He lifted his eyes toward the upper floor, then pointed at Ilsa Klausner. 'I left Gregor with his father,' he told her. Ilsa lifted her hand to her mouth to stifle her horrified gasp. 'Go and see to him, if he yet lives!'

Thulmann ignored the noblewoman as she raced up the stairway, several of her servants hurrying after her. He glared at the remaining staff. 'Did any of you see where they went?' he demanded. A grimy, dirt-covered man hesitantly raised his hand. The witch hunter fixed him with a harsh and impatient look.

'I was outside, in the courtyard,' the man sputtered. 'I saw the… the things…'

'Where did they go?' the witch hunter snapped.

'It… it looked like his lordship was leading the others… leading them toward the… toward the cemetery.'

The witch hunter turned away, the gardener's recollections no longer of any interest to him. He nodded toward Streng. 'Come along, you'll earn your gold tonight,' he said. The mercenary jogged alongside Thulmann as the witch hunter crossed the ravaged hall with long strides.

It was not long before they were outside within the courtyard, staring at the human debris strewn about the open gate. It seemed that the vampire had been quite thorough about slaughtering all who had witnessed its arrival, from gate guards to stable boys. Streng swallowed nervously as he realised that the injuries he saw had been done without benefit of a trebuchet or cannon. Thulmann was more disconcerted by the fact that the monster had shown no interest in disposing of those who had seen it leave.

'Where are we going?' the mercenary asked. Thulmann did not look at him, but continued striding toward the open gate.

'The only place Wilhelm could be taking them,' he said. 'The place where all of this started.'

CHAPTER TWENTY-ONE

MIST ROLLED ACROSS the graves, coiling about the headstones, clutching at faded and forgotten names with wispy tendrils of nothingness. From the wasted boughs of an old dead oak, an owl called out into the night while from the dried-out brambles that clustered about the walls of the cemetery a chorus of toads croaked and chirped.

All sound died away as three figures approached the gate, the aura of dread and malevolence exuding from the group crawling across the graveyard like the icy breath of Morr himself. The toads huddled against the ground, their warty skins burrowing into the soft soil, desperate to hide from the dread that clawed at their tiny amphibian minds. The owl gave one last cry, then took to wing, intent on continuing its mournful song in some less forsaken place.

The vampire struck the wrought iron gates with its hand, snapping the chain that lashed them together and throwing them open. Its smouldering eyes glared into the pale, perspiring visage of Wilhelm Klausner. The vampire's lips pulled away from its fangs.

'Here?' it scoffed.

'Where better than amongst the dead?' the old patriarch retorted, pushing past Sibbechai, his frail frame shivering from weakness and the cold that had set into his bones. The vampire followed close on the old man's heels, the thing that had been Anton Klausner striding silently behind them both.

Wilhelm tottered his way amongst the graves, sometimes lingering to consider a name, to recall a face or some fragment of family history.

Whatever the witch hunter had said, the Klausners had accomplished a great deal of good over the years, more than enough to atone for the ritual they had handed down from father to son. They were a noble line, with pure intentions and a fervent devotion to Sigmar.

The fact that in five hundred years not a single Klausner had used *Das Buch die Unholden* beyond employing the ritual of protection was mute testament to the fact that the family was not corrupt and tainted, not driven by the nameless promises of black magic and blacker gods. The fact that they had kept the profane tome from the clutches of creatures like Sibbechai for hundreds of years was justification for what they had done. It had to be.

The patriarch glanced behind him, finding the hideous shadow of the necrarch beside him, its gaze smouldering into his own. 'Where?' it hissed. The old patriarch pointed toward the massive marble crypt that stood at the very centre of the graveyard.

'Helmuth's mausoleum,' Wilhelm said, trying to regain his breath, the nocturnal excursion quickly depleting his thin reserves of strength. 'It was entombed with him and has never left the crypt.' The vampire's claw pushed the old man forward.

'For the sake of your family, I hope that is so,' snarled Sibbechai. 'I have had a very long time to consider how best to destroy this family. Some of the notions that have occurred to me are most inventive.'

The patriarch did not answer the vampire's threat, but continued to walk towards the old tomb. As he climbed the short flight of steps set before the squat marble structure, Sibbechai came towards him, hissing a warning into the man's ear. Then the vampire swept its claw through the cold night air, motioning for Anton to precede them. The vampiric thrall strode forward, exerting its increased strength upon the heavy stone doors. Slowly, the portal began to slide inward.

A foul, damp smell billowed out of the darkness within the crypt. Sibbechai's eyes glowed with an eager and desperate hunger.

'Take me to it,' the creature snarled, pushing Wilhelm forward once more. The old man stumbled up the steps, his eyes watering with regret and shame as he saw the sneering face of what had been his son waiting on the threshold to greet him. Anton snorted derisively as its father passed.

Wilhelm fumbled about within the darkness of the crypt until he found the lantern and tinder that had been left there. He was under no delusion that his monstrous companions could not see him in the shadows. They would allow the lantern only because they still needed the old man to guide them, but they would not suffer it to allow Wilhelm an advantage. As soon as the old man had the lamp lit, Sibbechai muttered an inarticulate snarl and Anton ripped the lamp from his hands, shoving its father against the wall.

'Lead the way, old one,' the Anton-thing snapped. Wilhelm nodded weakly, sickened by the empty, soulless sound of the vampire's voice. With slow, reluctant steps, he strode toward the flight of marble steps that burrowed downward from the small square anteroom. The two vampires filed after him.

The steps descended some twenty feet beneath the cemetery. Niches cut into the walls held the shrouded remains of past Klausner patriarchs. There were even a few empty niches that would have served Wilhelm and Gregor, had things proceeded along the path they had always followed. The fact was not lost on Anton, and Wilhelm could hear the vampire's snarl of envious wrath as they passed the empty places.

The corpses became less complete the deeper they descended, as the hand of time came to rest ever more heavily. Many were now nothing more than fragments of bone and cloth, cobwebs and dust. The stink of slow decay and grave mould managed to make itself known even above the stench of Sibbechai's rotten flesh.

A centipede scurried away from the light, creeping back into the crack that had snaked its way down the smooth marble surface. A rat gave a sharp squeak of fright as Sibbechai's unholy presence offended its senses, the rodent scrabbling at the walls in its desperate attempt to flee before falling dead from fear as the vampire's shadow fell upon it.

Ahead, at the bottom of the stairway, a small chamber opened. Wilhelm paused as he stared up at the name carved into the archway, the name of the man who had brought doom and dishonour upon the generations who had followed after him. Then he continued onward, into the clammy darkness of Helmuth's tomb.

The light of Anton's lantern fought to illuminate the tiny chamber, its beams flickering upon the massive stone sarcophagus that filled the centre of the room. Upon the lid of the sarcophagus had been sculpted a life-size image of Helmuth Klausner, depicted in the prime of life, wearing his armour and prayer beads, hands folded across his chest, the witch hunter's sword laid out atop his body with the blade pointing at his feet and the pommel upon his lips.

Sibbechai surged forward, the witch-lights in its face glaring down at the sarcophagus. It had been many centuries since it had last set eyes upon that face, but it was a face that the vampire would not forget should a thousand years come to pass. The vampire stared at the cold stone features, remembering them warm and coursing with a life every bit as perverse as its own…

* * *

THE CHILL OF black sorcery set the brooding crows flying into the darkening night above the cursed rubble of Mordheim, croaking their fright at the icy clutch of necromancy in the air about them. The old, crumbling facades of the buildings seemed to become still more decrepit as the years tugged at their decaying structures, hurried along by the foul magic swirling about the ruins.

Dead things twitched, rigid arms began to flex their rotting muscles and sightless eyes snapped open in decomposing faces. The mangled dead began to stir once more, their spirits dragged back from oblivion to provide a shallow mockery of life to the shells they had worn only moments before.

Sibbechai's corrupt visage contorted into a mask of scorn and contempt. 'More sorcery, Helmuth?' the vampire hissed. 'Is there no limit to your hypocrisy?'

The witch hunter captain continued to mumble his conjurations, allowing the zombie monsters to shuffle and shamble their way between himself and his undead enemy. 'The tools of your loathsome kind can be made to serve the cause of Light,' Helmuth Klausner snarled. 'By such perversions is this great land threatened and by such perversions shall every last witch and wizard be driven from the Empire!'

The vampire paid only partial attention to the witch hunter's words, watching as the zombie creatures of the madman closed in upon it. The monster's face twisted with wry amusement. 'Is this the best you can do?' Sibbechai laughed. 'I find your efforts insulting.'

Sibbechai launched its lean form forward, the vampire's clawed hands lashing out, tearing the head from the shoulders of the nearest zombie as easily as a child pulling wings from a fly. The necrarch snarled a word of power and the next zombie toppled, crumbling into dust before it even finished falling to the blood-soaked cobbles. Sibbechai spun about, gesturing with its clawed hand, sending another blast of dark magic searing into a pair of the shuffling corpses, the unholy power turning both cadaver-things into walking torches.

The vampire was spinning about to smash its way through the last of Helmuth's zombies when sharp, blinding pain surged through its body. The vampire stared down with revulsion as a pustulent mass spread across its chest, a green morass of goo alive with maggots and filth. The vampire ripped the robe from its withered body, hurling the tainted garment into the face of an approaching zombie, the creature shambling onward a few moments before the writhing corruption ate through its skull and consumed its festering brain.

Helmuth Klausner snarled as he saw the vampire's inhumanly quick reflexes react to the pestilential spell the witch hunter had directed at it. Klausner had travelled far to uncover and destroy the corrupted festival, had nearly been killed by the loathsome and bloated priest of Nurgle who had acted as the carnival's master. He had done so because he had imagined that the spellcraft of such a sorcerer might prove of great use against the restless dead. Fortunately, there was more than one way to burn a bat.

The witch hunter pulled his heavy blackpowder pistol from its holster of blackened leather. The vampire saw the man's reaction, the undead abomination not even deigning to consider such a crude device any threat. Sibbechai ripped through another pair of zombies, finding its path to Helmuth unhindered.

Helmuth returned the corpse-thing's stare, the fanatic zeal in his veins countering the aura of supernatural malice exuding from the vampire's eyes. With calm deliberation, Helmuth lifted the pistol, whispering the slithering words he had extracted from the mangled body of a wizard in Averheim, the words of an ancient and pre-human spell of guiding. The pistol cracked and roared as Helmuth depressed the trigger, foul black powder smoke blowing back into his face and causing his eyes to tear.

The vampire darted aside as the witch hunter's crude weapon fired. It had fought many men who employed the smelly, unreliable firearms before and had learned that even on the rare occasions when their bullets did strike, they could do the monster no lasting harm.

But Sibbechai had not reckoned upon the sorcerous augmentation of the witch hunter's marksmanship, nor the uniqueness of the shot he had loaded into his weapon. The golden ball smashed into the vampire's shoulder, spinning the necrarch around and slamming it to the ground. Sibbechai snarled in agony and disbelief as it tried to lift itself from the broken cobbles.

A strange paralysis seemed to spread from its injury, making even its wasted limbs seem as heavy as stone. The witch hunter laughed, slipping his smoking weapon back into its holster.

'Surprised, monster?' he sneered down at the struggling vampire. 'I've learned a few new tricks since last our paths crossed.'

The witch hunter's boot cracked Sibbechai's face, smashing the vampire's rotting nose and spraying filthy black blood about the ground. 'I employ a rather unique shot now, graciously provided by a Solkanite inquisitor I encountered in Nuln. Poor misguided fellow, he seemed determined that I was a servant of the Dark Gods, a depraved sorcerer. Can you imagine that?'

Helmuth kicked the vampire again before stepping away. A thoughtful expression flickered across his face. 'I killed him of course. I found that his golden mask, melted down and treated with certain prayers, had a certain amount of usefulness to a man of my calling.' The witch hunter glared down at his foe. 'But you've discovered that for yourself, haven't you?'

Helmuth Klausner called out, his lisping voice a deep and commanding boom. From the dirty shadows where they had hidden themselves, the witch hunter's followers appeared. They were, for the most part, miserable and dirty creatures, their clothing almost as tattered and ruined as the grave cloth hanging from the corpses of Klausner's zombies.

These men were the bitter, the desolate and the dispossessed, men to whom the light of existence had winked out, whose families and livelihoods had been consumed by plague, famine and war. They were men from whom everything had been taken except the hate that boiled within them, that kept their hearts warm and their blood hot.

They were men who had been only too eager to listen to the witch hunter, to join him on his crusade to purge the Empire by spell, fire and sword. They were men who did not question the hypocrisy of one who burned a witch after stealing her secrets, nor the heresy that seemed so obvious when the man they followed sent lifeless abominations given vitality and motion through the black arts to contend with the mortal attendants of a vampire. They had put aside such questions. They were no longer needed.

Helmuth Klausner gave them something more important than any moral debate, he gave them a way to lash out, a way to make their hate fulfil itself. Klausner made these men something nobler than simple murderers and thugs, and to question the correctness of his methods was to question the righteousness of the barbarities they performed on his command.

The dirty-faced rabble of warriors and zealots glared at the carnage strewn all about their leader, at the mangled zombies and the still-dripping bodies of those of Sibbechai's fold who had yet to breathe their last. Several of the thugs drew daggers and set to hastening the demise of the wounded men.

One among them, an elderly man with hollow cheeks and steel-grey hair, the soiled white vestment of a priest of Sigmar still fluttering about his spindly form, strode towards the still moving monster at Helmuth's feet.

Walther stared down at the vampire, trembling as he saw the necrarch's unholy orbs look back at him. The old priest stood his ground, however, lifting the long wooden shaft he carried, its end carved into a sharpened point.

The priest began to pray in a soft and solemn voice, calling upon his god to guide his hand. Sibbechai stared back, an air of resignation and something that might even have been expectancy seeming to enter the foul creature's face.

Walther leaned back, then made to drive the stake into the vampire's chest, the full weight of the priest's body behind it. He found his strike foiled, however, as a strong hand closed about the other end of the stake, thwarting its descent. Walther turned his head, finding himself looking into the cold eyes of Helmuth Klausner.

'No,' the witch hunter told him. 'I have hunted this filth too long to let the end be so quick for him.' Helmuth smiled malignantly at the paralysed vampire. 'There are things I need from him before I finish with him.'

Sibbechai felt a flash of rage boil up within its old, cold heart, a ghostly return of the emotions that had run through it before the vampire curse had completely consumed its humanity. By a supreme effort, the vampire lifted its head, mouth dropping open in a snarl of inhuman savagery. 'You have already taken everything!' the vampire spat. 'My wife! My daughter! My life! There is nothing left, finish it and be damned!'

The witch hunter's features spread into an expression of loathsome and ghastly amusement. 'Oh yes, dear brother, I most certainly have! I have taken from you everything that you won with your miserable sorcery, everything you tricked and cheated the gods of fortune into tossing into your lap. Your life, your inheritance of our father's trade contracts, his farms and businesses, awarded to you by the few minutes your sorcerer's gods made you my elder! And your lovely wife and daughter,' the witch hunter's lip twisted into a sneer. 'She should have been my wife! My child! Only by your heathen magic did you prevail, did you turn her affection for me into hate!'

'No magic in this world or the next could have done that any better than the cruelty and malice in your heart, Helmuth,' the vampire hissed. 'How could she love such a thing as you, a thing of bitterness and envy, coveting everything that was not your own and hating those you could not look down upon. Is it any wonder that a man such as you should rise above the fears of your neighbours, to rise above that fear in order to prey upon it?'

The vampire's eyes gleamed with contempt. 'Tell me, Helmuth, did any priest ordain you to torture and burn innocent women and children, or did Sigmar himself call down to you and tell you to become a monster?'

Wrath blazed up in the witch hunter's face for a moment, but swiftly faded into a cold and malicious spite. Helmuth sneered down at the vampire. 'Oh, I did more than torture that slut you chose to pollute our name,' the witch hunter declared, a note of pride in his voice. 'I waited until you had gone, of course, to confer with your sorcerer friends. Then I denounced her, her and her daughter. Denounced them as witches before the whole town.'

The witch hunter chuckled with sinister mirth. 'You know, not one of them spoke a word in her defence. That rabble you so loved and helped with your heathen magics, your elf lore and pagan prayers. Not one of them dared to defy me, for they saw that justice was within me. And before justice, no unclean thing can prevail!'

The vampire struggled against the power that pressed upon its limbs, struggled to rise and rend the gloating figure of its hated enemy. But it was a struggle the monster could not win. Helmuth watched Sibbechai's desperate movements for a time, then continued his tormenting.

'I am impressed,' the witch hunter mused in a thoughtful tone. 'I had imagined that all the humanity would have burned itself out of that rotting carcass of yours some time ago. Don't tell me that there is still enough of my...' the witch hunter paused, putting such an emphasis on the next word that it seemed to explode from his mouth, '*little* brother that he still feels some connection with that slut of his? Would it anger him to know that the favours she chose to deny me and bestow upon you are not unknown to me now?' The witch hunter laughed again as he saw the enraged vampire struggle once more to rise. Walther cast a nervous look at the vampire, then at his leader, uncertain which of the two was the greater menace.

'She was most forthcoming,' Helmuth continued. 'One might even say eager. I spent many a happy night before I tired of her incessant begging and pleading.' The witch hunter shook his head. 'I can't understand why you were so devoted to that boring cow. But, it might lift your spirits to know that they died together.'

Helmuth laughed. 'A single pyre is so much more economical,' he stated. Sibbechai growled, the creature's immobile claws scratching deep into the cobbles. A stern expression came upon the witch hunter.

'Don't deceive yourself, monster,' he snarled. 'You are no longer my brother Hessrich! You did not drive me from Gruebelhof, pursue me across the Empire, follow me into this place of horror and madness simply to avenge that carrion.'

The witch hunter pulled open a heavy leather satchel that hung from a strap across his chest. From it he removed a mass of paper and parchment, held together by an array of string and leather cords.

Helmuth brandished it before the vampire, watching with satisfaction as Sibbechai's eyes narrowed with lust and desire. 'Yes,' Helmuth cooed. 'The book you brought back to Gruebelhof after your *accident*. Of course, I have added to it since then, added to it with the rites and spells of a dozen sorcerers, the hexes and charms of a score of witches. But this is no longer some coffin-worm's grimoire, nor some magister's tome of profane lore! This is *Das Buch die Unholden*, Helmuth Klausner's book of unholy things, his weapon against the powers of Old Night!

I shall not use this vile tome as you would, vampire! I shall use it to give glory and honour to Sigmar, to destroy those who would mock and profane his holy name!'

Helmuth drew a deep breath, calming himself after his tirade. The witch hunter glanced aside, finding that his minions were staring at him. He gestured at the vampire. 'Seize it!' he snapped. 'Bind it!'

The witch hunter smiled as he watched his men overcome their hesitance and fall upon the vampire, winding chains of silver about its withered limbs. Iron spikes were driven into the cobbles, the chains wrapped round them. The men strained at their task, extending the vampire's limbs, forcing the monster to spread itself upon the ground.

The witch hunter nodded in satisfaction as he saw his followers complete their labour, retreating back in revulsion and fear as the vampire snarled up at them.

'Such a work,' Helmuth said, rubbing his hand across the weathered pages, 'should have a proper setting, don't you think? I have seen for myself that necromancers choose to enshrine their despicable secrets within covers of human skin. It should only be fitting then to entomb my great work within the hide of one of the loathsome monsters that threatens Sigmar's noble Empire.' Helmuth turned away, pointing to one of the most brutal looking of his henchmen, a grizzled bear of a man dressed in furs and mud. 'Skin it,' he ordered the warrior.

Walther grabbed the arm of his leader, flinching away when he saw the look of anger in his master's eyes. 'You can't do such a thing!' he protested. 'That sorry creature was your brother! Whatever it has become, surely you can extend it some small measure of mercy?'

The priest understood that the monster needed to be destroyed, but the savage horror of what Helmuth intended sickened him even more than anything else he had been witness to since joining up with the witch hunter. 'Even the most pious of Sigmar's champions can show pity. Destroy it, yes, but not this way.'

Helmuth Klausner's voice was like the cackle of one of the Dark Gods. 'Destroy it?' he laughed. 'I am rather hoping that it does not die. Some of the nosferatu are capable of suffering hideous injuries before meeting their end. I hope to amuse myself with this creature for quite some time.' The witch hunter laughed again as he saw the skinner cut away the tatters of Sibbechai's robe. The crescent-shaped knife sank into the vampire's rotten skin, flaying it from the flesh beneath.

A low howl of anguish rose from the undead creature.

'Destroy it?' Helmuth gave the priest an incredulous look. 'I've not even started with it yet!'

IT WAS IN the long dark hours when all was quiet and still that Walther crept his way toward the place where the vampire had been left.

It had taken many hours for Helmuth's men to fall asleep, revelling in their leader's victory. The witch hunter himself had retired to his own room within a half-collapsed tavern, there to consult his tome of sorcery. There had been no one to watch Walther go, no guard to prevent his departure. Yet it had taken many hours more for the old priest to justify what he intended, struggling to overcome beliefs that had been branded into his soul and the last lingering traces of faith and loyalty some dark part of him still felt towards Helmuth Klausner.

The witch hunter was mad. Walther had known it for quite some time, if he was fully honest with himself. It was only now, however, that he had the courage to accept the fact.

He had followed Helmuth for two years, at first believing that the witch hunter's plan to drive the pawns of the Ruinous Powers from the Empire by employing their own profane arts against them. He had believed because he knew the nature of those wizards and warlocks he had seen, selfish men who pursued their own interests, whether knowledge or power, with a reckless abandon, contemptuous of the gods and their fellow man. But Helmuth had been different, a man who had within him a great and zealous devotion to Sigmar.

Walther had believed in the witch hunter, believed his claims that a righteous man could bend the twisted powers of sorcery and use it in the name of justice and good.

Walther could only shake his head at his former naiveté. He had watched the foul knowledge Helmuth had collected consume the witch hunter, twisting him into the very likeness of those he hunted. He had watched as the corrupt power devoured the witch hunter a bit more every day.

What might he become if left to continue as he was? Would the evil of his outrages be any less for being consecrated to Sigmar? Or did it make them worse, fouler even than the devotions of depraved Chaos cultists and witches?

The old priest had seen far too much of Helmuth's black power, knew only too well the profane forces the witch hunter could command. It terrified him, for all his faith in Sigmar. He knew that he could not challenge Helmuth on his own. He did not have the courage or the faith. He worried that at the last moment, some fragment of his former loyalty to the man would assert itself and stay his hand, delay the fatal blow. Then the witch hunter would destroy him, and Walther shuddered as he considered how inventive the man would be when dealing with one who had betrayed him.

Walther stared at the unmoving figure that lay sprawled upon the street, arms and legs made fast to iron spikes driven deep into the cobbles.

He hesitated, trembling as he recalled the monster's screams. Perhaps it was already dead, perhaps he had risked discovery and damnation for nothing. No man could have survived what Helmuth had put the vampire through, no mortal could have endured such pain for hours on end. And even if it yet lived, how could it possibly have strength enough left within it to help him?

The old priest closed his eyes, whispering a prayer to Sigmar that he might have guidance, that he might be shown what to do. When Walther opened his eyes, he felt an impulse to run, to flee the accursed and damned rubble of Mordheim. The old priest turned to do just that, but a slight change in the vampire's shadowy figure caused him to hesitate.

Two glowing eyes were staring at him from the vampire's mangled form, shining out at him with a cold wrath. Walther stared back, feeling the faint traces of the monster's aura of fear prickle his skin and crawl along his spine. Sibbechai lived, and Helmuth might still be stopped. The priest walked toward the silent shadowy mass, feeling his stomach turn as he saw what remained of the vampire, a dry mass of bare meat and muscle, like the carcass of a dried-out toad. Sibbechai stared up at the priest, its stripped face incapable of any sort of expression.

'Come to finish my brother's labours?' a dry voice wheezed from the vampire's mouth. Despite the horror of its mutilated tones, Walther could detect a hopeful ring to Sibbechai's words.

The priest noticed for the first time that he held his long wooden stake at the ready, poised to thrust it into the vampire's chest. He smiled weakly, lowering his weapon. 'No,' he said at length. 'Only Sigmar can grant you peace,' he added with a note of genuine sympathy and regret.

'If Sigmar has chosen a man such as Helmuth Klausner as the instrument of his will, then I pity man,' Sibbechai sighed. The vampire stared intently at the expression that came upon Walther's face. 'You know what he is, I can see it in your eyes. I am a monster,' Sibbechai stated, 'but how much more so is my brother? He clothes his horror within the cloak of justice and beneath the banner of righteousness, but

is he truly so different from what I have become?'
The vampire might have smiled had it understood
how directly and precisely it had read the troubling
doubts boiling within the old priest's mind.

'Helmuth Klausner serves the Empire, serves holy
Sigmar,' the priest declared as he fought to regain his
composure. 'He turns the powers of the enemy against
themselves, fighting the fires of corruption with their
own flame.' The vampire hissed with bitter laughter.

'Is that so? Your noble champion serves Sigmar?'
Sibbechai's mangled form shuddered with the force
of its anguished mirth. 'Then tell me why I find him
here? I did not follow your master to Mordheim, I
waited for him. I knew he would come here, come
here to harvest the wyrdstone. To use it to attempt a
thing no sorcerer or necromancer has ever dared to
contemplate.'

The vampire itself seemed to shiver with fear as it
thought about the dark purpose that had drawn Helmuth Klausner to Mordheim. The old priest turned
pale at the mention of wyrdstone, for the witch
hunter had indeed been gathering as many of the
greenish-black shards of rock as he could find. But
unlike the mercenary rabble who conducted their
own wyrdstone hunts through the ruins, Walther
knew that Helmuth had no patron waiting to buy the
stones from him.

'Helmuth seeks only to cleanse this land of its pol-
lution, to drive corruption from the Empire,' Walther
insisted, fighting against his own doubts and fears.

'In his diseased way, that is what he hopes to do,'
Sibbechai said. 'He would burn the field to save the

crop.' The vampire's hiss dropped into a whisper. 'I know what it is that he stole from me, I know the ancient secrets he learned from my book!'

'You do not frighten me,' Walther swore at the monster, brandishing once more the wooden stake. The vampire shook its head slightly, all the movement it could manage.

'Then you are a fool,' it told him. 'For your master has had time enough to decipher that book, to unlock its most terrible lore. I tell you, Helmuth Klausner came to Mordheim with one purpose: he means to recreate the Great Ritual of Nagash!'

The wooden stake fell from the priest's hands, clattering upon the cobbles. Walther recoiled in horror as he heard the vampire whisper the ancient and blighted name of the First Necromancer, the undying father of the undead.

He staggered as the enormity of what Sibbechai had suggested struck him. The Great Ritual, a dark fable that was still whispered on winter nights, an event of such atrocity and infamy that its echoes still resonated through the souls of men, a story that was still remembered by men who had never even heard of the lands where it had unfolded.

The Great Ritual, the apocalyptic spell by which Nagash had destroyed the kingdoms of Nehekhara and transformed them for all time into the Land of the Dead, the spell through which he had slain every man, woman, child and beast then resurrected them as soulless abominations to walk the barren wastes until the ending of the world. Walther felt sickened even by the possibility that such knowledge had not been purged from all existence with Sigmar's smiting of the Black One.

'I heard Helmuth,' Walther snarled at the vampire. 'You hunted him here to reclaim your filthy book. You intend to work this abominable spell yourself!'

'I waited because I knew that he must come here,' Sibbechai corrected the old priest. 'I came here to avenge the outrages he committed upon my wife and daughter.' The vampire's voice seethed with rage as it spoke. 'I have hunted Helmuth all these years for revenge, not for some tome of cursed and blasphemous knowledge!'

The priest glared down at the monster, considering its words. At last Walther nodded to himself, drawing a dagger from his belt. 'You will help me to stop Helmuth if I release you?' the old priest asked, his voice quivering from the disgust he felt at what he was doing. The vampire nodded its head as much as it could. 'When it is finished, you understand that I cannot let you live,' the priest added.

'When Helmuth is dead,' Sibbechai told him, 'there will no longer be any reason for me to live. I will not hinder you from doing what must be done.'

The priest leaned downward, gripping one of the silver chains. He pressed the edge of his dagger against it, then hesitated, staring at the vampire once more. 'How can I be certain that you will honour your word?' he demanded.

'I swear by Sigmar, who I worshipped when I yet drew breath,' the vampire told him. Then, in a softer, pitiable voice it added, 'But if that does not bind me to you, then I shall swear upon the souls of my wife and child that I shall work no harm upon you.' Walther bowed his head, accepting the conviction and misery in the vampire's tones. He set to sawing through the silver links.

'The bullet,' Sibbechai hissed. 'It drains me of strength. Cut it from me first, or I can be of no use to you. If I am too weak to help you, you must leave the chains, leave me to Helmuth.' A growl of hate rumbled up from the vampire. 'Only promise me that even without my help, you will strike down the heretic!'

Walther rose from attacking the chain. He stared into the vampire's ruined face, seeing for the first time not a soulless monster, but a cursed and tormented man. He nodded his head, feeling a new strength flow through him. 'I promise it. I promise on my faith in holy Sigmar that Helmuth Klausner will answer for all he has done.' The priest knelt beside Sibbechai, staring now at the gory hole that had bored and burned its way into the meat of the vampire's shoulder. He looked over at Sibbechai's face. 'I suspect this is going to hurt,' he commented.

The vampire clenched its jaws against the agony that flashed through its ravaged body as Walther's knife probed into the wound.

It was some minutes later when Walther rose from his gruesome labour. The lack of blood had somehow added to the horror of the operation as the vampire's collapsed veins shed not a drop of fluid as the priest's blade worried its way past them. The priest held the gold bullet before his face, wondering how so small a thing might bring low so dreadful a being as a vampire.

The priest's face contorted with an ironic smile. This dreadful being was now his only ally against a man he had once called friend and mentor. Strange indeed were the twisted paths of fate.

'It is done,' he said, tossing the bullet away. 'Do you feel any change?' The question died unanswered as Walther turned back towards the vampire.

Sibbechai had leapt to its feet the instant the old priest's attention had wavered, ripping the iron spikes from the cobbles with inhuman strength. Sibbechai whipped one of the silver chains dangling from his wrists towards Walther, the heavy iron spike fixed to the end of the chain length smashing into the side of the priest's skull.

The man fell to the cobbles and in an instant the vampire was upon him, strangling the life from the old man with one of the chains, ignoring the burning wracking pain that sizzled into it every time the naked meat of its palms touched the metal. In a brutally short time, the priest's body grew slack. Sibbechai let the man's corpse slump into the street, Walther's neck nearly cut clean through by the action of the chain upon his flesh. The vampire stared hungrily at the puddles of blood that had already drained out from the corpse. It fell on its hands and knees and began to lap the crimson liquid from the filthy cobbles.

There really had been no hope that the fool's plan might have worked, the vampire told itself. It was too weak to confront Helmuth Klausner so soon, and even if they had accomplished some miraculous victory over the deranged witch hunter, Sibbechai doubted if it would have been able to escape with the book afterwards. That was what mattered. Not Helmuth's death, not some noble attempt to thwart the witch hunter's insane schemes.

The transcription of the Great Ritual was fragmentary, Helmuth's hopes of recreating it were nothing more than delusions. Far greater minds than his had tried and failed. Nor was revenge enough to spur the vampire to such foolish and suicidal action, though the old priest had been quite willing to believe it would.

No, Sibbechai decided, all that mattered was regaining that which had been stolen from it. It would take some time to heal the injuries done to it this day by Helmuth, but it would recover. And then it would reclaim its property, if not from its brother, then another. The book was all that mattered.

As the vampire reached that decision, and slipped back into the shadows of the night, a tiny voice deep inside it, a part of it that had grown steadily weaker and quieter, screamed as it faded into darkness…

SIBBECHAI ROSE FROM its study of the sarcophagus, withdrawing from its reverie. The vampire's claw scratched a jagged line down the unblemished stone face. 'How did he die?' it asked, not looking away from the disfigured sculpture.

'He was old,' Wilhelm Klausner said. 'Very old. He had lived a full and prosperous life, commended and decorated by the Grand Theogonist himself. He was given this district by the Elector Count of Stirland.'

The patriarch swallowed as he considered the haunted legend that had been handed down from generation to generation, the cautionary parable that warned against using *Das Buch die Unholden* for more than protection. 'As I said, he was very old. He took to keeping himself in his room, not even allowing his son to see him. The flicker of candlelight could be seen from his window at all hours. It was thought that he was trying to prepare for his death, to set his affairs in order or to leave a complete record of his deeds. Then one dark night, the keep was awakened by the sound of a pistol shot. Helmuth's door was broken down when he did not answer. Smoke rose from the pistol that lay upon the floor, and beside it lay the first Lord Klausner. He had put a golden bullet through his brain.

'He'd not been writing,' Wilhelm went on. 'He had been reading, reading from that accursed tome. He was afraid of death and knew that in that blasphemous body of profane knowledge he could find a way to defy death. A ghastly, abominable way, but a way. In the end, he triumphed against the temptation,' there was a note of pride in Wilhelm's tone. 'He chose to destroy himself rather than succumb to the lure of unlife.'

Sibbechai's filthy voice bubbled with a grim laughter. 'He could have been no more a monster dead than alive,' it hissed, a faint trace of faded emotion echoing through its twisted mind. For a moment, the monster idly considered whether the bullet its brother had ended his life with had been the same one that had nearly caused its own demise amidst the corruption of Mordheim. 'Long may he rot.'

The vampire turned its gaze about the remainder of the room, its head freezing in place as it sighted the large stone lectern that rested in front of the rear wall. The necrarch made a low cackle, like a starving man who has discovered a scrap of bread.

'At last,' its loathsome voice croaked. 'After all this time, it is mine again. Flesh of my flesh!' The skeletal apparition rounded the lectern, its grisly visage lifted into a mask of morbid rapture.

The smile fell away, supplanted on the corpse-creature's visage by an expression of such malevolence that might chill the spirit of a god. Sibbechai glared across the crypt at Wilhelm Klausner, seeing the glimmer of proud triumph that shone in the old man's eyes. The vampire's claws gripped the lectern, toppling the heavy stone pedestal to the floor.

The necrarch's thin lips pulled back in a howl of frustrated fury. Its fist slammed into the wall, crumbling the marble. Wilhelm Klausner fled, placing the stone sarcophagus between himself and the vampire. Anton withdrew several paces up the darkened stairs. Sibbechai's howl of anguish lingered as the vampire punched the marble wall again and again. Then its wrath turned toward Klausner.

'Where is it?' Sibbechai raged. 'It was here! What have you done with it?' Wilhelm cowered before the furious monster, watching as the embers of its eyes seemed to glow white-hot. The vampire's thin figure grew rigid, then it lunged for the old man, hurling itself across the small room.

The crack and roar of a pistol thundered above even the snarls of the vampire. Sibbechai's body was punched in mid-air, dashed against the wall as a bullet smashed into the vampire's breast. Anton turned his head, lips drawing back in a savage snarl as he saw the two men descending the stairway.

A look almost as rapturous as that which had come upon Sibbechai when the monster had reached out to claim *Das Buch die Unholden* filled Wilhelm Klausner's features as he saw Mathias Thulmann stalking down the darkened stairs.

'Doom and judgement are upon you!' the witch hunter shouted. 'This night, Sibbechai of the necrarchs, you atone for your crimes of sorcery, heresy and outrage upon the Empire!'

ANTON KLAUSNER HURLED himself at the witch hunter, hands curled into claws, face contorted into an animalistic leer. Streng fired his crossbow into the rushing monster, the bolt smashing into its ribs. The Anton-thing stopped, uttering a menacing chuckle as he tore the missile from his body, not so much as a drop of blood weeping from the wound.

'You can't hurt me!' he spat. 'So what do your little toys matter?' Anton watched with grim amusement as Thulmann pointed his second pistol at the monster. Before the witch hunter could fire, the vampire lunged up the dozen steps that separated them. Anton's claw forced Thulmann's hand upward, causing the witch hunter to fire his shot into the ceiling.

The vampire's other claw closed about the Templar's neck, forcing Thulmann's head back, exposing the warm pulse throbbing at his throat. Anton distended his jaw, exposing the chisel-like fangs.

Suddenly the vampire's face twisted in pain. Anton released his grip, retreating several steps. He held his hand against the bleeding wound that punctured his side, staring in shock as he saw the blood staining his pale claw. Mathias Thulmann firmed the grip upon his sword, stalking downward.

A look of fear pulling at his features, Streng drew his own blade, but was careful to keep well behind the avenging figure of his employer. Having seen the vampire already demonstrate its invulnerability to honest steel, the mercenary was resolved to allow the witch hunter to attend to it with his priest's tricks and Sigmarite mummery.

'Yes, you bleed, blood-worm!' the witch hunter spat. 'This is the sword of Sigmar, blessed by the Grand Theogonist himself. You are not the first unclean abomination to feel its kiss,' Thulmann told the vampire. 'Nor will you be the last,' he promised.

The sneer Anton had worn in life slithered onto its cold flesh as the thrall drew its own sword. 'It seems we shall finish that fight we started in The Grey Crone, old man,' he hissed. 'But I should warn you, I am not the same man I was a few days ago.'

With no further word of warning, the undead creature launched itself at Thulmann. The witch hunter's blade clashed against Anton's sword and so began the deadly game of lunge, parry and strike.

WILHELM WATCHED IN horrified fascination as what had been his son attacked the witch hunter. The blades of man and thrall were a blur of flickering steel, the ring of weapon against weapon echoing through the crypt, rebounding from the dripping walls. They were evenly matched, it seemed. The cold, calculating skill of a seasoned swordsman, a man who had learned his art from accomplished masters, was behind the witch hunter's blade. But behind Anton's was the savage strength of the undead and the feral swiftness of a thing from beyond the grave. It was hard to tell which would prove the deciding quality, but Wilhelm prayed with all his being that it would be Thulmann's sword that emerged victorious and granted to Anton the death that was now the only thing that could redeem the boy from the horror that had claimed him.

As the patriarch continued to watch the duel, he saw Anton's tireless strength begin to take its toll. The vampire could put its full power behind every sweep and still muster the same power for its next blow.

The witch hunter did not have such supernatural reserves to call upon. More and more of Anton's blows were slipping past the Templar's guard, delivering painful slashes to arm and thigh. The witch hunter had managed to avoid any of the vampire's more telling attacks, but Wilhelm knew that his luck could not endure forever.

The old patriarch reached out his hand to the cold stone lid of the sarcophagus, grasping the sword that lay upon the image of Helmuth Klausner. The chill grip of the sword felt like ice in the old man's hand.

He turned to lend his own meagre aid to the struggle, but even as he did so, a different sort of ice closed upon his left hand. Wilhelm gasped in pain as the vice-like grip of Sibbechai's clutching claw crushed the old man's bones.

'The book,' the ghastly vampire hissed. Its chest wept a thin black tar from where the witch hunter's blessed bullet had slammed into it. But after five hundred years, Sibbechai was not so easily defeated. Even a bullet of pure silver, blessed in the Great Cathedral of Sigmar, was capable of little more than stunning the monster. Where Helmuth Klausner's bullet had almost fatally paralysed the necrarch, Mathias Thulmann's had only immobilised it for a few minutes. The vampire's fangs gleamed as it exerted its strength and broke every bone in Wilhelm Klausner's hand.

'Where is my book?' Sibbechai hissed again, depraved madness blazing within its grotesque gaze.

The old patriarch crumpled before the might of the vampire, falling to his knees before it. Sibbechai closed its hand still more tightly, grinding the shattered bones against each other. The incredible pain caused Wilhelm to drop his ancestor's sword, the heavy weapon clattering upon the marble floor. He glared defiantly at the undead monstrosity.

'Where you will never find it!' he snarled. Maddened by rage, Sibbechai flung Wilhelm against the side of the sarcophagus with such force that the snapping of the old man's back could be heard even above the clash of swords echoing from the entrance. The vampire roared at the broken man, its rat-like fangs bared.

'Living or dead,' Sibbechai shouted, 'you will tell me!'

* * *

THULMANN DESPERATELY PARRIED the flash of Anton's blade, knocking the blow aside, feeling the power of the assault shudder up his arms. The witch hunter risked a quick glance at his henchman. Streng nodded in understanding, removing a small vial of coloured glass from a pouch on his belt.

With a grimace of uncertainty and dread Streng rushed forward, flinging the contents of the small glass vial ahead of him. The liquid splashed across the left side of the vampire.

Anton uttered a shriek of agony as his flesh began to steam and his skin began to bubble. The thrall dropped his sword, pawing at his steaming face. Thulmann did not hesitate, rearing back and putting his force into a brutal slash that severed the thrall's hands and caused its head to leap from its shoulders. The decapitated monster slumped against the wall even as its head bounced into the crypt below.

The witch hunter drew a deep breath, trying to regain his strength.

'You're going to get yourself killed playing with things like that,' Streng grumbled as he kicked Anton's body away from the wall.

'I wanted to save the Tears of Shallya for the other one,' Thulmann wheezed. The witch hunter collected himself, sprinting down the remaining steps with his sword held before him.

He found the necrarch leaning over Wilhelm's broken body, a great gash torn into the vampire's wrist.

Tarry black blood oozed from the wound. At the sound of the witch hunter's approach, the vampire's grotesque face turned upon him. Thulmann could feel the ageless malignancy of the monster clutch at him, seeking to drain his courage and resolve.

The witch hunter blinked away the momentary confusion. He had been here before, this place of doubt and despair, facing the black sorcery of Erasmus Kleib, the strength of his will his only defence against the dark sorcery of his foe, faith in Sigmar his only armour. He had not failed then and he would not fail now.

Thulmann forced his foot forward, forced his sword to rise. Words came pouring from his lips and it was only after they were spoken that he realised he was reciting a prayer of protection. The vampire twisted its body away from the broken figure of Wilhelm, surprise showing on its corpse-like face.

'I have killed more of your kind than I can count,' mocked Sibbechai. 'If you go away now, I might forget this pathetic display.' The witch hunter took another step forward.

'This sword has put an end to one blood-worm this night,' he retorted. 'It is hungry for another.'

Sibbechai drew back, its face contorting with fury. The smouldering embers of the vampire's eyes bored into the witch hunter's, probing for any trace of fear, any sign of weakness. Finding none, the vampire uttered a disgusted hiss.

'I should show you the foolishness of such a boast,' Sibbechai said. 'But I will concede that there is a slim chance that you could cause me harm with such a trinket.' The vampire gestured toward the toppled lectern, waiting for Thulmann to shift his gaze. When the witch hunter did not, it continued in an arrogant tone. 'There is nothing here to give me cause to entertain such a risk. The gods of fortune are fickle, after all.' The shadows darkened around Sibbechai as the vampire crept back toward the wall. 'But know that to every dawn a night must fall.'

Thulmann lunged forward, realising that while he had avoided the more obvious ploy of having his attention diverted, he had not escaped the subtle, disarming tone in Sibbechai's voice. As the vampire's soft hissing speech had crawled through the witch hunter's mind, he had let his guard down. Now, the darkness swelled and billowed about the creature, summoned from the shadows of the crypt.

Thulmann slashed at the pillar of darkness. In reaction to his stroke, a grisly shape fluttered past his head, a gaunt bat with ebony wings, leathery hide stretched tight over a skull-like face. Its tittering laughter bounced about the crypt.

The bat circled the chamber twice, then flew up the stairway, easily avoiding Streng as the mercenary swung at it with his crossbow. The thug shouted after the fleeing nightbird, raining every curse in his colourful vocabulary upon the creature.

THULMANN TURNED AWAY, walking to where Wilhelm Klausner's broken body had crumpled. Blood stained the old man's face, thick and dark with bile. Heretic or misguided servant of Sigmar, the old patriarch would answer to an authority higher than any to whom Thulmann could have sent him. As the witch hunter stared down at him, the old man's lips began to move. Thulmann leaned down to hear Wilhelm's feeble voice.

'Tha... thank you,' the patriarch whispered. 'Thank... you for... saving... Anton...'

'He is at peace now,' Thulmann assured the dying man.

'What... of... Gregor?' Wilhelm asked, voice cracking with despair.

'Your son will live,' Thulmann replied, not knowing if it was the truth or a lie, but praying that it was the truth he spoke. The statement brought a flicker of contentment to the dying man's face.

'It was all for them,' Wilhelm said, tears boiling up in his eyes. 'I did it all for them... destroyed the tradition, put an end to it all.' He looked at the witch hunter, his eyes filled with a deep shame. 'I... I know it should... should have been for Sigmar... for the poor people... but it was... for them.'

Thulmann stared intently at the old man, trying to discern his meaning.

'The... the ritual,' Wilhelm explained, coughing another quantity of bloody spray. 'There were never... six. There... were seven. The spell needed to feed... needed to feed. It fed on the trees... the life of the trees. But it needed a man to focus it... it needed to suck the vitality from a man.' Wilhelm's words drowned into another fit of coughing. Thulmann considered the old patriarch's words. It explained much, the so-called 'blight', the premature ageing of Wilhelm himself, all to feed some ancient pagan spell. And Wilhelm determined to prevent his sons from being consumed by the ghastly tradition as he had been consumed.

The old man lifted his heard, a pleading, intense energy filling his face. 'Sibbechai did not... did not get... the book.' Wilhelm closed his eyes against the pain that surged through him. 'Couldn't keep... it... here. I couldn't... destroy... it. Sent it away... to Wurtbad. Look... look for... the book... in Wurtbad. It's there.' The old man's head sagged downward, toward his chest. 'Forgive...' he hissed as the death rattle bubbled up from the back of his throat.

Thulmann put his fingers to the old man's face, shutting his eyes. The witch hunter stared down at the crumpled figure, uncertain how he should feel. The man's mixture of virtue and heresy was a puzzle the witch hunter doubted he would ever be able to accept or understand.

'He may have been a murdering heretic bastard,' Streng commented in his gruff tones, 'but he died like a champion.' The mercenary gestured at the room around them. 'We burn the bodies here, Mathias?' he asked.

Thulmann stared once more at the broken form of Wilhelm Klausner, the man who had defied gods and monsters for the sake of his sons, who had risked even his immortal soul to ensure their welfare and safety. The witch hunter glanced over at the corrupted remains of Anton. He almost felt sorry that the old man had seen his dreams die before him.

'No,' Thulmann told his waiting henchman. 'We will carry them out of here and burn them in the open. Somewhere clean.'

EPILOGUE

Two RIDERS SLOWLY made their way down the road that snaked away from the township of Klausberg, winding between small hills and fields of wheat. Eventually it would join up with the much larger main road that would return them to the city of Wurtbad.

The foremost of the two riders was quiet, his face hidden beneath the wide brim of his hat, his thoughts turned inward, contemplating things and decisions he did not wish to speak. The witch hunter's companion continued to grumble into his beard, bristling under the chill of the morning air.

'We might at least have waited for the frost to clear,' Streng groused. 'Why the haste, Mathias? You could make your report in a week and no one would complain.'

The witch hunter did not regard his henchman, his eyes studying instead the slopes of the hills, the clusters of rock and tree that huddled about and upon them and the cold breeze that slithered around them. 'I should think you'd be eager to fill your pockets with the temple's gold,' Thulmann returned, a note of reproach in his tone. As usual, Streng chose to ignore the witch hunter's distaste for his openly mercenary motivations.

'Aye, it'll be nice to have full pockets again,' the mercenary observed. 'Though we could have turned a better coin,' Streng added with a sullen grunt. Thulmann turned about in his saddle, fixing the man with a stern look.

'What larcenous drivel are your spouting?' Thulmann demanded.

'I was only remarking that we could have had a bit more coin for our efforts,' Streng said. 'Five gold for old man Klausner, another seven for his vampire son, and another nine for Kohl and his lads.' A greedy gleam twinkled in the mercenary's eyes. 'We could have done a bit better is all I was considering.'

'Speak plainly,' Thulmann snapped. 'I tire of your insinuations.'

'Well,' grinned Streng, leaning back in his saddle. 'That vampire did attack Gregor Klausner, and now the boy is sick. Might have gotten another seven gold if we'd waited around.' Thulmann shook his head in disgust, returning to his contemplation of the countryside.

'There was nothing about him to suggest that the vampire's taint flows through his veins,' the witch hunter stated. 'The violence of the creature's attack and the death of his father, coupled with the hideous truth about his family's legacy would naturally have undermined his health.' Thulmann's voice grew sombre. 'There are monsters enough in this world without you inventing more.'

'I rather did like the feel of his sword,' pressed Streng. 'Fine blade. Hated giving it back to him. If he'd been a vampire or involved in his father's heresy…'

'You can have half of my payment,' Thulmann snarled, 'if it will quiet that scheming tongue.' It was an old argument between the two men. The materialistic, hedonistic Streng saw ample opportunity to exploit the office of witch hunter for petty gain and was always quick to give voice to his suggestions.

Thulmann knew that there was no lack of men who did just that, exploiting the power and respect demanded by their profession toward their own selfish ends. It was a sore point with Thulmann, because it was a temptation that he was never entirely convinced he himself had not yielded to.

'Keep your filthy money, Mathias,' Streng sighed. 'You know me better than that.' There was a note of genuine injury and offence in the mercenary's tone. After a moment he regained his composure. 'Back to Wurtbad then, eh?' he asked.

Thulmann nodded, straightening in the saddle as new thoughts occurred to him. 'There is some chance that we may yet pick up Weichs's trail, and I'll not let that man slip through my fingers if there is even the remotest chance of catching him.' There was a venom in the witch hunter's voice, as he recalled the nefarious doctor and his disfiguring, corrupting experiments with warpstone.

He'd hunted the man for many years, and been forced to kill far too many of his tainted victims. Then there was the matter of Helmuth Klausner's book of unholy lore. With his dying breath Wilhelm Klausner had confessed that he had entrusted the tome to someone in that city. It might take quite a bit of investigation to discover who the old man had trusted enough to leave the book with. The fact that the vampire Sibbechai was still at large and still hunting for the book was enough to make the witch hunter doubly keen on tracking it down and destroying it.

The thought of the uses to which a necrarch would put such a blasphemous work caused Thulmann to urge his horse into a gallop, and soon he was many lengths ahead of his henchman.

'Ah well,' grumbled Streng, urging his own horse to greater effort. 'There's wine and wenches enough in Wurtbad, I suppose.'

GREGOR KLAUSNER LAY upon his bed, heavy fur blankets wrapped about him, his head propped upon pillows. He could hear the soft, concerned voice of his mother giving directions to her servants to attend her son. He could feel the soft towel that wiped away the feverish sweat beading upon his brow, and smell the heavy pungent aroma of the medicinal herbs smouldering in the urn beside his bed. But it was with a detached, almost unreal way that he perceived these things. It was like his mind was outside his body, observing it from afar.

His thoughts brooded upon the deaths of his brother and father, slaughtered by the filthy monster that had invaded their home and profaned their name. The ghost that had so haunted the Klausner line that for fear of its wrath, generations of noble Klausner men had practised a filthy and unspeakable ritual. The vampire had very nearly slaked its thirst for vengeance, but it had made one mistake. It had not finished what it had started with Gregor Klausner.

The young noble could still taste Sibbechai's vile blood upon his mouth, a few drops of filth forced upon his lips when the vampire had hurled him aside after threatening his father.

His father had led the monster away trying to save him, but the truth was that the vampire had already done its worst. The thought of the creature's cruel treachery brought a groan of anger from Gregor's feverish lips. At once, soft warm hands caressed his cheeks, trying to soothe his pain.

Somewhere within the back of his mind, Gregor was laughing. Why did they try? Couldn't they see? Didn't they know?

The witch hunter had known or at least suspected, which was why he had made his departure with such awkwardness and haste. He had known what he would have to do if his suspicions proved themselves. He'd left, hoping against hope that Gregor would recover, that his lust for life would drive out the filth that clawed at his soul.

But Gregor had no lust for life. Only one thing mattered now. He had to find and destroy the creature that had damned him and his family. He had to track down and destroy the vampire Sibbechai, for there was no one else left to do so and no other way to redeem the name of Klausner. Gregor could sense the vampire's presence, sense the creature as it fled through the early morning back to its refuge. There was a link between them now, a tether of corruption that bound them together.

Gregor would follow that bond, follow it back to its source and force Sibbechai to answer for all its monstrous sins. Before he could allow his own tainted existence to be put to an end, Gregor would see the necrarch destroyed.

The young noble sank back, staring up at the shadowy forms of his mother and their servants, ignoring the bright gleaming lines that burned within the grey and indistinct shapes, ignoring the warm flowing blood that called out to him. Gregor cried as he wondered how long he would be able to deny that call.

The shadows within the gloomy, dank cavern grew even darker, as though the nebulous pockets of blackness were striving to become things of solidity and form. The chill of the forsaken and blighted place sank into an almost icy atmosphere and the rank stink of the place became unspeakable in its foulness. The small wooded hill had been a barrow once, burial mound to the naked half-intelligent savages who had wandered the lands of the Empire in the aeons before Sigmar's birth. There was a power to such places of ancient death, and that grim power seeped into the stones and earth, making animals snarl and men avert their gaze. Such shunned places called out to their own, shining like black beacons to the creatures of night and horror.

A shape emerged from the shadows. Tall and thin, its body draped in a grim black robe, ghoulish adornments dripping from its garb. The vampire Sibbechai turned its head, its fiery eyes narrowing with disgust at the faint flicker of dawn that danced about the small opening to its refuge.

Unlike many of its diseased kind, the necrarch could endure the sun for limited periods, provided that the proper enchantments were invoked. But it did so at great peril, for the creature would lose much of its strength, and the ravages of the purifying rays of the sun could not be fended off completely. The sun was forever the bane of Sibbechai's kind, dispelling the night with which the vampire shrouded itself, providing the monsters with no shadows in which to hide but revealing them for what they truly were.

The necrarch hissed its anger. It had been cheated once again, cheated when it was so very close to achieving what had been denied it for so very long. But it would endure and it would prevail. It was only a matter of time now, and time was one thing that Sibbechai had an in abundance.

The vampire's withered face spread into a malevolent grimace as it considered the events that had unfolded in Helmuth's tomb. Its pet had been destroyed, which was irritating. But far worse had been the humiliation of being forced to retreat from that mortal swordsman.

Still, even so slight a risk as the witch hunter had posed was to be avoided when there was yet so much to accomplish. The vampire could afford to swallow its pride; there would be ample opportunity to claim restitution from the man's mangled bones in the future, when their meeting would be under circumstances of Sibbechai's choosing.

The vampire strode back into the gloomy tomb, its gaze fixed upon the large coffin of polished Drakwald timber that rested against the far wall. It was one of a matched set of twenty that Sibbechai had commissioned long ago. Its black surface was edged in gold, the griffon and wolf emblem of the Klausners worked upon the sides and the top of the lid.

The flawless wood had been polished to a sharp shine, so that even the tiny embers of Sibbechai's eyes shone back at the vampire from the walls of its casket. The vampire still smiled at the ingenuity of the device, the cunning lock it had taken a dwarf craftsman the better of a decade to design. It had been the dwarf's finest work, a perfection of craftsmanship that the fellow had never exceeded. The insidious traps in the lock were themselves tiny masterpieces: needles that would stab at the flesh of any would-be trespasser, delivering a lethal dose of a most unkindly poison, a small glass vial that would shatter and release a mephitic vapour, safeguards that had ensured the sanctity of the vampire's slumber for many years.

Sibbechai removed the iron key from the chain that hung about its neck, leaning down toward the dwarf lock then stepped away hissing in rage. The lock had been destroyed, nor by any simple, crude means. The ancient device had been reduced to a glob of molten metal clinging to the singed side of the coffin.

The vampire uttered a savage snarl of rage, its claw lashing out to rip the heavy lid of its coffin from its hinges. The panel of Drakwald timber crashed against the wall of the tomb and Sibbechai glared down at the velvet-lined bed of its coffin. The necrarch hissed again and flinched away as it saw the silver icon resting there.

'I thought it might be prudent to make certain changes in the décor,' a malicious voice called out from the darkness.

Sibbechai spun around, glaring at the shadows. The sneering face of Carandini greeted him. The necromancer had been waiting for his treacherous ally for some time, veiling himself in a cloak of sorcerous shadow that even the necrarch's unnatural gaze had not penetrated.

'Get rid of it!' Sibbechai demanded.

The necromancer laughed back at it.

'Patience,' he scolded the monster. 'Patience. You act as though a few minutes were a matter of life and death. Or undeath,' Carandini smiled, casting a sidewise look at the growing glow clawing at the mouth of the barrow.

'Take it away!' the vampire repeated, its words more snarl than speech. Carandini smiled back at the monster, apparently unconcerned by the creature's barely restrained fury.

'If I am to help you,' the necromancer observed, 'then you should help me.' The mocking smile fell away and the man was at once as serious as the grave. 'Hand over the book,' he told it. 'I could of course dig it out of your ashes after the sun has done its work, but I'd rather not risk the book coming to any harm.'

Sibbechai glowered at the necromancer, jaws clenching and unclenching. He lunged toward the gloating sorcerer, but flinched away as Carandini held up an identical icon. The vampire paced before Carandini like some caged beast, averting its gaze every time it chanced to glance at the silver hammer clutched in the necromancer's hand.

'You really should at least try to be helpful,' Carandini said. 'Otherwise I think things are going to go rather badly.' The necromancer laughed as Sibbechai again reached for him, then recoiled from the hurtful aura of the Sigmarite relic. 'One of the benefits of being a man in my position, vampire, is that one can enjoy the benefits of both worlds, that of the living and that of the dead.'

'I don't have the book,' the vampire snarled as it retreated before Carandini's holy symbol once more. 'It wasn't there.'

A blank look fell upon Carandini's features. The necromancer pushed a wisp of ratty hair from his pale face, then sighed in disappointment. 'I suppose we really have nothing more to discuss then. I must confess, however, that after your little trick with the wolves, I will find a great deal of enjoyment in watching you shrivel into a cinder.'

Sibbechai snarled at the man, more infuriated by the contempt with which Carandini dismissed the vampire's attempt to kill its partner than anything else. Its pride had been injured enough this night. Yet Sibbechai knew that if its pride did not suffer still one more time, then it would shortly discover the grave it had defied for so long.

'I know where the book is,' the vampire growled. Carandini's expression shifted between amusement and doubt as he heard the monster speak.

'Really?' the necromancer snickered. 'Why does this sound like something I've heard before?'

'The old man knew I was coming for it,' Sibbechai explained. 'He had it removed, gave it to a friend.' Sibbechai considered the fragmentary memories and images the necrarch had ripped from the dying man's mind, the secrets which by his very determination to keep from the vampire had risen to the forefront of Wilhelm's thoughts.

'And where might that be?' Carandini asked. Sibbechai looked away from the man, pointing once more at the casket.

'We bargain for that information,' the vampire snarled. 'Take that filthy thing away!'

The necromancer studied his undead adversary, pondering just how far he could trust the monster. It could not possibly be dealing false with him. It would know that he would search it as soon as it slipped back into its grave, and slipped into the half-sleep of its kind.

Sibbechai could be under no delusion as to what the necromancer would do to it if he found the book hidden away nearby.

A sly smile on his face, the necromancer strode across the cave, careful to keep the holy icon between himself and the vampire.

Still facing the necrarch, he put his hand into the open coffin, fumbling about until he grasped the Sigmarite symbol. Carandini held both symbols before him, staring in open challenge at the vampire. Sibbechai covered its eyes with one clawed hand. The glow of dawn was strong at the mouth of the barrow now, and the necromancer could see that the vampire's movements were growing slower and more ungainly by the second.

'What is your bargain?' the necromancer asked, a tone of mirth in his voice.

'I know where the book has been taken,' Sibbechai replied in a desperate hiss. 'We can still share its secrets!'

Carandini was silent for a moment, pursing his lips as he considered the vampire's offer. Sibbechai fidgeted before him, the vampire's body twitching and twisting with anxiety. 'Are you proposing a return to our earlier arrangement?' the necromancer's tone was incredulous. 'Just forget everything that has happened and let bygones be bygones? Is that what you are offering?'

'Yes,' hissed Sibbechai, a dry sound that seemed to wrack its lean frame. The necromancer smiled and stepped away. The vampire did not speak, but at once leapt forward, scrabbling into its coffin like a rat racing back into its hole. Carandini stepped away from the casket, smiling at the undead monster's refuge.

'That sounds agreeable,' the necromancer laughed, though he knew the vampire could not truly hear him. He patted the bottle of sacred water secreted within his robes. He was almost sorry that he wouldn't get a chance to use it now, but the possibility that the vampire was telling the truth was a bit too important to indulge his petty ambitions for revenge. *Das Buch die Unholden* was a prize that would more than compensate him for his near death beneath the fangs of Sibbechai's wolves.

Still, there were a few experiments that Carandini knew of that required the fangs and claws of a vampire to perform. The necromancer had been looking forward to attempting a few of them.

Of course, there was no reason he could not return to them after Sibbechai led him to the book. One could never quite tell what a new day would bring.

Carandini walked from the barrow, out into the cold morning air, an evil dream shining behind his eyes.

More Warhammer from the Black Library

BLOOD MONEY

A Brunner the Bounty Hunter novel
by C. L. Werner

A LONE RIDER made his way through the timber gate that led into the town of Greymere. The guards atop the walls eyed the man with looks of suspicion, for in the realms of the Border Princes it paid to trust no stranger. War between men in these lawless regions was almost as common as war with the marauding tribes of orc and goblin. The rider paid his coin to the sergeant at the gate, and suspicion or no suspicion, the man was allowed to enter the town, leading a dappled grey pack horse behind his own black and brown bay.

The merchants and peasants that ambled about the muddy lanes of the town paused to favour the stranger with curious glances, for he presented a compelling, almost sinister, sight. The man wore armour about his lean frame, his head was encased in a helm of blackened steel, and knives and other blades hung all about his body. On either side of the man's saddle, sheaths had been attached: one bore a large crossbow, the other a wood and steel frame of a blackpowder weapon. His second horse laboured under assorted burdens, barrels, packs and rolls of cloth. But with one look at the man, all could tell that those packs did not contain merchandise, and that he was not some sort of wandering peddler.

The stranger stopped before the crude timber face of the town's only inn. He dismounted. Casting his visored gaze about the street, as if challenging any thieves who might be watching, he left his horses and stalked into the building. Although several sets of eyes cast covetous looks upon the animals and the gear they carried, none did more than look.

Shortly afterwards a man emerged from the inn, his face as white as a sheet. Quickly and cautiously the man slunk away from the building into the nearest alleyway, losing himself in the confusing spaces between the town's maze of huts and pigsties.

Brunner, the man thought, smoothing the front of his leather tunic and wiping the perspiration from his swarthy brow. The Tilean licked his lips and placed a reassuring hand on the sword at his side. Then, a sudden thought of just who it was he feared brought a fresh burst of speed to the man's steps. *By Ranald and Morr, what is he doing here? Whose head is he after?* The answer came to Vincenzo's mind almost immediately. The meagre price on his own head would not have dragged the bounty hunter away from the city states, but there was someone in Greymere who did merit such a price.

THE GREY-HEADED MAN swept a bone brush through the massive moustaches that crouched upon his lip, training them back into the upward-pointing horns fashionable among the nobles of the Empire. It was unwise, he knew, to affect such an appearance, but years of habit were hard to escape and the former Baron of Kleindorf was not about to give up the few, miserable trappings of his former station that he was able to maintain.

Not for the first time, the man who had once been Bruno von Ostmark, and now called himself Drexler, considered his surroundings with a snort of disdain. The house he kept in Greymere was lavish by the standards of the Border Princes: it had a stone façade and wooden floors and roofing that did not consist of thatch and straw or logs thrown across support beams. Only the keep of the ruler of Greymere, Prince Waldemar, was more extravagant and sumptuous. Yet, the baron could not help but remember the castle that had once been his, the estates and private forests that had been his possessions. Even his kennels had been larger than his present home.

Drexler finished sweeping his moustaches into the desired shape and began to dress himself. Here, too, he thought of his fall. Once, three servants would have busied about his person, preparing him to face the day in whatever raiment he chose from closets larger than the bedroom he now sat in. The exiled baron sighed loudly and slumped into a velvet-backed chair and slowly pulled a leather boot onto his foot. Such extravagance was beyond him now. The few servants that he could afford had more pressing duties – matters of business, that would keep Drexler from slipping down the ladder of life. For the nobleman was realistic enough to understand that, miserable as his surroundings might seem, there were far more wretched levels of squalor into which he could sink, and never emerge.

A sharp knock at the door interrupted the nobleman turned merchant as he stuffed a stocking-covered foot into his other boot. He turned towards the door, snarling at this intrusion upon his routine. Drexler stifled the impulse to hurl the shoe at the door as it opened. The men now serving him were hardly domesticated, and hardly as meek as those who had cowered before the Baron von Ostmark. One had to be careful about berating and insulting them, lest the dogs snap at the hand of their master.

The wiry, dark-skinned shape of Vincenzo, Drexler's Tilean aide, assistant and confidant slipped through the portal, slowly closing it behind him. Drexler stared at the Tilean, suspicious of his furtive manner and quiet steps. The merchant reached under the fur blankets of his bed, fingering the dagger hidden within the bedding.

'Well?' the merchant demanded. 'What news is so important as to drive you to disturb me before I have properly risen? What troubles you that you cannot await a more decent time to speak to me?' Drexler tensed his grip on hilt of the dagger as Vincenzo sidled across the floor towards him. The Tilean licked his lips and a cold sweat glistened on his face.

Drexler could practically smell the fear dripping off
the man.

'Have you ever heard of a man named Brunner?'
the Tilean said at last. Drexler shook his head, staring
at the thief and smuggler with a questioning gaze.

'He is the most notorious bounty hunter in all of
Tilea,' Vincenzo explained.

Drexler pursed his lips in thought. 'And you think
this killer, this Brunner has come to Greymere looking for the Baron von Ostmark?'

'The reward offered by the Count of Stirland is
quite substantial,' Vincenzo pointed out. 'What other
reason could there be for the bounty hunter to come
to Greymere?'

A troubled expression grew upon Drexler's features. He pounded his fist in his palm. 'No, of course.
Somehow he heard of me, found me. But he won't
get me!'

'I could ask Savio to attend to it,' Vincenzo offered.
Drexler smiled.

'Yes, do that,' the merchant said. 'I have never seen
a man who could match Savio's blade. Now, leave
me. We have to negotiate with the dwarfs again
regarding the transport of their beer to the Moot and
I want to look my best.'

THE STRANGER SAT at a small table in the rear of the
large tavern that dominated the ground floor of the
two-storey structure. A few off-duty soldiers from the
prince's guard eyed the armed bounty hunter with
thinly veiled antipathy. Mercenaries were a common
sight in Greymere, and their arrival often heralded
the replacement of one of the other soldiers in the

pay of Prince Waldemar. The other occupants of the tavern, a trio of dishevelled peasants who were nursing their beers in order to savour the expensive luxury for as long as they could, did their best to avoid looking at the black-helmed man.

A buxom barmaid made her way between the largely empty tables and set a stein of beer before the bounty hunter. The visored head lowered, staring at the frothy mug for a moment before setting a few copper coins on the table. The woman leaned forward, scooping up the coins with one hand, while her eyes maintained their hold on the face. The cloth covering her massive chest hung loose as she bent over the table, and the woman licked her lips with a wet, pink tongue. She hesitated a moment, lingering over the table, watching for any sign of interest the warrior might exhibit.

The bounty hunter reached a gloved hand forward and closed it about the body of the clay stein. He drew his hand back and raised the frothy drink to his lips. The barmaid stood, shaking her head in an angry gesture and stalked away – hopes of supplementing her wages diminished by his indifferent air. As she turned, Brunner let a slight smile play on his face. It had been a long ride here from Remas, but not that long.

The door of the inn opened, bearing with it the smell of dust and excrement from the street outside. A single man entered: short, but with wide shoulders and muscular arms. He was wearing a foppish-looking cap of red silk, with a purple falcon's feather sticking out from a gold button on its left side. A shirt of chainmail encased his body, the skirt falling to his thighs, where green leggings completed his costume. Leather shoes with bright brass buckles set a jingling echo across the tavern's earthen floor with each step the man took.

Bright blue eyes set in the dark-skinned face of a Tilean considered the tavern and its inhabitants. The face of the man was dominated by a bristly black beard, cut to a point. When his eyes closed upon the figure of the bounty hunter, the beard became distorted as his mouth curled into a predatory smile. The Tilean let his gloved hands caress the hilts of the long-bladed dagger and rapier that hung from his belt. He shrugged and the red cape he wore fell from his shoulders and onto his back. The man strode across the room, each face in the tavern watching his every step – save the bounty hunter, who continued to quietly sip at his drink.

The Tilean stopped beside the table, staring down at the seated warrior. Slowly, Brunner set the stein down, and peered up at the Tilean through his visor.

'Your name is Brunner?' the Tilean asked, his tone arrogant, his accent that of the merchant princes of Tobaro. Brunner let his left hand emerge from beneath the table, his small crossbow pistol now visible in his gloved hand.

'Who would like to know?' his icy voice asked.

The Tilean pulled a velvet glove from his hand. 'My name is Savio,' the man said, dropping the glove on the table. A light of recognition blazed in Brunner's cold eyes as the Tilean spoke. 'I make my challenge. If you are a man, you will face me.'

'Not in here!' bawled the massive bald-headed innkeeper from behind the bar. 'It stinks bad enough without blood seeping into the floor.' The off-duty guards seemed to share the innkeeper's thoughts, and Brunner let his grip on the crossbow relax when he heard the men draw their swords.

'It seems here is not the best place,' the bounty hunter said. The duellist nodded back at him.

'I shall await your pleasure outside then,' the man said, spinning about and retracing his steps across the tavern. Brunner watched him go. As soon as the door had shut behind him, the innkeeper strode to the bounty hunter's side.

'Whatever you have done to earn the notice of Savio,' the man shook his head. 'He is the most feared swordsman in all the Border Princes. He has killed more people in Greymere than dysentery.' The man's expression changed to one of mock regret. 'Could you please settle your bill before you go outside? And if you will add a little extra, I can send a boy to fetch the priest from the shrine.'

'That won't be necessary,' the bounty hunter said. He reached below the bench he sat on, and pulled a leather-wrapped object onto the table. The innkeeper stared as the bounty hunter removed a heavy object of steel and wood.

'If you don't pay for the priest, they won't bury you,' the innkeeper muttered. 'They'll just strip your body and toss it over the side of the wall for the wolves and the crows to pick at.'

'Well, they have to eat too,' the bounty hunter said, not looking at the bald man. He removed a small tube of paper from a pouch on his belt. The ends of the paper tube had been twisted closed. The gloved hands tore one end of the tube open and up-ended the paper cylinder over the mouth of the steel weapon. A foul-smelling black grain-like substance poured into the barrel. 'And if I can choose, I'd rather feed wolves than worms.'

'I am happy that you can joke about it,' the innkeeper said, wringing his hands on his apron and looking anything but happy. 'But if you think you can match swords with Savio, then you have no idea who you are facing.'

The bounty hunter packed down the grain in the barrel with a long wooden rod. He set the rod down and removed an iron ball from another pouch on his belt. 'I know who Savio is,' he said. He dropped the steel ball into the weapon, packing it down again with the wooden rod. 'In Tobaro, in Miragliano, in Luccini, his name is reckoned as that of the greatest duellist to ever practise the art of the vendetta.'

The innkeeper's eyes grew wide with alarm as he heard Savio's name associated with such great cities. Suddenly the professional swordsman had become more frightening than even the innkeeper had imagined. 'There is a back door,' the bald man said. 'You could slip through it and be out of Greymere without Savio seeing you go.'

A loud voice called from the street, demanding that Brunner emerge, and berating the bounty hunter as a rogue and a coward without honour.

'And keep him waiting even longer?' Brunner asked. He removed another packet of paper from a third pouch on his belt. He tapped the light, flour-like powder from the folded square of paper into a covered pan at the rear of the gun, just below the steel latch of the hammer. The bounty hunter rose from the table, bearing the loaded handgun with him.

'What are you going to do?' the bald man asked, voicing the question on the mind of everyone in the tavern.

'Before he left Tilea, Savio killed the son of one of Luccini's most prosperous guildmasters,' the bounty hunter replied, snatching up a shabby cloak from a hook beside the door, and draping it over his right arm to hide the weapon he now carried. 'More than enough to pay for the replacement of a bullet and some powder.'

Savio stood in the centre of the muddy lane, men and animals giving him a wide berth as they passed. The thin-bladed, lightweight sword was gripped in his still-gloved hand. His other arm was covered by the heavy fabric of the red cape, the slender fang of his dagger gleaming from the fist that emerged from the folds of the cape. As the duellist saw Brunner emerge from the tavern, he uttered a short, sharp laugh.

'I was thinking that maybe I would have to go inside and drag you out,' he laughed. 'Many is the time when some churlish cur would refuse to answer the demands of honour and unman himself before the duel even began.' The Tilean's blue eyes focused on the shabby cloak draped about the bounty hunter's right arm. 'Oh? You think to fight me in the style of a Tilean streetfighter?' The duellist laughed again. 'The trick is to employ the cape as not only shield but weapon. Catch your enemy's blade in its folds, if you can, but there is many another trick.'

The duellist made a quick swipe with his sword into the empty air, then pranced a pace forward, whipping the edge of the cape forward, like a boy cracking a wet towel. 'Strike the hand of some handsome noble and watch them recoil from so minor a blow, dropping dagger or sword from fingers stung by so little a thing.' The Tilean withdrew, then danced forward a step, unfurling the cape and casting it about an invisible foe, as the sword lashed out again. 'Then one can always cast one's cloak about the enemy. He will panic, trying to fend off your cloak, and exposing himself for one instant to the steel in your hand.'

'Your swordplay is as extravagant as your mouth,' Brunner's voice sneered. The Tilean lost the playful expression, and his words their jocular tone.

'I have never met my equal with the sword,' the duellist said, staring at the armoured figure of the bounty hunter.

'And you never will,' Brunner stated. He lowered the gun held upright at his side. The hammer responded to the tug of the trigger, smashing into the pan and the powder contained there. The powder lighted under the impact, in turn igniting the gunpowder in the barrel. The black powder exploded with a flash and boom, forcing the iron ball from the weapon. The bullet shot across the few yards separating the two men and crashed into Savio's breast, tearing through the chainmail shirt as though it were not there. The duellist toppled backward, his head crashing into a pool of mud and horse urine.

A stunned silence settled upon the street as the echoing report of the handgun slowly faded away.

Brunner stalked across the mud, crouched down beside the body of the Tilean and pulled the large knife from his belt. The serrated edge gleamed in the light for a moment before he brought the blade against the neck of the dead man. A woman screamed as Brunner set about his gruesome labour.

'Always make sure that the man you want to kill is playing by the same rules,' the bounty hunter said as he lifted Savio's head from the corpse.

Brunner looked about the street, his gaze canvassing the horrified onlookers. He settled upon a young boy standing near the door of the inn, and tossed a gold coin to him.

'Fetch me a sack of salt,' he told the boy. 'Keep a few coppers for yourself, but bring the rest back to me.' The boy rushed off, the menace in the bounty hunter's voice ensuring that he would return as speedily as his young feet would allow. Brunner pushed open the door of the tavern with the still-smoking barrel of his gun and disappeared into the darkness with his trophy.

Follow the career of Brunner the bounty hunter as he roams the Old World in search of profit and revenge in the novels Blood Money and Blood & Steel.

ABOUT THE AUTHOR

C. L. Werner has written a number of Love-craftian pastiches and pulp-style horror stories for assorted small press publications. More recently the prestigious pages of *Inferno!* have been infiltrated by the dark imaginings of the writer's mind. Currently living in the American south-west, he contin-ues to write stories of mayhem and madness in the Warhammer World.

More Warhammer from C. L. WERNER
BLOOD MONEY

IN THE GRIM and medieval Old World, few are feared and hated as much as the bounty hunter. Their world is one of deceit, treachery and random violence, where words are cheap and life even more so. Survival depends upon a unique blend of intelligence, animal cunning and brute force, with pain and the promise of pain maintaining their aura of fear. Brunner is one such man, a ruthless individual who will stop at nothing to catch his prey and claim his reward.

'Dark and dangerous in equal quantities.' – SFX

More Warhammer from C. L. WERNER
BLOOD & STEEL

ENTER THE DARK and dangerous world of ruthless bounty hunter Brunner, as he hunts down the Old World's fugitives without respite or mercy! Allowing nothing to stand in his way, Brunner battles against goblins, vampires and all other manner of dark creature in order to catch his quarry and claim his reward. But lurking in the shadows is the mysterious Krogh, a rival bounty hunter with a grim reputation who will stand for nothing less than Brunner's demise.

'Strong and highly atmospheric fantasy.' – **Starlog**